You Ca

By Carlene Thompson

You Can Run...

Carlene Thompson

St. Martin's Press

This is a work of fiction. All of the characters, organizations, and events portrayed in this novel are either products of the author's imagination or are used fictitiously.

YOU CAN RUN...

For information address St. Martin's Press, 175 Fifth Avenue, New York, NY 10010.

ISBN-13: 978-1-61523-039-6

Printed in the United States of America

St. Martin's Paperbacks edition / March 2009

St. Martin's Paperbacks are published by St. Martin's Press, 175 Fifth Avenue, New York, NY 10010.

To Rebecca Oldfield

The fairest English rose

Thanks to Pamela Ahearn, Anne Bensson, Keith Biggs, Patricia Nicolescu, and Jennifer Weis

Special thanks to Phyllis Sabellichi for encouragement when I most needed it

PROLOGUE

The child slid out of her bedroom window into the smothering folds of a hot summer night. Her mouth slightly open, she turned in a circle, gazing upward at the dome of sky, thinking that the stars looked like silver glitter sprinkled on Mommy's black velvet dress. She'd never seen so many stars twinkling around a fat moon as white as fresh snow. Maybe the moon *was* made of snow, she mused. Maybe up so high, it was too cold for snow to melt.

She pulled her thoughts away from the beautiful night sky and directed them to her task. The girl grasped a glass jar sitting on the windowsill. She checked to make sure the lid bore several tiny holes. Then she listened for a moment. The sounds of a song floated from the house. She knew the song was called "In My Room," sung by some boys who lived at the beach. Mommy always listened to that song when she was sad, and tonight she'd played it again and again.

Mommy wasn't just sad, though. For the last few days, while the little girl had been getting well from an operation on her tummy, Mommy hadn't laughed like usual. After Mommy had brought her home from the hospital that morning, she'd kept walking through their little house, sometimes crying. When the child asked what was wrong,

Mommy always said, "Nothing at all! Everything is fine, Willow."

But Mommy didn't look like she believed everything was fine. That's why Willow had decided to give her a surprise, even if Mommy might get a little mad because Willow was supposed to be in bed. She had to hurry, though, before Mommy looked into her room like she'd done so many times today. If she saw the bed was empty. . . .

Willow decided she just wouldn't think about that now. She had work to do, and if she moved real fast and tried real hard, she could be back before Mommy noticed.

Willow dashed across the yard as fast as her five-year-old legs would carry her. She loved the backyard, where she had a swing set and a little rubber swimming pool. She vaguely remembered once living in a big building—up high, with lots of windows. There was no yard and no swing set, but sometimes Mommy took her to a huge place called Central Park. Central Park had grass, but Willow liked her own grass much better.

She liked her grass so much, she couldn't resist smelling it. She winced with pain before she remembered she was supposed to bend at her knees, not from her tummy. Too late now, though, and her tummy didn't hurt very much. Besides, she'd spotted a dandelion. She sniffed it, too, loving its tangy smell. Willow thought dandelions were beautiful, all bright yellow and fluffy. This summer she'd often picked bouquets of dandelions for Mommy, who always put them in a glass of water.

Willow pushed aside her long red-gold hair and tucked the dandelion behind her ear. Then she headed farther back, toward the woods at the edge of the backyard. The moon and stars were so bright, she hadn't needed to bring along her little plastic flashlight. She held her precious glass jar with both hands. If she dropped it and it broke, she'd ruin the surprise. She knew she had to be very careful.

Willow stepped just inside the line of trees. Then she removed the lid from her jar and stood still, hardly breathing, waiting. And waiting. And . . .

There! A tiny yellow flash above her head, but not too high! She reached up, gently closed her hand around the insect, dropped it in her jar, and put the lid back on. She held up the jar and looked. *Blink, blink, blink!* Her friend called this a lightning bug. Willow thought that was silly. These bugs didn't shoot out scary spikes of blinding light. Some people called them fireflies, but they didn't set things on fire, either. No, these bugs were nice and they flashed soft, glowing colors that didn't hurt anyone. Mommy called them sparkle bugs and so did Willow. This sparkle bug she named Dandelion.

Willow took one more step into the woods and stopped. Mommy didn't like her to go into the woods at all, which made them even more enticing to Willow. The woods were darker than the backyard, though, and Willow had to admit they looked a little bit scary at night. Besides, she didn't need to go into them. If Dandelion had been floating around right here, other sparkle bugs would be, too.

Willow again went completely still, trying to take little, silent breaths. Little breaths weren't easy, though. The night was so hot, she felt as if a blanket covered her head. A breeze blew, but it was hot, too. Sweat had popped out on her forehead, and she didn't feel as good as she had when she climbed out the window. She thought briefly that maybe she should have waited one more night after her operation before she'd come out looking for sparkle bugs. Mommy needed cheering up *now,* though.

At that moment, a tiny light blinked right in front of her face. Willow giggled, quickly took off the lid, gently grasped the bug and put him in the jar with Dandelion. The bug blinked again, his light the color of the cantaloupe slice Mommy had given her with lunch. Willow named him Cantaloupe. Cantaloupe and Dandelion blinked at the same time. They'd made friends!

Willow wanted to get at least one more sparkle bug. She'd planned to get five because she was five, but she was just too hot, and all at once very tired. Just one more bug would be perfect. She'd have three sparkle bugs, and they would make Mommy as happy as five of them.

"Willow!"

The little girl almost dropped her glass jar when she heard her mother yell from the back door of the house. Willow whirled around and hurried out of the woods. She saw Mommy coming down the three steps from the back porch, heading directly for her. *Now I'm gonna get in trouble,* Willow thought dismally. She'd get in trouble, she didn't feel good, and she had only two sparkle bugs. Her wonderful plan shattered.

"Willow Conley, what are you doing out here?" Mommy's usually soft, sweet voice sounded high and sharp. "You know you're supposed to be in bed. Do you want to end up in the hospital again? Because that's what will happen if—"

Just at that moment, as Willow stood frozen in the face of Mommy's anger, a tremendous blast shook the earth. Her mother pitched off the bottom step into Willow's little rubber swimming pool, as a funnel of fire shot through the roof of their house. Vicious yellow flames darted like snakes' tongues out of the shattered windows and burst through the open back door.

Stunned, the little girl stood rigid, paralyzed by shock and fright. Burning pieces of wood soared through the night, some landing only inches from her. She did not retreat into the woods though. Willow simply clutched the jar of sparkle bugs, her terrified eyes fastened on Mommy, lying motionless in the swimming pool as the hungry fire swept over her.

CHAPTER ONE

Twenty Minutes Earlier

1

Diana Sheridan had watched from behind her windshield as the horizon turned from bright blue to dusky lavender to violet, before the sunlight completely disappeared behind the tree-covered Appalachian Mountains. Now night had come and she was relieved to be almost home, her late arrival caused by a three-car collision on the interstate.

Behind a pile of crushed metal, and police cars and emergency service vehicles, Diana had waited in a line of cars full of people who were at first curious, then sympathetic, then cranky, trapped behind the wreck for over an hour in the August heat and humidity of Friday afternoon. Diana had stopped a passing state trooper and learned that one person had died in the accident and three were critically injured. Getting victims out of the mangled cars was a time-consuming feat requiring many expert hands, as well as the Jaws of Life.

Now, nearly two hours later, Diana soared off an exit ramp, happy to leave the speeding highway traffic. She spotted a fast food restaurant and longed to make a quick pass by the drive-thru window and order french fries. Her growling stomach reminded her that she hadn't eaten since the morning.

A glance at the dashboard clock stopped her, though.

Nine fifteen—almost the exact time that her friend Penny had called Diana's hotel room the previous night and, in an anxiety-edged voice, said she needed to talk in person as soon as possible.

"Is Willow worse?" Diana had asked, referring to Penny's five-year-old daughter who'd had an appendectomy late Tuesday afternoon. No, Penny had assured her, the sound of distress giving way to relief. Willow had undergone laparoscopic surgery without complications. They were releasing her from the hospital in the morning.

Something else was terribly wrong. "Diana, *please* come by my house before you go home," Penny had begged almost pitifully, her voice rushed and breathless again. "I can't talk about this over the phone, but I have to give you an explanation. I can't just leave you and Simon wondering what's become of us. . . ." Penny had paused. "I'm involved in a situation that could be a matter of life and death."

Deeply alarmed, Diana had urged Penny to go to the police, but Penny nearly shouted *no,* so Diana had promised to come by as soon as she arrived back in Huntington the following evening. She had said she'd be there by eight at the latest. Penny, sounding on the verge of tears, had thanked her and hung up so fast Diana didn't have time to say good-bye—or ask more questions, Diana thought later, puzzled. If Willow was on the mend, what could have gone so wrong in Penny's world during the last three days?

Diana grabbed her cell phone to let Penny know that she was on her way, even though she was running late. She cursed softly when she saw her phone battery hovering at death's door. Unfailingly, she'd misplace the phone, she'd need to use it in an area with no reception, or she'd forget to recharge the battery. Diana kept it only because her great-uncle, Simon Van Etton, a retired archeology professor with whom she currently lived, had been aghast when he learned that she didn't have a cell phone, and immediately presented her with one he'd chosen especially for her. At seventy-five, Simon was obsessed with every new technological gadget that hit the market. Diana looked hopelessly at his latest gift—an iPhone lying on the seat beside her. She'd never even tried learning how to use it. Her technical acumen seemed confined to cameras.

Diana sighed as she stopped at a red light. Another delay. When the light finally turned, she pressed the accelerator, concentrating on "Layla," by Eric Clapton, pouring forth from her CD player. She wouldn't be lucky enough hear anything like "Layla" at the country club dance club tomorrow night, and she wished she hadn't agreed to go with Glen Austen, a university history professor. Glen was nice looking, intelligent, warm-hearted, unfailingly courteous, and utterly predictable.

Even her great-uncle Simon kept telling her to stop seeing him. "I introduced you to Glen, although not as a potential love interest," he often said. "He's a nice fellow, but you need a man with some fire, girl. Someone more like me when I was twenty-five!"

To which Diana always replied, "Glen is *thirty*-five, but I'm sure even at that age you would have had too much fire for me!" The remark never failed to delight Simon, bolstering his already robust ego and sending him into a gleeful fit of laughter as he agreed with her.

Besides, she'd had "fire" once. She'd had passion and excitement, and for a short time, what she'd thought was true love. After a short engagement and three years of marriage, though, Diana had realized how naive she'd been. She'd tied herself to a man who resented her career and her deep ties to her family. He wanted to be the only meaningful part of her life. When he'd unceremoniously left her for an eighteen-year-old who thought the sun revolved around him, Diana had been almost relieved. Almost.

Annoyed with herself for dredging up an unfortunate part of her past, she cleared her mind of the old memory of disenchantment and concentrated on driving. Penny lived in Rosewood, a housing project built quickly at the end of World War II, like hundreds of others throughout the United States, when returning soldiers needed homes. In the late 1940's, the 1950's, and even the early 1960's, the houses had looked neat and were considered pleasing, if not fashionable. But now neighborhoods like Rosewood had begun to decline, the houses no longer looking fresh and inviting, and nearly a third of them displaying "For Sale" signs, as the paint peeled and shingles fell disconsolately from neglected roofs.

Which is why Penny had chosen this particular place to live. "I don't want to be cooped up in an apartment," she'd told Diana. "I want Willow to have a yard and space for a swing set, and Rosewood has the only houses within range of my budget."

Penny had told Diana that her young husband died instantly when he plowed his car into a telephone pole on a slick road. He'd left only a twenty-thousand-dollar life insurance policy and little savings, so money had become a problem for a woman with no conveniently well-off relatives and no college education. Penny had worked as a part-time waitress in a diner before she decided to get a college degree and began taking a summer composition class at Marshall University, where she had seen Simon's advertisement for an editorial assistant posted on the bulletin board. She applied for the job she found interesting, hoping it would allow her to build a regular schedule around her child.

The day Penny Conley came for her interview, Diana took an immediate liking to the attractive, vivacious woman, although when Diana glanced over her résumé, she'd felt that Penny didn't stand a chance of being hired. The composition class was her first brush with college, she had no secretarial or research experience, and she'd never held a job other than waitressing. Diana doubted that Penny had the skills Simon required of someone helping him write his fourth book about ancient Egyptian culture and his archaeological expeditions.

Diana had held her breath as Simon scanned Penny's résumé, afraid he might dismiss her without her a chance, although later she'd chided herself for not giving her great-uncle more credit. The man did not make hasty judgments, which was a blessing for Penny, because after she'd answered his first few cursory questions, he'd begun merely chatting with her. Half an hour later, Penny had left the house with orders to report to her new job on Monday morning. That had been over a year ago, and aside from her good looks and charm, Penny had proved to be the most conscientious and astute assistant Simon had ever employed. She and her daughter had also become like members of the family.

Diana reached Penny's neighborhood at last. She stretched behind the wheel, feeling like she'd been driving since early morning instead of early afternoon. The photo assignment she'd taken on had been more grueling than she'd expected. She'd thought it would be simple— just photos for a city tourism pamphlet. But almost every time she'd focused her camera and started to take a picture, the fussy male head of the tourism center would screech "Stop," after he'd spot a cloud moving to an unsatisfactory position or observe a shriveling petunia in a flower border. At the end of the first day, Diana had been ready to strangle him.

By the time she finished on the third day, she'd fled the town, her muscles aching with tension. She vowed that within the next year, she would take only the commercial assignments she found appealing. A few galleries in New York City, Chicago, and San Francisco were already showing her photographs, and in the last year, sales had begun to climb beyond Diana's expectations, if not beyond her hopes. She no longer had to scramble for money.

She turned onto Penny's street—dark without streetlights—and felt a chill pass over her. Diana stiffened, hearing her grandmother's dreamy voice from long ago: "I feel like someone just stepped on my grave," she'd say, after which, Simon, always the earthbound empiricist, would tell her affectionately such remarks made her sound like a simpleton. Now, though, Diana knew exactly what her grandmother had meant. Suddenly she felt weak, cold, frightened, and doomed, as if Death were whispering in her ear.

As if Death were whispering in her ear? The phrase caught Diana by surprise. She shook her head and told herself she was even more tired than she'd realized.

Diana sighed in relief as Penny's house came into view. Penny had turned on the outside light, which showed off an urn of red geraniums and the porch swing she'd painted light blue at Willow's request. Diana remembered stopping by during the painting process to find Penny impressively splattered with blue paint. Penny had laughed, saying this was her first experience with painting and should probably be her last.

Diana parked at the curb, avoiding a skunk sitting stubbornly in Penny's driveway. She turned on the interior car lights, looked in the rearview mirror, fluffed her long, curly honey-brown hair that had frizzed in the humidity, and wiped away a smudge of mascara beneath one of her heather-green eyes. Even in the dim light, she thought she looked tired and older than her twenty-eight years.

Later, Diana couldn't remember whether she first saw or heard the explosion. She'd turned off the engine and was reaching for her tote bag when Penny's small white house suddenly erupted into a blinding ball of fire. Diana screamed as her car rocked, burning debris raining over glass and metal. At first she ducked. Then she raised her head slightly to see gold and red flames devouring the house, igniting surrounding shrubbery, shooting across the lawn, leaping and frolicking with deadly joy against the still, ebony sky . . . creating a glittering, voracious inferno that Diana was certain no one could survive.

2

Thick, gray-black smoke plumed from the towering burst of flames, slowly floating away after their first, shocking eruption. The smoke spread in layers, the breeze sending it wafting toward Diana's car, enclosing her in a gauze-like shroud. She heard a pitiful mewling sound, then realized it came from her as she sat shuddering, clutching the steering wheel, waiting for . . .

Waiting for what? For Penny to come running toward her, holding Willow's hand?

Diana fumbled with the handle and opened her car door. She stepped out, realized her legs were too shaky to bear her weight, and dropped back onto her seat. She didn't even feel the swinging car door bump against her legs dangling outside of the car. *I should do something,* she thought. *I have to do something.* She looked at the cell phone with its dead battery, and which she didn't know how to use anyway. She looked at the little house, still burning gaudily in the hot night. Diana had closed her eyes for a moment when someone jerked the car door completely open and yelled, "Are you all right?" She jumped.

She saw a man with sun-streaked blond hair combed back from a wide forehead, and steely-blue eyes that were watering slightly from the smoke-filled air. "Miss, are you all right?" he asked again, his voice rough-edged and slightly Southern.

Diana swallowed. "My friend Penny. It's her house. I just pulled up and—" Her throat closed.

"Penny," the man repeated.

"Penny C-Conley," Diana managed.

"I don't live here. I was just turning onto this street when I saw the explosion." The man spoke rapidly. "Did you call nine-one-one?"

For a moment, Diana went blank. Call 911?

"Lady, did you call nine-one-one?" the man nearly shouted.

"No. My cell phone is dead." The words flowed out of Diana's mouth in a voice she barely recognized as her own—thin, high, without emotion. She sounded as if the explosion held no horror or surprise for her, but as the man nodded and disappeared, Diana realized she was crying. Tears flowed down her face to her trembling mouth and dropped off her jaw onto her blouse. She wiped her cheeks with her hands but more tears streamed, and finally she dropped her hands and simply sat, weeping silently, hating her helplessness.

The man returned a moment later. "Help is on the way, but we have to move your car and make room for the emergency vehicles," he shouted. Diana nodded and reached for the ignition. No keys. She'd dropped them when the house exploded.

"Scoot over." Diana did so without a thought. He jumped into the driver's seat, bent down and retrieved the key chain from the floor. "I saw it when your interior lights came on." Without looking at her, he said, "My name is Tyler Raines, by the way."

"Diana . . . Sheridan."

He started the car and pulled forward to the third house beyond Penny's. Diana again swiped at her tearstained face, then opened her window and peered out. An overweight fortyish man wearing baggy sweatpants and holding a beer can stood on his porch, gaping at the fire.

"Where's everyone else?" Tyler Raines yelled to the man as he leaped from the car. "Where are the people who live on either side of that house?"

Sweatpants gaped a moment longer, then said, "House on the right's vacant. Just an old lady lives on the left. Miz Hanson. Got rheumatoid arthritis."

Mrs. Hanson. *Clarice Hanson,* Diana thought. Penny's friend and frequent babysitter for Willow.

Tyler Raines began running toward Mrs. Hanson's house. Sweatpants squinted at Diana. "Wha' happened? Will fire get my house?"

By now Diana had managed to remove herself from her car and stood clutching the door for support, her stomach in a knot, although she'd finally stopped crying.

"Hey!" the man yelled blurrily at her. "I asked if the fire will get my place."

"I don't know!" Diana snapped. The beer he held was clearly not his first. Probably not even his fourth or fifth. "If you have a family, get them out!"

"But my *house* . . ."

Diana didn't need to argue anymore. A woman and an adolescent girl ran past the man on the porch, nearly knocking him down. He rocked unsteadily before his wife yelled, "For God's sake, Clyde, to hell with the house! Or do you care more about it than us?"

The man frowned as if he were pondering this dilemma, continuing to weave and peer at Penny's blazing house. Diana also looked toward it, feeling sick as she pictured Penny and Willow inside the inferno. Something else in the house had caught fire and shot another column of smoke toward the night sky, throwing sparks as it rose. The breeze turned into a sudden gust of wind that caught a piece of burning debris and sent it flying to Mrs. Hanson's house.

Fire began eating the old shingles, creeping across Mrs. Hanson's roof. How fast could that tiny line of fire burst into a blaze? Diana's heart beat harder before she saw Tyler Raines carrying a woman from the house. He headed toward Diana's car. She opened the door wider and he set the woman on the front seat, positioning her body straight ahead, directing her gaze forward, away from the fire. Penny had told Diana that Clarice Hanson was just over seventy. She had small, delicate features and amazingly clear, violet eyes, huge in her pale, horrified face. "My lord, what happened?" she quavered.

Diana crouched, enfolding the woman's frail hands with their swollen joints within her own larger hands. "Mrs. Hanson?" The woman nodded. "We don't know what happened. Penny's house just caught on fire."

"No, Penny's house *exploded!*" Mrs. Hanson's chin trembled. "I didn't have my draperies drawn shut. I saw it!"

"The fire trucks will be here any minute." Diana looked at Tyler Raines over the roof of her car and mouthed, "Her house." His vivid blue eyes shot in the direction of the house from which he'd just emerged. He glanced back at Diana and nodded.

Suddenly, Diana heard the blessed sound of sirens. She thought of the irritation she always felt when sirens awakened her at night, and knew she'd never experience that irritation again. Lights flashed in the night as a fire truck screamed its way toward them.

"Oh dear." Mrs. Hanson's voice wavered. Tears brimmed in her eyes. With shaking hands, she fumbled in the pocket of her much-washed flowered cotton dress and withdrew a dainty handkerchief. "I've never seen any-thing like this."

"I haven't either." Diana realized her own voice sounded thin and old. She wrapped her arm around Clarice Hanson's narrow, trembling shoulders, holding her firmly, blocking her view of the fire. "Everything will be all right, Mrs. Hanson."

"How can you say that when Penny and that sweet lit-tle girl—"

"Shhh." Diana tightened her arm around the woman. "We don't know anything about them yet. Maybe they weren't home."

"Yes they were." Mrs. Hanson stopped dabbing at her tears, her voice suddenly vehement. "Willow's room faces my house. Willow's light was on and I saw Penny come in and kiss her good night. Willow just got out of the hospital today. Penny wouldn't leave her alone. Penny is a good mother."

Penny wouldn't leave her alone. The words tolled in Diana's head. *Penny is a good mother.*

Of course Penny and Willow had been in the house. Where else would they be while Willow recovered from surgery? While Penny anxiously waited for Diana to come? Diana tried to draw a deep breath, failed, and mechani-cally patted Mrs. Hanson's shoulder. The woman buried her face in her handkerchief, and Diana turned to watch the firefighters leaping from the truck, yelling, connecting a huge hose to the nearby fire hydrant and sending a pow-erful blast of water at the blaze.

An emergency service van pulled in just ahead of the

fire truck. Mrs. Hanson lifted her head from her handkerchief-covered hands and whimpered, "I wonder if they've found Penny and Willow."

"I don't know." Diana frowned in frustration. "I wish Mr. Raines would come back and tell us what's going on, but he seems to be helping the firefighters. I don't know what he's thinking—he doesn't even have on protective gear."

"Oh dear, he doesn't, does he?" Mrs. Hanson sounded tearfully resigned and yet admiring. "It's foolish for him to be helping, but men are so brave."

"Some of them are brave." Diana looked at Sweat-pants finally stumbling away from his house, clutching his beer can as he passed in front of Diana's car. His wife and daughter were long gone. "Others don't know the meaning of the word."

Mrs. Hanson glanced at Sweatpants. "Oh, you mean him," she said scathingly. "I'm so glad that blond man came along to help us. Mr. Buckner, the drinker, is a waste of space, as my Henry would have said."

Mr. Buckner, who was more worried about his house than his family. Diana was surprised he hadn't gone back into his house for another can of beer to tide him over until he could safely return home. He was indeed a waste of space, Diana thought, and suddenly remembered Penny saying that he was the laziest man she'd ever known, although he always found enough energy to make passes at her. The other man, Tyler Raines, was a different breed. Diana wondered how she and Mrs. Hanson had been so lucky to have him appear at the exact moment when they needed him.

Mrs. Hanson said weakly, "You're Penny's friend, Diana."

"Yes. I was coming to visit." Her throat tightened. "I was late."

"Then thank the lord, child. Otherwise, you would have been in that house."

I would have been in that house. The full impact of the

realization suddenly hit Diana with dizzying shock. She felt sick with horror. If she'd exited her car one minute earlier . . .

Mrs. Hanson looked up at her, and obviously seeing Diana's stricken expression, she reached out, gave Diana's hand a squeeze, and quickly changed the topic. "Pardon me for being nosy, but is the blond man who's been helping us your . . . admirer?"

"You . . . You mean my boyfriend?" Diana said slowly, trying to focus on Mrs. Hanson again. "No. I've never seen him before. He said he'd just pulled onto this street to turn around when the house caught fire. His name is Tyler Raines."

"Tyler Raines. I've never heard the name, although he looks vaguely familiar. . . . At least I thought he did at first. My memory isn't what it used to be. Thank goodness he was here. I've been having a bad bout with my arthritis this week and I need my walker. I was shaking so much, though, I turned it over and I was standing there wavering back and forth, ready to fall on the blasted thing, when he swooped in and picked me up, as if I was no heavier than a little bird, and carried me out to you. If he could have only gotten to Penny and Willow. . . ."

Mrs. Hanson broke off, her hands trembling violently. "Oh, dear heaven, that little house simply blew up! We both have gas furnaces. Could her furnace have exploded?"

"Penny wouldn't be running the furnace in the summer. Maybe it was the water heater. It was gas, too, and in the basement as I recall. It could have been leaking all day and Penny didn't notice. All it would have taken was one spark to set off all that gas."

"A spark from what?"

"A frayed electrical cord or the water heater flipping on or a pressure valve malfunction or . . ." Diana glanced helplessly at Mrs. Hanson, who was looking at her expectantly. "I'm not an expert. I'm just speculating."

The woman's shoulders sagged. "Knowing the cause won't help Penny and Willow anyway. Oh, my lord, those poor things." Mrs. Hanson's voice shivered. "That explosion even made *my* house shake. My daughter makes beautiful ceramics and she gave me a figurine that looks just like Willow. She said it was the best thing she'd done. It fell from the curio cabinet and I know it shattered. It's like a sign from heaven."

The woman suddenly began to shake and sob, again raising her drenched handkerchief to her face. Diana, still crouching, stretched into the car and enfolded Mrs. Hanson in her arms, making comforting sounds that she would to a child.

Diana continued to rock and croon absently while keeping her gaze on the uproar around Penny's house. Emergency workers had hooked up giant lights that somehow made the scene look almost artificial, more like a movie set than Penny's familiar and very real house—or shell of a house. The right side had completely collapsed, and only two-thirds of the left side remained standing, drenched in water sprayed from the giant hoses. From where Diana stood, the insides of the house were black and glistening. The back of the house disappeared into darkness.

A few small fires still burned inside, and three firefighters entered, dousing the flames. Beyond the destroyed right wall, Diana could see that the three men walked along the inner left side of the house, taking small steps and repeatedly looking downward. She realized most of the living room floor must have collapsed, and the men were peering into the basement. They looked upward, too, dodging charred boards and shingles crashing from the roof. The men were obviously scanning the ruins for survivors, Diana realized. She closed her eyes. How she longed to hear one of them yell, "We've found a woman and a little girl and they're not hurt!"

No one said anything about a woman and a little girl, though. They simply moved slowly and silently through the ruin that half an hour earlier had been Penny's cozy little house where Willow had lain recovering from surgery, and her loving mother had hovered over her.

They had extinguished the fire at Mrs. Hanson's house, although Diana couldn't judge how much destruction the structure had suffered. The woman still didn't know that the conflagration had reached her own home. Diana dreaded telling her or letting her see it, no matter how minor the damage. The shaken woman seemed as if she couldn't handle more bad news. Still, someone had to inform her.

Diana took a deep breath and strove to speak as calmly as possible. "Mrs. Hanson, I'm afraid the fire got to your house. Or rather, to a small part of it." The woman gasped, but Diana smiled reassuringly. "A chunk of burning debris hit your roof. The firefighters immediately started spraying, and I think they've completely put out the fire," she said quickly. "Still, if you wouldn't mind sitting alone in the car for a few minutes, I'd like to see how much damage was done."

Mrs. Hanson clutched her arm. "Oh, no, Diana! You mustn't leave the protection of this car. It's dangerous out there. My house is just a little old thing, not worth getting yourself hurt over."

"I'll be extremely careful. Mr. Raines hasn't come back for a while. Maybe they've found . . . something."

"You mean *someone,*" Mrs. Hanson said dully. "And if they'd found Penny and Willow, I'm sure that young man would have rushed right back to tell us." Her throat worked as if she were choking back a sob. "Oh, I just can't bear it," she blurted.

"Maybe Tyler Raines is helping and he couldn't come back. I have to know *something,* Mrs. Hanson. That's why I need to go check for myself. Will you be okay if I leave for a few minutes?"

Mrs. Hanson drew a deep breath and said with feigned strength, "Certainly I'll be okay, dear. My joints are swollen but my heart is in good shape." She patted Diana's hand. "You go take a look if you want. I'll sit here quietly."

And cry, Diana thought as she stood, her legs cramping slightly from the crouching position she'd held so long. She closed the car door, hoping to shut Mrs. Hanson away from some of the noise and smoke. She wished she could just as easily block out the sight of the ruined house.

She glanced back and saw that she needn't worry. Mrs. Hanson held her head high and firm. Diana was certain the woman was gazing straight ahead with her lovely eyes—eyes that apparently didn't need glasses even though she was in her seventies, Diana thought as she tucked her thick, windswept hair behind her ears and tried to walk steadily toward the burned houses.

"What are you doing?"

Diana jumped at the sound of Tyler Raines's razor-sharp voice. She'd been trying to keep her mind off Penny and Willow by thinking only about Mrs. Hanson. She hadn't even seen Raines striding toward her. She drew herself up to her full five-foot-six frame, but she had to look up at least another six inches to glare at him. "I want to see Penny's house."

Tyler Raines stood firmly in front of her. Sweat streaked his dirty face, soot had settled into three shallow creases across his forehead, and his light blue T-shirt had turned an indeterminate shade of gray and stuck clammily to his wide chest. His damp, longish hair had parted unevenly in the middle and hung below his high cheekbones, almost to his earlobes.

The man looked exhausted and, to Diana's mind, surprisingly distressed about people he didn't know. But worst of all, he looked as if he was going to argue with her. She narrowed her eyes slightly and set her jaw.

They gave each other long, measuring looks. Then Diana thought she saw a flicker of understanding in Raines's eyes before he sighed and stepped aside. "Oh, all right, dammit. Go ahead. Be careful, though. Hoses are lying around, everything is soaked—"

"Which I can very well see for myself. I am not a child. I'm not going to run around willy-nilly—"

"I'm not afraid of you running willy-nilly. I'm afraid of you fainting."

In spite of the situation, indignation flashed through

Diana. "I am not one of those silly women who faint! I have never fainted in my life, and I've been on archaeological expeditions to Egypt!"

"Egypt, eh? Well, that's impressive, but you weren't far from fainting when you tried to get out of your car after the house exploded." Raines gave her a hard stare with his azure eyes, and Diana flushed at the memory. "If you insist on getting a closer look at this mess, though, I guess I can't stop you."

"No, you certainly can't," Diana huffed, grasping at her waning bravado. "And I'm not just some stranger who wants to get 'a closer look at this mess,' as you put it. My friend Penny and her five-year-old daughter were in that house, for God's sake!" Diana's voice cracked but she plowed on. "Do you expect me to just sit in my car for an hour until someone gets around to telling me something like whether or not they're still *alive*?"

Diana was almost certain the man flinched. Then his gaze softened a fraction. "Sorry about my wording. It's natural that you want to see about your friend, Miss . . . I forgot your name."

"Diana Sheridan," she snarled, exasperated with him, furious that again she was on the verge of bursting into racking, useless sobs—just what he'd expect from her. "Now will you stop blocking my way to the house?"

"Okay, but I'm going with you. I don't want you falling down and breaking an arm or a leg. People are too busy to stop and patch you up, on top of everything else."

"I know to be careful about where I'm walking, Mr. Raines," she seethed.

"It's Tyler. And I'm sure usually you are careful about where you're walking, but tonight you're upset and the area around the house is dangerous." He reached out and tightly closed his hand around her forearm. She stiffened, glaring at him. "Don't fight me about this," he said in a steely voice. "If you haven't noticed, you're trembling all over. Even your lips are twitching. You're more upset than you realize."

Diana made a sound she hoped conveyed supreme contempt for his appraisal, but secretly she felt grateful for the large, sturdy hand holding her arm as they began walking. Everything inside of her seemed to vibrate and her legs were shaky. She'd always been strong, emotionally and physically, which is why Great-uncle Simon had allowed her to accompany him on her first Egyptian expedition when she was only eighteen. Now, though, she felt weak and vulnerable, although she was doing her best to hide her unusual fragility.

Diana kept her gaze on the ground, determined not to trip over anything, as Tyler Raines had predicted she would. She wanted to show him she was totally in control. But she wasn't. She jerked to a stop as they neared the house and she heard wood cracking. A man screamed hoarsely before a crash came from inside the house, and Diana knew the floor had given way under one of the three firefighters who'd entered the building.

A general shout of distress mounted into the night, men rushing to the front of the little house, not daring to step inside and put more weight on what was left of the living room floor. Two firefighters, looking unreal in the glare of powerful electric lamps, stood plastered against the wall. Both gazed into the basement and one shouted, "Davis, you all right?"

Everyone seemed to hold their breath for at least ten long, silent seconds. "Davis! Are you all right?" the man yelled again.

After a moment, a feeble, breathless voice floated from the depths of the house. "I'm alive. Landed on my side." A pause, then a soft moan of pain. "Think I broke . . . couple of ribs."

"Don't move. You might puncture a lung." Pause. "Paramedics!"

No one came and someone else called. Once. Twice. Then two men and a woman came around the side of the house pushing a gurney. A firefighter rushed to them and began bellowing as if they weren't standing three feet away from him. "One of our guys fell through the floor! He thinks he's broken some ribs. You've gotta help him!"

The female paramedic looked at the firefighter. "I'm afraid your man will have to wait a few minutes until the second emergency team arrives," she said quietly, her young face immobile. "We found a woman in the back-yard."

"Penny!" Diana broke away from Tyler and ran toward the gurney where a motionless figure lay. She reached the gurney and looked at the motionless form covered by a white sheet, only the head exposed. The sight hit Diana like a hammer blow. A paramedic had brushed back what was left of Penny's short mahogany-brown hair to reveal her once lovely face, the left side of which now seemed to bubble with vicious, searing burns that stretched halfway across her forehead, destroying a cheek, annihilating her nose, obliterating the left eye.

Diana stepped back in shuddering horror. She went cold and rigid, as if turned to stone. Finally, she whispered desolately, "My God, Penny."

The female paramedic looked at Diana with compassion. "She was lying in a little rubber pool with a couple of inches of water in it. The right side of her face was in the water, but her nose was exposed or she would have drowned."

"Penny?" Diana leaned toward the burned woman, saying uselessly, "Penny, it's Diana."

"She's unconscious, thank the saints," the female paramedic said gently with a slight Irish accent. "She can't hear you, ma'am. Don't look at her any more than you have already. She wouldn't want you to see her this way, and you won't want to remember her this way, either."

" 'Remember her' " Diana asked vaguely, then louder, "She's not dead, is she?"

"No, but . . ." The woman trailed off and looked down at the wreckage of Penny's face.

A male paramedic intervened. "She's not dead, Miss, but she's sustained some bad burns."

"Not just to her face?" Diana demanded in agony.

"The whole left side of her body was exposed." The man gave Diana a sympathetic but authoritative look. "The burns are bad. Let's leave it at that. Right now, it's vital that we get her to the hospital as soon as possible. The doctors can tell you more later."

As they began cautiously moving the gurney toward the ambulance, Diana felt herself going limp. By now, Tyler Raines stood behind her and placed a firm hand under her elbow. She sagged against him, barely aware of his presence, only of his strength holding her upright.

As the paramedics wheeled Penny away into the hot, smothering darkness, Diana drew a deep breath and called, "Penny has a little girl. She's five. Have you found her?"

The female paramedic looked back at her. Their eyes met and Diana knew the answer even before the young woman said, "We've found no signs of a little girl. Maybe inside . . ."

Maybe inside, where the fire had raged in unchecked ecstasy, consuming everything in its ravaging path, Diana thought, including a sweet, innocent five-year-old girl.

And for the first time in her twenty-eight years, Diana fainted.

CHAPTER TWO

1

Diana jolted awake as cold water splashed over her face, into her ears, and across the delicate skin of her neck. She opened her eyes to see Tyler Raines holding a large, empty Styrofoam cup and gazing down at her, his head tilted slightly to the right, a vertical wrinkle lodged between his dark eyebrows. They stared at each other until he finally asked, "You all right, Miss I-Have-Never-Fainted-in-My-Life?"

"I'm fine. Don't you dare throw more water on me. And I *haven't* fainted until now!" Diana realized she was lying flat on the ground, legs and arms splayed. She pulled together all four limbs and quickly sat up, wiping at her wet face. "Where's Penny?"

"The ambulance just pulled away with her."

Diana looked around in time to see the ambulance turning the corner. "I should have gone with her!"

"No, you shouldn't have." Tyler grasped her hand, helping her clamber to a standing position. She pushed her long, dripping hair behind her ears and looked around frantically. "Have they found Willow?"

"No, but—"

"Oh my God!" Diana felt as if her chest was tightening, squeezing the air from her lungs. "They still haven't found her?"

"If you'd stop yelling and let me finish, I was going to say you were out for only a couple of minutes."

"You don't think Willow is..." Diana gestured vaguely at the ruin of a house, unable to look at it, unable to say more.

Tyler hesitated. For a moment, Diana thought she saw him waver behind what seemed to be only a veil of self-possession. "I don't know about the little girl," he said finally. "The mother was outside—maybe the child was, too."

"No, she'd just had surgery. She wouldn't have been—"

"Don't reject possibilities. We don't *know* anything for sure. The firefighters haven't had a chance to search everywhere. They're still trying to help the guy who fell into the basement when the floor gave way. They can't prop a ladder against that crumbling edge of the floor. I think they're using ropes to bring him up." Tyler reached out and touched Diana's arm. "You don't look so good. You need to go home."

"Go home! I can't go home until I know something about Willow. And if I were going anywhere, it would be to the hospital with Penny!"

"Settle down and get your breath," Tyler said sternly. His gaze seemed to grasp hers and hold it unrelentingly. "Now you listen to me. It could be half an hour or longer before they find the child, and there's not one damned thing you can do for Penny at the hospital besides sit and wait for them to tell you she's in critical condition."

Diana's face crumpled and Tyler's voice softened. "You're exhausted, you're frightened, and you've had a hell of a shock. You've already fainted. Unless you want to end up in the hospital, too, you'll go home. You're in no shape to hang around here and neither is Mrs. Hanson. *Especially* Mrs. Hanson. The fire burned a large hole in her roof and destroyed part of the kitchen and living room wall. Also, embers might be smoldering beneath some of the roofing and they could set another fire."

"Oh, no," Diana moaned.

"Oh, yes. That lady can't stay in her house tonight. Does she have any place else to go?"

"I don't know. I've barely met her." She paused. "I live in Ritter Park," she said, referring to the seventy-acre park stretching along the Southeast Area and up into the Southeast Hills of Huntington. "She could come home with me."

"Ritter Park, eh? The ritzy neighborhood. I should have known."

"The house belongs to my great-uncle," Diana said irritably. "I don't own it—I'm just a boarder for a while. Anyway, the house is large. There's plenty of room for guests."

"Fine. I know the area. Just direct me to the house."

"Mr. Raines, I know how to drive."

"I told you before that my name is Tyler, and I'm sure you're usually a first-rate driver, but not tonight. Now let's go tell Mrs. Hanson she's having a sleepover with her new best friend."

A few minutes later, they informed Mrs. Hanson that Penny was alive. "How badly hurt is she?" the woman asked. "She must have gotten burned."

"We don't know any details," Tyler said quickly, then, before she could ask more questions, he told her she would be spending the night at Diana's house. Mrs. Hanson widened her eyes and shook her head vehemently. "I can't just desert my home. Someone could break in!"

Tyler spoke to her gently and patiently. "Mrs. Hanson, firefighters and probably the police will be here most of the night. You see, they haven't found the little girl yet."

Mrs. Hanson's slender, thin-skinned hand flew to her throat in distress. "They haven't found Willow? I just assumed . . ."

Mrs. Hanson seemed to drift away from them for a moment. Diana and Tyler exchanged looks over the woman's head. *She can't bear this tragedy,* Diana thought. *Maybe she's going to have a heart attack. Maybe we should take her to the hospital.*

Abruptly, Mrs. Hanson interrupted Diana's thoughts with a crisp voice. "I thought of this when both of you were at the house, then I forgot about it when you came back with news of my house burning. I remember now, though." The woman took a breath, concentrating. "Earlier, I glanced outside and I'm almost certain I saw Willow climbing out of her bedroom window. Penny had left Willow's bedside lamp on. That's how I could see her room."

"Willow climbed out of her window!" Diana was incredulous. "But she just had an operation."

"I know, but Penny told me they were doing some procedure that didn't cause as much pain as the old-fashioned surgery. It also enables people to heal faster. I guess Willow felt all right."

"Where did she go?" Tyler asked urgently.

"She went toward the backyard. Penny has no outside lights, so I only saw Willow for a moment because she was walking very fast. Almost running. Maybe she was going toward the woods. On this street, the woods border all of our backyards. I went back to my chair—my phone is on a little table beside my favorite chair—and I was calling Penny to tell her about seeing Willow, when . . . when . . ."

The woman's eyes filled with tears. *When the house burst into a ball of fire,* Diana thought. She reached out and patted Mrs. Hanson's shoulder, frustrated that she couldn't think of anything more comforting to do for the woman. "Don't cry. It's going to be all right."

"How can you possible say that?" Mrs. Hanson demanded tearfully. "I could see them carrying someone—it must have been Penny—and putting her into the ambulance. Now you tell me they can't find Willow! I may be old, but I'm not senile! I know everything isn't going to be all right!"

Tyler bent down and looked steadily into the woman's

eyes. "You're not old—you're just older than us, but you're right. We *have* been treating you like you're senile. My grandmother would have thrashed the daylights out of me if I talked to her like she didn't have good sense."

Mrs. Hanson smiled slightly and Tyler went on. "I'll just tell you straight. Things aren't all right. Not by a long shot. Professionals are taking care of Penny, though, and after what you told us, I think Willow might be hiding in the woods. She's probably afraid to come out, but I'd bet a hundred dollars she's not hurt. If she was in the woods, she would have been too far away to get burned.

"You and Diana don't seem to be faring too well, though," Tyler went on. "You're trembling all over and Diana can hardly get her breath, although she's trying to hide it. That's why you both need to get away from here. You need quiet and rest. I don't think a stiff drink would do you two any harm, either."

"Oh, I don't drink," Mrs. Hanson protested.

"Then start. One drink won't turn you into an alcoholic. I'm going to drive you to Diana's house."

Mrs. Hanson looked aghast. "Oh, I couldn't impose. I can go to my friend Ella's. . . ." She trailed off. "Except that she's in Vermont visiting her daughter. My son and daughter's families met yesterday at Disneyworld for a vacation. Well, if someone will get my purse with my money in it, I can go to a motel."

"Where you'd have none of the amenities of a home," Diana said. "Come to my house. You need a comfortable night's sleep, and after the shock of tonight, you shouldn't be alone in some motel room."

"I could just watch television. I can't possibly sleep tonight."

"You can rest," Tyler stated. "I'll drop you two ladies off and come back here. The minute I know anything about the little girl, I'll call."

Diana snapped, "I told you I can drive home."

"We don't need any more disasters tonight," Tyler nearly

snarled. "If you're not going to think of your own safety, think of Mrs. Hanson's. My nerves are steadier than yours at the moment. Now get in the car."

Anger surged through Diana, but she knew Tyler was right. She felt herself nearly vibrating within. Her reactions and judgments no doubt suffered because of the shock, and only a selfish desire to prove herself capable would force her to insist on driving. Sighing, she got in the car without a word, wondering how Tyler Raines could remain so calm.

As they drove away from Penny's house, Diana glanced over at him, his jaw clamped tight, his tanned skin ashy beneath smudges of soot. He looked in the rearview mirror, back at the ruins of Penny's house, and Diana noticed his eyelids close for a moment, as if he couldn't stand the sight. No, she realized, she was wrong about Tyler Raines's uncanny composure. He might be putting on a good show for her and Mrs. Hanson, but he wasn't as unaffected by the possible deaths as he pretended to be, even if he didn't know Penny and Willow Conley.

Diana softened toward him a bit and asked, "Where are you from, Tyler?"

For a moment, he seemed startled. "Huh? Oh, New York. City, that is. I'm just down here visiting."

"Oh, who?" Clarice Hanson asked. "That's an impolite question, but I might know them."

"Uh, the guy that owns Al's Barbecue."

"Albert Meeks?" Clarice asked in surprise. "Why, he's older than I am!"

"He was a friend of my grandfather's, really. Grandpa's dead, but I still try to visit Al every so often. He seems to appreciate it. They used to go hunting together a couple of times a year. Al's one fine hunter. When I was a kid, they'd let me tag along sometimes."

Diana had known Al Meeks for years. Penny, Willow, and she often dined at his casual restaurant that served the best barbecued ribs in town. She frowned at Tyler's description of him, however. "Al is a fine hunter?" Diana asked, her mistrust of Tyler rising again. "How could he be? Al's been blind in his right eye for over thirty years."

Tyler paused. He gave her a sidelong look that told her he knew she was trying to trip him up, poke a hole in his story. Then he said casually, "You don't need good eyesight in both eyes if you use a scope on a rifle, Diana. I guess you don't do much hunting."

"No, as a matter of fact I don't," she answered. "I think unless you're in need of food, hunting is just an excuse for killing."

"It's a sport," Tyler parried.

"The sport of killing."

Tyler turned his eyes away from the road and looked at her. "Think you've got things all figured out, don't you? Even me."

She stared grimly ahead. "Not quite yet," Diana returned slowly. "But I will. You can be sure of that, Mr. Raines."

2

"Uncle Simon? I'm home!"

A voice boomed from a room on their left. "Well, at last, thank God! I've been going crazy here this week without you *and* Penny. Which reminds me, she hasn't called this evening to tell me about Willow's condition and she promised—"

Simon Van Etton strode into the foyer and jerked to a halt, looking in surprise at the three bedraggled people standing in front of him. Clarice and Tyler both hovered at least two feet behind Diana, as if they expected a beating from the elaborate cane Simon carried mostly for show. His thick silver hair gleamed under the light of the chandelier, and he raised a white eyebrow. "Good lord, what's happened?"

Without thought, Diana rushed to Simon and flung her arms around him, burying her face in the satin of his smoking jacket. For a moment, he seemed astonished and stood stiffly, then he encircled her waist with his arms. He touched his cheek to the top of her head and murmured into her thick hair, "Diana?"

"It's Penny, Simon." Diana suddenly felt as if her hold on Simon was the only thing keeping her on her feet. Her words poured forth in a torrent. "I'd just pulled up in front of Penny's house earlier when it . . . it *exploded*!"

Simon Van Etton held Diana out from him and stared at her, for once speechless. His dark green eyes looked at her first with hesitation, then doubt, then alarm. He opened his mouth once and closed it. When he opened it the second time, he asked with an eerie softness, "The house exploded?" Diana nodded. "You're certain it *exploded?*"

"*Yes,* Simon. For God's sake, I wasn't dreaming!"

"No, no of course you weren't." He hugged her again. "Penny? Willow?"

"I saw Penny." Diana leaned back and looked at him. "She wasn't conscious. She's so badly burned I don't think she's going to live."

The color washed from Simon's face. "Penny is burned?"

"Oh, yes." Diana wavered. "Her face—"

"Don't describe it," Simon ordered. "I do not want to hear it." *He can't bear to hear it,* Diana thought. "What about Willow?"

Diana had begun to shake. "They can't even find her!"

Simon tightened his grip on Diana as Tyler said, "We think the child might be hiding in the woods behind the house, sir."

Simon looked at him. "Who are you?" Simon swallowed. "Forgive my lack of manners. If I know you, young man, I'm sorry that I'm too astounded by this news to remember your name."

"You don't know me, sir. My name is Tyler Raines." He put his arm around Mrs. Hanson's shoulder and pushed the woman gently forward. "And this is Mrs. Clarice Hanson. She lives beside Penny."

Diana saw Simon try to smile reassuringly at the woman whose gaze was taking in the glistening Georgian chandelier shining down on a large circular Oriental rug and the eight-foot-tall antique grandfather clock in the corner. She looked ready to bolt out through the massive, carved double doors. "Of course, Mrs. Hanson. We met briefly at Willow's birthday party in June, but there were so many children around, I didn't get a chance to talk with you," Simon said graciously.

Clarice finally glanced at him and tried to smile, but tears overcame her.

Simon looked at Tyler. "Mr. Raines, you seem to be the calmest person here. Will you tell me what happened?"

Tyler told him quickly, not elaborating, not going off on tangents, just concisely, as Simon liked. When he finished, Tyler added, "Mrs. Hanson can't stay in her own home tonight. Your niece said she would be welcomed here."

"Mrs. Hanson is most welcome," Simon said. If Diana hadn't known Simon so well, she wouldn't have noticed the forced steadiness of his voice. He was trying mightily not to betray his horror. In spite of everything, his sharp eyes had even taken in the woman's infirmity. "Mrs. Hanson, we have a nice bedroom here on the first floor. Diana said it looked as if no one had touched it since the Middle Ages, and she redecorated it last year. It has an adjoining bathroom and a good view of the garden. I think you'll be comfortable there."

"Oh, it sounds lovely," Mrs. Hanson said, clearly intimidated by the size and formality of the house, "but I really hate to force myself on you."

"You are certainly not forcing yourself on me or Diana." Simon managed a reassuring smile for the woman. "I suggest we all go into the library and have some brandy. This has been quite a shock."

"Thanks, sir, but I'm going back," Tyler said. "They haven't found the little girl."

Simon looked at him piercingly. "And you think you can when no one else can?"

"I'd like to try." Tyler's voice was somewhat humble yet at the same time firm.

Diana pulled away from Simon and faced Tyler. "I'm going with you."

"No, you aren't," Tyler said with authority. "You have to pull your nerves together."

"My nerves are just fine," Diana argued, although she knew she sounded far from convincing. "If Willow is hiding in the woods, I'd have a better chance of finding her than you. She *knows* me."

Tyler tilted his head slightly, as if trying to make her see reason without offending her. "Even if you don't realize it, you're an emotional and physical wreck. I'm sure your uncle would agree that you need to stay here."

"Indeed I do," Simon agreed, his voice brooking no argument. "Diana, Mr. Raines is correct. You will stay here with Mrs. Hanson and me."

"Oh, *men!*" Diana exclaimed, suddenly acting furious to hide the fact that what she really wanted was to sink to the floor and cry. "You all stick together."

"When we're making more sense than the womenfolk, we certainly do."

"Womenfolk!" Diana spluttered. "Uncle Simon, I have never heard you sound like—"

"Like what?" Simon's commanding voice and sharp green gaze deflated an exhausted Diana.

"Like you just did," she answered meekly.

"We drove here in Diana's car," Tyler intervened. "Mine is back at . . . the scene. I'll call a taxi."

Simon made a face. "Oh, nonsense. It will take forever for a cab to arrive on a Friday night. This city is disgracefully short of taxicabs. I have two cars and I'm not going to be using either one tonight. Take one of them." Diana looked at him in disbelief. Was her great-uncle turning over one of his cars to this complete stranger? Apparently so.

"We'll worry about getting the car back here tomorrow," Simon continued, not even glancing at Diana. "Frankly, at the moment I couldn't care less if I ever get it back."

"I appreciate the loan," Tyler said, "and I'll make sure you get the car back safe and sound."

"I'm sure you will." Simon gave Tyler a long, measuring look. "And I have an odd feeling you will return Willow safe and sound, too."

3

Tyler Raines gaped when Simon Van Etton turned on the garage lights. A slightly dirty SUV dominated the middle of the three-car garage, but beside it sat a gleaming black Porsche. Simon, obviously watching Tyler's gaze lock on to the Porsche, managed a wry smile. "I bought that last year. Diana had a fit. She said I was going to kill myself. I replied, 'At my age, it doesn't matter, and if I do kill myself, at least I'll go out in style.'"

Tyler grinned. "I can see why you couldn't resist it. It's a beautiful car, Dr. Van Etton."

"Take either car you want, Tyler."

"The SUV would be the most practical."

"I suppose it would, although I know you'd like to take a spin in the Porsche." Simon walked about a foot away from the door and looked at a Peg-Board holding sets of keys. "Here are the keys to the behemoth over there. We'll save the Porsche for another time."

Tyler hesitated then said reluctantly, "That would be great, but I don't live here, Dr. Van Etton. Like I said, I just happened to turn onto that street when I saw the house blow up."

"So you actually saw the house explode?"

"Yes, sir."

"What do you think happened, Tyler?"

"I have no idea." Tyler looked into Simon Van Etton's keen, dark green eyes. "It could have been faulty wiring or a piece of defective household equipment."

Simon stared at him for a moment. "I can tell you're going to stick with that story, whether or not you believe it." He sighed. "Well, thank God you were there. Diana is a strong woman. Still, anyone can take only so much. And poor Mrs. Hanson—I don't even like to think of what could have happened to her. She looks frail enough to snap in two." The older man put his hand on Tyler's shoulder. "I want to thank you for taking care of Diana. She's the dearest person in my life. You also did a very brave thing, running in the house to get Mrs. Hanson."

"Anybody would have done the same."

"Hell, no, they wouldn't, and you know it." Simon paused, frowning. "Is Penny as bad as Diana said?"

"I didn't see her entire body—just her face. I'll be blunt: One side was hideously burned."

Color drained from the older man's complexion and he stiffened, as if marshalling all of his strength.

"The paramedics, especially one of them, looked as if there wasn't much hope," Tyler ended bleakly.

"Well, they might not believe there is, but I choose to believe there's always hope, and Penny is a strong girl, just like Diana. Also, they can work miracles with plastic surgery these days. Penny will live and she will be lovely again. I'm absolutely sure of it." Simon's volume swelled, as though if he said the words loudly enough, they would come true. He handed the keys to Tyler. "Now go find that little girl."

"I can guarantee I'll return the car, sir, but I can't guarantee I'll find Willow."

"But you'll do your best," Simon said earnestly. "That's all anyone can do."

4

Smoke. Burned wood. Wet ground.

Willow Conley kept her eyes tightly shut. She didn't have to see, but she did have to breathe. She tried taking only little breaths, keeping the smells out of her nose, but they were all around her, too much for her to conquer.

She sighed and scooted closer to a big tree trunk—a tree far back in the woods where she wasn't allowed to go. The tree limbs above her had begun to sway in the wind, and the leaves whispered to one another. Willow didn't usually pay any attention to leaves blowing, but tonight their murmurs added to her fright. She pulled up her knees and tried to bury her face in the clean smell of her pink cotton pajama legs, but scrunching up made the right side of her tummy hurt. Besides, her pink pajamas were dirty and they didn't smell clean and fresh anymore, not like they had when Mommy had put them on her. . . .

How long ago? Minutes? Hours? Willow knew only it was still night. Up high, the moon and the stars looked cool and peaceful, just like they had when she'd climbed out her window. If she stared only at them, she could pretend nothing bad had happened. But if she looked at the ugly place where her and Mommy's house had been . . .

Willow cringed and shut her eyes tight. Still, behind her eyelids danced the red and yellow flames, the pieces of burning wood shooting in all directions, poor Mommy flying off the bottom step of the porch and landing in the swimming pool. . . .

The pool that could not keep her safe from the fire that swept over her limp body, chewed at her hair, and danced on her face. Mommy's beautiful, laughing face—a face that Willow somehow knew would never laugh again.

Pain jabbed at Willow's chest—a pain that had nothing to do with her operation. Her heart must have broken, she decided, holding her breath as the pain stabbed again. She wondered how long it took a broken heart to stop hurting. Probably forever and ever.

Earlier, when the fire had captured Mommy, Willow had taken a couple of steps back into the woods. Shortly afterward, sirens wailed and swirling red and blue lights slashed the night. Then Willow had heard men yelling before huge arcs of water fell on the blazing house. The fire, the lights, the miniature waterfalls should all have been dazzling and exciting in the quiet of the night—like fireworks on the Fourth of July—but Willow had found none of it either dazzling or exciting. This wasn't the Fourth of July, and she knew all the color and the noise meant disaster.

Finally the flames got smaller and smaller until they were gone, leaving behind smoke and sharp smells. She'd seen people bending over her mother lying in the pool. They shook their heads. Then carefully, oh so carefully, they had lifted her, put her on a narrow bed on wheels, and taken her away.

Later, people with big flashlights walked around the backyard. They headed for the woods shouting, "Willow! Willow! Come out now, honey! *Willow!*" That's when Willow began retreating deeper into the shelter of the trees because she knew the people wanted to take her away. They wanted to make her walk past the little rubber pool where the fire had claimed Mommy, past her home, where she'd felt safer than in any other place in the world—the place that was now just a scary, smoky shell that didn't look anything like her and Mommy's dear little house. Willow knew what they wanted, and she couldn't bear to go. She *wouldn't* go, and they couldn't make her if they couldn't find her!

Deeper into the woods she moved. Mommy had said there might be bad things in the woods—snakes, maybe even a wolf. She did have the feeling that she wasn't alone—a twig snapped close by, and Willow thought that she heard movement in the tangle of weeds and creeping vines beneath the trees. Maybe it *was* a wolf or a poison snake. She didn't care about wolves and snakes after what she'd just seen, though. Willow almost hoped a poison snake would bite her or a wolf would eat her.

It didn't matter because now only Diana and Uncle Simon would miss her, and they'd probably soon forget her because she wasn't their real family. Besides, she didn't want to live if Mommy wasn't with her. Being a little girl wouldn't be any fun without Mommy—Mommy who sometimes raised her voice if Willow did something

wrong, but who mostly laughed, played Candyland whenever she had time, and sometimes at night let Willow
wear lipstick and dress up like she was a grown-up girl.
But what Willow loved most was when Mommy put on
music and danced like an angel, her feet barely touching
the floor and her eyes looking as if she saw some beautiful, magic, faraway land.

Tears stung Willow's eyes, inflamed and hurting from
all the smoke. She didn't want to start crying. She didn't
want to make a noise. Otherwise, all those people with
their yelling and their bright flashlights would find her. She
would be happy if she could just stay here forever; except
that forever was a long time, and she already felt loneliness
descending on her like a dark, cold cloud.

Willow lay her head against the trunk of the tree. It
seemed like the shouting had grown softer and the lights
were moving in a different direction. The people in
uniforms—the people who had taken Mommy and wanted
to take her, too—were finally going away. Willow rubbed
her head against the rough tree trunk, searching for a comfortable spot. Maybe she could just go to sleep and no one
would find her for days or even years.

She'd grown drowsy when she first heard the man's
voice. It was a nice voice, deep and soft and soothing, not
loud and piercing like the other voices had been, yelling
out her name so harshly they frightened even the night
birds into flight. No, this voice sounded kind and warm.
This voice sounded *safe*. And to top it off, the man was
saying a rhyme—a happy, pretty rhyme. Willow cocked
her head and listened:

> If I could capture that fat white moon
> I'd drag it down to earth so soon,
> I'd tie it up in a pink satin bow
> And give it to my pretty Willow.
>
> If I could capture that fat white moon
> I'd drag it down to earth so soon. . . .

Suddenly the man stood in front of her. He looked like a giant, so tall and straight. For a moment, Willow felt overwhelming fear. Then he stooped in front of her and, even in the moonlight, she could see his blondish hair and his bright blue eyes. He smiled at her—such a nice smile—and said very softly, "Willow."

Tremulously she held out her carefully tended jar of sparkle bugs. He took it, studied the bugs twinkling and winking, and he smiled his nice smile at her again. Finally he set down the jar and held out his arms.

Willow gazed back for moment. Then she ran her tongue over her dry lips and said just above a whisper, "It's you!"

CHAPTER THREE

1

When he returned from the garage, Simon looked at Clarice seated stiffly on a small, hard chair in the foyer. "Mrs. Hanson, please come into the library and have something to drink." He was already putting an arm around her shoulder and gently but firmly helping her rise, steering her toward the room at the left. "Do you like brandy?"

"I'll just have a glass of water," Clarice said almost shyly, not looking at him.

"Water!" Simon sounded as if she'd just asked for a glass of poison. "That's absurd. Water won't do a thing for your nerves, and they need soothing. So do mine. You'll be doing Diana and me a favor to have a drink with us. Won't she, Diana?"

"Yes," Diana said lifelessly, knowing a glass of liquor wasn't going to calm any of their nerves tonight.

Diana followed them into Simon's library, which was really the heart of the house where he spent most of his time. Mrs. Hanson took two steps beyond the entrance and halted. The room spanned the width of the house. The woman's gaze traveled over the soaring vault of the ceiling from where a large bronze-and-amber chandelier hung above a long, shining walnut table bearing stacks of books and small brass desk lamps with opalescent shades.

At the front of the room, a smaller version of the bronze chandelier gleamed over a grand piano placed near a floor-to-ceiling bay window bordered with opened cream-colored draperies. Quality antique and modern chairs and couches dominated the center of the room. The hodge-podge of styles and colors should have clashed, but instead they looked comfortable and inviting. Another bay window graced the back of the room. An outside light shone through a center pane bearing an inset of stained glass depicting a vibrant sapphire-blue water lily with a golden center. Beneath the window stretched a wide, dark blue velvet-covered window seat.

"Goodness gracious," Mrs. Hanson breathed. "This room is awesome, as my grandson would say."

Simon emitted a dry laugh. "Overpowering is more like it. My grandfather built this house. He demanded that his son and wife, my parents, live with him. I was born and reared here, so I don't pay much attention to it—not even this humdinger of a library."

"You and Penny worked in this room, didn't you?" Mrs. Hanson asked. Simon nodded. "She told me it was beautiful, but I didn't imagine it to be so grand."

Simon gave her a comforting smile. "Mrs. Hanson, you're hardly in the presence of royalty. I was a university professor. I never made enough money to build a house like this one—I simply inherited the place. My father believed the male child should have the house. I wanted to sell it and split the profit with my sister, but she wouldn't hear of my selling the old place. She said it's the family home."

"No wonder she didn't want you to sell it. The house is lovely."

"Thank you. Now please sit and make yourself comfortable, Mrs. Hanson." Simon led her to a large easy chair and offered her an arm to which she clung, as she slowly bent her stiff, arthritic knees and lowered herself.

She let out a sigh of relief then blushed. "I suppose I was more tired than I thought. And do call me Clarice."

"Clarice is a beautiful name. I'm Simon."

Clarice smiled shyly at Simon, but when he turned away from her, Diana saw the woman's face turn desolate again. Clarice was trying hard to be sociable and strong, not to fall apart in front of strangers, Diana thought, but she'd suffered the fright of her life, not to mention the crushing grief for Penny.

As Clarice's gaze scanned the room, Diana joined Simon behind the bar. "She needs her walker," she whispered to him. "We didn't get it out of her house."

Simon spoke softly. "Luckily, I bought the one that fool doctor insisted I use after I twisted my leg on my last expedition."

"You didn't *twist* your leg, Uncle Simon. You broke your thigh."

"A hairline fracture is nearly nothing!" Simon hissed back impatiently. "The walker is in the attic. I never wanted to see it again," he said, raising his voice. "Clarice, would you prefer cognac or armagnac?"

Clarice jumped in her chair and let out a startled "Oh!" She caught her breath. "I wouldn't know the difference. As I said, water would be fine."

"Cognac it is. I know armagnac is becoming more popular, but I've always preferred the lighter notes of cognac. . . ."

Impatience washed over Diana as Simon rattled on about cognac—trivial chatter, considering the circumstances. Then she noticed how his hands shook as he poured three generous servings, splashing some over the side of one brandy snifter. She had seen her great-uncle enter dark, frightening tunnels in pyramids—tunnels that had caused even a few seasoned explorers to balk—and he'd never shown the slightest hesitation, the tiniest tremor of apprehension. Yet now Simon prattled and quivered.

He'd loved Penny and Willow. Obviously, shock, horror, and devastation filled Simon tonight. Still, he refused to give in to his own emotions, using banal talk to hide

his feelings from the delicate, shaken Clarice Hanson.
Diana's annoyance with Simon vanished, as her love for
him grew even stronger on this dreadful evening.

Simon handed Diana a glass, and she immediately took
a gulp she couldn't swallow, her throat feeling like sand-
paper from the smoke and tight from the effort of holding back tears. She closed her eyes and rolled the liquor
around her mouth before letting it slowly trickle down her
throat. She had felt cold to her bones, but within a couple
of minutes, the liquor's warmth began to spread through
her. Slowly Diana's inner trembling lessened, and for the
first time since Penny's house had erupted into flames, she
was able to draw a deep breath.

"How's your cognac, Clarice?" Simon asked.

"Delicious," she said with a smile. "The last drink I had
was a glass of champagne on my seventieth birthday two
years ago. Actually, my Henry, God rest his soul, said I had
three glasses. I don't remember." Clarice's slight smile
disappeared. "But that was a happy night. Not like—"

"Tonight." Simon nodded as he looked down at the
fragile woman. "I know it seems wrong for us to be serving
drinks after what's happened, but it isn't as if we're having
a party. We're only trying to hold ourselves together. After
all, we aren't in a position to help Penny, and we have
young Tyler out looking for Willow." He frowned. "Diana,
who *is* this Tyler Raines fellow?"

Diana tried to hold her own glass steady, although she
knew her hand jerked at the mention of Tyler Raines.
Still, she tried for a nonchalant shrug. "All I know is what
he told you. He doesn't live here." She looked intently
into her great-uncle's face. "I don't know one thing about
him except what he claims is his name," Diana said sig-
nificantly.

"And that he's brave," Clarice added staunchly, seeming to miss the nuance of skepticism in Diana's voice. "He
carried me out of my house to safety, then he went back
and tried to help the firefighters, and now he's looking for

Willow. I'd say all of that is far above and beyond the call of duty, especially when he's doing it all for absolute strangers."

"Yes, it is," Simon said thoughtfully, picking up his own snifter of brandy and shifting his acute gaze from Clarice to Diana. "It certainly is."

2

Twenty minutes later, Simon sat in a chair across from Clarice as he sipped his second glass of cognac. "Yes, indeed, Diana was only eighteen when she accompanied me on an Egyptian expedition. Her parents died in a car wreck when she was fourteen. Afterward, she lived with her grandmother—my dear sister whom I could cajole into just about anything—and I persuaded her to let Diana go along. My niece was particularly mature and self-sufficient for her age—her grandmother knew it, too—but even I was shocked by what a trooper Diana was, Clarice! She didn't complain once, no matter how rough the conditions. And the photos she took were excellent! I used three of them in a book—"

"Mrs. Hanson, did you notice Penny acting strange this week?" Diana interrupted, unable to remain silent one moment longer while Simon surged on with the diverting story. Simon looked at Diana in exhausted surprise while Mrs. Hanson blinked with bewilderment. "I mean, did Penny seem upset?" Diana floundered, angry with herself for dragging Clarice back to the hell she'd witnessed earlier but unable to go on trying, like Simon, to act as if nothing was wrong. "Was Penny . . . well . . . afraid?"

Mrs. Hanson's slender hand started shaking, and Simon quickly took her brandy snifter before throwing Diana a severe look.

"Was Penny afraid?" Clarice repeated in a weak voice. "Well, of course she was concerned about Willow. The night they admitted Willow to the hospital, Penny came to my house after visiting hours. She was so worried. I told her about my own young granddaughter who'd had an appendectomy and done splendidly. I could tell that didn't help much, though. She only stayed about fifteen minutes, but I saw her lights on past one in the morning." Clarice paused, looking slightly embarrassed. "Sometimes I have trouble sleeping. I really *don't* watch Penny's house twenty-four hours a day."

"Well, of course you don't," Simon said reassuringly. "I have trouble sleeping, too, and it's only natural to glance out the windows when you're up and you feel like the rest of the neighborhood is snoozing comfortably."

Diana knew Simon slept like the dead, but he did not want Clarice to be embarrassed. Diana appreciated his concern for the woman's dignity, but she needed answers.

"But was there something besides Willow troubling Penny?" Diana persisted. "Did you get the feeling Penny was frightened of being harmed?"

Simon snapped, "Diana! What a question!"

Clarice Hanson raised her hand to quiet him. "No, Dr. Van . . . Simon. It's all right. I should have said something before now. Penny *hasn't* been her usual self, aside from her worry about Willow's operation," she said definitely.

"How was she different?" Diana asked.

Simon leaned forward. His expression told Diana that although she hadn't mentioned Penny's agitated phone call to her the night before, he'd already guessed something besides Willow's illness had been bothering Penny.

"To be accurate, I have to say Penny seemed different the past three weeks. Maybe a bit more." Surprise tingled through Diana, but she said nothing, not wanting to break Clarice's train of thought. "Maybe the week before last I noticed she was staying inside a great deal. That isn't like her. She loved the outdoors, no matter how cold or hot. When she wasn't working for Dr. Van Etton or at the university, she spent time outside, playing with Willow or gardening. Yet the little flowerbed she'd taken such particular care of this summer wilted because she didn't water it.

"This week she stayed in the house almost constantly, and she kept her lights on all night I only saw her coming from and going. She usually looks so neat, so carefully groomed," Clarice went on. "But every time I caught sight of her going out, she had on the same pair of ragged jeans and a loose wrinkled blouse."

Clarice frowned. "She came to my house on Thursday evening when she got home from the hospital. Willow's surgery had been performed Tuesday and she'd come through just fine. Penny was bringing her home the next morning. I would have expected her to be ecstatic, but she wasn't. She asked me if I thought Willow could travel safely by Sunday. I must have looked surprised because she quickly said Willow was bored, and she'd been thinking of taking the child for a car ride.

"Penny was terribly pale," Clarice went on. "Her jeans just hung on her. Clearly she hadn't been eating. Or drinking. Her skin and lips looked dry. I offered her iced tea or a soft drink, but she refused. She said she felt a bit nauseated—too much bad hospital coffee, she claimed. Then she said the oddest thing." Clarice frowned. "She said, 'You've been such a wonderful neighbor, Clarice. I hope you'll always remember us fondly.'"

"'Remember us!'" Simon repeated loudly. "What did that mean?"

Clarice looked startled at his tone, then raised her hands in bafflement. "I said, 'My goodness, dear, are you and Willow moving?' Penny flushed and burst into high-pitched laughter, saying she was just being sentimental. Then she started crying. Before I could say a word, she jumped up from her chair and ran out the door. I thought about calling her to make certain she was all right, but I decided she needed to calm down and get some sleep, so she'd be ready for Willow to come home the next day."

"You did the right thing," Diana said, thinking that Penny must have called her hotel room shortly after she ran out of Mrs. Hanson's house—called and begged her to stop by the next evening.

Diana snapped back to attention just as Clarice was saying, "No one who looked like they could be Willow's grandparents even stopped by to see Penny, much less stayed with her this week. There was only . . ." Clarice looked at Diana and stopped abruptly.

"There was only who?" Diana asked.

"Oh . . . no one."

"That's not what you were going to say."

"Yes, it was." Clarice's gaze shifted to a crystal ashtray on the table beside Diana. "I wasn't going to say anything else . . . important."

"Oh, Clarice, don't think you're protecting *me,*" Simon said. "*I* went to Penny's, Diana. I thought she would be too tired and worried to shop, so I raided our kitchen. I also picked out two bottles of good wine, and I stopped at the bakery to get baklava. Penny loves baklava."

"I know," Diana answered in faint surprise. Simon was a kind man, but it wasn't like him to haul around groceries for someone. "Was Penny home?"

"No, so I just let myself in."

"You let *yourself* in! You have a key to Penny's house?"

"*We* have a key, Diana. Have you forgotten that Penny gave us a key in case she ever locked herself out or lost her key?"

"Now I remember. I don't suppose you noticed anything odd when you were in the house."

Simon looked reluctant for a moment, clearly not wanting to discuss something troubling. Then he gave up. "First of all, I must say that I, too, noticed a difference in Penny the last two weeks she was here. Each day she was quiet and distracted. On Monday, her hands trembled so much she could barely work at the computer. I was going to ask her on Tuesday if there was a problem, but that very day Willow got sick."

Simon took a deep breath. "The day I went to Penny's house with the food, I put the cold items I'd brought in the refrigerator, set everything else on the kitchen table, and wrote her a note. As I left the kitchen, I noticed four or five large, packed boxes in the living room. Then I glanced at that awful recliner Penny had gotten at a yard sale. Her birthday is in two months, and I'd planned on buying her a new recliner—something sturdy, very comfortable. . . ." Simon's voice trailed off and he swallowed hard.

"I remember the recliner," Diana said quickly, knowing her great-uncle would be deeply embarrassed if he broke down in front of Clarice.

Simon promptly regained his composure. "There was an end table next to that awful chair. I saw an object lying on the table." Simon took a deep breath again then lowered his voice. "It was a very nice Glock 23 handgun, clean and loaded."

3

The phone beside Clarice's chair rang. All three of them jumped and Simon shouted, "Good God!" Then he flushed at betraying his nervousness.

"I gave Tyler Raines this phone number," he muttered before snatching up the handset and barking a loud, "Hello!" Diana watched his handsome, hawklike face relax slightly. He closed his eyes before saying, "Thank God. Where is she?" Diana was nearly tugging on his arm by the time he hung up after saying, "Thank you, Tyler. You must be exhausted. Forget about the car—we'll deal with it tomorrow."

"Did he find Willow?" "Is Willow hurt?" Clarice and Diana asked at the same time.

Simon took a deep breath. "Clarice, you were right. Willow was in the woods. Unfortunately she saw the explosion. She saw her mother . . . on fire." Simon paused. "Afterwards she went deeper into the woods, scared to death and refusing to answer the police or paramedics who were calling for her, but Tyler found her. He didn't say how. He said the paramedics looked her over and she seems perfectly fine—physically, that is. Still, they want her to spend the night in the hospital for observation."

"I'll go to her." Diana stood up. "I'm sure she needs somebody she knows."

Simon frowned. "I doubt if they'll let you see her until morning."

"I don't care. I'll ask someone to tell her I'll be there all night. That might be some comfort for her."

Clarice began to fumble, trying to rise from her chair. Diana noticed the woman looked exhausted. She also seemed extremely unsure of herself. "Clarice, I'll show you to your room and get you some nightwear," Diana said.

Clarice gave Simon and Diana a weary smile. "I accept your hospitality with gratitude."

"No gratitude needed." Simon offered Clarice his arm to help her up from the chair. "Diana will have you fixed up in no time. We have a housekeeper—a young woman named Nan Murphy. Her mother has worked for me for years but she had a mild heart attack, so Nan is taking her place for a while. Her demeanor is less than warm, but she does arrive on time. She'll be here in the morning."

"Just get up when you please," Diana added. "We don't have a routine. If you'll show Clarice to the bedroom, Uncle Simon, I'll run upstairs and get something of mine for her to wear."

Ten minutes later, Clarice sat on the bed in a large, soft gray and dusky blue bedroom. "This is lovely, Diana! Simon said *you* decorated it?"

"Yes. You should have seen it before—all velvet, tassels, valances, dried flowers under glass. It was my great-grandmother's room during the last months of her life. I didn't know her. I've heard she was rather stiff and formal, though, not at all like her daughter, my grandmother, who raised me after my parents died."

"Your grandmother was the sister Dr. Van Etton seems to have loved so much."

Diana smiled. "Yes. They quarreled constantly and

enjoyed every minute of it. They seemed as different as night and day, but underneath, they were very similar. Simon was heartbroken when she died four years ago. He never married, and I'm afraid I'm the last of his family. That's partly why I moved in with him. He would never admit to being lonely, but he was and it showed. Simon had always loved to entertain. He threw big parties for every possible occasion, but after Grandmother's death, he never even had a small dinner party.

"Two years ago, I was divorced, living in a small apartment and making do with a tiny bedroom for a darkroom. Simon did me a great favor by inviting me to live here, but he seemed to think he was the only one benefiting. He kept promising not to act like a parent and assuring me that this was a *big* house and he wouldn't get in my way." She smiled. "Not too long after I moved into the house, I asked Simon if I could redecorate this room."

"You did a fine job. The gray and blue are beautiful with the yellow and russet accents. You have excellent taste, Diana." Then she looked dubiously at the nightwear Diana had brought for her. Diana always slept in one of her many mid-thigh-length T-shirts. The only other thing she'd been able to find was a bright pink nightgown and robe with chiffon flounces and satin ruffles at every opening, embroidered all over with bunches of cherries.

"When I was married, my mother-in-law desperately wanted grandchildren," Diana said. "She gave me this negligee for Christmas the last year of the marriage. I believe she thought it would drive my husband wild with passion." Diana paused. "One of the last good times he and I had together was after his mother left and I tried it on for him. He said all I needed was a crown and a wand and I'd look like Glenda the Good Witch in *The Wizard of Oz*. We both howled with laughter."

Clarice smiled and held up the mass of chiffon and satin. "Well . . ." Her smile faded. "I was going to say something nice about it, but I can't think of one thing."

Diana couldn't help giggling. "I like your honesty. I'll

get you some proper nightwear tomorrow. What do you prefer—pajamas or a nightgown without ruffles and embroidered cherries?"

Clarice looked at her in surprise. "I wear short nightgowns so I won't trip over them, but I'll be going home tomorrow."

Diana said gently, "Your house suffered quite a bit of damage. You'll need a second home for a few days, and Uncle Simon and I would love having you." The woman looked unconvinced. "Frankly, Clarice, I think your presence would be good for Simon right now. He and I are close, but having someone nearer his own age to talk to at a time like this would be a blessing for him. I would really appreciate you staying."

"In that case, I'd be delighted." Clarice smiled, then her expression turned quickly to one of concern. "Diana, you don't need to play hostess to me. You're terribly anxious to go to the hospital and see Willow. You've been fidgeting with your hair and your watch for the last ten minutes. Please go. I'll be fine."

Diana had been sitting in a small boudoir chair and she almost jumped up, saying, "I *do* need to see Willow, and you need to get some rest. Promise me not to look at yourself in the mirror once you've donned that lovely gown. If you do, you really *won't* be able to sleep!"

4

Diana left Clarice's room and discovered Simon had abandoned the library. Maybe he'd gone to look for the walker. Or he may have decided to search for the walker tomorrow morning and simply retreated to his own bedroom, she thought. He had exhausted himself trying to keep Clarice from dwelling on Penny, but Diana knew that his own mind had not wandered far from the young woman. For the three of them, the chatter, the liquor, the comforting ambience of the library had merely formed a thin veneer under which lay the shattering knowledge that Penny had suffered unspeakable injuries and probably would not live.

Diana had washed her hands and soot-smudged face when she arrived home, but she did so again and changed her blouse before going to the hospital. She pulled her long wavy hair—smelling of smoke—into a ponytail, brushed her teeth, swiped gloss on her dry lips, and put some drops in her eyes—bloodshot from smoke.

As Diana left the house and got behind the wheel of her car, she felt oppression descend on her. She wished she could cry, which might be a release—poor, at best, but at least a slight release. She couldn't do it, though. Her tears had spilled at the site of the explosion and now her emotional landscape felt arid and bleak, like some of the vast deserts in Egypt she'd seen years ago.

Traffic was light at this time of night—or rather, morning—giving Diana a better chance to think. The gun. Ever since Simon had revealed he'd seen a loaded gun sitting by Penny's chair, Diana hadn't really been able to concentrate on anything else. She was certain Penny would not have left the gun out if Willow had been home, but Willow had been in the hospital. Diana imagined Penny sitting in the old recliner at night, tensed, all the lights on, the gun beside her, waiting for . . . For *what*?

Penny never seemed to be afraid of living without a man in the house. Diana hadn't asked her if she owned a gun, but Penny had known Simon owned a collection of guns and kept a gun in his room, insisting that Diana keep one, also. He believed in defending one's home—not depending on a security company or the police.

Diana deftly maneuvered the narrow, hilly roads of Huntington's large recreational and residential Ritter Park. In record time, she pulled into the well-lit hospital parking lot. She ran toward the glass-front emergency room and dashed through the doors, her mind filling with dread at the condition she might find Willow in. She nearly hurled herself against the reception desk.

"Willow Conley," Diana burst out. "I'm here about Willow Conley."

A nurse with brown hair nodded absently and continued to read the scrawled handwriting on a chart. She put the chart in a rack and slowly looked up at Diana, her blue eyes set in a long face showing fatigue. "Sorry, but I didn't want to break my concentration. How can I help you?"

"Willow Conley." Diana leaned on the counter and casually held two fingers over her mouth. She didn't want to take a chance of blowing the smell of liquor into the nurse's face. "She's a little girl, five years old, who witnessed a house explosion and saw her mother on fire. The mother is Penny Conley. They're both here. Or were." Diana watched the nurse's eyebrows rise. Diana knew she was talking at a rapid-fire rate, as she always did when she was upset, and tried uselessly to slow down.

"I'm sure Penny has already been taken to the burn ward, but Willow was hiding in the woods so thank heavens she wasn't burned. Someone found her and took her to the paramedics. He phoned us—the man who found her, not the paramedics—and said she seemed all right, but the paramedics were going to bring her here in the ambulance, so I think she could only have arrived about half an hour ago," Diana ended breathlessly.

The nurse spent at least five seconds looking into Diana's bloodshot eyes before asking in a cautious tone, "Are you family?"

"No. Penny and Willow have no family." Diana forced herself to take a deep breath and try to sound more calm and competent. "I mean, Penny and Willow have no family anywhere nearby. Penny works for my great-uncle, Dr. Simon Van Etton. He's a retired professor of archaeology. I live with him. My name is Diana Sheridan. Simon and I are the closest people Penny and Willow have to relatives in this part of the country."

Diana had no idea if the last part of her statement was true, but she did her best to look trustworthy. She wouldn't allow herself to blink as the nurse's intelligent gaze probed her face, obviously deciding whether to believe her. Diana knew she must look awful—messy hair, skin pale from shock and dry from recent washings with strong hand soap, her lower lip swollen from nervously pulling it between her teeth.

The woman finally seemed to make up her mind in Diana's favor. "Willow Conley is still being examined, Ms. Sheridan."

"I see." Diana tried to sound calm. "Which examining room?"

The nurse looked regretful. "I'm afraid you can't go in. As you said, you're not family."

Diana's artificial poise vanished. "But I'm the closest thing to family Willow has!" She hated the shrillness of her voice but was helpless to quiet it. "I mean, I'm the closest thing Willow has to family except for her mother! She needs me. Please!"

"I'm very sorry."

"Yes, but—"

"Rules are rules, Ms. Sheridan. You can't see Willow Conley." Diana drew back, wanting to be angry, but aware the nurse realized Diana would have argued for at least ten minutes unless cut off firmly. "Now try to calm down because the doctor needs to ask you a few things about Willow," the woman went on crisply, not giving Diana a chance to interrupt. "We know nothing about her except what the paramedics told us."

Diana forced down her ire, telling herself the nurse couldn't be as emotionless as she looked. The woman had to maintain her composure even if Diana couldn't maintain hers. Allowing herself to get visibly disturbed over every patient who came into the emergency ward wouldn't be good for the patient or the family, not to mention the nurse's own well-being. A nurse prone to hysterics wouldn't last long in the profession.

Diana felt her frustration begin to ebb before she said in a softer tone, "I'm sorry if I sounded unreasonable. Of course you couldn't know anything about Willow because Tyler Raines doesn't know Willow. Or Penny."

The nurse's eyebrows rose again. "Tyler Raines?"

"The man who brought in Willow. I'm sure he spoke to you as soon as he could after Willow arrived." The nurse continued to look at her quizzically and Diana felt her frustration level rising once more. "He's early thirties, at least six feet tall. He has blond hair and blue eyes. He had on jeans and a T-shirt. He would have been dirty because he helped the firefighters at the site of the explosion. . . ." Diana trailed off, watching a vertical line form between the nurse's eyebrows. "Maybe he didn't give his name—"

"Ms. Sheridan, no one came with Willow Conley. The paramedics who brought her in said a man handed her over to them, and then he drove away."

"Drove away?" Diana asked faintly. "He just drove away from the site of the fire?"

"Apparently, if that's where the child was found. The paramedics said he didn't even give his name." Diana stared, surprised, as the nurse continued. "Now if you'll have a seat in the waiting room, I'll let you know when the doctor who is examining the child can speak to you." Diana continued to stare at the woman, unable to close her mouth completely as shock ran through her. "Ma'am, if you will *please* just have a seat—"

"Yes. Okay. A seat. I'll have a seat," Diana said vaguely. She turned away from the reception desk and ambled toward a crowded waiting room, her mind whirling. Tyler Raines had called, told Simon he'd found Willow, and that the paramedics had said Willow seemed physically fine. He had appeared to be so concerned about Willow earlier that Diana had been certain he would come to the hospital and find out what the doctors had to say about the child.

But he hadn't. Tyler Raines had simply handed over the little girl to the paramedics at the explosion site and disappeared into the night.

CHAPTER FOUR

1

Diana didn't know Tyler Raines, but he hadn't struck her as the kind of man who would give a traumatized five-year-old girl to strangers, even if they were paramedics, then just abandon her. Driving Simon's car. Surely, he could have waited to see if the child he'd seemed to care about was all right. Instead, he'd vanished as quickly as he'd arrived. Why?

Because he couldn't do anything for Willow? Because he hadn't wanted to get involved? Diana wondered. That's certainly not how he'd acted when he helped at the scene of the raging fire, when he'd insisted on driving her and Clarice home, when he'd rushed straight back to Penny's house so he could search for the little girl. Why would he be so hellbent on finding Willow, then not wait to see what the doctors had to say about the child's condition? Why . . .

"Ms. Sheridan?" Diana jerked slightly in surprise. A slender man wearing a white coat and wire-rimmed glasses stood in front of her. His face was young, but streaks of gray laced his brown hair, and fine wrinkles surrounded his kind, dark-gray eyes. "Nurse Trenton at the desk tells me you're here about Willow Conley."

"Yes. How is she?"

"First of all, I'm Doctor Evans." He sat down beside Diana, his expression sober. "Ms. Sheridan, I don't mean to be rude, but what is your relationship to Willow Conley?"

"None." He blinked at her. "I mean, I'm not a blood relative, but I'm her mother's closest friend. I know there are hospital rules—Nurse Trenton reminded me—but I'm the only person available to come tonight."

The doctor smiled. "Usually we do abide by the rules, but there are always situations calling for exceptions. I think this is one of them." The doctor's manner immediately became cool and analytical. "Willow shows no signs of physical trauma—no burns, lacerations, or even bruises. However, I've ordered several tests to rule out internal injuries, especially because when I was examining her, I saw she'd had an appendectomy on Tuesday."

"She just came home this morning." Diana realized it was after midnight. "Or rather, yesterday morning."

"Willow's incision looks fine—no tearing, no signs of infection. Still, we want to be sure all is well with her, especially after such recent surgery." Dr. Evans paused. "Before the appendectomy, Mrs. Conley listed Simon Van Etton as the person to call in case of emergency if she was not available." He paused, adding reluctantly, "I know Mrs. Conley is in the burn unit. I caught a glimpse of her when they brought her in, but I didn't treat her."

"She's not going to live," Diana stated flatly.

"We don't know that yet. Even massively burned patients survive these days with all of the new broad-spectrum antibiotics available." He tried to look encouraging and failed, falling back to a detached, professional tone. "Ms. Sheridan, we know nothing about Mrs. Conley except that she's widowed and Willow is her only child. Her doctor will need more information about her. Do you know Simon Van Etton?"

"He's my great-uncle. I live with him. He's a former professor at Marshall University, an archaeologist, and he now writes books. He employs Penny as his research assistant. He's seventy-five, Doctor Evans, and what's happened tonight has devastated him. That's why I came alone. I wasn't certain he could stand the stress of being here."

"I see. Will he be able to give us more information about Mrs. Conley and Willow?"

"Maybe, but I don't think he can be of any more help than I can. Neither of us knows much about the background of Penny or Willow. I doubt if Uncle Simon even knew Penny had listed him as the person to call in case of emergency."

The doctor looked at her in confusion. "You said you are Mrs. Conley's closest friend."

"To the best of my knowledge I am, but not in the usual way people are close. I mean, I understand why Penny listed Uncle Simon as the person to call in case of emergency. He's as close to her as I am. She only began working for him a little over a year ago, though. Simon and I have grown fond of Penny and Willow, but Penny has never said much about her background except that she's a widow. She did tell me she lived in Philadelphia before she came here after her husband's death, but she never talked about her parents. I don't know if they're even alive. The same goes for her husband's parents." Diana frowned. "My goodness, I don't even know her maiden name. . . ."

The warm, compassionate gaze Dr. Evans had been giving her morphed into one of reservation. *No wonder,* Diana thought. *I sound like I don't even know Penny and Willow.* She wished Uncle Simon were with her. His very presence bespoke authority.

Diana felt as if she'd been awake for three days. She was worn, dirty, muddled, and almost too exhausted to speak. Penny needed her help, though. Diana took a deep breath and looked earnestly at the man beside her. "Doctor Evans, my great-uncle and I like Penny and Willow tremendously, and I consider Penny a good friend. But I'm a photographer and I often have assignments that take me all over this country and occasionally to a few others. I'm not home a lot—I don't see Penny every day or even every week. In fact, I left early Tuesday morning for a three-day trip. Willow was admitted to the hospital about two hours later and diagnosed with appendicitis. I'm certain that's why Penny listed Uncle Simon as the person to call in case of an emergency instead of me—I wasn't home."

The doctor nodded, his gaze never leaving hers. When she finished, he said expressionlessly, "Ms. Sheridan, you said Mrs. Conley has worked for your great-uncle and you have been friends with her for over a year. Haven't you learned *anything* else about her in all that time?"

"I know it's unusual." Diana realized she sounded as if she were exaggerating or possibly lying. The doctor had every reason to doubt her, but she was determined to keep trying. "You see, Penny has always been reticent to talk about her past. I've thought when Penny is ready to tell me more about her life, she will. She was—is—a wonderful mother, an excellent research assistant to my great-uncle, and she's a good and caring friend to me. As for details about her past . . ." Diana shrugged. "I'm afraid I just can't be of much help. You know, she wouldn't have listed my great-uncle as the person to call in case of emergency for her daughter if she didn't trust him, though, and I'm his niece. If you don't believe me, we can call him."

Dr. Evans hesitated a moment before he said, "Calling your uncle won't be necessary. I believe you. I also understand you not wanting to interrogate her, but we need to know more about Mrs. Conley and Willow. There are medical questions we must find answers to."

"I know Penny is in critical condition, but is there something wrong with Willow that you haven't told me?" Diana asked in quick anxiety.

"Willow is all right, unless the tests show something a routine examination didn't reveal. I'd like to have a more thorough history of her than I do, though. The child can't tell us much. Actually, she's giving me little more than 'yes' and 'no' answers right now. She keeps muttering about something she calls 'sparkle bugs.' "

Diana smiled. "That's what Willow calls lightning bugs. She likes to collect them in a jar and give them to her mother."

"Yes, she did say something about her mommy needing sparkle bugs. Of course, she has asked for her mother. And a few times she's mumbled 'bad' or 'badge.' Do you know what she means?"

Diana was quiet for a moment then said, "No. What happened was horrible, but to a five-year-old child, she might describe it as *bad*. As for *badge*. . . ." Diana cast her mind's eye over thoughts that felt like ragged, old playing cards. "Police officers came to the scene. Willow might be referring to their badges."

"That's what I thought." He frowned. "I have an idea, Ms. Sheridan. Because you know so little about her family connections, I think we should fingerprint both Willow and her mother. I believe one of Mrs. Conley's hands was not burned." Diana winced inwardly. Only one of Penny's small, amazingly dexterous hands remained undamaged. "If the police have the fingerprints, perhaps they can locate records that would tell us more and help us to find relatives. Is that all right with you?"

Diana felt a rush of relief. "I know you're just being polite. You don't need my permission for the fingerprinting, but I think it's a great idea. Even though Penny didn't mention family, I can't believe she and Willow are completely alone in the world except for my great-uncle and me. At least, I hope they aren't—it would be too sad." Diana felt her throat growing tight. "Do anything you think might help them, Dr. Evans. Anything . . ."

"I will." He put his hand over hers. "And so will everyone else here at the hospital."

The doctor started to rise and Diana blurted out, "I want to see Willow!" She blushed and lowered her voice. "I mean, may I see Willow? She's so young and alone without her mother. I know you're taking good care of her, but I just need to see that she's all right. Then I can call Uncle Simon and comfort him a bit. He's so terribly upset. *I'm* so terribly upset. . . ."

Diana looked into the doctor's eyes and saw that he was trying to make a decision. Finally he nodded. "I think that might help the child. She's young and she's terrified. Seeing a familiar face will probably make her feel secure."

"I hope so," Diana said, although she feared Willow would never feel secure again.

2

The earth shuddered. The scorching air roared. Someone screamed repeatedly. She shut her eyes but she could still see the red and gold tongues of fire leaping toward a velvety black sky, turning the peaceful night into an inferno. The fire inched closer—cruel, unnatural, destructive. She tried to escape but she was trapped, the hungry fire now scorching her hair, searing her clothes, blistering her skin— swiftly, voraciously, happily devouring her.

Diana awakened drawing long, raw gasps, her hands covering her face, her legs drawn up to her abdomen. She kicked viciously at something clinging and white— a shroud, she thought wildly. Once free of it, cool air gently washed over her sweat-drenched skin.

Slowly she lowered her hands, letting her gaze dart around the small, unfamiliar room. A glow from a sodium vapor lamp seeped through partially closed vertical blinds, and in the semi-dark Diana dimly saw a tiny nightstand beside her and, mounted on the wall, a dark square she somehow knew was a television.

She ran her hands over the coarse, damp sheet covering the hard mattress beneath her. The top sheet lay where she'd kicked it onto the floor. Diana flipped onto her right side and saw another twin bed. Even in the shadowy room, she could make out the short, still form beneath the sheet, and long, wavy hair spread across a pillow.

Willow.

Diana drew a deep breath. It was just a horrible dream, she thought in vast relief. *I'm not burning like Penny. I'm in the hospital watching over Willow.*

A few hours earlier, if Dr. Evans had any doubts about Diana's relationship with Willow Conley, they had vanished when Diana entered the examination room where Willow lay stiffly on a narrow bed, her eyes squeezed so tightly shut that furrows had formed in her porcelain skin. Diana had approached her slowly, leaned down, and said softly, "Willow, sweetheart, it's Diana. I'm here." Within seconds, the child had opened her eyes, rose up, and wrapped her arms around Diana, burying her head against Diana's neck, babbling about fire and her mommy and begging Diana not to leave her.

Dr. Evans had looked at them thoughtfully, then he'd whispered in Diana's right ear that if she would like, he would arrange for her to spend the night in Willow's room. Diana had nodded vigorously and mouthed *Thank you,* almost wanting to kiss the doctor for his empathy. She knew the kindness she'd detected earlier in his gray eyes had been genuine.

Now, her heart still pounding, Diana ran her hands over the cotton hospital gown she'd been given for the night. She would have slept in her clothes, but they had felt tight and smelled of acrid smoke. She wished she'd at least changed clothes, if not showered, before coming to the hospital, but the night's events had rattled her so much she hadn't given a thought to the state of her slacks and blouse.

Before she'd crawled onto the narrow bed in the room with Willow, the loose hospital gown had seemed comfortable. Perspiration had turned it clammy after her nightmare, though. For an instant, she thought of slipping out of the gown and sleeping just in her bikini panties, until she remembered the damp sheet she'd thrown on the floor. She didn't want to lie beneath it, and she couldn't sprawl nearly naked.

Metal clinked against ceramic.

The sound came from the bathroom. In a flash, all thoughts fled from Diana's mind, as she focused on the sound she'd just heard. She even stopped breathing. Nothing. Finally she heard a faint scrabbling sound and another clink.

Was someone quietly and carefully retrieving a metal object from the ceramic-tiled shower? The sink? The commode? Was the bathroom floor covered in ceramic tile? Diana couldn't remember. The bathroom door was closed, the light turned off, but she distinctly remembered turning on the light and leaving the door open about six inches. Willow had been afraid to go to sleep in the dark. Diana told herself not to panic. Perhaps a nurse had simply stepped into the bathroom to . . .

To do what? Stand in the dark with the door closed?

The sound seemed innocuous, Diana thought. Then why did she feel like a tiny animal trying to evade an aggressor? What made her certain someone regretted making the two nearly inaudible noises that she heard only because she was already awake?

Diana rose silently on the bed, holding her breath again. Something was wrong. Dammit, no matter how much her uncle would scoff at her for relying on a feeling, not evidence, she knew a malevolent presence hovered near.

The door to the bathroom began to open with deliberate slowness. Swallowing the impulse to scream, Diana leaped from her bed and ran to the other, scooping up the sleeping child. Diana thought she heard something behind her, just as Willow let out a drowsy murmur of surprise. She said nothing to Willow and didn't look back. She focused on holding the child and aimed for the door, fumbling for the handle then flinging open the heavy wooden door.

Diana burst into the hospital corridor, carrying the groggily frightened Willow, just as the sound of gunshots echoed at the opposite end of the hall. Diana had dashed from the room in such a frenzy, she plunged ahead at least eight more steps before she could stop. A female nurse hovered near her, rigid and emitting staccato shrieks. A thin male orderly stood splayed against a wall shouting, "What's goin' on? What's goin' *on*?" Two other women at the nurses' station stood motionless for a few seconds and then ducked behind the counter. Another nurse standing in front of the counter stooped with her arms locked over her head.

Diana froze, stunned, holding the now wide-awake, terrified child. In spite of her fear, Diana became acutely aware of the chaos surrounding her, including the fact that no one stood firing a gun in the hospital hallway. The shots must be coming from a room, she thought, but why would someone enter a hospital room and let loose a hale of gunshots?

Except they weren't gunshots. As soon as Diana had drawn a deep breath and quelled her raging fear enough to think for a moment, she realized she wasn't hearing the shots of a gun but the popping sounds of small firecrackers. She'd heard the sound every Fourth of July since she was a child. Simon always had someone set them off at his annual Independence Day bashes.

A burly orderly ran toward a door bearing a RESTROOM sign at the opposite end of the hall. When he opened the door, the sound grew louder and more metallic. He paused, as if taking stock of the room, then slowly entered. Diana had lost all sense of time, but glancing at the big clock on the wall across from her, she saw that two minutes passed before the popping sounds stopped.

The thin orderly remained pinned to the wall yelling, "What's goin' on?" The screaming female nurse kept shrieking.

Finally the orderly who had entered the restroom opened the door, leaned out of the room, and roared, "Everyone, *shut up!*" Deathly stillness immediately fell in the corridor. It lasted only seconds before a murmur of voices quickly intensified to a din.

Willow had begun to cry raggedly against Diana's shoulder. Diana hugged the child closer and kissed her forehead. "It's all right, sweetie. I have you—you're safe."

Safe. Diana wished she could say that with confidence. She yearned for the peaceful world she'd known just hours ago. In exhausted frustration, she staggered over and leaned against a wall, her heart beating so hard she thought it would crack a rib. Willow's crying had dulled to monotonous, hopeless whimpering. She sounded doomed, Diana thought, and no wonder. How could Willow calm down, when Diana couldn't even control her own rising hysteria?

"It's Black Cats!" the orderly yelled down the hall. "It's just the firecrackers Black Cats. Someone put them in the metal waste can and lit them up. Do you understand me? They're *harmless*! Everybody settle down. You're not in any danger!"

Willow pulled away from Diana's shoulder and wailed, "Somebody shot cats? Somebody killed kitty cats?"

Diana took another deep breath and tried to steady her voice. "No, honey. There are little firecrackers called Black Cats. You heard them last month at Uncle Simon's Fourth of July party. They don't have anything to do with kitty cats. Someone just gave the firecrackers a silly name. The firecrackers made all the noise."

"Firecrackers?" Willow wavered disbelievingly. "No guns?"

"No guns. No hurt kitty cats. I promise. Don't cry."

Willow sniffled, valiantly trying to stop her tears. At a loss about what to do next, Diana looked around. She felt invisible, as nurses, orderlies, and a few patients headed toward the restroom with the firecrackers. Diana glanced back at the door to the room she and Willow were sharing. She had no desire to see the remains of firecrackers, but she wasn't going to take Willow back into that room—where she was certain someone had lurked silently in the dark, waiting to strike at her or Willow, or both of them.

Diana began walking slowly, holding the trembling Willow tightly. Suddenly a nurse appeared in front of them.

The woman's hands shook slightly, and her middle-aged face showed stress, but concern, too, for Diana and Willow. "Everything is all right," she said, eyeing the sniffling Willow. "It was—"

"Firecrackers," Diana said. "I know."

"Yes, well, you can go back to your room. We have everything under control."

Diana shook her head. "We can't go back to our room."

"Of course you can." The nurse began trying to gently herd Diana toward the room. "It was just a prank. It gave me quite a scare, too, but everything is fine. Quit crying, honey," she said to Willow. "There's no reason to be scared. No reason at all—"

"We can't go back to our room because someone is in there. Or *was* in there. Someone was hiding in the bathroom," Diana, standing rigid, cut off the still ashen-faced nurse in the middle of another hollow reassurance.

The nurse blinked at her for a moment then tried to smile. "I think you had a dream, dear. Why would anyone be hiding in your bathroom?"

"I don't know, but someone was," Diana said firmly. "I did *not* dream hearing someone drop a metal object. I was wide-awake. Then the bathroom door started to open, so I grabbed Willow and ran out into the hall just as the firecrackers began exploding."

The nurse's color had begun to return, and one side of her mouth lifted in an attempt to smile. "You heard someone drop something in your bathroom?"

"Yes, I did." Diana looked at the woman stonily, knowing that if she seemed even faintly unsure, the nurse would dismiss her assertion. "Someone was in our bathroom. You need to call Security or at least have a couple of orderlies search the room."

"Someone from Security will come any minute because of the firecrackers, but—"

"Good. They can search our room. It's five-oh-one. I want someone to go in there immediately."

Diana felt as if the nurse was so anxious to get everything back to normal that she wasn't really listening. "I know your room is five-oh-one, dear. There is no reason to be snappish. I think you're letting nerves get the best of you."

Diana was on the verge of repeating her demand when two young nurses swept past them, talking loudly. "Who could have put firecrackers in the restroom?" one of them asked, her face flushed with excitement. "I didn't see anybody."

The other nurse shrugged tiredly. "It's been busy. That woman in five-oh-eight has buzzed for me at least ten times. All of the patients seem agitated and demanding tonight. No one working the floor noticed who went in and out of that restroom." She sighed. "It's not the Fourth of July or Halloween, so why tonight of all nights would someone go to the trouble of creating such pandemonium?"

A cold chill rippled down Diana's back. She clutched Willow even tighter, the young nurse's words echoing in her mind. *Why tonight of all nights would someone go to the trouble of creating such pandemonium?* Diana looked back at the door of Room 501, where she and Willow had lain, supposedly asleep—the room where someone had been hiding—and suddenly she knew why somebody set off the firecrackers. . . .

To produce chaos while they committed murder in Room 501, then slip out and escape down the back stairs completely unnoticed.

CHAPTER FIVE

1

"We'll have to break the law in order to get you home to-day," Diana said as Willow crawled into the back of the car and Diana fastened a seat belt around her. "You're supposed to be in a booster seat but I don't have one."

"I hate the booster seat. It's for babies."

"Nevertheless, the State of West Virginia says you must sit in an approved booster seat if you're under eight years old."

Willow looked glum then perked up a bit. "How long am I gonna stay with you and Uncle Simon?"

"Oh, a few days." Diana shut the car door quickly. She hoped her vague answer would satisfy Willow, but "vague" never worked with Willow. The child's insistence on exact answers had always amazed Diana.

"How long is a *few* days?" Willow asked as soon as Diana sat down in the driver's seat. She made a production of slamming the car door and fastening her seat belt while she tried to think of a satisfactory answer. Finally she said, "Until Romeo and Christabel get tired of you."

Willow giggled. Diana felt a wave of relief and encouragement. The child hadn't even smiled since Diana had hugged her in the emergency room. "Romeo and Christabel love me almost as much as they love each other," Willow informed Diana, referring to Simon's "mature" cat, Romeo, and Diana's young beauty, Christabel. "They won't want me to go home."

"Well, they rule the household, so that means a long visit for you, young lady. Uncle Simon and I want you to stay, too, Willow. And I forgot to tell you something. Your neighbor, Mrs. Hanson, is also staying with us!"

"Clarice!" the child exclaimed. "She told me to call her Clarice, not Mrs. Hanson, just like Simon told me to call him Uncle Simon. I like Clarice a *whole* lot. So does Mommy. But why is she stayin' at your house?"

"Her house got burned, too, but just a little bit." Diana backed out of her parking space and sped to the entrance of the parking lot. She felt as if she couldn't get home fast enough. "Clarice stayed up late and talked with Uncle Simon and me last night. She seems like a really nice person. She's funny, too."

"She's real funny. And she cooks good. And she's got lots of rel'tives. I'm friends with one of her gran'girls, Sue. Sue's big sister, Katy, is *real* old, like thirteen. She's sorta nice but she never wants to play with us 'cause she doesn't wanna mess up her hair. I don't know why—it looks like a bird nest." Willow sighed. "That's just how teenagers are, though," she ended in a world-weary voice.

Diana tried not to grin. "Did Clarice tell you about teenagers?"

"Yeah, she did." She paused. "When's Mommy gettin' out of the hospital?"

Diana looked in the mirror again to see the little girl's blue eyes full of sadness. The eyes also held a small, pitiful glimmer of hope, and Diana could not take that hope away from the child, even though she was almost certain she would be lying.

"Your mommy will come home just as soon as she's better. The doctors are doing everything they can to help her get well. We have to believe they can do it, Willow. Your mother needs for us to believe it."

Doubt flickered in the child's gaze for an instant. Then

Diana saw her take a deep breath before she said with res-
olution, "Then we *will* believe it. We'll believe it with all
our hearts like we believe Tinker Bell will live in *Peter
Pan* and she does."

"That's the spirit!" Diana knew an adult would catch the
loud insincerity of her voice, but Willow seemed somewhat
soothed. Her change of expression was well worth any lie,
Diana thought, and maybe, just maybe, she was telling the
truth after all.

The heavy mugginess of yesterday had lifted, leaving
the air warm, gentle, almost caressing. Diana looked at the
cloudless, crystalline blue sky with its pale lemon of a sun.
The world had turned beautiful, she thought, as if trying to
make up for the destructive inferno of last night. A comfortable temperature and a pretty sky could not mend Penny,
though. An image of her seared, blistered face flashed in
Diana's mind, and she felt a stabbing pain in her stomach.
She almost let out a small cry but caught herself, glancing
back at Willow.

The child's earlier chattiness had stopped abruptly and
now she sat looking small and somewhat ethereal with her
beautiful long hair and her big shadowed eyes. She stared
down at her clasped hands. Diana didn't know if she was
praying—she didn't even know if Penny and Willow were
religious—and she felt a prick of shame. How could
she know so little about the two people she loved most in
the world except for Simon? Was she so self-consumed
she hadn't bothered to learn who Penny and Willow *really*
were, to learn something about their thoughts, their beliefs, their desires?

Apparently so, Diana thought dismally, so ashamed of
herself she could have cried. *And now I want to shed tears
for my failure,* Diana chastised herself. *Do I always think
of myself? Tears can't change the past and tears can't help
the young child who seems to have no one else in the world
except for Simon and me. Well, we will take care of her,* Diana told herself fiercely. *We will put our very best efforts
into taking care of Penny's little girl.*

"Do you like the dress I'm wearing?" Willow asked, pulling Diana from her reverie.

"I think it's very pretty. The nurse was certainly thoughtful to bring some of her little girl's clothes for you to wear home today."

Willow fingered the blue gingham of her full skirt. "She was nice. She smelled good, too, like vanilla." She paused. "Do I have to wear this dress until Mommy gets well?"

Diana laughed. "Of course not, Willow. The dress is pretty, but it's not right for scrambling around on the floor with the cats or playing outside. Besides, the nurse's little girl might need the dress, so I'll have to return it soon. I'm going to buy you some new clothes this afternoon. Jeans and cotton shorts and tops. What else would you like?"

"Sneakers. And I want a crown for when I play queen. I had one at my house."

"Certainly, you may have a crown. Do you remember where your mommy bought it, Your Royal Highness?"

Willow giggled then said helpfully, "At a store."

"Oh. Well, maybe I can call some stores before I go shopping and see if they carry crowns for queens. And you need underwear and socks."

"And 'jamas," Willow said. "The people at the hospital didn't give my pink ones back. They were my favorites."

"We'll get pretty, new pink pajamas. Maybe some blue ones, too. I also have to buy a few things for Clarice, although maybe the fire didn't reach the bedroom where she kept her clothes." Diana could have bitten her tongue for mentioning the fire again and said quickly, "You should have seen what she had to sleep in last night, Willow! It was *the* funniest-looking nightgown and robe ever made!"

Diana managed to keep up a riotously exaggerated story about the negligee until they began climbing the narrow, circling roads of Ritter Park. At last she saw the large stucco, red-tiled roof of the Van Etton house sitting on a knoll in the center of its four-acre grounds, both the house and the lawn beautifully maintained and drenched in sunlight. Diana had never in her life been so glad to see the place. She pulled her car into the long driveway winding up to the house, parked, and before she'd been able to loosen Willow from her seat belt, Simon rushed out the front door to greet them. He gave Diana a glancing kiss on the cheek, then swept Willow up in his arms.

"How is the most beautiful little girl in the whole wide world?" he boomed.

"I'm real happy to get away from the hospital, and I'm extra happy to see you!"

Willow gave Simon a smacking loud kiss on his jaw and laughed as he swung her around in a circle, holding her away from him. "Do you know who else is staying here with us?" he asked.

"Clarice! Diana told me."

"Diana, you simply cannot keep a secret," Simon pretended to scold, winking at her. "Clarice and I have been up since *dawn* waiting on the two of you!"

Clarice emerged through the front door, leaning on the walker Simon must have found for her. She wore the dress she'd had on last night and had pulled her silvery hair back in a French twist. She looked paler and still tired, although she smiled brightly.

"Willow, darling!" she cried as she slowly made her way to the car. "I'm *so* happy you're here. I haven't gotten to see you since last Monday, the day before you went into the hospital!"

"That's was a long time ago," Willow replied. "I'm happy we both get to stay here with Diana and Uncle Simon."

Which would not have happened without Simon's influence, Diana thought. In circumstances like Willow's, Child Protective Services, CPS, normally took charge of the parentless child. Early this morning, though, Simon had reached Diana at the hospital and told her he'd spoken to one of his former students who now had an executive position with CPS. The ex-student had vouched for Simon and Diana, and the government agency had given permission for Willow to stay in the Van Etton home while they searched for her relatives. Diana knew that being taken away by strangers would have been terrifying for an already traumatized child.

"Clarice, you and Simon are looking well for two people who went to bed late and got up at dawn," Diana said.

Clarice's eyes widened. "Where did you get the idea we were up at dawn?"

Diana looked at Simon, who quickly said, "Seven thirty, dawn—so close together. And I agree that Clarice looks well, but you, Diana, obviously did not spend a comfortable night."

"That's a long story," Diana mumbled. When Simon's eyebrows went up, she said, "I'll explain later. Let's go inside. If I don't get a cup of decent coffee, I'll collapse right here in the driveway."

Nan Murphy, the temporary housekeeper, hovered in the entrance hall. As usual, Diana marveled at the nineteen-year-old woman with the body of a Las Vegas showgirl and the face of a horse. She always imagined there had been some terrible genetic mix-up in which one girl's head had been mistakenly placed on another's body. Diana felt ashamed of the thought, but she couldn't quash it, no matter how hard she tried.

Nan wore a slightly above-the-knee-length denim skirt from which her long, beautiful, tanned legs emerged, ending in white canvas tennis shoes. Her short-sleeved white blouse looked fresh and crisp although obviously a size too large, probably bought at her mother's insistence to hide Nan's voluptuous curves. Her thick, light-brown hair fell in glorious waves around her equine face with its elongated nose, wide nostrils, and broad, flat forehead. Her large dark eyes, which could have been her face's redeeming feature, sat far apart and bore no expression. Nan always appeared to be looking at a world that stirred absolutely no emotion in her.

"Our second guest has arrived," Simon announced to her gaily as he carried Willow inside.

Nan stared at Willow, who finally gave the young woman a shy "Hello." Nan merely nodded and stared some more.

Obviously annoyed, Simon asked sharply, "Is there plenty of fresh coffee for Diana? And I believe Penny told me Willow likes apple juice in the morning. Do you want apple juice, sweetheart?" Willow nodded. Nan stood rooted to the Oriental rug until Simon snapped, "Well, how about it, Nan? May we have coffee and apple juice?"

"Yeah, if that's what you want," Nan managed in her toneless voice. She'd opened her mouth just enough to show large, protruding teeth. "I guess you want me to serve it?"

"In the library, if you please," Simon said with strained patience. "And bring some cinnamon buns and the blueberry Danish I bought yesterday."

Nan turned and, without a word, walked slowly toward the kitchen. "Still service with a smile, I see," Diana muttered.

Simon rolled his eyes. "I cannot wait until her mother is well enough to come back to work. Honestly, I don't know how someone as energetic and pleasant as Martha Murphy could have a daughter like Nan. The girl must take after her father, whom I never knew."

"If Nan took after him, I'm sure you're glad you didn't know him." As Simon led them into the library, Diana smiled at Clarice. "How was your night?"

"I slept, although I was certain I couldn't. You do look tired, though, Diana. Hospital beds are so uncomfortable," Clarice went on. "I felt guilty sleeping in that lovely bedroom, thinking of you and Willow spending the night in a hospital room."

Willow piped up eagerly. "Where's Romeo and Christabel?"

Simon looked at Willow. "You know Romeo and Christabel run every time someone comes to the door. As soon as they hear your voice, they'll be back in two minutes flat."

"Maybe they forgot me," Willow mourned. "I haven't seen 'em for ages and ages."

"It's really only been eight days since you saw them," Simon corrected gently. "They certainly aren't going to forget their favorite little girl in eight days."

As if on cue, the two cats entered the library. Christabel, Diana's cat, pranced in with her long black-and-white fur freshly brushed and fluffy, her gigantic tail held high, and made her way straight to Willow. Romeo, as usual, trailed right behind her. He was gray, three times Christabel's size, and possessed only three legs, a fact that slowed him down only slightly. He followed Christabel to Willow, who immediately dropped to the floor and pulled both cats onto her lap.

"I've missed you so much!" she exclaimed rapturously, hugging the felines. Christabel uttered a soft, sweet trill. Romeo followed suit by emitting his usual greeting that sounded remarkably like a duck's unusually loud quack. Clarice, who had obviously not heard the cat's robust, bizarre vocals, looked at him in shock.

"See, Clarice, I told you he quacks!" Willow giggled.

"Yes, you did, but I believed . . . Well, I thought—"

"You thought she was exaggerating." Simon laughed, delighted. "I was stunned the first time I heard his dulcet tones, too. I thought he'd just eaten a very large duck."

"Romeo wouldn't hurt a duck!" Willow defended the cat passionately. "Romeo loves ducks."

"Actually, I don't think he knows any ducks." Simon looked at Clarice. "Several years ago Diana was here one weekend when he turned up. In his past, his hind leg had been professionally amputated and the wound neatly healed—someone had once taken good care of him. That day, though, his fur was tangled and he obviously hadn't eaten much for a while. He was flea-ridden, starving, and meowing—or rather, quacking—his head off.

"Diana rushed outside and had him in the kitchen, gobbling everything she put in front of him, before I knew what was happening," Simon continued. "She was married then and her husband claimed to be allergic to cats, so she couldn't keep him. I placed an ad in the newspaper and attached a few fliers to trees, but no one claimed him. A week later, I called Diana to tell her the cat had a permanent home with me. *She* named him Romeo."

"That's because I knew you would give him an impossible-to-pronounce name of some Egyptian pharaoh," Diana said defensively.

"So I would have, but considering that he's fallen head over paws in love with Christabel, I think you chose the perfect name for him."

Nan walked into the room carrying a tray with coffee, apple juice, and pastries. Her flat stare locked onto the cats.

"What's the matter, Nan?" Simon asked pleasantly. Diana stifled a smile. Simon knew Nan couldn't stand the cats.

Nan jerked her head at Romeo. "That gray one gets fur all over the rugs the way he drags himself around."

"Then it's a good thing we have an excellent vacuum cleaner," Simon returned equably, reaching for the coffeemaker's glass carafe, not the elegant silver coffee pot that he preferred when coffee was being served. "I don't see any sugar here, Nan. I already told you Mrs. Hanson takes sugar in her coffee. Also, you brought only one blueberry Danish."

"That's because you ate all the Danishes except for that one," Nan returned snippily.

Simon's color heightened. Clarice, clearly sensing the contentious atmosphere in the room, said quickly, "I know I ate at least three."

"You had *one,*" Nan maintained. "*He* ate most of them." Simon's face was growing red. "Nan, I did *not*—"

"Yes, you did," Nan interrupted firmly.

"It doesn't matter. I don't even like them," Diana lied— she could have eaten her weight in them. "Thank you, Nan."

As soon as Nan had cleared the doorway, Simon snarled, "I don't think I can take one more day with that girl!"

"You have to," Diana said, trying to sound pleasantly calm. "Her mother is spending the last two weeks of her sick leave in Portland with her sister, and you can't call her back to work. She'll resume her duties in exactly sixteen days. You can stand just about anything for sixteen days, even Nan Murphy."

"Mommy says Nan doesn't got charm," Willow offered.

"Your mother is absolutely right." The red in Simon's face began to fade as he looked at the beautiful little girl sitting on the rug gently stroking the two madly purring cats. "Ready for some apple juice, Willow?"

2

After Willow drank her juice and ate the lone blueberry Danish, her eyelids began to droop.

"You didn't get much sleep last night," Diana said. "I think you need a nap."

"I don't take naps so early," Willow informed her in a voice blurred by exhaustion.

"You can at least rest your eyes." Diana pretended to study the matter, although she and Simon had already talked over sleeping arrangements. "Would you like to sleep in the room next to mine?"

Willow looked at her, troubled. "Isn't your room upstairs?"

"Yes. You're not afraid to sleep upstairs, are you?"

"Well, no, but before we got here you said the cats could sleep with me but Romeo can't go up the stairs."

"Romeo usually sleeps in Uncle Simon's room and it's upstairs. Simon carries him up."

"But Uncle Simon doesn't want to go up and down the stairs all day for naps and playing and all the stuff I do in my bedroom. And Romeo's kinda heavy. I'm afraid I'll drop him if I try to carry him to my room upstairs."

Diana smiled. "I'll carry him up for now, but you've

forgotten this house has an elevator my great-grandfather had installed because he was in a wheelchair the last few years of his life. Romeo can take the elevator up and down."

The fact that Romeo did not operate the elevator didn't seem to cross Willow's increasingly tired five-year-old mind. Satisfied that the cat could ride to the second floor in the elevator whenever he chose, Willow followed Diana, who carried the fifteen-pound cat up the stairs. Christabel zipped up and down the staircase twice before she calmed enough to lead the way, her long, fluffy black tail waving like a banner.

Diana ushered Willow into a bedroom near the end of the hall. Sunlight shone brightly on the soft pink, pale green, and powder blue chintz decor that Diana's grandmother had chosen. "Do you like the room?" Diana asked.

Willow's eyes had widened as they swept over the room. "I sure do like it! I love beds with a lid on top."

"That's called a canopy."

"Oh yeah. I forgot. Mommy said someday I could have a bed with a can'py."

Mommy again. The child's smile faded again. Then she looked around sheepishly. "My room at home is lots littler than this one. I might get scared in here all by myself."

"Do you know what's really special about this room?" Diana asked exuberantly. She put Romeo down and walked to a side door that opened into a large yellow-and-white bathroom. "This bathroom adjoins my bedroom!" Willow frowned over "adjoins."

Diana took Willow's hand, crossed the bathroom, and opened the opposite door leading into her own tan-and-amber bedroom. "Wow. This room is pretty, too."

"I made it the color of the desert—tan for sand, amber for the sun. But the nice thing is that we can leave the bathroom doors open at night and it'll be like we're sleeping in the same room. You'll have a night light and the cats, and we can see each other from our beds. You won't be scared then, will you?"

"Well . . ." Willow frowned in thought for a moment then said decisively, "No. I won't be one bit scared."

"That's great!" Diana beamed. "It'll be fun, Willow, you wait and see!"

The child smiled, and the tightness in Diana's stomach eased a bit. She'd feared Willow would be totally withdrawn or nearly hysterical. She knew the little girl hadn't completely absorbed the enormity of the fire's destruction—that would come later, especially if Penny died—but at least for now Willow was coping better than Diana had expected. She appeared to be as strong as her mother, who'd seemingly been so alone in the world yet managed to give her child a good and happy home full of love, security, and also, most important, fun.

The doorbell rang, and within five minutes Simon appeared in the bedroom. "Glen is here to see you, Diana." He looked at Willow. "How about climbing into bed, young lady, and letting me tell you a story? I know dozens of them. When Diana was young, they always put her right to sleep."

Willow curled up on the bed, and Diana placed Romeo beside her while Christabel leaped up to claim Willow's other side. Simon sat down on the bed and began one of his interminable tales about ancient Egypt—tales that *had* always put a young Diana to sleep because they sounded like university lectures rather than children's bedtime stories. She still didn't have the heart to tell him. Besides, they were surefire sleep-inducers.

Willow will be snoring in less than five minutes, Diana thought as she descended the stairs. Glen Austen, the man Diana had been dating since March, sat in the library talking with Clarice. He was slender with ash-brown hair and even features. Most women would probably not have rememberd him unless they'd encountered his considerable quiet charm. Although usually restrained, as soon as he saw Diana, he jumped up and strode to her, taking her forcefully into his arms.

"My God, Diana, I turned off my phone and went to

bed early last night. I didn't hear the news about Penny until this morning. People say she's not going to live!"

Diana saw distress in his large brown eyes and the crease that always appeared between his eyebrows when he was worried. He'd met Penny when he'd dropped by to see either Diana or Simon during the day, and the two of them had formed a casual friendship. Diana and Glen had invited her to have dinner with them at the country club in May, a night that had been fun for all of them. They'd asked her to come with them to the dance at the club tonight, but Penny had declined, saying she'd be a third wheel.

"Glen, she is so terribly burned. When I left the hospital this morning with Willow, they told me there's been no change in her condition from last night." Diana's voice shook, and she felt tears threatening. "She's still unconscious and . . ."

The tears came and Glen again pulled her close to him. "I know it must have been awful, and this sounds cold, but try not to think about Penny right now. There's nothing you can do for her, and you need to stay strong for Willow." He leaned back and looked into her eyes. "But you're all right?" he asked anxiously. "When I talked with you on the phone early yesterday, you said you were going to stop by Penny's on your way home. When I heard about the explosion this morning, I thought you'd been in it!"

"I almost was. I was late and I'd just pulled up in front of Penny's house when it simply blew up. I've never been so shocked, Glen. I have *never* seen anything so terrible in my life. And poor Penny . . ."

Glen winced and handed her a tissue that Clarice had been waving in his direction for at least two minutes. Clarice skittered out of the room, and Diana mopped at her wet face.

"Please, no more about Penny, honey." Glen pulled Diana toward the middle of the room to the comfortable loveseat on which he'd been sitting with Clarice. "You're so pale and your eyes are sunken. You look like you might collapse. Try to concentrate on something positive." He paused. "Mrs. Hanson told me Willow is all right."

"Yes. She was back in the woods when it . . . happened."

"Why was she in the woods after just having surgery?"

"Something about catching lightning bugs."

"I'm glad she's okay." Glen took the damp tissue from her, and stroked her wet face. "I'm even happier *you* weren't hurt."

"Oh, Glen, I told her I'd be there around eight o'clock. If I'd been on time . . ." She shuddered. "I know I'm lucky but I feel so guilty saying it."

"You *are* lucky. Penny seemed like a nice woman, and I know she was a good friend. We're all sorry about what happened to her, but you have no reason to feel guilty because *you* are alive and well, sweetheart," Glen said, kissing her forehead.

Nan walked into the library and Diana realized the girl had been standing in the doorway for the last couple of minutes. Nan fixed her expressionless gaze on Glen. "Do you want coffee or anything?" she asked tonelessly.

Glen shook his head and Diana said, "None for me either, Nan, but thank you for asking."

"It's my *job* to ask," Nan snapped. She turned quickly and strode from the room, her back straight, her head held high, resentment emanating from every line of her body.

"I think this will be her last housekeeping job," Diana said drolly. "She hates it."

"Maybe that's a good thing. She'll probably come back to the university and try harder than she did her first year, knowing this might be the only kind of job available to her without a college degree. She was in my European History class. She's smarter than she seems."

Diana doubted his last statement, but she didn't argue when Glen smiled at her, shallow lines forming around his brown eyes. Puppy dog eyes, she always thought but never told him. Diana knew Glen wished he were the elegant, edgy ladies' man. That type definitely didn't have puppy dog eyes—eyes begging for affection, eyes so often betraying hurt and rejection.

She reached up, touched his light-brown hair, and looked fleetingly at the short stubble on his pleasant face. He must have noticed Diana's glance, because his hand immediately flew to his chin and cheeks. "I showered but I didn't take time to shave after I heard about the fire. I was so shaken up I would have given myself a few fairly bad nicks."

"You don't always have to be perfectly groomed, Glen. It's Saturday."

"We were supposed to go to the country club dance tonight."

Diana sighed. "Oh well, I don't think either one of us was looking forward to the dance all that much."

"I was. I thought it would be a nice change from the usual dinner and a movie. I even sent my best suit to the cleaners." Diana didn't meet his gaze. She hadn't given a thought as to what she would wear. "Should I send flowers to Penny?" Glen asked suddenly.

"No. She's in the burn unit. I'm sure they don't allow flowers." Diana paused. "I saw her briefly last night before they took her away in the ambulance. Mercifully, she was unconscious. She looked so awful. I didn't even try to see her this morning, although I did ask about her. She's still unconscious and her condition hasn't improved." Diana drew a long, ragged breath. "I'm certain she'll die."

"My God, what a shame." Glen's voice shook slightly, and Diana knew he was appalled. He'd been acquainted with Penny, but he hadn't known her well. Nevertheless, he clearly felt dreadful for the lovely young woman and her child. "Does anybody know what happened at her house?" he asked. "It couldn't have been faulty wiring. That doesn't cause a house to explode."

"No, it doesn't." Diana considered telling Glen about the gun that Simon had seen in Penny's house. Then she glimpsed the toe of a white tennis shoe around the corner.

Nan was standing just out of sight at the library entrance, eavesdropping again. This wasn't the first time Diana had caught the young woman listening to private conversations, and she knew that she should reprimand Nan, but not now. Still, she was glad she'd said nothing to Glen about the gun or the events at the hospital. She didn't know what Nan Murphy might do with the information—probably try to sell it to a newspaper. "An arson investigator will probably check the house today," she went on. "He'll be able to tell us what caused the explosion."

"I suppose so." Glen put his arm around Diana and gazed into her eyes. "I'm just so thankful you weren't in that house, Diana. You don't know how much I care for you."

Diana felt guilty, as Glen kissed her gently on the lips. His voice had deepened with emotion when he spoke of how much he cared for her. She wished only that she felt the same way about him.

CHAPTER SIX

1

"You found the SUV just parked in the driveway? No note? Nothing?"

"The keys were inside, which was a relief." Simon smiled at Diana, who sat beside him on a couch in the library after Glen had left. "I have no idea what time Tyler Raines returned the car. I don't know whether he left here on foot or he had a taxi waiting."

"I'd be shocked that he didn't even leave a note except that he also didn't follow Willow to the hospital. He seemed so concerned about her at the site of the fire. He even went back to look for her after bringing Clarice and me here." Diana shrugged. "I don't understand him, and to be honest, Simon, I don't trust him. His actions don't make sense."

"He seemed trustworthy to me when he was here, and I even understand him not going to the hospital with Willow—he'd already notified us, he isn't her family, and he must have been exhausted. I don't mean to belittle your woman's intuition about him, though."

"Oh, Simon!" Diana exclaimed. "You're not going to explain my feelings by attributing them to sexist nonsense like women's intuition."

"I wouldn't dream of it, my dear, even if I believe in it just a tiny bit." He grinned. "Your grandmother did have *some* influence on me. I do think sometimes, not often, intuition rather than provable data gives us the correct answer. And if you repeat that to anyone, I shall deny it with the last breath in my body!"

Diana giggled. "I promise not to repeat it, but I have to tell you, hardly a day goes by when you don't surprise me. I don't think anyone could ever completely know you, Simon Van Etton."

"No one ever completely knows anyone else," he replied, his tone growing serious. "But there is one person in this world I completely trust, Diana, and that is you." She felt her color heighten in surprised pleasure. "That's why when you tell me someone was in your hospital room last night, I know you're right. Good heavens, no one is certain yet that the explosion at Penny's was accidental. Didn't those hospital people see the connection between the firecrackers going off and your claim that someone was hiding in your and Willow's room at that same time?"

"Apparently not," Diana said dourly. "They thought the firecrackers were someone's idea of a joke, and I was an imaginative hysteric. To be fair, though, I didn't take time to explain that we think Penny is in trouble, and that somebody might have meant her and Willow harm."

"No, all they knew was that the little girl's house had caught on fire. But someone setting off firecrackers on the hospital floor where a child who has just escaped a fire is staying would have seemed quite a coincidence to me even if I didn't know the whole story."

"Unfortunately, not everyone thinks about coincidences that are just too suspicious *not* to be real coincidences like you do, Uncle Simon. Most people weren't interested in the *way* the firecrackers had been set," Diana went on. "The orderly who found the firecrackers also discovered cigarette ashes in a trail on the floor beside the trash can. He explained how someone probably had pinched off the filters of two extra-long cigarettes, fastened them together, and attached the fuse to them to delay igniting the fire-crackers by six or seven minutes.

"When I heard that, I realized the time delay would have allowed someone to hurry to my and Willow's room and hide before the firecrackers went off. In a lab coat, neither an unfamiliar man nor woman would have been noticed in that crowded corridor."

"But you couldn't convince anyone of this scenario."

"I didn't even try," Diana said morosely. "I insisted Security search our room, but whoever had been hiding in the bathroom was gone. I know he left when I ran into the hall with Willow. The hospital personnel acted like I was an idiot. I can't say I blame them. It does sound far-fetched, especially because I couldn't offer any reason for someone wanting to murder Willow and me. I still can't, but I didn't sleep the rest of the night. I sat up in a chair watching over Willow."

Simon clasped Diana's hand in his own strong, tanned one. "Of course you sat up watching over Willow if you sensed danger. I wouldn't have expected anything less of you. You could have called me, you know."

"So you could do what? Sit up with me? No, I needed you well rested today. You have to look after both Willow and Clarice."

"Clarice doesn't need me, dear. She's very self-sufficient."

"In her own home. This place is unfamiliar to her. I'm glad she's here, though, both for her sake and for Willow's. Even if her house were livable, I wouldn't want to think of her sitting there looking at the heap that was Penny's home, going over the experience time after time in her mind. Where's Clarice now?"

"In her room, reading." Simon couldn't suppress his slightly proud expression. "She's reading one of my books. I didn't push it on her. It was lying on a table, she picked it up and flipped through it, then said it looked fascinating and asked if I minded her reading it. If I *minded*! I was embarrassingly flattered."

"Your books *are* fascinating," Diana said seriously. Simon had always amazed her by his ability to write fast-paced, engrossing sagas of an ancient culture, when he couldn't tell a simple children's story to save his life.

Simon looked at her closely. "My dear, why don't you lie down and rest? I can see you're exhausted."

"I'm worn out but not sleepy. Besides, I need to buy some clothes for Willow and go by Clarice's to see if her clothes and medicine are salvageable. In the meantime, I should get going. The little energy I have left is definitely on the wane, and I don't want to wait two hours for Nan to make another pot of coffee."

2

Diana first bought a booster seat and had it installed in her car for Willow. She understood the child objecting to it—at five, Diana would have felt the same way about being forced to ride in a "baby seat." Nevertheless, even if the law didn't require the seat, Diana realized it provided safety for a young passenger.

Before she'd left the house, Diana had looked at the size of the dress the nurse had brought for Willow to wear home. She knew an experienced store clerk could help her select jeans, T-shirts, and shoes to fit the child. Clarice had insisted that if the fire had damaged her own clothing, she'd take a taxi downtown and choose a few new dresses for herself. "I can't stand being such a burden," she'd told Diana, who did not intend to send the woman off in a taxi for an extended shopping trip on a hot afternoon. She'd reassured Clarice for at least the fifth time that she was not a burden.

Before she would go shopping for Clarice, however, Diana needed to see if the woman's clothes were salvageable.

The living room and kitchen areas of Clarice's house faced Penny's, which meant her bedroom was nearly the whole house's length away from where the fire had damaged the living room and kitchen walls. She'd also told Diana she kept her medicine in the bathroom beside her bedroom.

After the booster seat installation, Diana drove toward the Rosewood housing development, hoping she might not have to shop for Clarice at all. She knew Willow would like anything she selected; a seventy-two-year-old woman might be more finicky, and saving time with the shopping would be a blessing. Diana desperately needed rest this evening and time tomorrow to begin developing the photographs she'd taken for the tourism board. Had she finished that annoying assignment just two days ago? She felt as if it had been weeks ago.

Diana had promised herself that she would slam a door against her memories, but as soon as she turned onto Penny's street, a finger of horror touched her neck. In her imagination, the calm, clear afternoon turned to night, and wild, ravening flames leaped to the darkness above—higher, higher. . . .

Diana veered to the edge of the street, braked, and closed her eyes. She took three deep, bracing breaths and let her eyes drift open. She saw a clear, cornflower-blue sky, a gentle yellow sun, a few clouds looking like fluffy meringue—an unusually beautiful summer day presented like a gift to compensate for the horror of the previous night.

"So much for gifts," Diana muttered bitterly. There weren't enough gifts in the world to even the score.

I cannot go past Penny's house, Diana thought in near panic, although she'd let up on the brakes and was beginning to creep forward. *I'll just tell Clarice the police or the fire department has declared her house isn't safe. They refused me entrance. She can call her doctor and get a refill for her medicine. If she checks out my story or asks a neighbor to go in the house and she finds out I'm lying . . . well, it will just be the end of a beautiful friendship.*

Diana's thoughts raced until she neared the ugly, charged remains of Penny's small home. She'd expected to see a secured site protected from curious children who would clamber around and get hurt, as well as curious adults who should know better but who'd also poke around. She had not expected to see official-looking cars pulled into the driveway and parked in front. She had not expected to see a news van and a leggy woman with every brunette hair sprayed in place interviewing a stiff-faced police officer.

And Diana certainly hadn't expected to see Tyler Raines leaning carelessly against a police squad car, gazing at her with a smile that said he'd known she would come.

3

Diana whipped her car to the side of the road, jumped out, and marched up to Tyler. "What the hell are *you* doing here?" she demanded.

Tyler raised an eyebrow, smiling. "Just takin' in the sights," he said with an exaggerated Southern drawl. "Why? Miss me?"

An impossibly young cop standing beside Tyler glanced away, smirking. Diana felt like slapping him. She felt like slugging Tyler Raines. Instead, she let loose a barrage of words. "Where did you go last night? You found Willow, turned her over to the paramedics, and then just deserted her!"

The glint in his eyes vanished. "I didn't desert her if I turned her over to the paramedics, now did I? I'm not a doctor. I couldn't do anything for her. And I'm not family. My going to the hospital would have been a complete waste of time. They wouldn't have let me stay with her." He paused, smiling again. "But I'm sure you went to the hospital. Are you mad I wasn't there waiting for *you*?"

Diana spluttered, "Are you crazy? Why would *I* want to see you?" The young patrol officer had completely turned

away as Tyler continued to lounge against his car, his
tanned arms crossed, his sun-bleached blond hair shining
in the light, and dimples forming on either side of his infuriating grin. "I'm just angry because everyone was puzzled. People at the hospital needed to ask you questions—"

"About a child I don't know?"

"They thought you did. And you had Uncle Simon's
car—"

"You're not going to try having me arrested for car
theft, are you? It won't work. If you didn't notice, I returned the car."

"I *know* you returned the car. But you never called to
check on Willow. . . ."

"How is she?"

Diana gave him a scorching look. "She's all right,
which you would know if you'd waited in the emergency
room until she'd been examined. She spent the night at
the hospital—I stayed with her—and they released her
this morning. She's at Uncle Simon's house. Penny is still
unconscious, thank God. I even checked on the firefighter
Davis who fell into the basement last night. He has two
broken ribs and a broken wrist, but otherwise he's fine.
Not that *you* care."

"You met me less than twenty-four hours ago but you
know all about me," Tyler said in an exasperated tone.
"Of course I don't give a damn about those people—not
if Diana Sheridan says I don't."

"Well, you don't act like you give a damn." Diana realized she sounded silly, as if she expected him to stand
outside their hospital rooms holding bouquets of flowers.
She decided to counter with questions. "Who are you?
What do you do in New York City?"

"I'm Tyler Raines. I thought we'd already established
who I am. As for what I do—I'm an international spy."

"Dammit, this isn't the time for jokes. What is your
occupation?"

"I don't answer personal questions."

"That's personal?"

"I consider it so, yes."

"Why do you keep turning up here?"

"I don't 'keep turning up here.' I only came by about twenty minutes ago. Young Officer Patterson here can verify the time of my arrival. Officer?"

"Twenty minutes, ma'am."

"Thank you so much for the information," Diana returned sarcastically. She looked at Tyler. "That doesn't answer why you're here just like you were last night!"

Tyler cocked his head. "I ended up getting just as involved with the situation last night as you did. More—I helped the firefighters and I found the kid. I don't think it's unreasonable that I'd stop by this afternoon to see if anyone has discovered what was responsible for that inferno. That's why I'm here." He paused, his smirk fading. "Now, why don't you try telling me the truth. Why are you so mad at me?"

"Because . . . Because . . ." Diana felt her eyes blur with tears. "Because what happened last night was so awful and you were right in the middle of it. You saw the horror. You seemed to really care about those people. Yet you just dumped Willow off and you've never even asked about Penny, who's probably going to die! That's why I'm so mad. You're not even worried about them!"

Diana's fatigue, the shock caused by the explosion, the terror she'd experienced at the hospital, and the overwhelming grief she felt for Penny all seemed to come down on her, nearly crushing her beneath the weight. Suddenly she began to cry—humiliated yet unable to stop the sobs coming from the depths of her being, the tears washing down her face like a sudden rush of rain.

Vaguely, she saw the young cop move away as Tyler stepped toward her, stood uncertainly for a moment, then wrapped his strong arms around her, pulling her against his tall, muscular body. Diana knew she should shake free of him—she barely knew him and she was quite sure she didn't like or trust him—but at the moment all she wanted was for him to keep holding her, to let her cry against his chest as he rested his chin on the top of her head and murmured, "Don't cry, darlin'. Don't cry."

"I can't help it," she wept into his T-shirt. "And I'm not your 'darlin', dammit!"

"Maybe you are and you just don't know it. Miracles do exist."

Diana leaned back and looked at him fiercely. "Then what happened to Penny? What was *her* miracle? Why couldn't she have been farther away from the house and closer to Willow? Willow told me she'd been at the edge of the woods looking for sparkle bugs when Penny spotted her and headed toward her."

"Why was she trying to catch sparkle bugs?"

"Because Penny was so upset last night."

"Penny was upset? About what?"

"I don't know. I talked to her briefly the night before. She was really worried but she didn't tell me the problem."

Tyler's hands moved to her waist and pushed her back a few inches. "You must have some idea."

Diana was regaining control of herself, the sobs quieting, the tears beginning to slow. "Why are you asking me all of these questions?"

"I'm curious."

Diana looked at his brilliant blue eyes now grown narrow and suspicious. She felt the tension in his arms and saw the muscles in his jaw tighten. "You're not curious the way most people would be. You aren't casually curious. You're almost desperate to find out why Penny was so upset."

"I am not. Why would I be? I don't even know the woman."

"Don't you?"

A short, sharp silence fell between them. Tyler's eyes narrowed even more, his gaze seeming to bore into hers. "What does *that* mean?"

"It means that even the most empathetic person couldn't sound as fierce as you did about finding out what was upsetting a young woman he doesn't know."

"I was here. I helped the firefighters—not much, but I tried. And the mother of a young child is so badly burned she's probably not going to live. I know you think I don't have a heart, that I can't feel for her even if I don't know her, but you're wrong. You're not as smart as you think you are."

He held Diana's arms and she did not pull away. Both of them had wary looks in their eyes, and a thin, tingling wire of anger and distrust seemed to vibrate between them. Diana's heart pounded, but she was determined to show this man he didn't intimidate her. She was not going to pull herself free and dash for her car. She would stand there matching him look for look for an hour. Longer.

Gradually, his breathing growing lighter, the ferocity in his eyes dying, he said slowly, "I didn't mean to scare you."

"You didn't scare me. You also had no right to demand I tell you *anything* Penny said to me. You have no rights here at all!"

"I . . ." Tyler looked down, drew a deep breath, then raised his azure gaze. Diana could feel him fighting for composure, trying to harness what she could sense were natural instincts to get the information he wanted, no matter what methods he had to use. He was an unknown element and she had no doubt he was dangerous. No doubt at all.

Still, he looked at her with a trace of sad gentleness in his eyes. "I guess my behavior hasn't been the best, but there's a reason for it. If you have *any* knowledge of what was bothering your friend, you have to tell the police. I mean it, Diana, because—"

"Yes? Because?" she asked, trying to sound haughtily dismissive.

He glanced around as if to see if anyone were near

them. "Because the fire marshal has determined this house didn't catch on fire because of a gas leak or anything accidental," Tyler said softly. "Diana, the explosion last night was caused by a bomb."

4

Bomb. The word felt like a sword thrust. She stared into Tyler's eyes, but she really didn't see him. She saw Penny's seared, blistered face against a background of blinding flames on the black canvas of night.

"Diana, did you understand me?" Tyler asked finally.

"Yes," she said vaguely, trying to fight her way out of her vision and back to the present. "You said it was a bomb." She forced herself to focus on Tyler. "But how do you know there was a bomb? I don't think the fire marshal is discussing his findings with *you*."

"I overheard him telling one of his men."

"You could have misunderstood."

"I didn't. Do you see that guy over there? Tyler nodded toward a middle-aged man with thick, graying brown hair and a grim expression. "He's with the ATF—Bureau of Alcohol, Tobacco, Firearms and Explosives."

"I know what the ATF is, Tyler."

"Then you know they don't come to the site of an ordinary house fire. They are sent for when the cops find something suspicious—in this case, a bomb."

"But how do they know? On what are they basing this bomb theory?"

Tyler looked around again and kept his voice low. "They found a big, jagged hole in the basement floor. A bomb would have a concentrated blast point, causing a crater in the concrete. An explosion from a gas leak—"

"Would be more diffused," Diana interrupted, lost in memory. "I once saw a house whose basement had filled with gas from a leak and something ignited the gas. There was no 'ground zero,' I guess you'd call it, no specific point like the hole in the concrete floor where the explosion must have ignited." She frowned, feeling as if she were speaking weakly from the depths of a well. "Don't tell me you overheard the fire marshal discussing the basement floor, too."

"I didn't, but that young cop Patterson heard him, and sometimes cops new to the job get a little too chatty when they're excited."

"And how do you know so much about cops new to the job?"

Tyler hesitated then said reluctantly, "I had an uncle on the force. He lived and breathed the job. He died a long time ago. . . ." Tyler seemed to mentally catch himself, and Diana saw his eyes become veiled. "This house was bombed, Diana. I suspected it last night because of the force of the blast. That's why I came back today. I wanted to know for sure. I probably shouldn't have told you just now. The police don't want the information released to the public yet."

Still feeling dazed by the news of a bomb, Diana said, "*I* certainly won't run to the press, but what about that policeman over there talking to the newswoman? Will he tell her?"

"Not if he wants to keep his job. He's probably just giving the usual line about this being an ongoing investigation and saying the police will release a statement when they know more."

Diana glanced at the newswoman dejectedly walking back to the news van as the cop strode toward the remains of Penny's house. "Looks like she didn't get much information."

"What did I tell you? You won't be hearing about a bomb on the evening news. Maybe tomorrow . . ." Tyler shrugged. "They won't be able to keep a lid on this for long. And you have to promise me you won't tell anyone. I probably shouldn't have told *you*."

"Why? Because you think I can't keep a secret?" Diana flared. "Well, I can! I am totally trustworthy, Mr. Raines."

Tyler gave her a satisfied smile, and she suddenly felt bewildered by her girlishly earnest assurance of her trustworthiness. What was wrong with her? After all, she didn't trust *him,* she reminded herself sternly.

He was still smiling when embarrassment caused her to snipe, "You helped the firefighters and found Willow, but that still doesn't explain why you're involving yourself so much in this situation. You don't even know Penny and Willow. Why do you care if their house was bombed?"

Tyler's smile turned into a look of deep annoyance. "Damn, Diana, are bombings a regular occurrence in this town? I don't think so. Wouldn't you be interested if a bomb had been set off in someone's house, even if you didn't know the people whose home had been bombed? Besides, maybe I don't know Penny and the little girl, but I do know Al Meeks, my grandfather's friend, *my* friend who lives not too far from here. I found out last night he knows Penny. Then there's you, Clarice Hanson, and your uncle. All of you know Penny."

Diana gazed at him uncomprehendingly. "Okay, we all know Penny. So what?"

His face tightened in frustration and he spoke slowly, as if explaining something to a child. "You're a smart woman. Use your head. Obviously someone tried to murder Penny—someone so vicious he didn't care if he killed her little girl, too. That person may have wanted to kill Penny because she knew something dangerous to him. If so, he might think she'd told Al Meeks, or Clarice, or your uncle, or especially you. And there's still Willow. Even if she's only five or six, she could know something." He paused. "Diana, every one of you is a target."

5

Diana stood in the main concourse of the mall, her hands trembling, her head aching, her thoughts skittering like frightened mice. Normally, the mall would be extremely busy on a Saturday afternoon, but the day was so beautiful many people had opted to stay outside. Still, in spite of the lack of a crowd, Diana could not seem to get her bearings. She paced through the concourse, looking blindly into store windows, trying to remember what she needed to buy for Willow and the proper sizes.

A bomb. Bomb. *Bomb.*

The word tolled in Diana's head until she couldn't concentrate. She read newspaper stories about bombings in the Middle East or in Europe. Sometimes bombings in places she'd never visited claimed lives. Occasionally bombings occurred closer to home. Even though she'd been young, she remembered the stunned sadness she'd felt over the bombing of the Federal Building in Oklahoma City in 1995—a bombing that had claimed 168 lives and injured over 800 people.

Still, she'd never really considered a bombing could never directly affect *her.* *How naive,* she now thought scornfully. Not only had a bombing occurred close to her, she'd almost lost her life because of it, and her closest friend would most surely lose her own battle to survive it.

What had happened at Penny's home seemed impossible. *But it wasn't,* Diana thought, her steps lagging, her desire to simply sit down and sob almost overcoming her. The bombing *had* happened, and her only comfort was that Willow had escaped, physically at least. Who knew what long-term emotional effects the violent tragedy would have on her?

And what about Tyler's claim that everyone who knew Penny could be a target for a killer? He might still be in pursuit of Willow. At that moment, Diana had almost told Tyler about the night in the hospital when she'd been certain someone had hidden in the bathroom. She'd stopped only because her story sounded so flimsy. Why would someone come into a crowded hospital and hide in a bathroom, waiting for the right moment to murder her or Willow or both of them?

Her belief that the firecrackers had been a diversion for the would-be murderer's escape also sounded melodramatic on this sunny afternoon. Add to it the fact that two orderlies and two security people had searched her room and found absolutely no trace of an intruder, and she certainly sounded like a hysterical woman. That didn't change Diana's mind—she knew she hadn't been dreaming—but she couldn't stand to be laughed at by Tyler Raines. For some ludicrous reason that she didn't understand, she wanted his respect.

Diana's cell phone buzzed in her tote bag and she jumped. Of course, Simon would have recharged the battery, she thought in weak amusement as she rummaged through the bag until she found it.

"Hi, Uncle Simon," she said. "Couldn't stand the thought of me carrying around a cell phone with a dead battery, could you?"

"I'm sorry to have invaded the inner sanctum of that saddle bag you call a purse, but a cell phone with a dead battery is of no use. I just thought I'd make sure you're all right." His voice was tight with the effort of trying to sound offhand when he was obviously worried. "You've been gone longer than we expected."

"I'm fine," Diana tried equally hard to sound at ease. "I thought I was going to need a presidential mandate to get into Clarice's house. The living room and kitchen will need some work, but the two bedrooms and bathroom are fine. The fire marshal accompanied me into the house and I gathered up everything I thought Clarice would need."

"That's wonderful. I'm certain Clarice will be glad to have her own possessions." He paused then asked offhandedly, "Did the fire marshal say what caused the fire at Penny's?"

"No," Diana answered truthfully. The fire marshal had said nothing about a bomb. That revelation had come from Tyler. "They're still investigating."

"They should know something! It's after five o'clock," Simon said irritably.

"Maybe they've come to some conclusions now," Diana

returned evenly. "I left there a couple of hours ago. Traffic was heavy and the mall is crowded," she lied. "I'll be home soon, though."

"Good. I shouldn't have checked on you. I promised you I'd never act like your parent."

"You aren't. My parents never noticed how long I'd been gone."

"They were a bit self-involved," Simon said mildly. "Anyway, I'm sorry for being a bother. After what happened last night, I'm acting like a mother hen."

For the first time all day, Diana laughed. "Uncle Simon, the last thing I can imagine you as is a mother hen." She paused as he chuckled. "How's Willow?"

"Fine. My story put her right to sleep!"

Diana grinned, thinking the child probably immediately fell unconscious in self-defense.

"Don't wear yourself out shopping, dear. You looked dead tired when you left here today."

Diana felt dead tired by the time she finally discovered a store filled with novelty merchandise. A sales girl quickly produced rhinestone crowns, and Diana bought one that she knew would fit Willow. Normally she would have been delighted with her find. But today she felt only tired relief. Willow had lost so much. At least Diana could restore one of her favorite playthings.

At 6:45, Diana pulled into Simon's driveway beside an unfamiliar blue Lincoln Town Car. She couldn't think of any of Simon's friends who had a blue Lincoln unless one had a new car.

When she entered the house, Simon called out for her from the library. He sounded tense and imperative. Diana walked into the room carrying two large shopping bags and nearly stopped in her tracks as a muscular middle-aged man with white-streaked brown hair and metallic-gray eyes rose, looking at her with an unnerving mixture of curiosity and fury.

As Diana and the man locked gazes, Simon hurried to her side as if trying to protect her. He clasped her arm with a strong hand and said tightly, "Diana, this is Jeffrey Cavanaugh." Simon paused. "It seems Mr. Cavanaugh is Penny's husband."

CHAPTER SEVEN

1

"Her husband?" Diana asked faintly.

"Yes." The man's sharp voice lashed at her. "I'm Penny's *husband,* Mrs. Van Etton."

"Mr. Cavanaugh, I explained earlier that we were waiting for my niece," Simon said coolly. "This is Miss Diana Sheridan."

"And Penny's husband is dead," Diana added.

"Do I look dead?" Jeffrey Cavanaugh returned aggressively. "We were married for seven years. We never divorced."

"But . . . But that's not possible," Diana insisted.

Jeffrey Cavanaugh took a step toward her. "Exactly eighteen months ago, while I was on a business trip, Penny took our daughter and disappeared. She didn't even leave a good-bye note. She just vanished."

Diana stood silent for a moment, stunned. Then instant hostility bubbled up within her. "No. Penny would not do something like that. Why are you lying?"

The man glared at her. "I am *not* lying. For eighteen months, I've been looking for them. Do you know how that woman has made me suffer? She took my child. My *child*! Your uncle said you're Penny's close friend. Don't you dare tell me you don't know what she did."

"I have no idea what you're talking about, Mr. . . . Cavanaugh, was it?"

The man's silvery eyes seemed to glitter. "You know damned well who I am."

"I've never heard of you until today. I don't know who in hell you are," Diana said furiously. "Where are you from? How did you hear about Penny?"

"I'm from New York City. Manhattan."

Diana glared at him. "You act like that explains everything. I asked you how you found out about Penny."

"Shortly before noon, the authorities contacted me to say they'd located a match to my wife's fingerprints. She'd been living in Huntington, West Virginia, under the name of Penny Conley. They told me Penny had been seriously burned in a house fire but Cornelia was unharmed and staying with Penny's employer."

"Cornelia?" Diana repeated blankly.

"My daughter."

"Willow," Simon murmured to Diana then looked sternly at Jeffrey Cavanaugh. "I think we should sit down and discuss this situation calmly. I don't believe any of us knows exactly what is going on, and arguing isn't helping matters."

"I agree. Jeff, please don't get so upset."

For the first time, Diana noticed a woman sitting on one of the couches. She was a younger version of Jeffrey Cavanaugh except for her large dark-blue eyes, so different from Jeffrey's narrow, almost eerily silver gaze. Beside the woman, an elegantly good-looking dark-haired man glanced away from Diana, obviously ill at ease with the tension vibrating between her and Cavanaugh.

Simon instantly became master of the situation, his look of confidence returning. His voice held a note of self-assured old-world courtliness when he said, "Diana, this is Lenore Wentworth, Mr. Cavanaugh's sister."

Although the woman strongly resembled her brother, her expressive blue eyes transformed her face from plain to almost pretty. "How do you do, Miss Sheridan?" she said in a soft, lilting voice and with a sweet smile. She could have been a little girl at a party.

"Hello," Diana snapped.

Simon continued smoothly, nodding to the man seated beside Lenore. "And this is Mrs. Wentworth's husband, Blake Wentworth."

The man rose from the couch. His patrician facial structure with its high cheekbones and slightly aquiline nose seemed exactly suited to the ambience of the formal library. His hair—coal black and wavy—gleamed in the fading sunlight flowing through the bay windows. The depthless, ebony pools of his eyes conveyed an almost intimate compassion for her feelings in this bizarre situation. As they shook hands, he gave her a small, genuine smile revealing teeth just a shade away from being perfect, and she noticed a tiny dimple in his chin. Blake Wentworth was without a doubt the most classically handsome man Diana had ever seen. *Lord Wentworth should be his name,* Diana thought distantly, *and he should own a giant English estate.* When he said, "Pleased to meet you, Miss Sheridan," all she could manage was a nod.

Jeffrey Cavanaugh remained standing—imposing, and breathing hard. He clenched and unclenched his large hands. Simon, still holding Diana's arm in a protective gesture, gave him a cold look. "Mr. Cavanaugh, as I said earlier, I believe we should all simply sit down and try to sort out this dilemma."

"It's not a dilemma," Cavanaugh boomed.

Simon took a deep breath and drew himself up to his full six feet. "Sir, I realize you're extremely distressed, but you are in *my* home, and if you cannot conduct yourself in a civil manner, I must ask you to leave. Now, we are going to talk calmly about this matter, or do you prefer the alternative?"

Jeffrey Cavanaugh stood, rigid and angry, his piercing gaze fixed on Diana. His sister, Lenore, looked at him anxiously. Blake Wentworth fell into a deep study of a small alabaster carving of the Great Sphinx of Giza

placed on the table in front of him. Just when Diana
sensed that her great-uncle was stiffening in preparation to
evict his three unexpected and unwanted visitors, Jeffrey
sighed, took two steps backward, and seemed to deflate
into a large armchair behind him.

"Nan," Simon called. "Nan offered to stay an extra hour
when our guests arrived," Simon murmured to Diana before repeating, "Nan!"

The young woman tripped on an untied shoe lace and
stumbled clumsily into the library, her cheeks flaming.
"Yes . . . sir."

Nan never said "sir," and Simon glanced at her in surprise before he asked, "Will you fix tea, please?"

Jeffrey looked stonily at Simon. "I don't like tea. I
don't want any tea."

"Well, *I* do," Lenore Wentworth said with gentle peev-
ishness. She gave her husband a practiced smile. "I'm sure
you'd like some also, wouldn't you, darling?"

Blake tore his gaze away from the carving and just
missed making eye contact with either Diana or Simon.
Diana had the impression he was deeply embarrassed by
the scene playing out in front of him. He looked at his wife,
who gave his arm tiny, loving strokes, and managed to
stretch his lips stiffly. "Yes, tea would be . . . nice."

"I gotta' leave no later than seven-thirty." Nan's loud,
toneless voice crashed like a brick through glass. "That's
a half hour from now."

Simon didn't give the girl the satisfaction of looking at
her. "Then if you start on the tea right now, you can serve
it long before your quitting time. Do run along, Nan."

Lenore and Jeffrey both glanced at Diana, who refused
to utter a word of apology for Nan's attitude. She was grateful when Simon took the two bags she'd carried into the
house and still clutched in her arms like shields.

"Did you find all you wanted?" Simon asked pleasantly.

"Yes. Clarice's things are in the bags. Willow's new
clothes are in my car."

Jeffrey Cavanaugh's eyes narrowed. "My daughter's name is *Cornelia*. Who is Clarice?"

"I'm sorry if we've offended you, Mr. Cavanaugh, but we're accustomed to calling your daughter Willow," Simon returned with dignity. "Mrs. Clarice Hanson is Penny's next-door neighbor and good friend. The fire badly damaged her house, too, so she's staying with us. She and Willow—Cornelia—are quite fond of each other. I believe Mrs. Hanson's presence makes Wil-Cornelia feel more secure."

"I want to see my daughter," Jeffrey said flatly.

Simon's tone remained even. "Clarice is playing a game with her upstairs. Don't you think it would be better to leave the child alone rather than force her to come down here when tempers are still running high?"

"No!"

"Yes," Lenore said sternly then looked surprised at herself and added coaxingly, "Jeff, I know you're anxious to see Cornelia, but Mr. Van Etton is right. We certainly don't want to frighten Corny."

Diana flinched. Corny? Did the Cavanaughs really call that beautiful little girl *Corny*? She had a giddy impulse to giggle.

"I agree with Lenore." Blake Wentworth spoke up for the first time. "The child has been through a horrible experience, Jeff. Although, thank God she wasn't physically hurt, we can't be certain at this point of her emotional state." His deep, mellow voice sounded of a cultured home and prep schools without being pretentious. "Why don't we leave her with her friend right now? I'm sure the Van Ettons won't object to you seeing her later."

"Of course we won't," Simon said cordially.

Diana expected Jeffrey to bark an objection. Instead, he gazed at Blake for a moment then nodded. "You're right, as usual."

Annoyance flashed over Lenore's features. "He's not saying anything I didn't say." She sighed and suddenly looked tired and about five years older. "If you're finally listening to sense, though, I guess it doesn't matter whether it comes from Blake or me."

Yes, it does, Diana thought. *You love your husband but you resent that your brother listens to him, not to you.*

"Lenore, Jeff doesn't value my opinion more than yours. He's simply accustomed to taking my advice." Blake looked from his wife to Simon. "Jeffrey and I are business partners."

"What business would that be?" Diana asked.

"Cavanaugh and Wentworth. It's a real estate developing company. Jeff is the chief executive officer and I'm the chief operating officer."

Diana stared at Blake. "You're *the* Cavanaugh and Wentworth?" she exclaimed as Nan walked into the room carrying a massive silver tray. "You're claiming Penny was married to the CEO of Cavanaugh and Wentworth?"

"I don't *claim* to be married to her," Jeffrey said challengingly. "I *am* married to her."

"Well . . . Well, that's just not possible!"

Nan drowned out Diana's shocked shrillness by slamming down the tray on an antique table in front of Simon. China rattled, milk splashed, and sugar spilled.

"See? I'm no good at serving tea," Nan proclaimed loudly, her face crimson. "I'll make a mess."

"I believe you all ready have," Simon muttered. Then he gave her a smile. "I think we can manage now. No doubt you have all kinds of exciting plans for your evening."

Simon's voice bore an edge of sarcasm that Nan would have never caught. Lenore did, though, and she sent Diana a tiny grin.

Nan unexpectedly announced, "I guess I can stay a while longer in case you need something."

"Such as?" Simon asked politely.

"Well, I won't know till you need it, now will I."

Simon managed to look unruffled. "Then please retire to the kitchen, Nan, until we decide what we need."

"I guess I'll be serving." Diana reached for a cup and saucer after Nan shot Simon a narrow-eyed look then plodded sulkily from the room. "I don't know what kind of tea Nan chose."

"It doesn't matter to me," Lenore said affably. "My mother is absolutely addicted to tea and so am I, especially since I've been around her like I have for the past two weeks. She lives in Connecticut and she hasn't been feeling well lately, so she sent for me, as usual, even though she has a full-time caregiver. I was at her house when Blake called me with the news about Penny." Diana noticed Blake nudge his wife. "Oh!" Lenore blushed slightly. "I ramble when I'm tired or nervous or feeling awkward. . . . Oh, here I go again!" She giggled then sighed. "I'll take my tea clear with some artificial sugar."

Diana poured for Lenore and Blake. Lenore looked at her brother and asked, "Jeff, are you sure you won't have tea?"

"I don't *like* tea."

"Yes, we've established that fact," Simon replied blandly, offering the man nothing else to drink. "Diana, fix yours next. You look like you're ready to drop. I think I'm up to pouring my own cup."

So much ceremony went into serving the tea, Diana felt as if she were at Buckingham Palace. By the time all of the pouring and stirring had stopped, Jeffrey sat rigid, his face looking like a stone carving.

"May we discuss my daughter now that everyone has their damned tea?" he asked, seething.

"Willow is fine physically," Simon answered pleasantly. "What we need to establish is that she is really your daughter and that Penny Conley is really your wife."

Jeffrey's face turned a dark red. "I have established that information to the satisfaction of the FBI. I should think that would be good enough for you."

"Jeff, it's obvious these people care a lot about Cornelia. They're only being careful." Lenore gazed at her brother pleadingly. "Can't we be a little less antagonistic? Why don't you show them Corny's birth certificate? And show them a picture of her."

"A birth certificate and a picture of Cornelia won't prove anything to them."

"Nevertheless . . ." Lenore said.

Jeffrey shot them all a look meant to turn their blood to ice, then he lifted a beautiful briefcase, opened it, and removed a folder. He handed it to Simon, who removed first the marriage certificate of Jeffrey William Cavanaugh and Penelope Ann O'Keefe. Next, Simon picked up a birth certificate for Cornelia Ruth Cavanaugh. Finally, Simon withdrew a large studio photo of a child around three years old with strawberry-blond hair and dark-blue eyes. With her pretty, babyish features, she resembled Willow or any number of little girls.

Diana and Simon looked expressionlessly at the material. Then Diana glanced up and caught Blake Wentworth's incredibly expressive dark eyes fixed on her. "Jeff, this stuff isn't proving anything to Dr. Van Etton and Diana," he said gently. "Show them the picture of you, Penny, and Cornelia taken the Christmas before Penny left." Jeffrey tensed, and Blake's gaze shifted to him. "That photo is more convincing than a ton of documents. Please do it."

Jeffrey sighed and slowly removed a photograph from the briefcase, glancing at it for a moment before nearly tossing it at Simon. Diana leaned over her uncle and they both stared at it as if mesmerized.

"I took it. I'm the amateur photographer of the family, and Blake says I'm getting better every day!" Lenore's voice trilled with pride, although Diana immediately noticed that Lenore had made the background of the shot so defined, it drew attention away from the three people who should have been the focus.

They'd posed in front of a brightly lit Christmas tree. Jeffrey was stockier, his hair was darker, and his jaw more prominent. He wore a red crew neck sweater with a white reindeer on the front. His gaze dodged the camera, and his stiff semi-smile bespoke self-consciousness. *No wonder,* Diana thought in amusement. Jeffrey Cavanaugh looked ridiculous in whimsical holiday garb.

In the photo, Jeffrey stood beside a child—a little girl of three or four—with shoulder-length strawberry-blond hair, sparkling blue eyes, and a smile of pure delight. A woman held the child—a woman with long, thick bronze-colored hair only a couple of shades darker than the child's, and eyes just as blue, but enhanced with shimmery bronze eye shadow and chestnut-brown liner expertly drawn with a tilt at the outer edge, giving her a cat's-eye look. Her peach blush blended perfectly with her peach-gold lipstick, glistening with a layer of gloss. Her left hand firmly gripped the child at the waist—a hand wearing an engagement ring with a multi-carat center stone and diamond-encrusted wedding band.

She was flashy. She was glamorous. She was the embodiment of confident happiness.

She was Penny.

2

Glen Austen checked the digital clock beside his bed— 7:35 p.m. Then he looked at his bedroom window. Daylight shone around the edges of the closed flimsy miniblinds. God how he hated daylight saving time. He liked it when darkness fell softly somewhere around seven o'clock. Ever since he was fifteen, he'd thought night was romantic, although he would never have admitted such a "girly" emotion. That was twenty years ago, but he still resented having the sun glaring halfway to midnight.

He didn't want to stay cooped up in his house tonight, but he also didn't want to drop by a restaurant or bar and be drowned by a deluge of questions about Penny Conley. Glen could not bear to hear about Penny Conley. He wished he hadn't let Diana say anything about Penny's condition because he couldn't stop picturing the horrible burns. He hoped Penny would die. Otherwise, what would she be? A once-lovely, animated woman who now would cause people to avert their eyes, unable to bring themselves to look at her hideously scarred face.

Glen thought he might throw up. After a couple of whirling minutes, though, his stomach calmed. He groaned and took another gulp of the expensive single-malt scotch he'd been saving for no particular occasion—certainly not one like this. As if Penny's disaster wasn't enough, he'd been politely but firmly ousted from Diana's life. Oh, not for good. She hadn't told him she no longer wanted to date him, but if she hadn't wanted to be with him this evening—an evening when she should have needed his love and comfort—then she really didn't need to say anything more.

Glenn finished his third glass of scotch. He could take a hint. He was a Ph.D., dammit. He sure as hell could take a hint!

He poured more scotch and tried to concentrate on the movie droning from the portable television in his bedroom. The movie starred a young Sean Connery, and Glen had seen it at least five times. He usually enjoyed imagining himself as the dashing Sean, but not tonight. Tonight he should've been getting dressed for the dance at the country club—*the dance at the country club.* How 1950's or '60's that sounded. Classy people in old movies that he'd loved growing up always went to dances at the country club—the height of cultured glamour and sophistication. Long ago he'd promised himself that one day he, too, would be a suave and significant part of the country club crowd; the handsome, debonair guy who turned the air electric as soon as he walked in the door.

Glen realized that belonging to a country club these days didn't have the cachet it once did, but Simon Van Etton, whom Glen admired beyond measure, belonged to one and had introduced him to the most important members. Within weeks, Glen could boast that he also was a member. Later, when he began seeing Diana, he'd been overjoyed that he'd paid the yearly membership fee, which was rather high, even though he didn't play golf or tennis, and he couldn't swim or dance.

He'd taken ballroom dance lessons and invited Diana for dinner and dancing on her birthday in February. She'd looked beautiful in a lavender chiffon dress, her wavy brown hair rippling halfway down her back, and her heather-green eyes alight when he'd had the waiters bring out a small cherry cheesecake—which he'd learned from Simon was her favorite—to sing "Happy Birthday."

The phone rang. Glen cursed quietly, though he was glad he'd unplugged his bedroom telephone. He definitely did not want to have a conversation tonight—not unless that conversation was with Diana, and he wasn't certain he even wanted to hear from *her* tonight. He was afraid she would say what he knew she would eventually say, and he wasn't up to hearing it tonight.

The two phones on the first floor of his small house continued to ring. Persistent. No doubt somebody claiming to be "calling to see how you are," when they were really calling to gather more information about the explosion and Penny's awful condition. Old Glen would know, the caller probably thought, mistakenly believing Glen was nearly engaged to Diana Sheridan and she'd know all about Penny. Outsiders would think Diana had told Glen every morbid detail about the fire.

The ringing continued. *Pest,* Glen thought viciously. Didn't the caller realize that if he hadn't answered after ten rings, he wasn't going to answer?

Glen thought of going downstairs to unplug the other two phones, but getting out of bed seemed like a Herculean feat. The scotch was getting to him, sending him into a haze far more pleasant than reality. He stopped worrying about the phones ringing. Let them.

His mind drifted to early May, when Diana had persuaded Penny to dine with them at what he now casually called "the Club." The prospect had not excited him. He'd run into Penny a few times at Simon's. She'd struck him as pleasant looking, especially without her reading glasses, and she was young and cordial but *definitely* neither beautiful nor highly educated—in other words, not someone he really wanted to take to the Club. Diana had nearly begged Penny, though, and to please Diana, so did he. Penny had hesitated but he could tell she'd wanted to go. He didn't think she dated, and he knew she must've desperately needed a night out with adults, no matter how much she loved her daughter.

Glen remembered how amazed he'd been by Penny's appearance when they picked her up at her house, and how proud he'd felt when he walked into the dining room with a beautiful woman on each arm. Diana had worn something blue—he didn't remember the details. But he'd memorized how Penny had looked in a sleek Nile-green dress with a rather deep but tasteful V neckline. She'd applied makeup more heavily than usual. A delicate rose-gold shade emphasized the perfection of her lips, and a subtle bronze shadow and liner dramatized her eyes. Her dangling gold earrings sparkled against her mahogany-colored hair, and her spike-heeled shoes showed off her long, shapely legs.

During dinner she had been quietly charming, letting Diana and Glen do most of the talking but occasionally offering an amusing comment or an observation that shocked Glen with its intelligence and perception. He almost felt offended by Penny's acuity. After all, she was just Simon's research assistant and a former waitress in a diner, for God's sake. Still, he forgave her lack of education and former occupation when she danced with him. She danced smoothly, gracefully, almost sensually, and for a moment he'd felt almost dizzy.

By the end of the evening, he'd discovered that Penny Conley was a lovely, bright, amusing, and sexy woman. Still, she didn't have Diana's background or artistic talent, so he had no urge to replace Diana with Penny. But that hadn't stopped his attraction to Penny.

The phone began to ring again, and once again he

cursed it, wishing he'd gotten up earlier and unplugged all the phones. Getting down the stairs would be impossible, unless he wanted to risk plunging down headfirst. The ringing went on and on, harsh, relentless, maddening. He knew the caller's identity. He knew the caller would keep pursuing, trying to run him into the ground, but he wouldn't worry about that person now. Not tonight . . .

Finally Glen's eyelids began to droop, and he realized he'd drunk over half the bottle of scotch. The ringing of the phone had finally, mercifully stopped. He fumbled with the remote control until the television clicked off. He was in complete darkness. He sighed with fuzzy relief that no light shone between the flimsy window blinds. Night had come at last. He could close his eyes, slip into the oblivion of sleep, and, with some luck, have pleasant dreams.

Glen's last half-waking thought drifted to Penny. He wondered if she was dreaming, too.

3

"Well?" Jeffrey Cavanaugh asked defiantly. "What do you say now? Penny couldn't have changed all that drastically in eighteen months!"

Diana felt as if her heart was plummeting right out of her body when she saw the Christmas photo. So it was true—Penny had taken their child and run. Actually, she'd kidnapped Willow. The FBI, already involved, had found her at last, making the case even messier. The worst part of the drama, though, was what Penny had done to Jeffrey Cavanaugh. For a year and a half he hadn't known if his wife and child were alive or dead, and when he finally found them . . .

"Well?" Jeffrey demanded again. "Is that Penny or not, Miss Sheridan?"

"This woman has blondish hair and blue eyes," Diana said vaguely, still fighting to reject what must be true.

"Penny's hair was—is—short and dark brown. Her eyes are brown."

Lenore nodded. "She has natural strawberry-blond hair and blue eyes. She must have dyed her hair and worn colored contacts. Otherwise, does she look like the picture?"

"Not really," Diana maintained weakly. "Penny wears hardly any makeup, and most of the time she wears glasses. She also dresses plainly—slacks or skirts and a sweater set. Low-heeled shoes, no jewelry."

"The country club," Simon urged gently. "Remember the night she went with you?"

Dammit, Diana thought in a moment of fury. Did Simon have to bring up a description of Penny that evening? Of course he did. Simon was scrupulously honest.

"One time I saw her look like she does in this picture," Diana said reluctantly. "She went with a friend of mine and me to a dance at the country club. She wore a green cocktail dress and dangling earrings, more makeup . . . I was shocked by how different she looked—how glamorous. And also . . ." Diana searched for a phrase to describe the mysterious quality about Penny she'd noticed that night.

"She seemed so relaxed, so much in her element in those clothes and socializing in that ambience. I'd expected her to be a little daunted—not that an evening at our country club is like being at a White House state dinner—but still. She wasn't the least bit nervous. And she danced so beautifully, so gracefully, so . . . professionally. I was amazed. Later she told me she'd taken ballet lessons for a few years."

Diana saw Blake and Lenore exchange a significant glance, then Blake quickly looked away.

Meanwhile, Simon peered at the photo, squinting because he always refused to wear his reading glasses in front of guests. "The high cheekbones, the slightly tilted nose, the shape of the eyes and of the lips—this is definitely the woman we know as Penny Conley." Regret resonated in his voice.

Diana knew he must have felt as disappointed in the woman as she was right now. "She even has the same tiny mole beside her left eye, just like Willow. Really, the resemblance between Penny and Willow is remarkable. But the birth certificate says Cornelia Cavanaugh was born in November. Willow just turned five in June."

"Just turned five?" Jeffrey repeated in surprise. "My daughter, *Cornelia,* will be six in November!"

"Why would Penny lie about Corny's age?" Lenore asked.

"Penny must have gotten hold of another child's Social Security card for Cornelia," Blake said thoughtfully. "The card was for a child born in June, not November."

"And Penny is twenty-nine?" Simon asked.

Jeffrey shook his head. "Thirty. We married when she was twenty-three. She would have been thirty-one on December twenty-fifth. She used to laugh about being an unwanted present from Santa Claus."

"Unwanted?"

"She said her parents didn't want her. Her early childhood was rough—or that's what she claimed," Jeffrey said bitterly. "Now I don't know if anything my wife told me was true, or why she married me, except for money."

The baldness of the statement embarrassed everyone. Color stained the top of Jeffrey's cheekbones, even though the rest of his face was chalky. Lenore looked with pity at her brother's bleak expression, while Blake stared at a large framed photo of the sun dazzling off the ice-swathed branches and twigs of a maple tree—a photograph Diana had taken the previous winter. Blake seemed extremely uncomfortable when Jeffrey showed strong emotion.

Finally Lenore leaned forward and took her brother's hand. "Jeff, I admit at first I thought Penny was after your money, but later I changed my mind. I watched her and I couldn't ignore the way she touched you, looked at you— well, so many things she did that you just can't fake unless you're a great actor."

"Maybe she was."

"She wasn't," Blake said, looking away from the framed photo. "I'm not saying this as your brother-in-law or your closest friend for over twenty years, Jeff. I felt the same way Lenore did at first about Penny. After you were married, though, I saw that Penny loved you. Love is one of those things you can sense between two people. You don't have to ask yourself if they're in love—you *know*. And I know you and Penny were in love. *Both* of you— not you alone."

Lenore looked at her husband with almost unbearable tenderness. Diana had to glance away, her desire for such depth of feeling so great that it almost hurt. The emotion surprised her—she hadn't realized how much she longed for love. Maybe the awareness came tonight because all of her feelings were raw, she thought. They were raw with the knowledge that Penny was dying.

Diana swallowed hard. "The Penny I know would only have married for love. I'm glad you agree."

"Well, love *and* money," Lenore offered almost apologetically. "If she'd married only for love, she could never have treated Jeff the way she has. Money was *very* important to Penny."

Her shock giving way to loyalty toward her friend, Diana said staunchly, "I would like to point out something. Penny lived on a small income. Her house was modest. I can remember going shopping with her several times. Penny bought things for Willow as she grew, but only two or three outfits for herself and those weren't in upscale stores. She drove a twelve-year-old car with almost a hundred thousand miles on it."

Penny's relatives simply stared at her. Diana sighed impatiently. "If she was a gold digger who married you for money, Mr. Cavanaugh, it certainly doesn't appear as if she ran off with any of it!"

"Well, she did!" Jeffrey's moment of weakness had fled. He looked at Diana unflinchingly. "Cash. Jewelry."

"A lot?" Diana asked in surprise.

"I don't think that's any of your business."

Lenore cast her brother an uneasy glance then spoke up. "Jeff, no matter what Penny *did* do, I think we have to be fair about what she *didn't* do." She looked at Diana. "She took fifteen thousand dollars from her personal bank account that only contained thirty thousand. Jeff kept her on a budget—he never let her have access to his bank accounts."

Jeffrey flushed, and Blake rushed to his rescue. "That was my idea," he said. "He hadn't known Penny long when they got married, and . . . well . . . I just thought it would make everyone feel more secure about the money issue. Also, it isn't as if she was living in poverty. The thirty thousand dollars was hers to spend on clothes, entertainment, whatever she wanted. It wasn't a household fund."

Lenore nodded. "Oh yes, Jeff was very indulgent. I didn't mean to imply he wasn't. Still, Penny only withdrew half the money in her bank account, as I said. She didn't take any of her designer clothes—none of the Chanel suits, the Armani, the Versace. She didn't even take one piece of the Vuitton luggage."

New money, Diana thought, almost smiling at Lenore's designer-name dropping. Diana glanced at Blake, whose color had heightened, but Lenore surged on, oblivious.

"As for jewelry," Lenore continued, "Penny took a pair of small diamond-stud earrings from Cartier—a gift from Blake and me. She also took a little gold cross she said her grandmother had given her when she was a child, and a pendant Blake and I had made at Tiffany's for Cornelia when she was born—a ruby rose with an emerald stem set in gold. Oh, and we got her the traditional, engraved platinum rattle from Tiffany's along with an engraved cup supposedly from my mother." Lenore finally tossed a glance at Blake. "I don't think we ever fooled Penny with that cup. She knew it didn't come from Mother." She looked back at Diana. "Penny took the rattle but not the cup. I don't think I was clear about that. And let me think if there was anything else—"

"Oh for God's sake, that's enough!" Jeffrey exploded.

"You sound like you're making a report for an insurance company."

Lenore's face flamed and her gaze dropped. "I'm sorry. . . ."

Blake jumped to his wife's defense. "Jeff, don't take out your anger on your sister. She hasn't done anything to deserve it."

"Yes, I did." Lenore looked up and spoke meekly. "I was babbling. Again. I'm sorry, Jeff. I know how upsetting this is for you."

"It is, but you upset me even more, acting like Penny didn't do anything wrong because she didn't take a Chanel . . . whatever." Jeffrey's big right hand whipped through the air, sweeping away Penny's designer clothes as his rough voice boomed relentlessly. "She left without a word! She deserted me after I gave her everything! When, because of me, she went from being a stripper to being a princess!"

"A *stripper!*" Diana and Simon exclaimed in unison.

Jeffrey glowered at them. "Don't tell me you didn't know."

"How would we know?" Simon nearly shouted. "We didn't even know she had a husband!" He paused, looking as if he was trying to absorb a byzantine concept. "Penny was a *stripper?* Are you sure?"

"Am I *sure?*" For the first time, Jeffrey looked almost amused. "Good God, man, she was my wife. I met her in a club after she'd finished her act, which I watched from demure beginning to scorching close."

Diana glanced at Simon, whose mouth remained partly open in surprise. She'd never seen him looked so astonished, and she couldn't concentrate on her own shock.

Lenore gazed at Simon, too her eyes widening in apprehension as if she thought he might have a heart attack. "Dr. Van Etton, Penny wasn't actually a stripper," she said quickly. "She was an exotic dancer. There's a *big* difference. She explained it to me. Exotic dancers really *are* dancers and they *don't* take off all of their clothes. Really, they don't. Penny didn't dance naked on a bar or give those disgraceful, grinding lap dances or—" This time Blake nudged her so forcefully he nearly knocked her off her seat. "She was an exotic dancer," Lenore ended, face flaming.

"What did her parents think of her profession?" Diana asked. Simon still seemed unable to say a word.

Jeffrey took a deep breath. "Penny said her father died when she was seven. Her mother was murdered by a boyfriend, to put it politely."

Diana wondered if Penny's mother had become a prostitute. No wonder she never mentioned her parents.

"She had no other relatives, so when she was ten, she was put in a foster home. At eighteen she was on her own," Jeffrey went on. "She waitressed for a while, and when she turned twenty-one, she started dancing. She made a reputation for herself and went by the name Copper Penny. It was a perfect name with her copper hair. One evening an important client insisted on taking me to the club where she danced, and the rest is history."

"Except that our mother and a lot of our friends were horrified," the irrepressible Lenore began. "Jeff was strong enough to ignore everyone, though. He married Penny and the both of them seemed very happy, especially when Corny was born, except that Jeff insisted on naming her Cornelia Ruth, our mother's name. Penny wanted to name the baby Willow Rose. That's why Blake designed the rose pendant—to sort of cheer up Penny about the name."

"Naming the baby Cornelia didn't make his mother accept the little girl, though," Blake said, for the first time sounding angry instead of placating. "The woman refused to see the baby more than three times and always when Cornelia was alone with Jeff. Mrs. Cavanaugh only met Penny once."

"And your father?" Diana asked Lenore.

"He's been dead for almost seventeen years," Lenore said. "He—"

Jeffrey held up his hand to silence her. "We don't have to bare the family history with these people." He looked piercingly at Simon. "I demand to see my daughter."

Diana grew taut. Of course she feared that Jeffrey Cavanaugh would simply take Willow away tonight, and she would never again see the child. That wasn't Diana's only fear, though. Another apprehension tingled throughout her, one she couldn't exactly identify but whose reality she trusted.

"Mr. Cavanaugh, it's getting late," she said. "Wouldn't it be better to see Willow—Cornelia—tomorrow, when she's not tired?"

He glanced at his watch, although she was certain he knew the exact time. "It's just past eight o'clock. She can't be too exhausted to see her own father. I want her brought to me *now!*"

Everyone stared at him, startled. Simon finally spoke, resignation in his voice. "Would you mind getting her, Diana? If Mr. Cavanaugh wants to see her, it should be before her bedtime."

Upstairs in Willow's room, Clarice sat in an armchair. Willow lay curled on the bed, both cats cuddled beside her as everyone watched a Disney movie. Or rather, everyone except Romeo, who usually never made it past eight at night and now lay, a seemingly boneless gray mass, snorting slightly every time Christabel's plumy tail brushed across his nose.

Clarice looked at Diana. "Is our company gone?" she asked with false brightness.

"No, not yet. They would like to see Willow before they leave." She tried to match the cheerfulness in Clarice's voice but failed. "Hey, kid, can we stop the movie long enough for you to go downstairs and meet some people?"

Willow gave her a reluctant look. "Do I have to? The movie's really good and I don't want to wake up Romeo and Christabel."

"You can start the movie right where you left off." Diana strode to the DVD player and stopped the movie, although she wasn't at all certain they would be turning it back on tonight. "And nothing will wake up Romeo."

Willow emitted an exaggerated sigh and gently pulled away from the cats. She still wore the dress the nurse from the hospital had given her, although now its skirt fell in wrinkles. Her smooth face showed shadows of fatigue around the big blue eyes, and her mouth was set in a slightly petulant expression. "Okay, but Mommy would say I'm tired and fussy. I'm just tellin' you."

"Well, thank you for being so considerate. I'm fore-warned." Willow walked toward her and put her hand in Diana's. Before heading for the door, though, Diana kneeled and looked into Willow's eyes. "Honey, do you remember your daddy?"

Diana felt, rather than saw, Clarice stiffen in her chair as Willow frowned. "I kind of remember a man I was s'posed to call Daddy," she said slowly. "I remember Mommy takin' me to see a big man in a real tall building in a great big city. He sat behind a desk. Willow paused. "But it was a long time ago and I didn't see him very much. Then Mommy said that big man wasn't my daddy at all. She said my real daddy died a long time ago. And then we came here and I liked it here a lot better."

Diana didn't have time to sort out this tangle of infor-mation and determine what Penny had actually said and how Willow had misinterpreted it. She took a deep breath. "Well, this will come as a surprise, Willow, but it seems your mommy made a mistake. She didn't mean to, of course. Your mommy loved you more than anything in the world. You must always remember that, Willow."

"I know Mommy loved me best of anything. What do you mean about Mommy makin' a mistake?"

"Your daddy isn't dead. He didn't know where you were for a long time, but he's finally found you. He's right here in this house, and he just can't wait to see his little girl—who's not such a little girl anymore!"

Willow merely stared at her before saying suspiciously, "A man who says he's my daddy is here?"

"Yes, honey. I know you want to see him."

"If it's my real daddy, then he's a ghost."

"Willow, he is *not* a ghost!"

"Then he's not my daddy."

"He *is* your daddy and he isn't a ghost. I know a ghost when I see one," she ended lamely.

Willow gazed at Diana steadily. "You're gonna make me see him, aren't you?"

"Well, he wants to see you, sweetheart. If you don't go down to see him, then he'll just come up to your bedroom."

"No! He can't come in here!"

Diana drew back. "Why can't he come in here?"

"Because . . ." Willow's eyes filled with tears. "Because even if he really is Daddy, he's still a ghost. I can't let ghosts in my bedroom!"

"Okay, sweetheart, settle down," Diana crooned. "I say he's not a ghost, but just in case I'm wrong, let's see him downstairs. Wouldn't that be better?"

Diana hated forcing the child to meet a man she had no desire to see. Willow had been through too much already, but if she didn't go down to see Jeffrey, he would certainly come up to the bedroom, and the possibility of that seemed to terrify Willow.

"Willow, I know you're a little nervous to see your father, but I'll be there and so will Uncle Simon."

Willow gave her a defeated look. "I guess I *have* to go," she said lifelessly just as Diana reached for the door.

Christabel leaped off the bed, ran to the door, trilled in her musical little voice, and circled Willow's legs twice. "Chris wants to go, too," Diana said cheerfully. "Are you ready, Willow?"

"Yeah," Willow said with a quaver in her voice. "I'm ready."

Willow clung to Diana's hand as they descended the stairs, Christabel running ahead of them, and Clarice watching them from the top of the staircase. Willow stopped dead at the foot of the stairs. Simon, Lenore,

Blake, and Jeffrey all stood in the foyer, the light from the chandelier shining down on them. Lenore broke into an ecstatic smile and chortled, "Corny! Oh darling, you're just *beautiful*!"

But Willow looked past her. Her blue eyes fastened on Jeffrey, who stood still but sent the child a tense, slitted smile. He held out his hands and asked, "Cornelia? Do you remember me?"

By now Willow's eyes had grown huge, horror in her gaze. Blood drained from her face, turning it parchment white, and her whole body went rigid, as if with an old, remembered terror. She lifted her hand and pointed a finger at Jeffrey.

"Him!" she screamed. "He found me! He must've found Mommy, too!"

Lenore drew back in shock, and Diana kneeled, pulling Willow close to her. "Of course he found you, honey. I told you there's no reason to be afraid. He's your daddy. Your *daddy* found you."

Willow shook violently then threw back her head and began a weird, almost unhuman keening that ripped through the house, rising and falling, going on ceaselessly. Christabel shot up the stairs, her fur on end in pure cat panic. Finally Willow caught her breath and shrieked, "He's not my daddy! He's the *Bad* Man and *he* killed Mommy, just like she told me he would!"

CHAPTER EIGHT

1

Diana held the child as tightly as she could. Willow buried her face against Diana's chest, and for a moment everyone in the foyer stood frozen, aghast. Willow's cries even drew a white-faced Nan from the kitchen to stand gazing at the child with a weirdly lifeless surprise. Finally Lenore lifted her voice above the child's crying and said, "Corny, it's Aunt Lenore and your daddy!"

Willow let out another blood-curdling shriek. Diana looked at Jeffrey, whose shock seemed to have vanished remarkably fast as his silvery eyes malevolently fastened on Simon, then on Diana. "I want to know which one of you turned my daughter against me. Who told her this despicable lie about me—"

"Jeff, you're shouting." Blake's voice was low pitched yet commanding. "You're frightening her even more. Besides, no one here told her anything about . . . what she said. Look at their faces. Can't you see they're as stunned as you are?"

Jeffrey stared at his sobbing, terrified daughter. He closed his eyes for a moment, and when he opened them again, the unnerving, flashing silvery look had vanished. "Cornelia, did your mother tell you awful things about me?"

Willow let out a wail, and Lenore shook her head at her brother. "Don't question her, Jeff. Let's just take Corny back to the hotel." She looked at Diana. "We're staying at Pullman Plaza. I remembered to bring the family album I've kept since Cornelia was born. We'll show her pictures and make her remember the three of us and how we loved her."

Willow screamed again.

"You cannot possibly be thinking of taking this child with you tonight!" Simon declared. "Look at her. She's nearly hysterical!"

"Right now," Lenore said with a shaky smile, "but maybe we'll get her some ice cream and then we can go back to our rooms and play games and look at the photograph album and—"

"Cornelia!" Jeffrey stuck out his hand for her to grasp. "Stop acting like a baby and come along with us!"

"Not tonight," Blake said firmly. Lenore glanced at him in irritation, and Jeffrey shot him a look of fury. "I'm sorry for taking over here, Jeff, but I can't help it. You've had an awful day and an even worse night. I'm not the Rock of Gibraltar, but I believe I'm thinking a bit clearer than you are right now. Cornelia feels happy and safe with these people. They obviously love her. Let the situation cool down for a while—at least for tonight. Please, Jeff, for all of our sakes. Let's think this through and decide over the next few days what's best for the child. She's the person who is most important right now—not any of us."

"I am her father," Jeffrey stated. "She belongs with me."

"Yes, but not right *now*." Blake's face tightened. "You've seen that she's healthy—"

"Healthy!" Jeffrey exclaimed. "She's—"

"Crying uncontrollably because she doesn't want to come with *us*. We're strangers to her," Blake said earnestly. "She's understandably frightened, so let's leave her where she feels safe. That's what a loving father would do, Jeff."

Diana expected a furious reply from Jeffrey. When,

after a few tense seconds he merely mumbled an unhappy "All right," Diana whisked Willow into her arms and ran upstairs. She shut the door to the child's room and placed her on the bed, where a still-frightened Christabel lay close to her nearly unconscious lover, Romeo.

Grabbing a handful of tissues, Diana began wiping Willow's tear-drenched face. "You're staying right here tonight, honey," she said, her heart pounding.

"But they said—"

"You were crying too much to hear Mr. Cavanaugh say you can stay here tonight."

"But he might change his mind," Willow wailed.

Diana looked her straight in the eyes. "Willow Conley, *no* one is taking you away tonight. You'll sleep in this bed, the cats will stay in here with you, we'll open the bathroom doors so we can see each other and wave and talk back and forth from our beds, and we'll be cozy and safe with Uncle Simon and Clarice."

"But they said I had to go to a hotel," Willow insisted tearfully. "That woman and the Bad Man." Just saying "the Bad Man" set Willow off again. "I don't wanna go to a hotel and . . . and look at . . . or be . . . ."

"Willow, you are not going anywhere." Diana decided to take another tack, one less serious. "Christabel and Romeo absolutely will *not* allow anyone to take you away!"

Willow, sniffling, turned to look at the cats. Christabel immediately crawled onto Willow's lap and began purring, and Romeo, God bless him, managed to open and close one golden eye as if he was giving Willow a wink of reassurance. She smiled through her tears. "No, maybe they *won't* let me go."

"Of course they won't. People underestimate these cats, but I can tell you, they make quite a team when they're protective of someone, and they're certainly protective of their favorite—their *only*—little girl. *I* certainly wouldn't want to meet them in a dark alley if I were a big, bad person after Willow Conley." Diana shivered. "They'd tear that person to shreds and eat him for dinner!"

Willow burst into giggles at the image of little Christabel and three-legged Romeo making mince meat of a grown man, not to mention then dining upon him. They both ate only the most expensive cat food and drank French bottled water.

Children could be so resilient, Diana thought as Willow continued to giggle and lovingly stroke the cats. But even a strong child like Willow could only take so much. One more trauma might put her over the edge. Diana quickly turned on the Disney movie again and pretended to have forgotten all the trouble downstairs, as she laughed uproariously at mildly funny parts and imitated the voices of the animated characters. After fifteen minutes, Simon came into the room and announced that they had left.

"They won't come back and get me, will they?" Willow asked nervously.

"You will be spending the night in the distinguished company of Diana, Clarice, and me," Simon said, being careful not to reassure Willow that she would never have to leave. "And, of course, Romeo and Christabel. Nan fled out the back door without even saying good night."

"No charm." Willow smiled, looking desperately relieved. "I'm glad it's just us here now."

"Me, too." Simon smiled broadly. "You know, Clarice had an excellent idea. She told me that sometimes when she babysits for you at night, you two have hot chocolate. Does a hot chocolate party with the four of us sound good to you, Willow?"

"It sounds wonnerful!"

Fifteen minutes later the four of them sat in the kitchen with their steaming drinks. Willow, with a chocolate mustache above her mouth, announced that this was the best hot chocolate party she'd ever attended. Simon pretended to think before proclaiming it the best party of its kind that he'd ever attended, too. "It's not just the hot chocolate," he said. "It's the charming company. I'm in the presence of three breathtakingly beautiful women. That's my idea of heaven."

"Wanna know my idea of heaven?" Willow piped up. They all nodded. "Mommy, Diana, Clarice, Uncle Simon, Romeo, and Christabel way up high with me havin' a picnic on a cloud."

She immediately turned her attention to catching a miniature marshmallow on her tongue. Tears had risen in Clarice's eyes, and Simon's throat worked furiously. Diana closed her eyes, feeling bleak and empty and hopeless.

Later, Diana bathed Willow, putting vanilla-scented candles around the tub and using lots of bubble bath. The festive bath delighted Willow, especially when Christabel came into the bathroom and sat on the vanity to watch her. Afterward, Diana showed Willow her new pink pajamas. The little girl insisted on donning them herself, and after a spin in front of the floor-length mirror, pronounced them be-*u*-ti-ful.

Diana settled Willow in bed. Romeo slept so deeply that he didn't even open his eyes when Diana moved him from Willow's bed and gently placed him in his own elegant cat bed. Occasionally he lifted his tail and smacked it down as if smashing an insect, and at other times he let out a soft, sleep-muted quack. Christabel, with her youthful energy and enthusiasm, always refused to settle in her kitty bed until they turned off all the lights and Diana was in her own bed, so she curled near Willow as Diana told the child a rambling bedtime story of her own creation.

Willow's eyelids gradually closed, and her breathing became even and slow. When Diana was certain the child was sound asleep, she kissed Willow lightly on the forehead then went downstairs, Christabel wide-awake and following on her heels. She found Clarice and Simon sitting in the kitchen over steaming mugs topped with marshmallows. "Good heavens, *more* hot chocolate?" She laughed. "We each had two mugs with Willow."

"Clarice and I are going on a hot cocoa binge," Simon announced enthusiastically. "A real bender. I can't guarantee what shape we'll be in tomorrow morning, but I think we deserve to cut loose after the mind-shattering evening we had with the Cavanaugh crew."

"I couldn't agree more." Diana put out two tiny cat treats for Christabel, who threw her a look of rebuke. Softening, Diana added three more into the bowl. Then she fixed another mug of hot chocolate for herself. *I'll pay for this,* she thought. Even in her late twenties, eating chocolate still caused her skin to sprout at least two pimples, but that's when concealer came in handy.

"Willow is sleeping peacefully," she said, sitting down at the kitchen table. "An hour ago I wouldn't have believed it, but I think sheer exhaustion overwhelmed her fear."

"Her fear of the Bad Man." Anxiety showed in Clarice's violet eyes. "That's what she called her father."

"She doesn't think Jeffrey *is* her father. She thinks her father is dead and Jeffrey is the Bad Man."

"The dear child took two years off my life with her shrieking," Clarice said. "Why do you think she called Mr. Cavanaugh the Bad Man?"

"Penny must have taught Willow the name," Simon said.

"Willow said she kind of remembers a man in New York—that must have been Jeffrey—but she didn't seem frightened of him," Diana said.

Simon nodded. "I think the key words are *kind of.* Willow was only three when Penny ran away with her. She couldn't count on the child clearly remembering Jeffrey, so Penny probably showed Willow photos of him to keep his face fresh in her mind. Then she told Willow he was bad and dangerous and that if he found them, he might try to kill them."

"Why would Penny do that?" Clarice asked doubtfully.

A furrow formed between Simon's arched silver eyebrows. "She'd want to make certain that if Jeffrey ever tracked down Willow, she wouldn't go with him. She'd run like hell and hide."

"Yes, that makes sense." Clarice frowned. "I simply can't believe Penny deserted her husband and took their child. Maybe they weren't getting along, in which case she could have divorced him, but to take his *child*? To leave him wondering where Willow was, how she was, for this long? Then to teach her daughter to fear her own father? I simply cannot imagine Penny being so cruel."

"Unless she wasn't being cruel at all." Diana stared beyond Clarice and Simon, seeing only the powerful love in Penny's eyes every time she looked at Willow. "We know Penny didn't steal Jeffrey's money. So why else would she literally run from the man, give up the luxurious lifestyle she had as Penny Cavanaugh, bury her and Willow's identities?"

"Fear," Simon said softly. "Penny was *terrified* of Jeffrey Cavanaugh."

2

The bomb. Diana almost blurted out that a bomb had caused the explosion at Penny's house, but she'd promised Tyler Raines she wouldn't tell Simon. She felt guilty for lying by omission, but looking at Clarice and Simon, she realized how desperately each needed a somewhat calm night's sleep. They looked exhausted, and the evening had been unsettling enough without her announcing that someone—maybe Jeffrey Cavanaugh—had planted a bomb in Penny's house.

The silence spun out, and Diana finally asked, "Simon, did you call the hospital this evening to check on Penny's condition?"

"Yes, I did, but Jeffrey Cavanaugh had already been there and established that he is her husband. The hospital will give out information about a patient's condition only to family, so you and I are no longer privy to updates about Penny. Before you came home from the mall, though, Lenore told us the doctors said her condition hasn't changed."

"She's going to die," Diana said miserably. "We all know it."

"We do not *know* it," Simon flared. "Today I read extensively about burn cases. These days even people burned as massively as Penny often live. What used to cause certain death was infection. Now we have powerful broad-spectrum antibiotics. There is always hope, Diana."

"You sound just like Grandmother."

"No, I don't. I'm not talking about getting odd feelings and messages from beyond the grave as she did. I believe in science, and science has made tremendous advances in the medical field. You are simply giving up on Penny without knowing all that can be done for her, and I will *not* have it!"

Clarice lowered her gaze and fumbled nervously with her napkin, obviously afraid Diana and Simon were going to burst into a fight.

This is only her second day with us, Diana thought in sympathy. *She still doesn't understand Simon and me.*

Diana smiled. "Clarice, don't look so uneasy. Simon and I have at least one argument a day. It keeps us from getting bored with each other."

Simon grinned at Diana, and Clarice gave her a small, wavering smile. "I'm fine if you two aren't really angry with each other."

"I don't think we've ever been really angry with each other," Diana said. "Except Simon was against my marriage."

"And I was right! That fellow was all wrong for you—childishly self-centered, jealous of your talent. Anyone could see it—anyone except you, blinded by what seemed to me a rather adolescent love, for which you were too old and far too smart. Diana, I never did understand—"

"Excuse me," Clarice interrupted softly but firmly. "Diana, do you know anything about Jeffrey Cavanaugh?"

Diana suppressed a smile as Simon immediately stopped talking. "I don't know anything about Jeffrey Cavanaugh except that he's president of Cavanaugh and Wentworth, which is one of the largest real estate developers in the country. They own hotels in Florida and California and properties in New York. I'm certain that's not all, but I've never made a study of the company."

"Obviously Jeffrey isn't a publicity hound like Donald Trump," Simon said dryly.

"Unfortunately," Diana returned. "If he were, we'd know something more about him."

Simon looked at them seriously. "That is the problem. We don't know what that man is. He certainly didn't make a good impression on me. Oh, I don't mean the ranting or the hostility. I could excuse such behavior in a case like this. Something deeper about him troubled me—something about his fundamental nature."

"He's a creep. That's what wrong with his fundamental nature," Diana stated. "He gave me bad vibes. I agree something is definitely not right about the man. That must be why Penny ran from him."

"And now he's here and Penny is near death. The house explosion is supposed to have been an accident, but I don't like coincidences." Simon looked at Diana with his penetrating green eyes, and she felt her color rising. She felt as if he knew that she was withholding important information from him. . . . "That is why we *all* have to be ready to defend ourselves and each other," Simon said decisively.

Twenty minutes later, Simon, Diana, and Christabel all stood with Clarice in her bedroom. "Now you have no reason at all to be afraid of this," Simon said, trying to hand Clarice a revolver. "It has a barrel length of just three inches and it weighs less than two pounds."

"I don't care how long its barrel length is! It's a *gun!*"

"A very small gun, Clarice, not a rifle." Simon tried once again to make Clarice take the gun, but she clenched her hands behind her back like a little girl. "Clarice, you are a grown woman, please take it. Of course, you need to be careful when handling it, even with the safety on, but it isn't nitroglycerin that will explode if you make an accidental move. All you have to do is let me give you a few pointers on how to shoot it, and then not touch it again unless you need it."

"I won't need it! Who am I going to shoot? Nan?"

Simon pretended to think then looked at Diana. "That isn't a bad idea. I don't know how much longer I can tolerate the girl."

Diana nodded. Clarice looked at both of them like they were crazy. "How can you joke about this?"

Diana smiled. "Because we're trying to make you relax. Guns certainly *can* be dangerous in the wrong hands. Children's hands, the hands of people who just want to shoot other people for the hell of it, high-strung people who would shoot at the slightest sound in their house, thinking it was a home invader—thousands of people should *not* have guns.

"But in this case, I think Uncle Simon is right," Diana went on. "Many people can't afford security systems. You didn't have one, Penny didn't have one, I didn't have one when I lived alone. And even with security systems, the police can't arrive in the blink of an eye. Simon has always believed—as do I—that it's best for you to learn how to protect yourself with more than a baseball bat. I know millions of people would say Simon and I are out of our minds, and we're reckless and irresponsible to keep guns in the house. But again, I agree with Simon that we need them considering our current situation. We can't forget what happened to Penny, and I know Simon told you what happened to Willow and me in the hospital last night. Remember, Clarice, we're not just protecting ourselves but also Willow."

Clarice slowly unclasped her hands and let them drop to her sides. "Well, when you put it that way, it doesn't sound quite so bad . . . except for one thing. You said a gun should not be in a child's hands. Have you forgotten we have a child in this house?"

"Not for a moment." Simon picked up a box he'd set on her dresser. "I keep most of my gun collection locked in a safe especially built for it, but I keep one handgun by my bedside in a box like this. So does Diana. I tried to give Penny a gun, but she told me she already had one. However, I gave her one of these boxes for storage."

"Oh, Simon, if something happened I'd be too nervous to get a key in a lock or remember a combination," Clarice almost wailed. "I'd be just *useless*."

"You are absolutely *not* a useless woman, and I don't want to hear you say such a thing," Simon said with a mixture of sternness and affection.

Diana could not help smiling, pleased. She knew her great-uncle wasn't just being kind—he genuinely liked and admired Clarice Hanson.

"Now, Clarice, this is called a fingerprint gun safe," he went on. "You don't have to worry about a key or a combination. This safe is new and unused. We will program it to recognize only *your* fingerprint. All you have to do is touch the box here," he said, indicating an indentation in the front of the box, "and it opens in as little as three or four seconds. The box saves the fingerprint even if we have a power outage. Now, what could be simpler?"

"Well, opening the box certainly seems simple," Clarice said reluctantly. "It's handling, and perhaps shooting, the gun that worries me."

"I'll give you a brief lesson showing you how to hold the gun and to aim. No bullets. In five minutes you will know everything you need to know. Then I'll load the gun and put the wretched thing in the safety box. Will that make you feel more comfortable?"

"Comfortable? You must be joking again, Simon," Clarice answered, showing her first smile in the last half hour.

Simon smiled back. "Everything will be fine, Clarice. Trust me."

"Well, I'm exhausted," Diana said. "I think it's my bedtime."

Upstairs, she tiptoed into Willow's room. The child lay curled in the middle of the big bed, sound asleep and holding her cubic zirconia queen's crown. Diana gently pried it from her small fingers and kissed the child's warm forehead. Was it too warm? Or did children's temperature normally rise slightly at night? Diana had no idea. Penny would have known, of course. *If only she were here to look after her little girl,* Diana thought, tears clinging to her lashes.

Both cats slept in their beds, wound into seemingly impossible positions that made them look as if their necks were broken. Romeo had a paw over a closed eye. "Take good care of your charge tonight," Diana whispered, although the cats did not look like defenders of the helpless.

She was careful to leave both doors of the adjoining bathroom open and to turn on a nightlight so that if Willow awakened, she could see Diana in her own bed. She did not want to turn on the bright bathroom light and perhaps awaken Willow, so she skipped her nightly bedtime ritual of cleansing cream, a moisturizer for the face, another for the neck, yet a third for the under-eye area—a ritual her mother had considered as important as breathing.

Instead Diana doused her face with soap and water and brushed her teeth. Then she headed for her bedroom and, still guided only by the night light, stripped down to her panties, pulled on a big, soft T-shirt, and literally dropped onto her bed. She didn't think she'd ever been as tired in her life, not even on one of Simon's expeditions.

She dreamed of trudging across an endless vista of sand, so hot that she didn't even feel the heat anymore, lugging her photographic equipment, determined not to complain, wondering how Simon, could walk faster than anyone else and never seem to need rest. He's a machine, she thought in the dream. He's not a man at all. Or maybe the ancient Egyptian gods blessed him with unflagging energy. Maybe he really was one of them, as some of his expedition companions used to joke. Simon Van Etton was a being from another world and time, an entirely different and superior species. . . .

Diana's eyes snapped open. For an instant, she thought she was still in the middle of the desert. Then her eyes began to adjust to the dim glow made by the night light, and she recognized her dresser, her chest of drawers, her stereo, and . . . Christabel sitting on the broad back of Diana's bedroom chair in front of the window. Chris's tail curled around her in the age-old pose of a cat silently, motionlessly, unflinchingly watching.

Diana slid out of bed and, keeping low, made her way to the chair. She hadn't pulled shut her draperies tonight. Often she left them open when the lights were turned off, liking to look out at the soft black night sky. But she'd never found Christabel on the back of the chair, also looking into the night.

Diana slipped her knees onto the seat of the chair and raised her head just enough to look over the chair's back. She followed the direction of Christabel's gaze to see a figure standing beside a giant oak tree about a hundred feet from her window. A muted glow of light grew brighter then dimmer. The figure was smoking. Smoking and watching.

A chill ran down Diana's spine, and the cat, sensing her fear, hissed gently then began growling low in her throat. "Who is that, Chris?" Diana asked just to hear something beside the unnerving hissing and growling that warned of danger. "It's one in the morning. Who's standing by the tree, smoking and staring up at us?"

A car answered her question as it whipped around a curve and its headlights caught the watcher. With sinuous speed, he darted behind the tree, but he was still too slow to escape their quick, piercing beam.

It was Tyler Raines.

CHAPTER NINE

1

Blake Wentworth emerged from the bathroom wearing a navy blue velour robe and towel-drying his wavy black hair. His wife, propped up in bed with two pillows behind her, the top of her pink lace-and-satin nightgown showing above the blanket, smiled although he was not looking at her.

"You're the handsomest man I've ever seen getting out of the shower."

Blake lowered the towel and glanced at her, grinning. "I believe that's what they call a backhanded compliment. Exactly how many men have you seen emerging from the shower, Mrs. Wentworth?"

Lenore blushed. "Oh! That compliment certainly didn't come out as intended!"

Blake sat down on the edge of the bed. "You're compliments often don't. It's cute." He touched her cheeks. "So are you when you blush. You look like a little girl."

"And you look like a *very* young man."

"I didn't think so when I saw four gray hairs in the mirror after I showered." Blake shook his wet hair at her and laughed.

"Half of my father's hair was gray when he was fifty and you only have *four* gray hairs?"

"That's because I'm a mere forty, darling."

"And I'm a wrinkled, overweight forty-four," Lenore mourned. "That's why I sometimes think you'd like to trade me in for a younger model."

"*Sometimes!*" Blake grinned. "Lenore, you let me know at least once a day you think I want a younger woman! 'Don't you think that young woman is attractive, Blake?' " He'd made his voice higher to imitate her, but there was no ridicule in the imitation and she started to giggle. "Other times it's, 'My, so-and-so is prettier at thirty-five than she was at twenty-five. Don't you think she's looking especially pretty?' " Lenore's giggle grew louder. "And on days when you're in a bad mood or have a headache, you just burst out with, 'Admit it, Blake, you wish you were married to a woman in her twenties! Let's just get it out on the table. Go ahead. Tell me the truth! I can take it!' " She was laughing now, unrestrainedly, although her face flamed.

"Honestly, darling, you amaze me," Blake continued. "If I were one of those men who is always looking younger women up and down, or staring at the cleavage some of them flaunt at parties, I could understand it. But I've *never* given you reason to be jealous."

"You're too polite to ogle other women with me around."

"No, I don't do it because I never even think about it. I am completely happy in my marriage." Lenore gave him a doubtful look and he leaned down. "I would be absolutely lost without my darling Lenore," he whispered before kissing her deeply.

She ran her hand through his damp hair and gave him a tender smile. Abruptly her smile disappeared. "Oh my, I haven't brushed my teeth yet!"

"See how much I love you?" Blake laughed.

Someone knocked at the door and Blake answered it. A waiter pushed in a cart, Blake gave him a tip, and after closing the door behind him, spread his arms out over the white cloth-covered table. "Room service. I ordered strawberry pancakes for you. You're not on one of those silly diets again, are you?"

"Well, I was, but strawberry pancakes are too much to resist."

"I also ordered you bacon, and I got us two pots of coffee. I know last night you were madly in love with tea, but the Lenore I know prefers coffee in the morning."

"Oh, last night," Lenore groaned as she climbed out of bed and slipped a beautiful pink matching robe over the nightgown. "Wasn't that excruciating?"

"The perfect word for the scene."

"I do like tea, but I've drunk gallons of it since I've been with Mother the last two weeks. And Jeffrey was acting like a bad-mannered two-year-old, constantly announcing he didn't like tea. He was upset. I noticed the old man didn't offer him anything else, though."

"That was deliberate and well called for, I'd say. He wasn't going to give in to Jeffrey. He wouldn't even let Jeff see that his rudeness bothered him."

"I don't think Jeff's rudeness *did* bother him—Simon Van Etton, that's his name. It's a distinguished name. He's a distinguished man. Very polished."

"And much more confident than Jeff, I'm afraid." Blake poured coffee. "I'm surprised those people didn't know about Penny. They seemed to have *no* idea about her past, not even that young woman Diana."

"I know." Lenore smiled ruefully. "They were genuinely shocked about Penny's stripping."

"I thought we were calling it 'exotic dancing.' "

"It's just you and me now, sweetheart. We can call it what it was." Lenore took the lid off the warm plate on which lay her pancakes topped with huge strawberries and whipped cream. "Oh my goodness, they look heavenly."

"I want you to eat every bite. You need your energy. You look a bit pale, and yesterday you had circles under your eyes. Your mother never gives you any rest."

"Thank goodness I'd just left to catch the plane for home when you called with the news about Penny. I can imagine Mother's reaction."

"I can't. I don't want to imagine it." Blake heaped

blueberry jam on his toast. "She won't shed a tear for Penny."

"Oh, Blake, she will. What an awful thing to say! She'll be glad that Penny's out of Jeff's life and that Cornelia is alive, but she won't be glad Penny is probably going to die."

"She won't say so, but she *will* be glad. Your mother can be fairly awful."

Lenore cut a strawberry in half, chewing it and thinking. Yes, her mother probably would be glad, but Lenore had trouble admitting this even to herself. She'd never come to terms with her mother's unforgiving nature. Instead, Lenore changed the topic. "What do you think of Diana?"

Blake laid down his fork. "Oh no, not again."

"No, not again." Lenore smiled. "She was Penny's friend and Cornelia seemed crazy about her. I just wondered what *you* thought of her."

"Well, I know the first thing you're interested in is whether or not I thought she was pretty. I did. She has magnificent hair, and the eyes are very arresting—they can look soft and feminine one minute and hard as granite the next. She's feminine, but I can also see her in cowboy boots or climbing trees—"

"Or going on Egyptian expeditions, just as her uncle told us about while we were waiting for her to come home."

"Yes." Blake took a bite of his eggs. "I also see a good bit of her uncle in her. But wait—he's her great-uncle, isn't he? She's not easily intimidated. Jeff didn't scare her any more than he did the uncle. She's not a hard, masculine woman, but she's not a delicate flower, either." He shrugged and smiled at Lenore. "What more can I say?"

"I wish she looked like that housekeeper."

Blake burst out laughing. "Why do they keep that girl? My God, her manners! She was atrocious!"

"Diana said she was new."

"There has to be more to the story than that." Blake

was still laughing. "I can't see Van Etton putting up with her more than a day unless he had a better reason than that she's inexperienced!"

"Well, we really don't know these people. We've been told they're highly reputable, we've seen that they live well, we've even seen how much Corny loves them, but still. . . ."

"But still, we haven't gotten to know them for ourselves." Blake paused, crunching a piece of bacon. "And by the way, I know this might make Jeff angry, but may we *please* call that child Willow instead of Cornelia or, even worse, Corny? Penny hated the name but Jeff insisted on it because he thought it would please your mother, who, true to form, was insulted that he named the daughter of that 'slut' after her. Since apparently everyone has been calling her Willow for the last eighteen months, will the world stop turning if we call her Willow, too?"

"I suppose not." Lenore frowned. "Penny kept her own first name. Why do you suppose she didn't change it, too?"

"The FBI said Karen Hope Conley is the name on the Social Security card she was using. The card for Willow belongs to a Deborah Lee Conley. I guess if anyone asked, Penny said Penny and Willow were nicknames."

"But where did Penny get the Social Security cards?"

"I don't know. We don't know a whole lot about her life before she married Jeff, Lenore. In her line of work, she could have met all kinds of underworld types who would know how to pull off an identity change. I've always believed she turned to one of those people—people who knew Copper Penny and were still willing to help her."

"For a fee, though. A criminal wouldn't take a risk for free."

Blake smiled. "I hope you don't know that from experience."

"In spite of all of my father's rumored shady contacts, I know criminals only from television and in movies—"

"Where criminals are always portrayed with absolute accuracy." Blake shook his head. "I don't know how she did it, Lenore, but don't forget the fifteen thousand dollars missing from her bank account. Maybe she used that money to buy the new Social Security cards."

"Maybe so." Lenore took a sip of coffee then poured more in the dainty china cup. "Penny didn't leave to steal Jeff's money. I've always thought she went away with a rich boyfriend. According to the Van Ettons, though, she lived a lower-middle-class life. Of course, that doesn't eliminate the possibility of a lover, but he couldn't have been a rich lover. And where would she have met him? I don't think she often visited Huntington, West Virginia."

"She'd probably never heard of it."

"Then why did she come here?"

"I have no idea, honey."

Lenore looked at Blake. "Why were you saying all those wonderful things to Jeff last night about knowing real love when you see it, and you saw it in Penny when she looked at Jeff? Were you just trying to calm him down?"

"Partly. That's why I laid it on so thick. But I'm certain Penny did love Jeff when she married him. I just didn't see that look of love in her eyes the last few months before she left."

"Then you think she might have left him for another man."

"I did at first, just like you did. When so much time went by and Jeff never heard anything from her about a divorce, though, I thought maybe she was with someone who wouldn't marry her. The only thing I was sure of was that if there was another man, he had a lot of money," Blake said. "Penny didn't marry Jeff for money alone— I'm sure of it—but she'd gotten used to a certain lifestyle and she'd also want the best for her daughter. It appears, however, that I was wrong. If there *was* another man, he certainly didn't keep her in style."

"No, she ended up being someone's research assistant and living in a tiny house with faulty wiring that caused an explosion."

His mouth full, Blake shook his head then swallowed.

"Faulty wiring could cause a fire, but not an explosion. Faulty wiring putting off sparks in a room where there is a gas leak could cause an explosion. We'll probably get a full report from the fire marshal today." He paused. "I think we're ready to start on the second pot of coffee."

Lenore pretended to toy with her pancakes as if not certain she could take another bite. She caught Blake looking at her, grinning. "You know I'm going to scrape this plate clean, don't you?"

"Yes. Why not? You always lose at least five pounds when you stay with your mother."

"I *need* to lose the five pounds. You don't, but you've lost at least that much. Of all the times for this to happen—when I'm just coming home from Mother's and you've been down with the flu. You're not over it, you know. You looked utterly worn out when we left the Van Etton house and you coughed throughout the night."

"It wasn't exactly a restful evening, Lenore. The icing on the cake was having Cor—Willow—scream that Jeff was the Bad Man, that he killed Penny."

"Oh, God, that was dreadful! Penny is to blame. She tried to turn Cor—Willow—against Jeff out of revenge."

"Revenge for what? Jeff didn't do anything to Penny except treat her like a queen."

Lenore sighed. "I just wish I knew what Penny was like during her months here in Huntington. I don't mean that she lived in a modest house and wore inexpensive clothes. I mean what she was really like—what she thought, what she talked about, where she went, what her interests were, if she had any."

"Well, you've met the two people she seemed to know best—Simon Van Etton and Diana Sheridan. If you want to know about Penny, I think Diana's the best person to ask."

"But I can't just go up to her and say, 'Tell me all you know about Penny.'"

Blake laughed. "That would lack finesse."

"Besides, Diana didn't strike me as being a gossip. I have a feeling getting information from her—about

Penny—would be extremely difficult, especially because I'm Jeffrey's sister."

Blake popped the last piece of jam-loaded toast into his mouth and poured another cup of coffee. "Lenore, you are an expert at getting information out of people. It's one of the reasons Jeff put you on the executive staff of the company. You seem charmingly innocent. Guileless. That disarms people—even very savvy business people. You learned more from some of our competitors than Jeff or I ever could."

"Talk about backhanded compliments! I'm great at finding out information because people think I'm stupid."

"I didn't say stupid. I said guileless. And charming. And completely candid and forthcoming. People blab everything they know to you without realizing they're doing it. Also, when someone says something vital we need to know, you give no sign that you even realize what they've said. You just chatter on as if the information didn't register."

"I repeat, people think I'm stupid."

Blake sighed then smiled at Lenore affectionately. "Okay, they don't think you're the sharpest knife in the drawer. They think you have a cushy upper-level job because your brother runs the company."

"My brother *and* my husband."

"Yes, but Jeff was already running things when he brought me on. Sometimes I'm not even sure he needs me. He feels an obligation to me because my father and his father started the business. But that aside, you are a gem, Lenore. Your brother and I know you are responsible for some of the smartest moves ever made by Cavanaugh and Wentworth." Lenore smiled at him. "So, just how hard a nut do you think Diana Sheridan will be to crack compared to some of the other coups you've pulled off so successfully? She doesn't have a chance at withholding information from Lenore Wentworth."

"My goodness, maybe I should offer my services to the CIA. Then they could stop torturing people to get information."

Blake grinned. "Marvelous idea, darling, but they don't pay as well as Cavanaugh and Wentworth." His grin faded. "So how about trying to get information about Penny from Diana? I don't think it will be all that hard for you."

Lenore took another sip of coffee, looking beyond Blake to the window, the draperies open to a beautiful day. "Last night Jeff said he wanted to see Penny today. He wanted us to go with him, but in spite of what Penny did, I just cannot stand to see her horribly burned. Jeff will let me bow out of the visit if you go with him. I know you don't want to go, either, but he'll insist. He worries me. He's getting almost pathological about social interaction and having you or me do the talking for him. But this time he really will need a family member with him if he's going to see Penny."

"So what's your plan?"

"You will go with Jeff to the hospital. I'll beg off, call the Van Etton house, and ask if I can drop by and see Willow. I don't see how they can say no. I'm the child's aunt and I'll be coming instead of Jeff, which should be a relief to them." Lenore looked at her husband and smiled. "And I'll act as charmingly ignorant and chatty and disarming as possible until I find out all I can. All right?"

"Better than all right." Blake reached across the table, hand held up. Lenore raised her own hand, which he clasped and squeezed. "Pure genius, dear Lenore."

2

Diana awakened to Willow standing beside her bed regarding her intently with big blue eyes. "I didn't think you'd ever wake up, and Christabel and Romeo and me are starving." Romeo, somewhere on the floor beside Willow, let out one of his stentorian quacks. "See? Starving."

"I didn't realize the situation was so dire," Diana mumbled as Christabel jumped up on her bed. "What time is it?"

"Breakfast time."

Diana glanced at her bedside clock. "It's nine o'clock. Really *past* breakfast time, but you and I had to catch up on our sleep. Besides, Romeo usually likes a late breakfast."

The big cat let out another resounding quack, as if proclaiming Diana wrong. "Romeo says he's hungry now," Willow told her. "He'd better eat soon or he could get all weak and shaky from not having any food."

"That'll be the day!" Diana laughed. "Okay, you three pitiful beings, I'm getting up right now. We'll all be having breakfast in ten minutes."

She was slipping on her robe when someone tapped lightly on the door. A moment later Clarice called, "Diana?"

"Yes, come in, Clarice."

The woman stepped into the bedroom without her walker. She wore a light-blue suit—the only dressy outfit Diana had taken from Clarice's closet the day before—and low-heeled pumps. She'd pulled her hair into a more elaborate French twist than usual, with small wavy tendrils at her ears and a deeper wave at the left side of her forehead.

"My goodness, you dress well even on a lazy Sunday morning. You look lovely," Diana said.

Clarice smiled. "Thank you. I always attend Sunday services, and your uncle has offered to be my escort."

"Uncle Simon is driving you to church?"

"Actually, he insists on attending with me and afterward taking me out for lunch, since I'm having little arthritis pain today. I told him lunch out was entirely unnecessary, but . . . well . . . you know Simon better than I do."

"Yes, I do," Diana said faintly. Simon who probably hadn't been in a church since his sister's wedding was now not only offering but *insisting* on taking Clarice? The man who Diana had left on Tuesday morning was not the same man who now waited to take Clarice Hanson to church and out to lunch. Diana smothered a smile. She couldn't have been happier that her great-uncle was no longer burying himself in his work. "Well, Willow tells me she and the cats are starving. We were just coming down for breakfast."

"*Starving*," Willow repeated for emphasis. "*All* of us."

"I'm glad your appetite has come back," Clarice said to Willow. Christabel trilled sweetly, already prancing toward the door with Romeo scooting top speed behind her. "Actually, Willow, Simon has told me Diana usually doesn't eat breakfast. She takes a shower then she goes on a long walk and takes pictures with her camera. That's why I went ahead and made scrambled eggs for you, and Simon will fix the cats' breakfast. Is that all right?"

Willow looked doubtfully at Diana. "You really don't eat breakfast?"

"Well, not a real breakfast. Just a piece of toast and some coffee."

Willow sighed. "Grown-ups! Yes, I would like scrambled eggs, Clarice."

"Fine. The three of you are going to ride down in the elevator." Willow clapped her hands. Clarice looked back at Diana. "I'll send them down and then I'd like a word with you, if you don't mind," Clarice said.

Diana had shrugged out of her robe, already heading for the bathroom and the glorious large shower stall, but she froze. Clarice's face had lost the smile that Diana now realized had been false. *Penny is dead,* she thought. *Penny is dead and Clarice wants to tell me before she tells Willow.* She nodded at Clarice, put on the robe again, and thumped down on the edge of the bed, already bracing herself for the news. After the elevator had descended, Romeo let out a triumphant quack. He loved riding in the elevator. Simon shouted up, "Cargo has arrived safely, ladies! We're off to the kitchen."

Clarice came back into the room and closed the door behind her. Diana glanced up and said, "Penny has died, hasn't she?"

Clarice looked at her in surprise, then sympathy. "Oh, heavens, no! Diana, dear, do you think your uncle and I would run off to church and lunch out and leave you and Willow alone if such a thing had happened? We haven't heard anything from Jeffrey Cavanaugh, but as far as I know, Penny's condition hasn't changed."

Diana realized she'd been holding her breath. She let it out and whispered, "Thank God."

"Yes, well, that's what I intend to do at church." Clarice hovered near the foot of the bed. "Dear, there's something I need to discuss with you. I wasn't certain, but I talked with your uncle after you went to bed—after he tucked that fearsome gun away in the fancy box—and he told me you had a right to know what I've been withholding from you. Not for very long, but withholding, nevertheless."

Clarice looked miserable, twining her fingers together, frowning, her violet gaze direct but also reluctant. Diana motioned to the chair across from her bed.

"Have a seat and tell me, Clarice. And please don't look so unhappy. I'm sure what you have to say can't be that dreadful."

"I hope it isn't." The woman sat down and looked at her directly. "It's about Glen."

"Glen?" Diana repeated in surprise. "Glen Austen?"

"Yes. I didn't know his name or his connection to you until he came by here yesterday when he heard about Penny. I've seen him before, though, Diana." Clarice hesitated. "I've seen him come to Penny's house."

"Glen and I took Penny with us to dinner at the country club in May. We picked her up at her house. . . ."

Clarice shook her head. "Not then. Later. When you asked me the night of the explosion if I'd seen anyone come to Penny's house, I hesitated. Then Simon said he'd been to the house to leave food for Penny the week Willow was in the hospital.

"I didn't say anything more at the time, but I've seen Glen come to her house four times starting around two months ago," Clarice continued in a hesitant voice. "Two of those times, Willow had told me she was spending the night with her friend. Each time Glen came, he stayed at least an hour. Another time, Penny had just come home from a lecture held at the university and she'd left Willow with me. Glen arrived immediately after she'd pulled in her driveway. They went inside and he stayed about an hour."

Clarice looked at Diana cautiously, as if she expected a cry of distress or a stricken expression. When Diana didn't respond, the woman went on a bit more confidently. "After he left, Penny rushed over, apologizing profusely, and saying someone she knew from a class she took during the school year had been at the lecture, too, and simply invited himself home with her.

"But she was flustered and embarrassed and I knew she was lying, Diana. I knew it and I was surprised," Clarice went on. "I could not understand why Penny would lie to me if she'd met someone she liked, someone she wanted to date. She would have known I'd be happy for her. I was also puzzled that although he'd been to her house before, they didn't seem to be having a normal dating relationship." Clarice took a breath. "Do you want me to go on, Diana? You look pale. . . ."

"I'm surprised but I'm fine," Diana said flatly. "I want to hear it all."

"All right. The last time I saw Glen was Wednesday night—two nights before the explosion. He arrived around nine o'clock—it was still barely light out. The evening was cooler than usual and so quiet. I'd turned off the air conditioning and raised my window and . . . well, I was spying, I might as well admit it."

Clarice colored faintly. "Penny didn't immediately let him inside. I overheard her saying she was tired after spending so long at the hospital with Willow, she didn't feel well and would just like to go to bed, but Glen said he'd only stay a few minutes. From what I could see, he had pushed himself halfway in all ready. Finally, Penny opened the door.

"I'm not ashamed to say I kept watching," Clarice said almost defiantly. "Glen had been so . . . well, almost aggressive when Penny obviously wanted to be alone. I was worried about her. Then I saw another car pull up and park across the street. By then daylight was almost gone and I couldn't see the figure in the car until the door opened briefly. Someone got out, looking as if they were going to Penny's, hesitated and then got back in the car. When the car's inside lights came on, though, I saw that the driver was a young woman. You can imagine how astonished I was when on Saturday morning your housekeeper arrived and she turned out to be the woman I'd seen watching Glen when he was at Penny's—Nan Murphy."

By now Diana was sitting so far forward on the side of her bed that she slid and almost fell on the floor. She caught herself and Clarice gasped. "Oh, dear, I've shocked you! I told Simon this would be too much for you. Please don't faint, Diana. Glen isn't worth *one* of your tears."

Diana scooted back on the bed, but her thoughts spun so fast for a moment that she couldn't form a coherent sentence. Meanwhile Clarice went into the bathroom and came back with a Dixie cup full of cold water. "Sip this slowly," she ordered. "Oh, I just feel *terrible* for upsetting you, but Simon said you could handle it, you can handle anything. He thinks the sun rises and sets on you and somehow you're not like other women at all—you're emotionally stronger and able to cope with all situations and—"

"Clarice, I'm all right," Diana finally interrupted. "I'm not all those things Simon would like to think I am, but I certainly can handle the news that Glen was pursuing another woman. Or maybe two other women." Diana tried for a smile, although she was still too stunned for it to be genuine. "Clarice, I have no strong feelings for Glen. I like him but I've just been drifting along with him for months, too lazy to break things off between us. I was *never* in love with him—not even close. Honestly, I'm not hurt and you mustn't feel bad for telling me all of this. Simon was right—I needed to know."

"Oh, thank goodness." Clarice dropped back onto the chair and began fanning herself with a magazine she'd grabbed from Diana's nightstand. "I could hardly sleep last night—I'd seen both Nan and Glen yesterday and I realized they had a connection even though Glen appeared to be *your* young man. I just had to ask for Simon's advice because he knows you better than anyone does. Even when Simon said I should tell you, though, I wasn't sure."

"You did the right thing." Diana paused then began talking almost to herself. "Penny knew exactly how I felt about Glen. I don't know why if he'd begun to pay attention to her, she wouldn't have told me. She couldn't possibly have thought I would be hurt."

"Penny seems to have had many secrets," Clarice said sadly. "I wonder if any of us really knew her."

"Well, I know most people would think I'm an absolute fool for believing this, but I think we knew the *real* Penny—her soul or spirit or whatever you want to call it, which lay buried under all her secrets. I can't help feeling that she was essentially a good person, but something had her trapped, Clarice. After all, she didn't run off with Jeffrey Cavanaugh's money. Also it's easy to say Penny taught Willow to fear Jeffrey so Willow would never go looking for him, but Penny wouldn't *terrify* her five-year-old daughter just so she'd never seek out Jeffrey when she got older. That would be cruel, and Penny was not cruel, I don't care what anyone says. I believe she had a good reason for leaving Cavanaugh. Maybe another man was involved, but Penny felt that flight and a life of concealment were the only way to escape Jeffrey. And something or someone had her scared out of her mind this week."

"But it couldn't have been Jeffrey," Clarice said. "He didn't know where she was until after the explosion."

"Or so he says. I don't like him and I don't trust him. I don't trust any of them—not Jeffrey, not Blake, not Lenore." And not Tyler Raines, Diana knew she should add, but for some reason she couldn't include him with the

Cavanaugh group. She didn't know what part he played in this drama, but he didn't seem to fit with the three people she'd met last night.

"As for Glen . . ." Diana shrugged. "For some reason, I can't imagine Penny being attracted to Glen. He's not at all the kind of man I would pick for her. Of course, I dated him for months, and he isn't the kind of man I'd fall in love with, either. And as you said, they certainly weren't having a normal dating relationship. A few sexual trysts? Maybe. After all, Glen and I weren't involved sexually." Clarice turned pink again. "Maybe Glen was wildly attracted to Penny. Frankly, I just wasn't paying enough attention to him to notice."

"He's a nice-looking young man," Clarice offered weakly. "And he's your uncle's good friend."

"Uncle Simon likes him—that's not the same as Simon considering him a good friend. He wasn't even too happy that I dated Glen for so long. He always told me I should be seeing someone else—someone with 'fire.' " Diana smiled ruefully. "If Glen was involved with *both* Nan and Penny, I guess Simon underestimated his amount of fire."

Clarice glanced down at her clasped hands, clearly embarrassed. "Well, I wouldn't know. When I spoke with Glen yesterday, I really wasn't thinking of him in those terms," she said almost primly.

Clarice's head jerked up when Diana laughed. "No, I guess you weren't! My lord, how astounded you must have been when he arrived presenting himself as *my* boyfriend. After you'd already discovered the woman who'd followed him to Penny's—Nan—was our temporary housekeeper, I don't know how you managed to maintain your composure at all. You're a wonder, Clarice!"

Clarice smiled. "I don't think I'm a wonder, dear. I was terribly uncomfortable having to talk to him while Simon went up to Willow's room to get you. I fled the library as soon as you arrived."

Diana let the silence hang, thinking. Then she asked,

"When Nan was parked outside of Penny's house, did Glen see her when he left?"

"Oh, no. She'd started her car and crept away around ten minutes before he came out the front door."

"What was Glen's parting with Penny like? Did he kiss her at the door?"

"Heavens, no! Penny's screen door flung back so hard it hit the house. Glen stomped out onto her porch, stood for a minute, then turned around and nearly yelled, 'You're making a big mistake, Penny.'"

Diana stared at Clarice. "He said she was making a big mistake?" Clarice nodded. "Of course, you couldn't know what he meant. Maybe it was her leaving Huntington. Simon was in her house—he said packed boxes were sitting around. Glen would have seen them. He would have known Penny was leaving even if she hadn't told him."

"Glen could have thought she was just moving to a different house. Maybe she was."

"If that were so, she would have told one of us. She didn't tell you, Uncle Simon, or me. And why would Glen think that was a big mistake? Also, don't forget she did say something to me and to you that sounded as if she'd never see us again." Diana shook her head. "I'm sure Penny wasn't moving to a different neighborhood, Clarice. She was on the run again."

"And Glen didn't want her to go."

"Either that, or he didn't want her to go and leave him out of the picture. Even if she was having a sexual relationship with him, if she thought she needed to get out of town, she probably wouldn't tell him where she was going. That would let him know just how little she cared about him. Or maybe she was leaving *because* of him. That would really set him off because Glen does not react well to rejection."

"Oh my," Clarice almost whispered. "Do you think he's capable of violence?"

"I really don't know. Then, to top off the mess, Nan knew Glen was seeing Penny. She watched him that very night." Diana hesitated, suddenly feeling as if something hard and cold was settling in her stomach. "Clarice," she said softly, "Glen got mad at Penny, and Nan saw Glen at Penny's house on Wednesday night. Tempers must have been running hot. On Thursday night, I got a call from Penny saying she must talk to me—it was a matter of life and death."

Clarice's eyes widened. "Do you mean on Thursday night she was afraid because either Glen or Nan had threatened her?"

"Maybe," Diana said vaguely, but she wasn't thinking about threats. She was thinking about the bomb that had exploded in Penny's home the very next night.

CHAPTER TEN

1

Diana and Willow walked out to bid Simon and Clarice good-bye as they set off for church. Willow waved as if they were leaving on a world tour. When they'd cleared the driveway, Diana took a deep breath, proclaimed it a beautiful morning, and suggested they amble around the lawn. When they came to the oak tree where Tyler Raines had stood, Diana found two mashed cigarette butts. She picked them up, certain he'd stayed longer than to smoke only two cigarettes. He'd collected the rest of the butts.

"Have the squirrels that live in the tree started smokin'?" Willow asked.

"I certainly hope not. Cigarettes could give them lung cancer."

"But if they did start smokin', where would they buy their cigarettes?"

"Shop-a-Minute," Diana returned straight-faced.

Willow laughed. "No, they wouldn't! Shop-a-Minute wouldn't sell cigarettes to squirrels!"

"You never know," Diana said seriously. "They'll do anything to make a dollar."

"Is that how much a pack of cigarettes costs?"

"More. Or three acorns, unless the price has gone up recently to four acorns."

Willow, still in stitches at their silliness as they entered
the house, soon settled down to tell the cats a story, while
Diana went into another room and found the telephone
directory. She looked up the number for Al Meeks, found
only one listing for Al's Best Barbecue and another for
Albert Meeks. She hesitated about calling now—maybe
this afternoon would be better—but her fingers pushed
numbers almost without her realizing it. A moment later,
a man's deep, scratchy voice said, "Hello there! What can
I do for you?"

"Mr. Meeks?"

"Yes ma'am."

"May I speak with Tyler, please? Tyler Raines?"

After a moment, Al Meeks said hesitantly, "Well, he's
not here right now."

So surprised by his not asking who Tyler Raines was,
Diana felt temporarily thrown. After a beat, she asked,
"Do you know when he'll be back?"

"No."

Too quick, too definite, Diana thought. Now Al was
lying.

"I see. Mr. Meeks, I'm Diana Sheridan. I ate in your
restaurant four or five times with Penny and Willow Conley."

"Oh! Diana Sheridan! Sure, I remember you." Immediately the enthusiasm left his voice. "My God, I'm sick
about what happened to poor Penny. I just loved that girl.
Thank the lord little Willow was spared." He paused. "And
you! Tyler told me how you missed bein' in that house by
less than five minutes."

So Tyler Raines did know Al Meeks. Tyler had even
told Al the details of the night of the explosion. She'd
been sure, so sure, that Tyler was lying about knowing Al.
She could feel the man on the other end of the connection
waiting for her to say something. "I was supposed to be at
Penny's house over an hour earlier, but I was late. If I
hadn't been and Willow hadn't crawled out a window to

get lightning bugs for her mother, there would have been two more casualties that night. Not that Penny is dead, but . . ."

Annoyed, Diana felt tears ready to flow again. She would *not* burst into sobs on the phone with a man she barely knew. She swallowed hard and said, "The doctors say there's no change in Penny. She's still unconscious. Of course, no one can see her or even get direct information about her except family members."

"What a shame," Al said mournfully. "I'll be prayin' for Penny."

"I'm sure she'd appreciate that. And it's really why I called. Not about praying, but to express my appreciation and Clarice Hanson's, and what I know would be Penny's, for all the help Tyler was that night. He pulled my car away from the fire, he went into Clarice's house, which was burning, and carried her out—"

"He did *what*?" Al nearly shouted.

"He carried Clarice Hanson out of her burning house."

"That boy! He didn't say a word about doin' a thing like that. Well, I'll be! Just like his grandpa. We were great friends. Guess it's better he died quite a few years ago. It would've broken his heart if he'd known what Tyler went through when he was younger."

"What Tyler went through?"

She could almost see Al Meeks's expression growing wary. "Oh, never mind me. I'm just an old man who talks too much. Well listen, Miss Sheridan, I'll tell Tyler you called and thanked him for his help. He'll like that." He paused. "He's a good boy, Miss Sheridan. I'd be proud to call him my own grandson."

"Could I ask one more question, Mr. Meeks?"

"Sorry, the Missus here is nearly pullin' me out the door. Time for church. Thanks for callin' Miss Sheridan. You take care now. Good-bye to you."

"And good-bye to you," Diana said softly as she hung up the phone, Al's words echoing in her mind:

He's a good boy . . . I'd be proud to call him my own grandson.

"Well, I'll be damned," she muttered, shaking her head and smiling.

2

"Can we go visit Mommy today?"

Diana looked at Willow, turned out in navy blue shorts, a blue-and-pink blouse with flutter sleeves, and her rhinestone crown. "I don't think they're letting your mother have visitors yet," Diana said as she held the Sunday morning newspaper. The front page bore a banner headline about a bomb causing the explosion of a house in the Rosewood neighborhood. She no longer had to keep the secret.

"But I wanna see Mommy."

"I know, sweetheart, but we don't always get what we want."

Willow's mouth trembled slightly. "Can't Mommy have visits because she's not getting' well? Is that what it means?"

"It means the doctors want her to use all her strength to get well and not use it visiting with people. She's still weak."

"But getting well." It wasn't a question. Willow seemed almost defiantly pronouncing that Penny would recover. Then she wavered. "Mommy *is* getting better, isn't she? You wouldn't tell me a fib, would you?"

Being completely truthful versus making a little girl feel better fought a flashing battle in Diana's mind. Then she looked at Willow's questioning eyes in her sad, innocent face and knew she couldn't dash the child's hope.

"The doctors and the nurses are putting all their efforts into getting your mother well. You know she wants desperately to come home to her little girl that she loves more than she loves anyone else, and she's a strong lady, Willow. *Very* strong."

"I wish I could see her for just a minute," Willow said droopingly. "If I told her I love her it might help."

"She knows you love her, Willow. Believe me—she knows." Diana smiled and put the newspaper aside. "Are you ready to go for a walk and take pictures with me? Uncle Simon and Clarice won't be home from church and lunch for at least a couple of hours."

"Yeah, I guess. Can the cats come?"

"Well, cats don't usually take walks with people like dogs do. Besides, long walks are too hard for Romeo."

"You could buy a wagon and pull him," Willow suggested.

"That's a very smart idea, but we have Christabel to consider. She'd run off. She'd hide in the woods and we'd never find her."

"I hid in the woods and I got found."

Diana's senses sharpened but she tried to sound casual. "Yes, you did. A man found you. How was he able to find you when no one else could?"

" 'Cause I hid from everyone else."

"But you didn't hide from him. Why?"

Willow's gaze drifted around the room for a few seconds. "I was tired of hidin' and I was scared of snakes."

"I see. Did you know the man who found you?"

"Well . . . no."

"That didn't sound like the exact truth."

Willow looked at her, and Diana saw a quick flash of apprehension in her eyes. She faltered then said, "At first I thought I knew him but I didn't. I got mixed up."

"Who did you think he was at first?"

"Well . . . I thought . . ." Willow took off her crown and began inspecting the rhinestones sparkling in the sunlight. Not looking up, she said, "I thought he was a friend of Mommy's but he wasn't."

Diana knew the child was telling either a half-truth or a complete lie. But Willow was not a child who lied even when she'd done something wrong and wanted to escape punishment. Diana knew if Willow was lying now, she was following Penny's orders. But why would Penny want to deny knowing Tyler Raines? And why did he want to deny knowing Penny?

Willow slowly edged away from Diana, growing more absorbed in watching her crown sparkle, when the phone rang. *Just as well,* Diana thought. Obviously she'd pushed Willow enough on the subject of Tyler Raines.

Diana answered the phone to hear a woman with a bubbly voice ask, "Is this Diana?"

"Yes. Mrs. . . . Wentworth?"

"Lenore, please. I hope I'm not calling too early."

Diana glanced at her watch. "It's eleven-ten. Hardly too early."

"Some people I know sleep until noon on Sundays. Others—a very few—go to church."

"Today I'm doing neither."

"Then I'm so glad I was able to reach you!" Lenore paused and her voice grew more serious. "Diana, I always loved my niece dearly. I was so looking forward to being with her last night but things didn't work out, to say the least. Jeff is going to the hospital to see Penny, and Blake is going with him. I know I should go, but frankly, I just can't bring myself to see Penny in her condition."

Conscious of Willow's closeness, Diana merely asked, "Any word on her condition?"

"Jeff called the hospital but he's in a 'yes' and 'no' mood this morning. He said they told him there's no change in Penny. I got no other details. Maybe he didn't either. I wish he wouldn't try to see her, but when he makes up his mind, there's no changing it. Anyway, I wonder if it'd be okay if I—just me—come by and see Cornelia."

Dread washed through Diana. She didn't want to cause more trouble by refusing, but she would not have Willow upset again. "Could you wait just a minute until I ask Willow?" she asked pleasantly.

"Oh! Well, I guess not." Lenore must have known her voice betrayed a trace of irritation. "I mean, of course you should ask her!"

Diana put her hand over the receiver. "Willow, your Aunt Lenore is on the phone. She was here last night but I don't think you even saw her." Willow's gaze grew wary. "She seemed nice and she says she always loved you and she'd like to see you." Willow frowned. "She made a point of saying she'd come by herself."

"No Bad Man?" Willow asked fearfully.

"Absolutely not."

Willow appeared to think for a moment. "Only if she *promises* it's just her."

"Lenore, Willow says it's all right with her if you *promise* you'll come alone."

"Oh, dear, it's as bad as all that? Well, we can't do anything about it now. I promise to come alone. Cross my heart."

"She says she crosses her heart."

Willow seemed to think it over then finally nodded.

"Well, there goes our walk," Diana muttered a minute later, after she'd said good-bye to Lenore. She'd been planning to leave in about fifteen minutes, thinking of how much Willow would enjoy playing in the park on this beautiful day, and the good photographs she could get of the child. Instead, they would be stuck in the house making uncomfortable conversation with Lenore Wentworth. . . .

Sister of Jeffrey Cavanaugh, Diana thought with abrupt uneasiness. Jeffrey, with his cold, silver eyes, his hostility, his determination to see his daughter—who'd called him the Bad Man and had a shrieking fit when she had seen him. Lenore had promised she would visit by herself, but Diana didn't know how seriously this woman took a promise made to a child. Lenore might come by herself, and shortly afterward Jeffrey would show up while Diana sat there alone in the house with Willow.

For one flashing instant, Diana wished Tyler Raines were still standing out by that oak tree gazing at the house. She dismissed the wish as ridiculous—she should have called the police when she saw him last night, but she'd told herself that she didn't want to throw the household into an uproar.

After her immediate desire for Tyler's presence when she felt threatened by Lenore's visit, though, Diana wasn't so sure that not wanting to disturb everyone had been her real reason for not calling the police. When she'd crawled back in bed, leaving Christabel to watch him watching the house, she'd felt . . . safe.

"Safe!" she burst out, stunned by the thought.

"What? What's wrong?" Willow squealed right beside her.

Diana pulled herself back to the moment and laughed. "Nothing, honey. I was just thinking of something and a word popped out of my mouth. Ignore me. I'm silly today."

"That's 'cause you didn't eat breakfast," Willow said wisely.

"Right," Diana agreed, and thought she probably *was* being silly. Reason told her that she couldn't trust a man who wasn't telling the whole truth. She could not believe he didn't know Penny and Willow, at least casually. He said he lived in New York—where Penny had lived with Jeffrey. He refused to tell her his occupation, but he'd gleaned information about the explosion from the police over twenty-four hours before they were ready to make a public announcement.

She knew nothing about this man . . . except how the night of the fire he'd pulled her car to safety; or that he'd run into Clarice's house and carried her out before she became trapped by flames; that he'd gone back to the site of the explosion to find Willow; that in the face of her irrational anger and tears yesterday because he hadn't stayed with Willow in the emergency room, he'd pulled her close and said, 'Don't cry, darlin'.' Most of all, Diana remembered that in spite of herself, she'd felt secure in his arms and both soothed and touched by Tyler's deep, Southern voice murmuring those words with tenderness, that did not sound phony or patronizing.

Willow stood regarding her gravely, her crown listing to the right. "Diana, are you all right?" she asked cautiously.

"Yes, honey. I was just thinking about Lenore coming."

The child immediately tensed. "You think she fibbed to us? You think she's really gonna come with the Bad Man?"

"No," Diana lied. "Still, I don't believe we want to sit around here all afternoon, especially because we planned on a walk and taking some pictures." She paused, thinking. "Willow, how would you like to have a picnic?"

"I love picnics, but maybe we should just hide in the house and not go to the door when the lady comes. I know you're scared about the Bad Man, no matter what you say."

The child was acutely perceptive, especially when it came to her mother and Diana. "Well, the Bad Man—I mean Jeffrey—*can't* come into this house and cause trouble if we're not here. We had a walk planned. It's too pretty a day to miss a walk. There's no reason why Lenore can't come with us, and we'll make a real occasion of it by having a picnic."

Diana stood up and was talking as she headed for the kitchen, Willow right behind her. "I know we have lemonade. You like lemonade. And peanut butter and jelly and . . ." Diana opened the refrigerator door. "And turkey cold cuts! We can have two kinds of sandwiches! And potato chips—Nan thinks we don't know she has a bag stashed in this cabinet but we do—and she has sugar cookies, too! Oh, bless you, Nan!"

"Bless Nan?"

"For bringing in food we need for our picnic. I don't want to go to the store. I want to have everything ready when Lenore gets here." *So we don't have to spend more than a few minutes alone in this house with her and God knows who else might show up,* Diana thought. "It'll be a surprise for her. She'll get to see you and have a nice day in the park. Oh, where's the picnic basket?" Willow pointed to a large pantry. "How did you know that?"

"Sometimes when I came with Mommy and she was

workin' with Uncle Simon, Mrs. Murphy let me explore. She's way nicer than Nan."

Nan. And Glen, whose class Nan took spring semester. Glen seducing a student, unless she simply had a crush on him and followed him around. Diana had a hard time believing Glen was merely the innocent object of a crush, now that she recalled a few awkward times when he and Nan had been in the same room and exchanged uncomfortable glances. She also recalled the afternoon they seemed to spring apart in the hall when Diana came down the stairs, and she'd told herself that they'd merely passed too close. And she remembered a day when every time she left the room, she came back to find the nonsocial Nan talking to Glen.

Glen was definitely involved with Nan. Diana knew she had to face it and she had to do something about it, even if it only meant she had to force Glen out of her own life. She couldn't make Nan give up on a relationship that Diana was certain would only give the girl pain, but she didn't have time to dwell on those two now.

Twenty minutes later, Diana had assembled a less-than-elegant collection of food in the big picnic basket. She'd just added a handful of paper napkins and three plastic cups when the doorbell rang. She opened the front door to see Lenore Wentworth waving away her husband, Blake, driving a white sedan.

She looked back at Diana. "Jeff took the Lincoln, of course. He left the car with the faulty air conditioner to us," she said, rolling her eyes. "My! I didn't even say hello!" She laughed. "Hi, Diana. I wish I was thin enough to wear such tight jeans and look so *great* in them!"

Diana laughed, slightly taken aback by Lenore's exuberance but unable to receive her coolly. "Hello, Lenore. As for the tight jeans, I have a habit of getting busy and skipping meals. I'm glad you think I look nice. Uncle Simon complains that the modern woman is obsessed with denim. He claims he's forgotten what I look like in a dress." Lenore had stepped into the foyer. She smoothed her beige linen slacks and matching short-sleeved belted top that looked simple but Diana recognized as designer garb.

"It seems awfully quiet around here," Lenore commented. "Are we alone?"

Diana spent a moment wondering if the question had significance before she decided to answer honestly. "Simon took Clarice to church."

"And your housekeeper? Ann, is it?"

"Nan. Short for Nanette. Her mother, Martha Murphy, has been our housekeeper for twelve years, ever since she became a widow. Martha had a mild heart attack the first week in June, and she begged Simon to let her daughter fill in for her. All I can say is that we will be grateful beyond words when Mrs. Murphy returns in two weeks."

Lenore burst into laughter. "So *that's* the answer! Blake and I were baffled as to why you would have a housekeeper like Nan. She certainly has a style of her own!"

"That's putting it mildly. Aside from being totally inexperienced, she doesn't like us and doesn't care about letting us know it. Oh well, we don't have to endure her for much longer."

"And there's my niece right behind you. Darling, how cute you look!" Lenore effused. "When did you become a queen?"

Willow smiled tentatively. "I'm not really a queen. I don't know if my crown's got real diamonds. Diana bought it for me."

"So it's definitely not made of real diamonds," Diana said dryly to Lenore.

"Who cares? The stones look like real diamonds and you look wonderful Cor—Willow. My husband and I decided this morning that because your mother wanted you to be named Willow, and it's what you've gotten used to, we'll both call you Willow instead of Cornelia."

Willow smiled. "Good. I don't like that other name."

"That's very considerate of you, Lenore," Diana said.

"Well, I'd hate to be called a name I didn't like." Lenore looked at Willow. "Do you remember my name?"

Willow had heard Diana say "Lenore" twice in the last five minutes, but when she said, "Len-ore," the woman clapped her hands.

"Even when you were little more than a baby, you were determined to say 'Lenore,' not 'Len' or 'Nore,' " she exclaimed. "My husband, your uncle Blake, sometimes calls me Len, but you never did."

"Oh," Willow said, looking as if she didn't really know how to respond to this information.

"I usually walk around the park on Sunday mornings and take pictures," Diana intervened. "You said you're an amateur photographer so I thought you might be interested. Then Willow and I decided it would be fun to have a picnic. Is that all right with you?"

When Lenore seemed startled and not pleased by this sudden change in plans, Diana felt a tinge of relief that she and Willow would not be staying alone in the house with this woman they didn't know. Maybe someone else *was* supposed to arrive.

But Lenore's expression quickly morphed into one of pleasure. "That does sound like fun. Maybe you'll give me a few tips about photography. I'm sorry I didn't know last night how accomplished you are, but it turns out my husband saw some of your photographs in a gallery in New York. He was very impressed with them. I felt like a complete idiot for bragging about the Christmas picture I'd taken."

"You didn't brag and the photo was quite good." Lenore gave her a chastising look. "All right, it showed promise."

"I consider that a compliment coming from you." Her blue eyes darted around. "Well, I guess we have some gear to gather up for our excursion."

Diana picked up her newest camera and a blanket, while Lenore insisted on carrying the picnic basket. Willow removed her crown and they loaded into Diana's car and drove down the hills to the parking lot beside the wide, flat land at the front of Ritter Park. Across the street stood some imposing, beautifully maintained homes. Near the entrance to the park, a large fountain sent sparkling jets of water into the air. Several stone bridges arched over the narrow Four Pole Creek and led to rustic steps ascending a hill to rose gardens.

"My goodness, this is just idyllic!" Lenore exclaimed, looking at the acres of lush grass and towering trees. "I had no idea. Last night we focused on finding your house and today I was chattering to Blake, as usual, and not paying attention to my surroundings. How big is this park?"

"About seventy acres," Diana said as they climbed out of her car and looked for a good picnic spot. "There are tennis courts, the rose gardens—you can see a bit of them from down here—an amphitheater, and an impressive museum at the top of the hills above the park."

"And see those steps over there?" Willow said, abruptly showing some of her usual ebullience. "There's about a hundred of 'em goin' up that hill—"

"I think it's more like twenty-five or twenty-six steps," Diana corrected, smiling.

"Yeah, well, a lot. They go up to the rose gardens, Lenore, and there's this building up there with lots of glass called A Room with a View where people have weddings and parties after the wedding and the guests come out and walk around the roses and look over the hill and the fountain's all lighted up and that's where I'm gettin' married when I pick out the right boy," Willow ended breathlessly.

"My goodness"—Lenore smiled—"you certainly have things well planned, Willow. Do you have any boys in mind?"

"Mommy says I have plenty of time, but I know I want a prince or a movie star or a rock 'n' roll singer. There's a place here where they have rock 'n' roll concerts and Diana and Mommy took me to *three* of 'em and I like the guys that sing. And play guitar. If I marry one of 'em, I'll sing with him and his band."

Diana raised her eyebrows at Lenore, both of them swallowing laughter. "You've really thought this through,

Willow," Lenore said. "That's good. But remember what your mommy told you—you have plenty of time."

Diana cleared her throat and looked beyond Lenore and Willow. "I see a nice spot near the park entrance. No Frisbee players or sunbathers anywhere near it. We can just enjoy the day."

"Yeah, that's a good place," Willow agreed, running ahead of them.

"Well, she certainly doesn't seem afraid of *me,*" Lenore said, pleasure in her voice.

"I guess she isn't. She let you in on her plans for the next twenty years of her life. Even the site of her wedding. I hope you like rock music in case she doesn't meet a suitable prince or movie star."

"I'm afraid my taste in rock froze when I was in my early twenties. I don't like most of the modern stuff. Heaven knows what it will sound like by the time Willow gets married."

When they reached the spot, they set down the picnic basket and the blanket. "I'm afraid the picnic was a last-minute idea, Lenore, and we don't have any fancy food."

"No chocolate-covered strawberries? No caviar? Well! I'm going back to the hotel," Lenore laughed.

"Who eats chocolate-covered strawberries?" Willow asked.

"People who want to get fat," Lenore answered, helping Diana spread the blanket on the grass. "I like simple food."

Lenore seemed to doubt her own claim when she saw the peanut butter and jelly sandwiches, the bag of chips, and the Thermos of lemonade. She stared at the sandwiches with disdain before she remembered to smile. "I haven't had a peanut butter and jelly sandwich since . . . I can't remember!"

"We have turkey cold cuts, too. And sugar cookies!" Diana said grandly, amused by Lenore's attempt to look enthusiastic. "I just love sugar cookies!"

"I'm watching my weight. I wish I were statuesque

like you, but I'm only five-four and usually carry twenty pounds too many. I exercise like mad and even do weight training. I get stronger but not thinner. Blake says I look perfect, though," she emphasized. "I lost five pounds staying at my mother's, and I don't want them back, so I think I'll just have a turkey sandwich."

"I'm five-six. I'd hardly call that statuesque." Diana laughed, handing Lenore a plastic-wrapped turkey sandwich then pouring her a plastic cup full of lemonade.

During the picnic, the earlier chatty Willow ate silently and steadily, occasionally casting half-shy, half-reflective glances at Lenore. Finally she asked, "Lenore, do you go to a place like this called Central Park?"

"Central Park! You remember!" Lenore cried out, laying down her sandwich. "Central Park is in New York City and it's even bigger than this park. Your mother took you there at least three times a week when you lived in New York. Sometimes I would come with the two of you."

"Oh." Willow regarded Lenore with a pensive gaze. "But other people came sometimes, too."

"That's right! Your uncle Blake came with us a couple of times. Then your daddy started sending a man to go along with you to protect you."

"To protect me from what?"

"Sometimes bad people loiter in the park—muggers, homeless people who are crazy and dangerous. Not that all homeless people are crazy and dangerous—just some."

Clearly, Willow didn't understand "loiter," "muggers," or "homeless people," but she didn't ask for any explanations. Instead she asked, "Did my daddy ever go with us?"

"No. He was always busy, but he loved you very much." Willow frowned. "Honey, you remember him. You saw him last night."

Willow went still and said distinctly, "The man you said was my daddy last night wasn't my daddy. He was the Bad Man."

"Honey, he *is* your daddy. He's a *good* man. What makes you think he's bad?"

"He just is. You can't fool me because I'm a kid," Willow maintained stubbornly. "He is the Bad Man."

"Willow, he isn't bad. He loves you. He wants you to be with him always."

Willow drew back. "I don't want to be with that man! I'm scared of him! Diana, don't let her take me to him!"

"Lenore is not going to take you," Diana said in her most authoritative voice, hoping to pierce through the armor of Willow's fear. "She didn't come here to take you or to talk about your daddy. She came for our afternoon in the park. Didn't you, Lenore?"

Lenore looked at Diana's stern expression and seemed to pull away slightly. "Yes, Diana is right." She sounded disappointed but she clearly knew that Diana thought she was pushing the child and wouldn't allow any more talk of "daddy." "I'm just here for a visit today, Willow. That's all."

The child gave Lenore a penetrating look for a moment then began to relax slightly. She made a few bland comments about the people jogging by them, and threw some pieces of bread to the small, almost tame, gray squirrels. A little girl about Willow's age carrying a disposable camera ventured over and asked if Willow would take her picture. Diana nodded and Willow jumped up delightedly. She often said that when she grew up, she wanted to be a "picture taker" like Diana. The two girls ambled away, talking as if they'd known each other for years and looking for the perfect background for the photo.

"I didn't want to mention this in front of Willow," Lenore said, lowering her voice although no one was near, "but I saw the morning newspaper. The police claim a bomb caused the explosion at Penny's house!"

"I saw the paper, too," Diana replied carefully.

"My God, do you believe it?"

"According to the newspaper, the fire marshal has no doubt and neither does the ATF."

"But it's incredible! A *bomb*?" Who could have built a bomb?"

Diana watched Willow showing the other little girl how to pose in front of a tree. "I didn't get the impression from the newspaper that it was a sophisticated bomb. Dynamite, a fuse, and a timer. Anyone could learn to build a simple bomb like that from the Internet."

"But why? Did Penny have enemies?"

"Not that I knew of, but she must have had at least one."

"You knew her so well, though," Lenore persisted. "You must have known about her other friends and people she knew, so you must have *some* idea of who could want to harm her."

A warning bell had begun to chime loudly in Diana's mind. Lenore was trying to sound innocently shocked and curious, but her almost childlike persistence about the matter struck Diana as insincere. She decided to let Lenore know that pumping her for information was useless.

"Lenore, the only person I know who might want to harm Penny is your brother."

Lenore looked as if she'd been slapped. Then astonishment turned to anger. "You think Jeff might have done this to Penny? My God, Diana, he didn't even know where she was!"

"He was still searching for her and he had a lot of people searching, too," Diana said calmly. "Are you absolutely certain Jeffrey didn't find out where Penny was living before the authorities called him to say his wife had been in an explosion?"

"Of course I'm certain!" Lenore's voice lifted, and someone jogging by turned to look at her. "I can't believe you're even insinuating that Jeff had something to do with Penny's mishap!"

"Mishap? Is that what you call Penny suffering what are probably fatal burns? A mishap?"

"I misspoke. A . . . catastrophe. A tragedy."

The little girls laughed and traded places. Willow began striking poses while the other child snapped photos.

"Yes. I would say both of those words apply to what happened to Penny."

"And almost happened to Willow. Are you forgetting that if she'd been in the house, the explosion would have killed her? Do you think Jeff would kill his own daughter?"

"I don't know what Jeffrey Cavanaugh might do," Diana said enigmatically, this time turning the tables on Lenore, getting her flustered so she might reveal all that *she* knew about Penny and Jeffrey.

"If you think Jeff would harm Cor—Willow, then you don't know one thing about him!"

"That's been my point all along," Diana said, reaching for the camera that lay beside her. "I *don't* know one thing about him, and I certainly don't know why Penny had to run away from him and live in hiding instead of getting a divorce. There had to be a reason, Lenore. I don't know what it was, but no one can convince me Penny wanted to live that way."

"There wasn't a reason!" Lenore said loudly. "Jeff was finally happy and she nearly destroyed him and no one knows why the hell she would do such a thing! Of course we want answers and you were her friend."

"I was a friend who thought Penny was a widow from Pennsylvania. I had no idea she was the runaway wife of Jeffrey Cavanaugh. I know none of you believe me, but it's the truth and no matter how hard you try to draw out information about Penny, that's all you'll get because that's all I know. Now, please lower your voice, Lenore. People are beginning to look at us. If you want to fight with me more over what you think I know, I'll be glad to oblige you but not now. If you love your niece as much as you say you do, you won't ruin this day for her."

While Lenore seemed to be fighting for self-control, Diana peered through her camera lens. The girls looked delighted, laughing, long little-girl hair shining in the bright sun, the giant tree trunk behind them, and the creek beside them, one of its banks formed by a rock-covered, light-dappled hill. They were only about seventy feet away, so the depth of field was not extreme. The camera had automatically preset for medium depth of field, so all Diana had to do was set the aperture. She immediately shot five frames in one second. Diana lowered the camera, smiling.

Lenore said nothing while the girls changed poses and Diana shot two more frames. When Diana put down the camera, she noticed that Lenore's breathing had slowed down. Finally Lenore said, "I'm sorry we've badgered you if you truly didn't know more about Penny. It's just that everyone says you were her closest friend, and she was hiding a very big secret. I knew Penny, and I find it hard to believe she was capable of such confidentiality."

"Then apparently neither one of us knew her as well as we thought we did," Diana said evenly. "We've both learned she was very good at keeping a secret."

"Yes . . . Yes, I guess we have." Lenore took a couple of deep breaths then said, "I'm sorry I flew off the handle, Diana. It's just that my brother's life has been hell since Penny left and took the baby. Sometimes he holes up in the apartment for a week—he doesn't even go in to work. He can carry on business fine from home, but he won't even let anyone come see him. He simply withdraws from the world and it frightens me. I'm always afraid one day he'll go inside and never come out again."

"It sounds as if he needs some serious psychological help."

"I know he does, but I think he believes his troubles started too long ago to ever be *fixed*. My brother hasn't had an easy life, Diana. Our father was a cold, hard man—a self-made man who didn't really admire anything in another person besides strength. He thought Jeff was a weakling because under that stony facade, my brother is kind and principled. Dad thought those qualities were signs of fragility and he tormented Jeff unmercifully when he was growing up."

"That's too bad," Diana said, never taking her gaze off

the little girls who'd come together for a quick conference and now began to walk slowly toward Diana and Lenore, their arms around each other.

"Yes, it was *very* bad," Lenore said bitterly. "Then my father was murdered when Jeff was thirty. And guess who the police's number one suspect was? Jeff. In spite of all my father's shady connections, even his links to the Mafia, the cops seemed to think Jeff killed Dad so he could take his place at Cavanaugh and Wentworth."

"That's awful," Diana said faintly, shocked. She also grew a fraction more afraid of Jeffrey Cavanaugh. "Why did they jump to the conclusion that Jeff wanted to replace your father at such a young age? The board of the company couldn't have believed Jeffrey was ready for so much power."

"Jeff certainly didn't. But apparently, Dad had made some remarks to people about his son, I quote, 'wanting to take over the throne.' I'm sure my father, Morgan, thought he was being funny. He would have found the idea of Jeff replacing him ridiculous. Morgan Cavanaugh thought no one could replace *him*!

"The police dogged Jeff for over a year, but they could never find evidence to link Jeff with Dad's murder," Lenore went on. "Meanwhile, although a few of the board members grumbled, Jeff *did* replace Dad, which was lucky for the company. Jeff is a genius, Diana, and I'm not saying that lightly. He has quirks—everyone does, but especially people with genius-level IQ's. He'd nearly doubled the company's business and taken it public by the time he was thirty-five. But he never recovered from the stigma of being his father's possible murderer. And then there was Yvette."

The little girls had almost reached them before they stopped to take a few shots of two squirrels darting in circles holding acorns. "Who is Yvette?"

"Who *was* Yvette, you mean. Yvette DuPrés. She was Jeff's first wife. He married her when he was thirty-three. Three years later, she plummeted out of the eighth-floor window of a hotel in San Francisco. She was as unstable as she was beautiful. Their marriage was a mistake to begin with and only got worse over those three years. She committed suicide, but . . ."

Diana jerked around to look at Lenore. "But what?"

"But the police believed Jeff threw her out of that window."

CHAPTER ELEVEN

1

Tyler Raines leaned back against a tree holding a book—a battered paperback copy of *Watchers* by Dean Koontz. He'd read the book three times over the past ten years and he enjoyed it every time. Today, though, he wasn't really reading. He was using the book as a prop while he kept an eye on Diana Sheridan. She sat on a blanket with another woman some distance away. The child Willow was taking pictures of a little girl of about the same age.

Tyler's gaze lingered on Diana. She wore jeans and a light-green blouse open over a cream-colored tank top. Her honey-brown hair shone in the sunlight, parted on the side and left free to curl halfway down her back. He couldn't see her eyes, but he remembered their exact shade of gray-green and the long, tilting lashes. He remembered the gentle curve of her nose, the shape of her lips over the straight white teeth, and the sprinkle of light freckles across her nose and cheeks. On the night of the explosion, when she was frantic and pale and eventually smudged with soot, she'd still been beautiful, and he'd cursed himself for even noticing her looks in the presence of such tragedy.

After they ate, the woman beside her talked animatedly, using her hands, her body leaning toward Diana, her face in constant movement, changing expressions. Diana sat motionless, never taking her gaze off the little girl Willow. Occasionally she said something to the woman, but she never relaxed her posture or looked around the park. She was no doubt listening to the woman but not for an instant dropping her alert observance or her attitude of curled intensity ready to burst forth if anything or anyone threatened the child. Tyler wondered if Willow could feel the force of Diana's vigilance.

The little girls had been taking pictures with what Tyler thought must have been a disposable camera. They put their heads together for a no-doubt serious chat, then they began walking back to Diana. Suddenly Willow stopped, stared into the distance, and began taking small, almost robotic steps backward. Her gaze locked onto a man stalking toward Diana—a tall, heavily built man with sandy-brown-and-gray hair, a strong-featured face suffused with blood, and big hands clenched into fists.

Diana watched Willow as she raised her hands to cover her mouth, probably to prevent a scream. Diana followed the little girl's gaze and leaped to her feet just as the man stopped within a few feet of her and bellowed, "You bitch!"

Diana stiffened and said something. At the same moment, Tyler stood up, ready to take a run at the man if he came closer toward Diana. But he didn't. Instead he yelled, "You *knew* about Penny! Do not stand there and tell me you didn't know about her and a man. Who is he? I'm her husband, dammit. I have a right to know!"

The other woman had now stood up beside Diana and held out her arms beseechingly toward the man. She resembled the man. He paid no attention to her, though. He stood solid and implacable in front of Diana, his head lowered slightly as if he planned to charge like a bull. Diana shook her head and said something, then looked at Willow, who was still walking backward. Even her little friend had retreated, clutching her camera, looking bewildered.

The man yelled, "You do know and you will tell me if I have to beat it out of you!"

Tyler launched into motion, bolting away from the shelter of the tree, heading straight for the man who'd taken another step toward Diana, his fists raised. Just as Tyler reached the midpoint between the tree and Diana, a slim black-haired man appeared behind Diana's tormenter, wrapped his right arm around the heavier man's neck, and jerked. The big man made a slight convulsive motion then dropped to his knees. *A classic chokehold,* Tyler thought. The sleek, black-haired man had disabled the big, muscular lout not with swinging fists and sloppy lunges, but by calmly, expertly exerting just the right amount of force on one of the body's pressure points.

While the sandy-haired woman cried out and rushed to the man still on his knees in front of Diana, Tyler pulled out his cell phone and called the police. They made regular passes by the park. Tyler was not going to let this guy just catch his breath, clamber back to his feet and leave. Or worse, go after Diana again.

He couldn't let that happen because he knew the man was Jeffrey Cavanaugh, and he was dangerous.

2

Diana stood motionless while Lenore and Blake helped Jeffrey up, Blake keeping a firm hold on him while Lenore cried, "Are you all right, Jeff?" Jeffrey waved her away, trying to get his breath. She turned to her husband. "Blake, how could you?"

"How could I? Lenore, didn't you see you the same thing I did? Your brother going for Diana? Getting ready to punch her?"

"That's idiotic. Jeff would never hit a woman."

"Then why was his fist aimed right at her abdomen?" Blake demanded furiously. "Sometimes you seem like some sickeningly doting mother when it comes to Jeff, oblivious to what he can do—"

"Shut *up,* you son of a bitch," Lenore hissed.

Diana's lips parted. She was as shocked by Lenore's suddenly feral tone as she was by Jeffrey's behavior.

Lenore looked at her husband, who drew back stiffly, his face blank of all emotion. She turned to Diana, clearly trying desperately to subdue her temper. "I'm sorry, Diana. Jeff didn't mean—"

"Don't apologize to her and I meant everything I said!" Jeffrey snarled, struggling to his feet without Blake's assistance. Jeffrey looked at her as if he was going to start yelling again, but in astonishment, Diana caught the glint of tears in his tortured eyes. He suddenly reminded her of a helpless, wounded animal.

Blake finally reached out with both hands, got a firm grip on Jeffrey's middle, and turned him around. "We're leaving now, Jeff," he said in what sounded like controlled rage.

Jeffrey said nothing. He began to shamble away with Blake, his head lowered. Lenore rushed to Jeffrey and put her hand on his shoulder, looking with concern at his face. Then she flung over her shoulder, "I'll go with them, Diana. Thank you for the day."

Yes, it was lovely day, Diana thought sarcastically as she watched the three stumble toward the street, Jeffrey's feet dragging, neither Blake nor Lenore letting go of him, all of them ignoring the heads turning to look at them, then back at Diana. She turned and scanned the area for Willow, quickly locating her standing on the bank of the winding creek, looking into the water as if she planned to jump. Diana ran to her and kneeled beside her. "Honey, he's gone. Don't be scared."

But Willow was more than scared. She stood tearless and rigid, abandoned by her little friend and now looking at Diana without seeing her.

Diana hugged her. "Willow, will you answer me, please?

Are you all right?" Nothing. "Willow? Your arms are cold. I know you were scared when your daddy—"

"He's *not* my daddy!" Willow shrieked. "He's the Bad Man! I told you, he's the Bad Man! He wants to kill people! He wants to kill me!"

She finally burst into a storm of tears and buried her face against Diana's neck. Diana hugged her tightly and crooned softly, knowing they were the object of everyone's attention and not caring. All she cared about was this little girl whose own father had fiercely approached Diana with clenched fists and yelled accusations in a public place, oblivious that the child he supposedly loved was watching and listening.

She let Willow cry until the sobs seemed to weaken of their own accord. Finally Willow lifted her face and said in a snuffling voice, "I got your hair all wet."

"It'll dry." Diana lifted up the loose bottom of her blouse and wiped Willow's tear-drenched cheeks. "So will your face. We should both look beautiful again in about two minutes."

Willow smiled, sniffled, let out one more choking sob and then relaxed. "I want to go home now."

"Me, too. I'll just get our blanket and picnic basket and we'll be on our way."

As Diana folded the blanket and Willow carried the used plastic cups to a nearby garbage can, Diana looked toward the street and saw a police cruiser stop beside the blue Lincoln where both Lenore and Blake were helping Jeffrey into the passenger's seat. A policeman emerged and they all seemed to freeze in place as he approached them. *Thank goodness,* Diana thought. *Someone in the park called the police. Jeffrey can't simply go back to the hotel as if he's done nothing.*

She turned and saw Willow staring at the policeman in his uniform and sunglasses. "Is he gonna take the Bad Man to jail?"

"I don't know what he's going to do," Diana said. "I don't know what happens to people who scream at you and try to scare you in public, but the policeman will do something. Don't worry, Willow. Your—that man will suffer some kind of punishment."

Diana carried the picnic basket and her camera, and Willow clung to the folded blanket and kept her eyes down as they walked back to Diana's car. For an instant, Diana thought she saw a tall, slender man with sun-streaked blond hair—Tyler Raines—out of the tail of her eye, but when she looked around, he'd vanished. Tyler had a habit of vanishing, though. Wondering if he'd been there all along, seen Cavanaugh's display and called the police.

I hope it was him, Diana mused, puzzled by the path her hopes took but too tired to again mentally list all the reasons she shouldn't trust him. Reason seemed to have abandoned her when it came to Tyler, and for once, she decided to let emotions govern the path she would take with him in the future. If Tyler Raines would even reappear in her future. . . .

3

Relief washed over Diana when she arrived home and saw Simon's Porsche in the driveway. She smiled, wondering how Clarice had felt arriving at church in a sports car with a tall, dashing escort by her side. Diana believed Clarice had experienced few luxuries in her life. And even though she always referred with affection to her "dear Henry," Diana had seen his photo in Clarice's house and thought that he looked genial and pleasantly round-faced, but he didn't have the still rakish mien of Simon Van Etton.

"Uncle Simon and Clarice are back," she said to Willow, who had not uttered a word on the short drive home. "I'm glad we won't be going into an empty house."

"Romeo and Christabel didn't go to church and then out to lunch," Willow finally uttered. "It wouldn't have been empty even if Uncle Simon and Clarice weren't back yet, but I'm happy they are." As Diana turned off the ignition, Willow looked over with her unusually large eyes set in a tight little face. "I'm scared. The Bad Man won't leave me alone."

Diana couldn't truthfully tell the child she would never see Jeffrey Cavanaugh again. After all, the man was her father. But his actions today would have an effect on whether he could simply sweep into the Van Etton house and take away Willow. Diana thought of Simon's ex-student who'd pulled strings to get Willow released into their custody until the police found her blood family. She would ask Simon to call that student again and make sure he knew what had happened in the park. Someone *had* to stop Jeffrey from forcibly taking this child and whisking her back to New York.

"Willow, a policeman came to talk to that man. I'm sure he's going to tell the man not to come near us, and he'd better do what the policeman says or he can get in very big trouble. That man might want to cause trouble for other people, but he doesn't want to get in trouble himself, and that's what will happen if he doesn't just go back to his hotel room and stay there. You don't have to think about him any more today."

"But what about tomorrow? Just 'cause he's scared today doesn't mean he'll still be scared tomorrow," Willow said with maddening logic.

"We won't worry about tomorrow until tomorrow comes," Diana said briskly and was relieved when Simon opened the front door and strode to the car.

"I thought you were going for a walk," he boomed. "Where were you?"

Diana immediately realized he'd been worried because her car was gone, and she berated herself for not leaving a note. "Lenore called and asked to come and see Willow. I thought it would be best if we all went down to the creek and had a picnic. Lots of people around," she said with a wink.

"Ohhhh." Simon winked back. "Much better than the three of you just sitting alone in the house."

Diana climbed out of the car and grabbed her camera and the basket while Willow clutched the blanket and ran inside the house without a word. "We tried to have a picnic," Diana muttered to Simon.

"Tried? What happened?"

"Jeffrey Cavanaugh happened. Let's leave it at that for now."

Once they entered the house, a flurry of information broke out about how everyone had spent the early part of the day. Willow said nothing, but instead walked to the piano, sat down on the bench, and touched the keys so softly Diana could barely hear the notes. When Diana began to tell Clarice and Simon that Willow had made a friend in the park, the child suddenly burst into tears, laying her head down on the piano keys as her body shook. "I want my mommy." She sobbed hopelessly. "I just want my mommy *so* much."

Diana felt as if a giant hand squeezed her heart. She rushed to the child and picked her up. "It's okay, Willow. We're home now. We're safe."

"But I don't get to stay safe." Willow wept. "The Bad Man will take me one day. He almost got me today. He would have hurt you and taken me except that man made him fall down before he could."

Diana saw Simon and Clarice looking aghast and knew she couldn't delay an explanation. "We were having a lovely day in the park when Jeffrey arrived. I don't know how he found us—we were in plain view of the park entrance, I guess. He started with his same old mantra about me knowing more than I was saying. He stepped toward me like he was going to hit me, when Blake Wentworth seemed to come out of nowhere and got Jeffrey in a chokehold. Blake and Lenore took Jeffrey back to their car, but someone in the park must have called the police. An officer was talking to them when Willow and I left."

"Good God!" Simon burst out. "That's intolerable!"

"He's gonna get me." Willow sobbed. "They keep sayin' he's my daddy and he's gonna take me away with him."

"We will see about that!" Simon's color intensified and his eyebrows had drawn together above his fierce green eyes. "Jeffrey Cavanaugh may believe I'm a doddering old professor capable of nothing except giving lectures to bored students, but he'll find I'm more of a contender than he thinks!"

"Are you gonna try to hit him?" Willow looked horrified. "You can't! He's mean and you're old!"

"She means you're older than Jeffrey," Clarice said quickly, although Diana could see her great-uncle had taken no offense. "Darling, you mustn't cry," Clarice crooned to Willow. "You have all of us to protect you."

Willow turned her face away from them and began to sob heartbreakingly that all she wanted was to see her mommy. Diana, on the verge of tears herself, looked at Clarice. "Maybe some time resting with you and the cats for company?"

Clarice nodded. "That's just the thing. I'm sure Willow is tired and the cats have missed her. They're upstairs waiting for her. Willow, would you like to go upstairs and see Romeo and Christabel?" After a moment, Willow nodded. "Would you like to go up in the elevator?"

Finally Willow turned and looked at them with her mottled little face and swollen eyelids. "Yes, please."

Diana held Willow as they creaked to the second floor in the elevator that had gotten more use in the last few days than in the last few years. Diana carried her to her canopied bed and was glad to see the cats were already in their beds, napping. They both awakened immediately, and Christabel jumped on the big bed beside Willow. Diana lifted Romeo onto the bed, then chose a DVD and left Clarice trying to look cheerful through her distress, telling Willow she had *always* wanted to see this movie about talking insects.

Diana came downstairs and headed straight for the

kitchen, where she poured a glass of ice water and searched for the bottle of aspirin. As she swallowed two pills, considering that three might be necessary to stop the headache pounding at her temples, someone knocked on the back door. Diana peeped through the curtains to see Nan. Surprised, she unlocked the door. Nan stood in front of her wearing ragged jeans, running shoes, a much-washed T-shirt, and no makeup. She'd pulled her hair straight back into a ponytail. Without its shiny waves to soften her face, she looked even more unattractive than usual.

"Nan, what are you doing here?" Diana asked bluntly.

"I wonder . . . I mean, I know you don't like me much but . . . well, Miss Sheridan, I gotta talk to you."

She broke something and didn't tell us, Diana thought. *She stole something and she has a guilty conscience. She wants the next few days off. . . .*

"Nan, I've had a very rough morning. Well, I guess it's afternoon now. . . ."

"It's almost two o'clock," Nan said. "And I promise I won't take up much of your time, but . . . well, *please,* Miss Sheridan. It's real important." She paused then said barely above a whisper, "It's about Penny Conley."

CHAPTER TWELVE

1

Diana opened the door and motioned for Nan to come inside. The girl's face was dewy with perspiration and her hands trembled. "I need to tell you something."

"You look like you need a cold drink," Diana said. "Lemonade?"

"Yeah. I'll get it."

"No, this time you sit at the table and I'll get the drink. Ice?"

"Yeah. I mean please."

Diana poured two glasses of lemonade. *She's going to tell me Glen was seeing Penny,* Diana thought as she added ice to each glass. *She's going to break it to me that Glen was "cheating" with Penny. Is she going to tell me he was cheating with her, too? Is she going to ask me to let him go so he can be with her? Or is she hoping that hearing about his involvement with Penny is going to make me end our relationship so he can rush into her arms?*

Diana placed a glass in front of Nan then sat down across from her. "All right, Nan, what's the problem?"

Nan took a long drink of her icy lemonade and looked down at her hands. "I know you really liked Penny. You don't like me and she didn't either."

"You don't let people like you, Nan. You never smile,

you're rude—even hostile—and, I'm sorry to say this, you have a tendency to be sneaky."

"I never stole anything from you people!" Nan flared.

"I know, but you eavesdrop. You even bring in food and *hide* it, like your potato chips. We don't care if you keep potato chips or sugar cookies or soft drinks or just about anything you like. It's the fact that you keep it hidden that bothers us."

"I thought you'd get mad."

"Your mother has worked in this house for twelve years. I know she didn't tell you that either Simon or I ran such a tight ship. Simon doesn't have strict rules and I certainly don't. I think you do it because you like to feel that you're getting by with something. You don't like having to work for people, and hiding things gives you a sense that those people don't have ultimate control over you."

Nan gave her a bleak look. "You sound like a psychologist."

"I think a psychologist would have a more sophisticated analysis of the problem. I'm just giving an uneducated opinion."

"Well, you're right, of course. You're pretty, you're smart and educated, you've done all kinds of exciting things, and your life is just a bowl of cherries so of course you'd be right. You don't even know how to be wrong, how to fail."

"Nan, you don't know as much about my life as you think you do. Believe me, I've failed at quite a few things and my life hasn't been the nonstop thrill ride you seem to think." Diana took a sip of her lemonade, watching as Nan nervously drummed the fingers of her left hand on the table. "But you didn't come here to talk about whether or not I like you. You said you wanted to talk about Penny."

"Yeah. Well, I do—want to talk about Penny, that is." Nan took a deep breath as if girding herself for what she had to say. "I guess I'd better start at the beginning, which was around April. You know I didn't do too well my first year at Marshall. I hated school except for one class—my

history class from Glen . . . Dr. Austen. I didn't love the
subject, but . . . well . . ."

"You thought you loved Glen."

Nan flashed Diana a startled look. "How did you
know? Did he tell you?"

"No," Diana said flatly. "He did not."

"Oh. Well who?"

"I don't think that matters."

"Was it Penny? You have to tell me if it was Penny."

Diana not only didn't like the girl's demanding tone,
but it made her suspicious. Was Nan here really to get information about Penny, perhaps for Glen? She decided to
see where the conversation led and answered. "It was not
Penny."

"Oh." Nan sounded relieved. "That's good."

"Why?"

"Well, it just is. You'll understand when I tell my story."

The doorbell rang. Diana felt a tinge of alarm. Would
Jeffrey Cavanaugh dare to come here after the scene in
the park? She knew Simon would go to the door and she
wished he wouldn't. If she'd been with him, she would
have somehow prevented him from opening the door. He
thought he was invincible, but at seventy-five, she didn't
think he was a match for a bulky, enraged man almost thirty
years younger.

"You're not even listenin' to me," Nan accused.

"Yes I am. My attention wandered for just a couple of
seconds when the doorbell rang. We had some trouble earlier today with Jeffrey Cavanaugh—I hope that isn't him."

"What kind of trouble?" Nan's face bore a look of fear
rather than mere curiosity.

"It doesn't matter. Go on with your story."

"Yeah, well, like I said, it starts in April when I got up
my nerve to go see Glen—Dr. Austen—in his office. I
pretended to be all worried about a paper I'd turned in,
but I really just wanted to see him, to see if he . . . well, to
see if he was interested in me. As more than a student.
You understand?"

"I think I get the picture," Diana said dryly.

"Well—"

Simon appeared at the kitchen doorway. "Why, hello, Nan! I didn't know you were here."

"Nan thought she left her wallet here last night," Diana said quickly, not wanting to embarrass the girl into silence. She would tell Simon the truth later.

"Well, you can't be without your wallet. No money, no driver's license—what a nuisance."

Nan nodded then turned her attention to her lemonade. She took a drink that went down with a loud gulp.

Simon looked at Diana. "I'm sorry to interrupt you, Diana, but you need to come into the library for a few minutes. Blake Wentworth is here and he says it's imperative that he talk to you and he doesn't have much time."

Simon had to know that one of the last people she wanted to see was a Cavanaugh minion. Still, Simon must have had a good reason for letting the man inside.

Diana looked at Nan. "I'm sorry but I have to go for a few minutes. Please don't leave."

"Yeah, well . . ." Nan's agitation seemed to have grown. Her lips twitched slightly. "Okay. But I can't stay for very long."

"I'll be *right* back. I promise."

Blake sat on the only uncomfortable chair in the room. He leaned forward, elbows on knees, balancing his chin on his clasped hands. The shining black waves of his hair were tousled, and his skin was pale and seemingly drawn more tightly over the patrician bones of his face. When Diana entered the room, with Simon right behind her, he stood and gave her an uncertain smile. "Hello, Miss Sheridan."

"I can't imagine why you're here."

Blake's smile vanished and his face took on a look of intense discomfort. "I came to apologize for Jeff."

"He couldn't do that for himself?" Diana asked as she sat down on a couch, keeping her voice cool. "Or he doesn't feel he should apologize to me?"

"Both," Blake said, lowering himself to the edge of the

chair. "He's at the hotel with Lenore, which is why I can't stay long. I don't want to leave Lenore alone with him if he decides to do something else stupid. But for right now, he doesn't think he owes you an apology. In fact, I don't believe he's thinking clearly about anything."

"Diana told me about the scene in the park," Simon intervened. "I can't feel sorry about Jeffrey's emotional state when his behavior sent his daughter into a state of complete terror. At first, we couldn't calm her. Finally, we were able to make her rest with Clarice in attendance and a movie playing to divert her attention. Willow won't forget today's scene any time soon, though. Jeffrey certainly doesn't act like a man who wants to win back his daughter. He doesn't act like a man who cares at all about her emotional state."

"He does care about her," Blake said sincerely. "I'm not saying that he was ever a great father. He wasn't harsh with her. He simply doesn't know how to express affection, especially for a baby. He has no experience with children and his own life has been rather bizarre—"

"Lenore told me a bit about his trials and tribulations," Diana interrupted. "It's all very sad, but it doesn't have anything to do with how he's treating his daughter. And frankly, I wonder how he *really* treated her when she still lived with him. You say he wasn't harsh, but how do you know? Maybe Penny ran away to protect Willow from him."

"I don't know why Penny ran away. I had my opinions at the time, then I changed my mind when we came here and learned about Penny's life in Huntington. Today, though, I believe my original opinion was correct."

"You thought she had a lover," Diana said flatly.

"Yes. That's what I thought at first. That's what I think now."

"Why?" Simon asked.

Blake hesitated. "I'll tell you about earlier today. Then you might understand Jeff's state of mind when he came to the park. After I'd dropped off Lenore, Jeff expected me to join him at the hospital as soon as possible. Not long after I got there, Penny woke up."

"She woke up!" Simon and Diana said in unison.

"Yes. You're both smiling. You wouldn't be if you'd been there." Blake closed his eyes for a moment before continuing. "I have never seen anyone in such agony. The doctor said some of the burns were so deep they'd destroyed the nerve endings and she felt nothing from them, but all the others—well, her thrashing, her shrieking in agony, her one remaining eye looking as if it were going to explode from her face were the most horrific things I've ever seen in my life. I'll remember that scene until I die."

"My God," Simon said softly, painfully.

Diana, too stricken to speak, felt as if a shard of ice had pierced her heart. Penny with her lilting laugh and twinkling eyes. Penny.

"Jeff was frantic, almost hysterical. The doctor said Penny couldn't stand this much pain—he had to give her a drug to put her back to sleep. I can't remember the name but it was something very powerful. Of course, Jeff told him to do it, do it *now*." Blake hesitated. "Then the doctor told Jeffrey the drug could have adverse effects on the baby."

"The baby?" Diana whispered.

Blake nodded. "It turns out that Penny is about two months' pregnant."

2

Glass crashed in the kitchen. The three of them looked at each other blankly for a moment before Diana jumped up. "Excuse me, Blake. I'll see what's wrong."

Diana found the shattered glass in the doorway between the kitchen and the hall, a mere two feet from the narrow second entrance to the library. Ice cubes lay scattered amid the glass, and the back door hung open about two inches. Diana rushed to it in time to see Nan jumping into her old car that she'd parked behind the house. Nan had rolled down her window and Diana called out to her, but Nan didn't turn her head. She simply picked up speed and flew past the house, headed for the paved driveway down to the road.

Eavesdropping again, Diana thought. You couldn't change old habits in a day, and Nan's compulsion to eavesdrop had gotten the best of her again. This time, though, she'd heard that Penny was pregnant, an announcement apparently so startling, or appalling, that the girl had dropped her glass of lemonade and run.

Diana decided to clean up the shattered glass after Blake left. He'd said he couldn't stay long and she had questions for him. Just as she reentered the library, the phone rang, and she motioned to Simon, who was seated, that she would answer. After her "Hello," Glen asked in a falsely cheerful voice, "How are you today, Diana?"

She briefly imagined Glen lying in bed with his nineteen-year-old student who no doubt adored him, but whom he no doubt found merely useful. She barely managed, "Today has been bad."

"Bad? How?"

Although she had not talked to Glen since the police located Jeffrey Cavanaugh, she was certain that Nan had told him about Cavanaugh and the scene he'd created when he came to collect his daughter Saturday night. Still, she didn't want to say more than necessary. "Penny came out of her coma—"

"What!" Glen sounded stunned. "How is she?"

"Horrible. All she did was shriek in agony. Awake, she can feel the burns. They had to put her back to sleep just to keep her alive. You can die of pain, you know."

"Oh God, sure."

"And finally, Nan came by here to speak with me."

She could almost feel Glen tensing. "Speak with you about what?"

"I don't know. We got a visitor who can't stay long and

she dashed away." Diana hesitated, but she couldn't help saying, "I'm sure she'll either call me or come back. She seemed almost desperate to get something off her chest."

"Is that so?" Glen tried for a mocking laugh that sounded something like a chicken cackling. "I can't imagine what the bright and beautiful Nan Murphy so desperately wants to confide."

"Neither do I. I'll just have to wait until tonight, or probably tomorrow when she comes to work." Diana looked over at Blake, who was talking quietly with Simon. "I'm afraid I have to get back to our company, now. I'm being rude."

"Who's there?"

"I'll talk with you soon, Glen. Good-bye."

Diana hung up and almost smiled, thinking about the state Glen must be in right now. Of course, Nan had wanted to tell her about the affair, and of course, Glen knew it. His perfect little world was about to pop—no more Diana, no more Simon Van Etton. *Whatever happened to him, he deserves it,* Diana thought.

Now her first concern was Penny. Diana returned to Simon on the couch. "In spite of the horrible scene at the hospital, did the doctor say if Penny is improving?"

Blake gave her a sympathetic but direct look. "He said infection has started. It's what they expected. They're giving Penny too many antibiotics for me to name, which often save people who wouldn't have stood a chance twenty years ago. The doctor said with burns as extensive as Penny's, though, the infection is often too much for the antibiotics to fight."

"Then I suppose worrying about the effect of the sedative on the fetus is pointless." Blake nodded and continued to look at her, the question in his eyes. "I didn't know she was pregnant, Blake." Diana knew that he was wondering if she had any idea about the baby's paternity. She was certain she did, but although she was furious with Glen, she would not set an enraged and dangerous Jeffrey Cavanaugh on him. "I didn't know Penny was seeing anyone."

"Well, this news has just devastated Jeff," Blake said. "He still loved her. I think he would have taken her back. He's always thought there was another man, but thinking and knowing aren't the same, much less finding out she was carrying another man's child. That's why he completely lost his head today. First the doctor told us infection had set in, then Penny woke up with those blood-curdling shrieks, and then Jeff found out about the baby. He literally ran out of the burn unit and out of the hospital. I was right behind him, but still I couldn't grab him before he got in the car and locked the doors. I was certain he was headed for your house, Diana, and I followed him straight to the park."

"I wish you could have reached him before he confronted us in the park," Diana said. "Willow was actually having a good time. She opened up to Lenore and even told Lenore her wedding plans. She made a new friend her own age. She was giggling like a normal, carefree five-year-old." Diana paused. "Then Jeffrey arrived."

"I'm sorry, Diana. I got to him as fast as I could."

"I know that now. But ever since, we've all been tense and waiting for him to come back."

Blake gave her a small smile. "I wouldn't worry about that. Lenore forced two of her tranquilizers on him. He was calming down when I left without saying where I was going. I hope he'll sleep for the rest of the afternoon—I don't think he's had more than a few hours of sleep since the FBI called him Saturday morning." He gave her and Simon that small, bleak smile again then stood. "I really have to get back. I don't like leaving Lenore alone with him."

"You're afraid for your wife's safety around her own brother?" Diana asked sharply. "Then even you must think he's dangerous."

"I think he's upset. Terribly upset and angry, and Jeff doesn't handle anger well. He's a little like his father in that way."

Diana and Simon also stood and walked behind Blake to the library exit, where he paused and looked back at the rear bay window with its stained-glass inset of the blue-and-gold water lily. "That's unbelievably beautiful," he said wonderingly.

"I got my interest in all things Egyptian from my mother," Simon told him. "When I was very young, she told me a myth about a blue water lily. She loved the myth so much, my father ordered new glass for the center window with the lily inset. He said this way my mother would be able to look at her blue water lily every day." Simon smiled. "Father usually acted like a man totally without sentimentality, but I think he was a closet romantic."

Now Blake laughed softly. "I've always thought the same thing about Jeff."

3

When dinnertime rolled around, no one seemed to have much appetite. Simon surprised Diana by suggesting they order pizza. Willow was delighted, and Diana remembered that the little girl loved pizza, hence Simon's suggestion, so she phoned in an order for an extra-large pizza with five toppings and two liters of soft drinks.

The delivery of the pizza caused great excitement, well acted by Diana, Clarice, and Simon but genuine for Willow. Simon carried the box into the kitchen as if it were a five-tier wedding cake, and everyone inhaled deeply when he lifted the lid. "Oh, it smells wonnerful!" Willow exclaimed. "I might eat the whole thing." After her third large slice of pizza, she announced she was stuffed. Everyone else declared they felt the same, and the rest of the pizza was stored in the refrigerator.

Afterward, Clarice and Simon sat down to watch a long-running weekly news program. Willow took her coloring book and giant box of crayons and sat down at one of the small tables in the library. Diana decided to put in some time on the computer, searching the Internet for information on Jeffrey Cavanaugh.

She came up with the most basic information: Cavanaugh's date and place of birth; parents, Morgan and Cornelia Webster Cavanaugh; first wife, Yvette DuPrés, death ten years previous ruled a suicide; marriage three years later to Penelope Ann O'Keefe. None of the articles mentioned Penny's disappearance. Cavanaugh had received an MBA from Harvard and had become head of Cavanaugh and Wentworth real estate developing company at age thirty, after his father had been murdered. Police had never apprehended Morgan Cavanaugh's killer.

Most articles remarked on how the shy, reclusive Cavanaugh had proved himself a master of finance, doubling the worth of Cavanaugh and Wentworth by the time he was thirty-five, and assuming the title of chief executive officer after taking the business public. That same year, Blake Wentworth, son of Morgan Cavanaugh's late partner, Charles Wentworth, became chief operating officer of the business. Because Cavanaugh had recently started a small aeronautics company, some effusive articles referred to Cavanaugh as a twenty-first-century Howard Hughes.

Diana knew if she searched further, she would find more information, but she couldn't concentrate. She kept seeing Jeffrey in the park, facing her with his fists clenched, and the flash of tears in his eyes. She thought about Blake telling them of Penny's horrific awakening and the announcement that she was two months' pregnant. And she thought about Nan. Homely, ungracious, seemingly impassive Nan sitting in the kitchen drenched in nervous perspiration, her usually detached gaze filled with anxiety.

And I just walked off and left her, Diana thought. True, Blake had said he couldn't stay long and he seemed to have something important to say, but so had Nan. Diana didn't like Nan, but then she didn't really know Nan. There had to be more to the girl than she'd seen during the months Nan had worked in this house. Even if there wasn't, Nan was the daughter of Martha Murphy, who'd been a loyal and beloved employee of Simon's for twelve years. Diana knew she owed Nan more consideration if for no other reason than just because she was Martha's daughter.

Guilt descended on Diana. She tried to fight it off by making excuses for her cavalier treatment of Nan that afternoon, but nothing worked. Aside from the guilt, she felt a twinge of concern. Nan had said that she wanted to start her story at the beginning, and her involvement with Glen had been the beginning, which meant she had more to say—and it involved Penny.

Maybe Nan meant to tell Diana only that Penny, too, had been involved with Glen, but while that would have caused Nan pain, it couldn't have been responsible for her look of apprehension. And hearing that Penny was pregnant had caused the girl to drop her glass. Diana could see how learning of the pregnancy might have been a surprise, but not enough to make Nan send a glass shattering to the floor and then flee at top speed. No, only fear could be responsible. But fear of what?

Diana abandoned her Internet search and went up to her room. She looked up Nan's cell phone number in her address book and called three times, only to be sent to voice mail. Nan still lived with her mother, so Diana looked up Martha's home phone number in the telephone directory and called. After seven rings, she hung up. Even Martha's answering machine had apparently been turned off.

By eight o'clock, Willow had begun to yawn, and Romeo could not open his eyes beyond slits. They went through the ritual of carrying him up in the elevator, putting him to bed where he immediately fell into unconsciousness, and dressing Willow in her pink pajamas. She crawled under the covers of her bed and said in a regretful voice, "I'm sorry, Diana, but I'm too sleepy for a bedtime story."

"That's all right, honey." Diana hoped that Willow didn't hear the relief in her voice. She was too preoccupied to come up with any kind of story that might entertain the little girl. "Do you want me to just sit with you until you go to sleep?"

Willow nodded and Diana took her place in the comfortable chair where Clarice had spent so much time watching movies made for the younger set. Tonight Diana had vowed to free Clarice to do what she pleased, which seemed to be spending her time with Simon discussing current events. She and Willow had left the two in a lively discussion of the situation in the Middle East.

Within fifteen minutes, Willow had drifted into a deep sleep. Diana tiptoed out of the room, leaving the door cracked so they could hear Willow if she called out. The night owl Christabel followed Diana downstairs and into the kitchen, where, out of habit, Diana opened the refrigerator door and looked for a snack. She settled on a glass of Coke then paced back upstairs to her room and tried Nan's phone number again. No answer.

Diana tried to read the latest murder mystery she'd bought, but she couldn't concentrate well enough to follow the plot. She decided to straighten out her closet and managed to group all of her summer tops together before she tired of that task. She closed the doors to the bathroom connecting her room to Willow's and put on a CD. She lay down on her bed to listen to Evanescence, waiting for "My Immortal," to which she usually sang out her heart. Tonight, though, she kept mixing up the words and finally stopped the CD at the end of the song.

At nine o'clock she tried Nan's phone again. Still no answer. Diana knew that worrying about a nineteen-year-old not answering her cell phone was ridiculous, but she worried nevertheless. She couldn't forget Nan's anxiety, her frightened eyes, the glass she'd broken in spite of her carefully maintained air of unconcern about the world in general. The girl had been desperate to open her heart, and Diana might as well have turned her away at the door. She'd put Nan on hold while she listened to a more important visitor—someone she barely knew—and she felt shame as well as a sense of neglected duty. She'd already let down Penny; and she didn't want to let down another woman who seemed to need her help.

Diana grabbed a light jacket and her tote bag, which she'd never gotten around to cleaning out after her trip last week. She casually descended the stairs and walked into the library, where Simon and Clarice now were watching a mystery show on the gigantic high-definition television that Simon had bought the previous year. They both looked up when they heard Diana's keys rattle.

"Going somewhere?" Simon asked.

Diana didn't intend to tell them that she was worried about Nan. If they thought there was cause for worry, they would immediately begin trying to talk her out of going to the Murphy home. Simon would suggest asking the police to check on Nan, although Diana knew that the police would not find the fact that a young woman wasn't answering her cell phone a little after nine o'clock reason enough for sending a patrol car to her house. Diana hated lying to them, but if she told the truth, then overcame their objections and left for Nan's, their enjoyment of the television show would be ruined by their concern for her, and for the first time in forty-eight hours, they both looked relaxed and almost happy.

"I have a sudden craving for ice cream," Diana lied blithely. "Also, a tabloid. Maybe two. I'm woefully behind on what all of my Hollywood friends are up to these days. I think I'll go to the convenience store and do a little shopping. I'm also restless, so I might ride around for a while before I stop at the store. Is there anything I can get for you two?"

Clarice immediately turned worried eyes to her. "Are you sure you should go out alone, dear?"

"I can't let fear of Jeffrey Cavanaugh make me a prisoner, Clarice. Besides, I don't think he'll try anything else tonight. Even *he* knows better than to push his luck."

"Is your cell phone charged?" Simon asked.

Diana smiled. "Charged and located in a convenient pocket in the lining of my bag."

"Well, all right. What kind of ice cream are you craving?"

"Uh, cherry swirl. Clarice, do you like cherry swirl?"

"I rarely eat ice cream, but tonight cherry swirl sounds delicious."

"Get a gallon," Simon ordered. "And none of the cheap stuff."

"I wouldn't dream of it." Diana smiled. "Be back soon."

The night air was warm but lacking the humidity of Friday evening. Diana took a deep breath. Although it was late August, she thought she could smell the coming autumn. She loved fall, when the leaves changed colors and the mornings became crisp without being cold. Tonight the stars were so bright they almost twinkled, and the iridescent three-quarter moon glowed. Neither the warm air nor the panoply of light could ease Diana's sense of dread, though. She had a dark feeling that the Nan she had seen today—the Nan she had never seen before—might do something to herself. *And all because of Glen,* Diana thought furiously. All because of the unprincipled, deceitful man whom Diana had been seeing for months. How glad she was she'd never let the relationship become intimate, but that's probably what had sent him looking for sex in an easy target like Nan.

And Penny? *She wasn't an easy target,* Diana thought as she swept down the narrow, curvy road through Ritter Park. Why had Penny become involved with him? Clarice had said she'd first seen Glen come to Penny's house about two months ago. And how old was the baby that Penny carried in her wreck of a body? Two months. Was the baby the reason she was running away? Diana had no idea how Penny felt about abortion, but she was certain that if Penny decided to have one, it would not be something she could do without guilt. Maybe she couldn't do it at all.

The Murphy house sat on an acre of land west of Huntington on a knoll overlooking Interstate 64. The house and land had belonged to Nan's paternal grandparents, who'd bequeathed both to their son and made him promise not to sell so much as a foot of the land. After Nan's father died when she was seven, Mrs. Murphy had told Simon that she wished she could sell half the land for money she desperately needed, but she'd made the same promise to her husband that he'd made to his father.

Diana turned onto the short, neglected lane leading to the house Nan shared with her mother. She passed two houses with lights burning in the windows, another one that sat in darkness, and finally reached the Murphy house at the end of the lane. Two lights shone in the house that wasn't much larger than Penny's—one light in what Diana guessed to be a bedroom, and another filtering dimly from farther back in the house. Diana pulled in the driveway behind Nan's old Pontiac, took a deep breath, and walked up the two steps leading to the front door of the ugly yellowish-green house.

She knocked. No one came to the door, but Diana heard music playing loudly inside. Perhaps Nan hadn't heard her, she thought, and knocked again. Still no answer, but Diana knew Nan must be inside. So why wouldn't she come to the door?

Diana glanced around. The moon and the stars did not seem to shine as brightly on this drab little lane, and the other two occupied houses looked far away. Diana felt her palms grow wet, and suddenly she knew that she should not have come alone to this relatively isolated spot at night, but she'd had no choice. After Jeffrey's demonstration this afternoon, she couldn't ask Simon to leave Clarice alone in the house with Willow. Her only real friend lay dying in the burn unit at the hospital and her "boyfriend" was not an option.

Leaving wasn't an option, either, she told herself, even though she wanted to make a run for her car and get away from this place. When had Nan become a priority with her? After what happened to Penny, Diana mentally answered herself. She hadn't taken Penny's anxious tone seriously enough Thursday night on the phone. She wasn't going to make the same mistake with Nan.

Diana twisted the doorknob. To her surprise, the front door swung open. Music washed over her. Barry White sang "Never, Never Gonna Give You Up" in his fathomless, seductive voice as Diana stepped into the small living room dimly lit by a hall light. To her right, a long, sagging couch huddled beneath a wildly flowered slipcover, and beside it was a well-worn recliner. The coffee table looked as if it might tumble over with its load of magazines, tabloid newspapers, dirty cups and glasses, a couple of bodice-ripper romance novels, and two heaping ashtrays. No doubt before Nan's mother left for Portland the previous week, the room had been spotless.

She called out loudly, "Nan!" but received no answer. Diana felt like an intruder, and hesitated actually searching the house for Nan, but she thought if she'd come this far, she should make an all-out effort to find the girl before returning home.

Diana glanced at the front door and decided to leave it open. Somehow, the open door made her feel less like a trespasser. It also made her feel less cut off from the rest of the world, she admitted to herself, although that world was oddly dark and quiet. She called for Nan again then decided to check out the room with the light—the room she was certain was a bedroom.

She left the living room and started down the hall, noticing the pull-down stairs that led to the attic. The attic light funneled through a narrow hole in the ceiling and down the stairs, and a dusty suitcase sat in the hall. Perhaps Nan had retrieved it from the attic and made a second trip up those stairs.

Diana stuck her head into each of the small bedrooms and found them empty. She called for Nan again but still received no answer, and sighing in frustration, she decided to check out the attic. As she grasped the side of the stairs, she felt as if a raindrop hit the top of her head. Diana reached up and touched the side part in her hair. Wet. She pulled her hand away and looked at it. Red. Then another drop landed on her temple and rolled lazily down her face. She wiped it off with the back of her hand and looked up to see more drops falling, faster and faster.

Diana's heart beat harder. Her first instinct was to run out of the house, get in her car, and leave as fast as possible, but she couldn't. Nan was hurt—maybe fatally, maybe not. If she wasn't dead, Diana could not run away from an injured girl who could bleed to death.

Diana began to climb the steps, dread settling over her like a heavy cloak. She thought about calling 911, but she could not tell them anything except that someone—or something—was bleeding in an attic. She needed more information. She wouldn't linger. She wouldn't actually go into the attic. If she could just peep over the edge of the flooring . . .

At last, she was high enough. The naked bulb in the center of the room lit up the shabby attic as if it were a movie set, showing layers of dust, cobwebs, torn insulation, years' worth of discarded furniture, and knickknacks sitting on the grit-covered floor.

Diana saw all of this within five seconds. Then she climbed one more step, her feet still on the ladder, her sweating hands gripping the attic floor. She glanced to her left, from where the blood had dripped on her. Shock dealt Diana a hammer blow as she looked at Nan Murphy, lying inches away from the attic opening, her vacant eyes fixed on Diana, a long gash nearly severing her neck, a pool of violent red spreading around her and oozing toward the attic opening.

Raging fear sucked the air from Diana's lungs. She couldn't have screamed even if it would have helped. She felt dizzy and held tightly to the edge of the attic floor for a moment, trying to regain her equilibrium. Starting to hyperventilate, she carefully stepped down onto the next stair and loosened a hand from the edge of the attic floor to place on the stair rail. Suddenly Diana heard a rushing noise before a burst of dust and dirt flew into her eyes, blinding her. Then she heard an almost inhuman grunt as someone placed a shoe against her chest and thrust. Her sweating hands lost their hold, and the steps seemed to disappear. Diana heard herself screaming thinly as she crashed to the floor of the hall.

CHAPTER THIRTEEN

1

"Diana! Diana!" A voice called faintly down a long, dark tunnel. "Diana, can you hear me?"

Yes, I can hear you. She thought she said it aloud, but the voice asked again, "Can you *hear* me?" A man's voice. Deep. Familiar. Coming closer to her through the tunnel. Closer. *"Diana!"*

"Tyler?" she managed barely above a breath. "Tyler . . ."

"Thank God!" A hand smoothed her hair away from her face. Lips gently touched her cheek. She waited for the lips to touch her again, but instead he asked, "Can you open your eyes?"

With great effort she lifted her eyelids, which felt as if they weighed five pounds each. Through her blurred vision, she could see him leaning over her, his blond-streaked hair falling forward around his tanned face, a line forming between the dark eyebrows over his laser-blue eyes. "Where are we?" she asked foggily.

"You don't remember?"

"N-No. I think I was looking for someone. . . . Yes, that's it. Who was I looking for?"

"It doesn't matter now. I want you to lie still." She promptly tried to lift her head, and Tyler snapped, "I said lie *still*, dammit!"

"Don't be mad," she mumbled. "My head hurts."

"I'm sure it does. And I'm not mad. I'm worried. Now don't move while I call nine-one-one. We have to get you to the hospital."

"Okay. Whatever you want, Tyler." She smiled weakly at him, ignoring his command not to move and running a shaking finger across his cheekbone. The last thing she remembered was saying dreamily, "Just don't leave me. Don't ever leave me. . . ."

Diana recalled nothing about the arrival of the ambulance, her ride to the hospital, or her admittance to the emergency room. Slowly she became vaguely aware of a light shining in her eyes, someone placing her body over hard rectangles before somebody else called, "Take a deep breath, hold it, and don't move." Finally she felt a sharp pain in her wrist, opened her eyes, and yelped, "Ouch!"

A pair of kind, dark-brown eyes looked at her through glasses. "Ah, you're back with us, Ms. Sheridan."

"Have I been somewhere?" Diana asked fuzzily. "I don't remember going anywhere."

"Right now you're in the hospital."

"Oh," Diana said without alarm. She looked at him closely. "I know you."

The doctor smiled. "Indeed you do. We met Friday night when you came to be with your friend's daughter, Willow."

"Willow . . . Willow." Diana looked at the ceiling for a moment then said in triumph, "Willow Conley, and you're Dr. Evans!"

"Very good! Do you remember what happened to you earlier this evening?"

Diana frowned. She felt as if she was trying to dig bare-handed through concrete covering the memory of the evening, and it was too much for her. "No. I don't remember," she said with growing agitation. "Why can't I remember?"

"Don't be upset. It's only natural."

"Natural not to remember what happened a few hours ago?" She tried to sit up but a nurse gently pushed her down. "Just lie quietly, dear. You have no reason to be afraid."

Diana looked up at the woman with intelligent dark-blue eyes. "Nurse Trenton!"

"Right again!" The nurse smiled at her. "I was at the desk the night you came to see Willow. You were upset with me because I wouldn't let you go to her immediately because you aren't family."

"Rules are rules," Diana said in a perfect imitation of Nurse Trenton's voice.

Miss Trenton and Dr. Evans looked at each other and laughed.

"She hasn't lost her sense of humor," Dr. Evans said.

"But I've lost a big chunk of my memory," Diana mourned. "I can't remember this evening and it scares me. I'm here all alone and I hurt and I'm scared!"

Dr. Evans glanced at his chart then said gently, "You aren't alone. A young man came with you. He's been very worried about you. Tyler Raines. Do you want to see him now?"

Diana looked at Miss Trenton. "May I? He's not family."

Miss Trenton laughed again, her cheeks turning pink. "My goodness, I didn't know I sounded like such a tyrant!"

"Not a tyrant." Diana smiled. "Just firm. And I would very much like to see Tyler."

A moment later, Tyler Raines entered the room almost tentatively. Although her vision was slightly blurry, Diana could see his eyebrows drawn together in worry. He didn't look at the doctor or the nurse—just at Diana. "Hi, there," he said awkwardly. "How do you feel?"

"Fabulous. I'd like to leave here and go out dancing. I'd also like to know what happened to me." She held out her hand. Tyler stared at it in bewilderment for a moment then seemed to realize that she wanted him to take it in his own. He stepped closer to the examination table and enfolded her hand in both of his. "Tyler, what happened?"

Tyler looked at her uncertainly before he said, "You had a bad fall."

"A fall? Down the steps at home?"

"Down steps, but not at home."

"Well, where?"

"I think Tyler should tell you what happened later." Dr. Evans smiled at her. "Most patients can't wait to find out what's wrong with them."

"I'm the exception to the rule, but I guess you're going to tell me anyway." Diana sighed. "Fire away."

"First of all, you have a concussion. You have what we call a goose egg on your head. It needed three stitches but we only cut a small square out of your hair. You have so much hair, the bald spot will never be noticed."

"Why do I have a concussion?"

"We told you—you fell down some stairs."

"Doctor?" Tyler said, sounding alarmed.

"It's all right, Mr. Raines. This is to be expected." Dr. Evans looked at Diana. "Concussions can result in confusion, nausea, headache, blurred vision, loss of short-term memory, and perseverating, which is the repetition of a question that's already been answered several times."

"I don't feel nauseated," Diana said. "I have a headache."

"And we'll give you something for that headache in a few minutes," the doctor said patiently. "As for your other injuries—"

"Oh no, not *more,*" Diana wailed.

"Yes, I'm afraid so." He picked up her left wrist and turned it slightly. She yelped in pain. "You have a sprained wrist. You landed on it and I'm surprised it isn't broken, but the X-rays tell us you were lucky. We'll bandage it tightly and you will use it as little as possible. You are right handed, aren't you?" She nodded. "Then the injury to the left wrist shouldn't cause you too much trouble. And you have one more injury," Dr. Evans said.

"Oh no," Diana groaned.

"It's called a hip pointer. We see it a lot in football players. It's caused by a direct blow to the pelvis, more specifically, the iliac crest. The bony ridge you can feel along the waist and the overlying muscle are bruised. We took X-rays and you're lucky again, since there's no fracture. You'll need rest, ice applications, and anti-inflammatory medication."

"And I'll be just like new?" Diana asked hopefully.

"In time. Don't rush your recovery. Don't forget the ice packs."

"We can give you handouts explaining all of these conditions and their treatment," Nurse Trenton said to Tyler.

"I'd appreciate that." He gave her his drop-dead grin—deep dimples, white teeth against tanned skin, twinkling eyes—the full package. The nurse's color heightened.

"Am I done?" Diana asked. "I'd really like to go home now."

The doctor frowned. "We've finished with your tests, but it would be safest for you to spend the night in the hospital."

Night in the hospital. Diana's memory of events immediately preceding the blow to her head might be impaired, but she remembered every detail of Friday night when she stayed in Willow's hospital room. The mysterious clinking of metal on ceramic in the bathroom, the closed bathroom door she'd watched slowly opening before she'd grabbed Willow and rushed into the hall where she immediately had been greeted by what had sounded like a hail of gunshots. No, she could not bear another night in the hospital.

"No," she said firmly. "I will not stay here tonight."

"Diana, if it's what the doctor thinks is best—" Tyler began.

"No. Absolutely not."

"You'll be leaving against medical advice," Nurse Trenton said.

"So be it. I'm going home if I have to walk there!"

Tyler sighed and looked at the doctor. "Diana's stubborn and hot tempered," he said as if he'd known her all of his life. She glared at him. "But we do have some cops waiting to talk to her."

"Cops!" Diana exclaimed. "The police want to know why I fell?"

Dr. Evans ignored her. "She's in no condition to talk to them. She can't really help them now, anyway. She has memory loss." He looked at Diana. "Do you remember anything else about what happened this evening?"

"No, I honestly don't. I wanted to talk to somebody. I don't even remember who." She looked at Tyler. "Where was I when I fell?"

He hesitated then said, "Nan Murphy's house."

"Nan's!" Images of a messy coffee table, attic stairs, and Nan's expressionless eyes swirled for a moment, then seemed to sink in mud. "I don't know why I was at Nan's."

"It doesn't matter now," Tyler said, looking slightly relieved and not giving her a chance to ask any more questions. "I'll go out and talk to . . ." He broke off. "The people wanting to visit Diana, and tell them they have to hold off until tomorrow."

Diana tried to sit up quickly, groaned, and lay down again. "I feel like someone ran over me."

"That's why we'd like for you to spend the night," the doctor said.

"Will I hurt any less here than I will at home?"

Dr. Evans smiled. "You've got me there, Ms. Sheridan. I'll give you a prescription for an anti-inflammatory drug and a painkiller. And remember that when you get home, you *must* rest."

A short while later, Diana was signing forms attesting to the fact that she was voluntarily leaving the hospital against the doctor's advice. She got dressed with Miss Trenton's help while Tyler had her prescriptions filled at the hospital pharmacy. Then she and Tyler made a slow trip to his car—Tyler keeping both arms around her, and she not making any effort to shake them off. She still did not remember what had happened, and Tyler would not tell her. "Not tonight," he kept saying. "Maybe tomorrow, if you don't remember on your own." As they drove to the Van Etton house, Tyler called Simon and told him Diana had refused to stay in the hospital. She realized he'd called Simon earlier, too, telling him what had happened. This time Tyler also alerted him to Diana's memory loss. "Diana and I have agreed not to talk about what happened to her until later," he told Simon.

"Traitor," Diana said as they pulled out of the parking lot. "*I* did not agree to anything. You simply told me how things were going to be."

"Yeah, I'm bossy," Tyler said equably. "Also stubborn, headstrong, and hot tempered." He looked at her, grinning. "Sound like anyone you know?"

"Uncle Simon," she answered promptly. "No one else."

"Okay, darlin', whatever you say. I don't want to get you riled up and make that goose egg on your head start thumping again."

Diana touched the large lump on her head. "I just want to know why I was at Nan's."

"And your brain just wants you to give it a rest. It's not as if you're going to have amnesia for the rest of your life like some character on a soap opera. Everything will come back to you in a couple of days. Maybe even hours. Just settle down and go with the flow."

" 'Go with the flow,' " Diana muttered in irritation.

Tyler sighed and said, "Let's stop with the questions and listen to some music." He pushed a CD into the player and Nickelback's "Someday" poured through the car.

"That's one of my favorite songs!" Diana exclaimed. "I didn't think . . . well, it's not what I expected you to like."

"You thought it was all country music for me. Well, surprise!" He looked at her and smiled. "I'm just full of surprises, Diana."

"So I'm finding out."

The Van Etton house seemed to be lit from basement to attic, and all of the landscape lights glared as well. When they reached the house and Simon rushed out to greet Diana, she laughed and said, "What's with all the lights, Uncle Simon? Are you expecting a dignitary?"

"Yes. You." Simon flung his arms around her and hugged her fiercely. "What on earth made you go—"

"Tomorrow," Tyler interrupted. "Plenty of time for questions tomorrow."

"He's driving me crazy," Diana said in a half-annoyed voice. "I can't remember anything and he won't tell me what happened, and he won't let anyone else tell me, either."

"It's best that you concentrate on resting," Simon said. "Come inside out of the night air. You need to go straight upstairs to bed."

Diana shook her head as she crossed the threshold. "I want to sit down in the library for a while, first. I'd like a glass of cognac, Simon."

"Well now, I guess you would but it's not recommended for people who've just gotten a concussion and are taking medication. And I know you aren't yourself yet, my dear, because you have *never* asked me for a glass of cognac." He looked up at Tyler, beaming. "Who did you bring home instead of Diana?"

Simon lowered Diana on a couch as if she was an invalid, while Clarice appeared with a heavy afghan that she tucked tightly around Diana. Simon disappeared and almost immediately returned with a glass of beer for Tyler and ice water for Diana, along with one of her anti-inflammatory pills and a painkiller.

"Where's Willow?" Diana asked after obediently swallowing her medication.

"You tucked her in before you left to get *ice cream*," Simon said with a hint of sarcasm. "Don't you remember?"

"Sir, she has short-term memory loss," Tyler said quickly. "I told you—"

"Yes, you did, and I sound like *I'm* the one with short-term memory loss."

"Diana, would you like a glass of milk or more ice water?" Clarice asked.

"No. If Simon is going to be stingy with the cognac, I'd like to go to bed." Diana suddenly felt ill-tempered with everyone fussing over her, and the pain in her head and hip abruptly rising a few notches. She slowly stood up.

"Oh, dear, you must let Tyler and Simon help you up the stairs to bed," Clarice cried. "You don't want to fall *again!*"

"I don't remember falling down stairs the first time," Diana returned, angry with herself for sounding so cross. Everyone was simply trying to help her. She forced the semblance of a gracious smile. "I'll take the elevator. Good night, Uncle Simon, Clarice. And Tyler, thanks for a lovely evening. We'll have to do it again sometime when I remember what it is we did."

2

"I made a complete fool of myself today." Jeffrey Cavanaugh sat in his dimly lit hotel room, holding a glass of bourbon in one hand and rubbing the other through his rumpled hair. His complexion was ashen and his eyelids puffy. "Now you're supposed to tell me I wasn't all that bad."

Blake Wentworth, seated across from Jeffrey, looked at his brother-in-law with clear, ebony eyes and said, "I can't tell you that you weren't all that bad. You were, Jeff. You almost hit Diana Sheridan, which was bad enough, but to make things worse, your daughter was watching."

Jeffrey winced and closed his eyes. "God, how could I? I barely even remember what I was doing. All I felt was rage and a sense of betrayal. Betrayal! It's ludicrous. Penny betrayed me a long time ago. Why did I find her pregnancy such a shock?"

"Maybe because you always said she ran away because of another man, but I don't think you really believed it."

"I did. I think there were always other men, just like with Yvette."

"Well, today, you had proof. Before, you just *thought* there was another man. Today, you had no choice but to accept the truth."

"Maybe that was part of it," Jeffrey said miserably, taking a sip of bourbon. "But I saw her, my beautiful Penny, so grotesquely burned. And when she woke up, she was in such agony." He squeezed his eyes shut. "When the doctor said she was pregnant, I knew for certain there was a man. If she hadn't run off to be with him, she wouldn't be dying a horrible death."

Blake frowned. "Why do you think Penny is dying because of another man?"

"Because if she'd stayed home with me where she belonged . . ." Jeffrey shook his head as if confused. "If, if, if . . . So many things could have been different *if*."

"For instance, if Yvette hadn't died, you never would have been with Penny."

Jeffrey looked at him sharply. "If Yvette hadn't died, we would have divorced. The marriage was wrong from the first month. People tried to tell me about her—that she was wild, unstable, incapable of love. But all I saw was her beauty." He took another sip of bourbon. "She was beautiful, wasn't she, Blake?"

"Yes, I'll have to say that for her."

"She was the most beautiful woman I'd ever seen. Still. Even Penny wasn't as beautiful as Yvette.

"Yvette's physical beauty just hid the ugliness underneath."

"Ugliness is too harsh a word!" Jeffrey flared. "She could be charming, lighthearted, and so much fun. She wasn't some exquisite doll meant to be dressed up and shown off like her parents seemed to think. And what her father did to her as a child! I get nauseated even thinking about it." Jeffrey hung his head. "Blake, she was sick and no one did anything for her. Not even me. The psychiatrists said she was schizophrenic. They said she should be put in an asylum—but I couldn't do that to her. There had to be another answer, but I didn't find it in time."

Blake leaned forward. "Jeff, she *needed* to be hospitalized. Medicine wasn't enough for her—she wouldn't take it regularly and she needed a controlled environment with no late hours at parties, no alcohol, and no chance to act like a complete hellcat the way she did the last few months of your marriage."

Jeffrey closed his eyes. "I can still see her that last night before the trouble began. Yvette with her blond hair pulled up, that flowing blue cocktail dress, the necklace—She loved that necklace."

"No wonder. What woman wouldn't love a five-carat canary diamond surrounded by countless blue diamonds?"

"I designed it for her, you know, because she was so intrigued by that Egyptian myth about a blue lotus with the golden center."

"I do know, Jeff. Can we please not talk about this *again*?"

"Yvette never took off the necklace," Jeffrey said as if he hadn't heard Blake. "Not when she slept, not even when she bathed or showered. When she was lying dead on that sidewalk in San Francisco, though, she wasn't wearing it." Jeffrey's voice turned angry. "People said I tore the necklace off her before I threw her out the hotel window, Blake, but I *didn't*."

"I know you didn't."

"After she jumped, people were swarming all around her. Someone in that crowd *stole* it. That's what happened to the necklace. I didn't take it from her and I certainly didn't *murder* her!"

Blake closed his eyes for a moment and sighed. Then he looked piercingly at his brother-in-law. "Jeff, whenever you drink too much, you start talking about Yvette and that damned necklace," he said in a steely voice. "We have been over this a thousand times since Yvette died. Who are you trying to convince? Surely not *me*. I've never doubted you for an instant. You know I haven't, so stop declaring your innocence, and for God's sake, pour out the rest of your bourbon. Then you can try thinking about Penny. *She's* still alive!"

After a tense moment, Jeffrey said quietly, "I have not forgotten Penny—not since she left me and certainly not today. But thinking about Penny makes me also think about Yvette. Mother thought Dad was the devil incarnate and she believes I'm just like him. Maybe she's right. I've brought tragedy to both of my wives."

"Jeff, you're not only being morbid, you're also talking like a lunatic. You didn't hurt Yvette *or* Penny. The only thing you're guilty of is marrying two women who weren't right for you. End of story."

"Well, don't mince words, Blake," Jeffrey said without rancor.

"I never do when I'm talking to you or Lenore." Blake tried to stifle a yawn but couldn't. "It's nearly midnight and I'd be dead on my feet if I were on my feet. Think you can sleep now?"

"When I finish my glass of bourbon, I'll go to bed. I promise. Sorry I took up so much of your time. I forgot you have a lovely lady waiting for you."

"Actually, I don't," Blake said leadenly. "Your sister is still furious with me for throwing that chokehold on you in the park. She took another room for the night."

"Another room?" Jeffrey looked flabbergasted. "Doesn't she realize you kept me from assaulting that woman? That you did me a *favor*?"

"Apparently she doesn't see it that way. She only knows I was mean to her big brother." Blake smiled grimly. "She even got a room on a different floor."

"I'll call her." Jeffrey rose quickly and headed for the phone. "What's her room number?"

"Forget it, Jeff. She gets like this sometimes. Nobody

is perfect, but she's as close as you can come and I'm lucky to be married to her. That's why I simply give her time to herself when she's angry with me. She'll get over it." He sighed. "I hope."

3

Raindrops hitting the window . . .

Barry White leaned in close to Diana, his deeper than deep sensuous voice singing "Never, Never Gonna Give You Up" in her ear. Red. Red dripping down her face. Red pooling on the floor and a face . . . lifeless eyes . . . empty eyes . . .

Raindrops hitting the window . . .

Diana's nose tickled. She rubbed it and turned her head slightly. More tickling. Fumblingly, she reached up and shut her hand around Christabel's fluffy tail. "Wha' are you doing?" she mumbled. "Go sleep."

The cat maneuvered her small body next to Diana's ear and trilled. Then she trilled louder. Louder. Then the trill turned into a demanding "Quack." "Romeo?" Diana muttered. "Go 'way. Both of you." Another trill. Then "Quack. Quack! *Quack!*"

Abruptly, Diana reached full awareness. She looked at the window. Darkness. No raindrops. She looked at the clock: 2:10. Christabel now stood on her chest, looking balefully into her eyes, and Romeo scooted in a circle on the floor, quacking.

"What's wrong with you two?" Diana asked as if they could answer her. "Why aren't you asleep in your beds? Why aren't you with . . ." Her gaze flew to the open bathroom door. "Willow. Where's Willow?"

Christabel jumped off the bed as Diana threw back the sheet and light summer blanket. She turned on her bedside lamp and flew through the adjoining bathroom into Willow's bedroom. The night light glowed enough to show her Willow's empty bed. She flipped on the overhead light, wincing at the glare. As soon as her eyes adjusted, Diana looked around the bedroom and even in the closet. Then she noticed a window opened about six inches. Willow never wanted a window open at night.

A shiver of apprehension rushed through Diana as she opened Willow's door and started out. The cats tried to come with her, but she shut them in the room. She didn't have time to carry Romeo downstairs, and she didn't want him tumbling down as he tried to keep up with Christabel. On the first floor, Diana padded barefoot through the library, the room officially known as the drawing room, the dining room, a little-used room that had been her great-grandmother's "office," and every inch of the kitchen, including the pantry. She looked at Clarice's shut bedroom door and thought about waking her, but the woman had looked exhausted when Tyler brought Diana home from the hospital.

As she walked back toward the kitchen, she noticed the back door open about an inch. *Simon checks all the doors before going to bed,* Diana thought. *He would have never forgotten this one.* She opened the door wider and looked into the night. Two acres of the Van Etton property stretched to a large wooded area—much larger than the woods behind Willow's house. Would she have gone back there at night?

Immediately answering her question, Diana saw a flash of light-colored cloth at the edge of the woods. It was there, and then it vanished. Was she seeing the new light-blue pajamas that she'd bought for Willow? Had Willow worn them tonight? Diana cursed her faulty memory. Then she caught another glimpse of something light, something darting among the trees at the edge of the woods.

Willow.

Diana grabbed an old raincoat hanging on a coat tree near the door. She wrapped it around herself, ignored her bare feet, and ran out the door. The night felt warm and somehow luxurious. Diana's head ached. She tried to run but her hip hurt. That was because of her fall, she told herself, and it didn't matter now. She needed to forget the pain and concentrate on Willow.

She crossed the concrete terrace and stepped onto the lawn. The grass felt cool and damp with dew. Diana tried again to run, but the jabbing pain in her hip wouldn't let her. She managed a trot, which was painful but bearable. She passed by the concrete pedestal holding an old and valuable sundial and automatically looked up at a crook between a limb and the trunk of an oak tree where a robin kept watch over her four newborns.

While looking upward, Diana stepped hard on a rock that sent a red-hot blade of pain up her leg, almost causing her to fall. *If I'd only grabbed my shoes before I left my bedroom,* she thought. But the shock of having the two cats waking her in the middle of the night with a "trouble alert" seemed to have wiped all good sense out of her injured head. If the situation were not so dire, she would be marveling with Simon over the cats' perceptiveness. Diana was certain Christabel had snapped awake either when Willow raised her window or left the room. The little cat had sensed something was wrong, and had managed an incredible feat—dragging Romeo from his nightly coma in order to awaken Diana. Standard procedure for most dogs but quite an accomplishment for two cats.

Diana had trotted, limped, and staggered two-thirds of the way to the woods, when she caught a glimpse of light blue and heard Willow's sweet, high voice. "Where are you?" she called. "Where did you go? You said you'd take me to see Mommy."

Take her to see Mommy? Diana felt the cold breath of fear blow over her. Someone had lured Willow out here with the promise of taking her to see Penny. The thought of seeing her mother was the only thing that could have made Willow overcome her fear of the Bad Man and caused her to come running alone into the night.

"Willow!" Diana yelled. "Willow, come here!" The child did not answer. Diana stepped on something long and narrow and wriggling—a snake—and let out a shrill scream of surprise. She wasn't afraid of nonpoisonous snakes. Still, she didn't like stepping on one barefooted. The sound of her scream must have reached Willow, though, because the child called, "Diana? Is that you?"

"Willow, come to me," Diana yelled, stopping to catch her breath, the pain in her hip and the ache in her head muddling her sense of direction. She couldn't tell exactly from where Willow's voice had come. "Come to me *now,* sweetheart. I'm not mad at you—I just want to be with you," she shouted, knowing it was important not to frighten the child with the fear of anger or punishment.

"I'm gonna see Mommy!" Willow's voice sounded closer. "My guardian angel is gonna take me to see Mommy!" Willow emerged from the woods wearing her blue pajamas and the fuzzy slippers Diana had bought for her. She ran to Diana and grabbed her hand. "It's supposed to be just me, but the angel will prob'ly take you, too, if I ask—"

A gunshot split the silence of the night. Birds suddenly screamed and flapped up from their nests, as Willow sucked in a mouthful of air and flung herself against Diana. A second shot ripped through the air, so close that Diana heard it whiz past her head. She dropped to the ground, pulled Willow down, and rolled on top of her. Willow started to scream but Diana put a hand over her mouth. "Be quiet. Your voice might be letting the person know where to shoot."

Another shot, right above them, and Willow tried to shriek beneath Diana's hand. Diana lowered her head, wondering frantically who could be shooting at them. Willow must have been the main target. *I just got in the way,* Diana thought. And the person trying to kill Willow was the same person who'd tried to kill her in the explosion on Friday night.

A fourth shot, coming from a closer distance, missed them by only inches. Diana thought of trying to reach the cover of the woods, but the edge was about ten feet behind them. She couldn't scoot backward and also keep her body over Willow's, and right now Diana's body was Willow's only protection.

Diana heard shoes moving through the tall, damp grass. They were easy targets, two figures flattened on the ground, just waiting for Death to walk right up and claim them. Diana had an impulse to raise her head, to look their killer in the eye before he fired the fatal shots. But she did not want her last sight on earth to be of the face of their murderer.

"Close your eyes, baby," she whispered to Willow. "Close your eyes and think of the prettiest place you've ever seen in your life. Remember the colors and sounds and how you felt. Make that your world right now. That's your only world."

Amazingly, the child's body went totally still. Under Diana's hand, Willow's facial muscles moved as she scrunched up her face, shutting her eyes as tightly as she could. Diana did the same. She thought of a lake she'd seen in New England—a big lake on a beautiful, sunlit day. A grassy knoll sprouting daisies and Queen Anne's lace had run down to the bank of the lake, and the water had been so smooth it reflected the sky and fluffy clouds like a giant mirror. She'd been happy that day. So happy . . .

Another shot tore through the night air, but this one seemed to be coming from farther away. Then another. Diana couldn't help opening her eyes, her vision of the beautiful lake dissolving into the sight of wet grass and darkness and suddenly light—artificial light—from inside the house, and the landscape lights set all around the terrace. She heard Simon yelling from what seemed miles away, she heard another shot coming from what must have been halfway between her and the house, and finally, she heard the pounding of feet that couldn't have been more than a yard away from her. She imagined she could feel the ground vibrating as their potential killer charged toward the woods. Another shout from a voice that wasn't Simon's. Another shot.

Then nothing, until a man bent over her and said gently, "He's gone. You're safe now, darlin.' "

Diana raised her head and looked into the perspiring, distraught face of Tyler Raines. Just as she rose up to throw her arms around him, Willow, weeping, cried, "Badge! You always save me, just like Mommy said you would!"

"Badge?" Diana mumbled. Then she looked at the weapon lying on the ground beside him. "You have a permit to carry a gun in West Virginia?"

"In all states," Tyler said softly. "Diana, I'm a New York City undercover cop."

CHAPTER FOURTEEN

1

"Was the person outside your window a man or a woman?"

Willow, sitting on the biggest, most comfortable couch in the library with a cup of hot chocolate beside her, looked at Tyler in frustration. "It was my guardian angel. I already told everybody."

The police had left fifteen minutes earlier. Willow had attempted to give them a description of the evening, but between tears, shuddering, and a case of hiccups, her story had been nearly incomprehensible. Tyler had decided that since she'd calmed down a bit, they had to try again while the events were fresh in Willow's mind.

"Was the angel a man or a woman?"

"Angels aren't boys or girls. They're just angels," Willow explained with a pained expression. "How come you don't know that?"

Tyler sighed. "A lapse in my religious education, I guess. Okay, honey, tell me exactly what happened earlier tonight."

"I already did. And I told the policemen who came."

"I know you did but I'd like for you to tell me again. Please, Willow."

"Yes, dear," Clarice said when the little girl looked like she might go silent out of pure annoyance. "I didn't understand everything you said to the policemen. My hearing isn't so good."

"But your gran'girl Katy says you've got ears like a bat and bats hear great."

Clarice looked affronted while Diana and Tyler tried not to grin. "Katy is only thirteen and she doesn't know as much as she thinks she does," Clarice replied tartly. Then she drew a breath and smiled at Willow. "Please tell the story again so I can hear all of it."

"Oh, okay." Willow snuggled deeper into the same afghan that Clarice had earlier wrapped around Diana. "I was sleepin' and then I woke up real slow 'cause somethin' was makin' a sound at the window. Christabel heard it, too. She was lookin' at the window. I got up and looked out and I saw the angel."

"How did you know it was an angel?" Tyler asked. "What did it look like?"

"I didn't know it was an angel at first. It was dressed in a long, white robe—not a robe like you wear over your 'jamas but a flowy robe with big, flowy arms—"

"I'm sorry to interrupt," Diana said, "but by *flowy* do you mean flowing, or draping like a cape or a cloak?"

"I mean flowy," Willow returned irritably. "And a light shined on its face and its face glowed!"

"It glowed?" Simon repeated doubtfully.

"It *glowed,* Uncle Simon. Why can't anyone understand what I'm sayin' tonight?"

"We're sorry. We're just very tired and we were very scared for you. We're not thinking too clearly," Simon said, trying to soothe the exhausted, frightened, and cranky child. "Have another sip of your chocolate while it's still warm and then go ahead with your story and we promise not to interrupt you again."

Willow slurped hot chocolate, then somewhat mollified, continued. "I slid up my window. I just looked 'cause I was scared. Then it said, 'Don't be afraid, Willow. I'm your guardian angel and I've come to take you to your mommy.'

I said, 'But I've never seen you before,' and the angel said, 'People don't see me till they really need me. Now come outside real quiet and I'll take you to see your mommy.' Christabel was standin' on her back legs beside me. She saw the angel, too, and she'd tell you about it if she could talk. Then I said to the angel, 'I'm not s'posed to go outside at night by myself.' And the angel said, 'You won't be by yourself. You'll be with me.'

"I knew the angel was right and that no one could get mad at me for goin' out at night 'cause I was with my angel. So I put on my slippers and I shut my bedroom door so Christabel wouldn't follow me. I could hear her meowin' inside my room and scratchin' at the door and I felt bad, but I remembered Diana sayin' Christabel could get lost in the woods and might not come back for ages.

"I tiptoed down the stairs and all the way to the back door and I unlocked it and opened it and went outside, thinkin' the angel would be right there waitin' for me. But it was farther away from the house. I thought it was leavin' without me 'cause I'd been too slow, but then it turned and waved to me, you know, like to follow it. So I did. Then it went in the woods and I went after it, but I couldn't find it. I kept runnin' around the edge of the woods 'cause I don't like to go way back in the woods at night, but I didn't see it.

"Then I heard Diana callin' to me and I ran to her and told her maybe she could come to see Mommy, too, and then . . ." Willow broke off, her face paling, her hands starting to tremble as they'd done earlier. "And then someone started shootin' a gun at me and Diana, and she pushed me down on the ground and rolled on top of me.

"There was more shootin' and she told me to close my eyes and think of the prettiest place I'd ever been. I thought of a while ago when Mommy and Badge and me climbed to the top of the hundred steps in the park and saw the rose gardens with roses in every color, all bloomin' just when the sun was goin' down and the sky was sorta dark blue and had pretty pink and orange streaks. Then there was more shootin' and Uncle Simon yellin' and lights comin' on and then there was Badge." Willow ran down like a clock slowly stopping. She smiled sweetly at Tyler and asked, "How come you're here when you're s'posed to be a secret?"

"It was time for me to stop being a secret, sweetheart," Tyler said gently. "Your mommy wouldn't want me to be a secret anymore."

After Simon and Clarice had taken Willow and her feline companions up to bed, Diana said softly, "I know Willow is your daughter. I'm not judging you, Tyler, but it's so obvious. She looks like you."

Tyler took her hand and looked deeply into her eyes. "She looks like Penny."

"Willow loves you," Diana went on calmly. "It's clear you've been around for as long as she can remember. Penny told her to keep you a secret, but I should have guessed a powerful tie existed between you by how frantic you were at the explosion site. You weren't horrified the way a stranger would be—I knew it at the time. Then Willow came to you in the woods after hiding from everyone else. Whenever I ask her about you, she gets very cagy. I told you she was collecting sparkle bugs for her mother. Everyone else asked what sparkle bugs were, but not you. You *knew* she called fireflies sparkle bugs." Diana drew a deep breath. "I've finally realized you and Penny were—"

"Siblings," Tyler interrupted. Diana had been so close to saying *lovers,* she went completely blank, nearly gaping at him. "Oh, we weren't related by blood, but we might as well have been," he said earnestly. "When I was fifteen and she was thirteen, she came to live in the foster home where Child Protective Services had placed me."

After Diana's first stunning surprise, she asked incredulously, "You were in the same foster home? That's your connection to Penny?"

"Yes, Diana. But our 'connection,' as you call it, went deeper." He smiled at the memory. "She was a pretty little thing, but she nearly drove me nuts because she just attached herself to me and I didn't want a thirteen-year-old girl trying to hang out with me all the time. It wasn't cool, and I thought I was the height of cool. Then I got used to her. Later, to my horror, I realized I loved her—not in a romantic way, but the way I would have loved a little sister if she'd actually been my sister by birth. Probably more, because my sister wouldn't have been Penny, and I think you know how irresistible Penny is."

Suddenly, Diana's words came in a flood. "She told me she was an only child. I didn't know she was a foster child until Jeffrey Cavanaugh told us, but he didn't say anything about you. If she'd remained close to you, why wouldn't she want Jeffrey to know about you? Why did you have to stay a shadow in her and Willow's life?"

Tyler took a deep breath as if debating how much to tell her. He began slowly. "I told you I had an uncle who was a cop. That was true. I admired him and wanted to be just like him. When I turned eighteen and left the foster care system, I'd already finished a year of college—I majored in criminal justice—and I'd decided I wanted to work undercover. I wanted Penny to go to college, but she was too impatient. She wanted to go out and *live,* as she always said. Anyway, she worked in stores and was a waitress for a while. When she was twenty-one, she began the exotic dancing. By that time I was beginning to work undercover, and considering how many lowlives she came in contact with, we decided it would be safer if no one knew she had any connection to me, although I don't use my real name on the job."

"But after she married, why did you want her to keep your identity a secret from Jeffrey Cavanaugh?" Diana asked. "He's not a lowlife."

"Isn't he? Exactly how much do you know about the guy?"

"Well, not a lot except that when his father died he took over the company and—"

"And there the saga begins. Do you want to hear the whole story or do you want to go curl up in your bed and sleep for the next ten hours?"

"I couldn't sleep if you paid me," Diana said ruefully. "Aside from hurting all over, I can't remember anything about yesterday until I woke up in the hospital. I have no idea who was trying to murder Willow and me in my own backyard. I'm afraid Jeffrey Cavanaugh is going to storm in here and take Willow away and I'll never see her again. My best friend is dying a slow, ghastly death. . . ." Diana's voice broke and her eyes filled with tears. "In short, I'm a nervous wreck."

Suddenly Simon's voice came from behind her. "Then what you need is an ice pack for your head, one for your hip, one of your pain pills, a mild tranquilizer, and a nice glass of—"

"Wine? Please?"

"Warm milk."

"Oh that should finish me off," Diana said between crying and laughing. "I *hate* warm milk."

"Nevertheless, it will do you good," Simon said authoritatively. "Clarice and I will have you medicated and comfortable in fifteen minutes flat, then we shall retire and you two can sit here and talk all night long. And Tyler?"

"Yes, sir?"

"Number one, you must call me Simon, not 'sir.' Number two, you look like you could use a drink. What's your poison?"

"Vodka."

"A double Grey Goose vodka it is. And I'll leave the bottle on the counter in the kitchen if you care for more. Number three, I would like to thank you with all of my heart for saving Diana's and Willow's lives. The world would not be the same without them."

Tyler looked into Diana's teary eyes, smiling tenderly. "I'll certainly drink to that, Simon."

2

Diana sat curled on the couch, wearing Clarice's long-sleeved heavy fleece winter robe that she had insisted Diana put on before the police arrived. In spite of the warm night, Diana felt cold to her core and the robe was comfortable.

"How did you happen to be here when Willow and I needed you?" Diana asked.

"I've been your shadow since Friday night. I thought you knew that by now."

"I think I did." Diana dutifully took her pills, held an ice pack against the lump on her head, and drank a third of her milk. "Tell me more about Penny *and* you."

"Penny never talked to me about the years before she became my foster sister. I'd be boring you with a story mostly about me."

"I'd like to hear it if you don't mind telling it."

Tyler leaned forward, picked up his glass of vodka from a coffee table, and took a sip. "I've only told a few people about my childhood. Because finally you seem to be putting your trust in me, though, I guess it would be best if you know everything." He leaned back and grinned at her, his dimples deepening. "Everything suitable for a lady to hear."

"I'm not easily shocked, Tyler. I promise not to flounce off to bed if I find out you weren't a choir boy."

"Well, that's comforting because I certainly wasn't." He drew a deep breath and looked straight ahead, as if reluctant to meet her gaze. "My parents both wanted to make it big on Broadway. They were from small southern towns and very young. They met at an audition and married shortly afterward. I don't think they were really in love—they shored each other up in a city they couldn't handle, but they refused to go home. They just turned to drugs.

"I was born two years after they married. My mother's parents had turned their backs on her. My dad's father was a widower but he kept taking me in, and so did my dad's big brother, Don. He was the cop. Don was seven years older than my father and I thought he was a god. He still lived down South in the same town as Grandpa and I spent a lot of time there with them."

"Hence your Southern accent," Diana said.

Tyler nodded. "My parents never lost theirs, and the happiest times of my life were spent in the South, so I hung onto that accent for dear life. Silly, but true. Grandpa and Don wanted to keep me, but my parents would get clean and demand they give me back to them. They never stayed clean, though. When I was twelve, they were hooked on crack, scraping out a living. They were ready to let me go to Uncle Don's or my grandfather's when Don was killed in the line of duty. Three months later, my grandfather had a fatal heart attack. By the time I was thirteen, all of my parents' efforts were concentrated on raking up enough money to support their habit."

Tyler paused and swallowed hard. When he began again, his voice had roughened. "I came home from school one day and they were gone. The apartment we lived in was a rattrap, but I managed to hang on in it for a month until the rent was due. Then I hit the streets. For nearly a year I begged, I slept in boxes in the summer and abandoned buildings in the winter. Finally I got a job cleaning up at a diner. The owner's wife turned me in to Child Protective Services. I hated her then, but it was the best thing that could have happened to me.

"Lots of times when I was with my grandfather we used to visit Al Meeks, and he became like a second grandfather. After Grandpa died, I'd write to him. When he hadn't heard from me for nearly two years, he tracked me down. By then I was in the care of the CPS. He wanted to take me, but he wasn't a relative, he was divorced and they prefer two-parent homes, and he wasn't approved to take in foster children, so I ended up in a home in New York. Lucky for me, it was a good home." He stopped, looked at Diana and smiled. "About a year later, along came Penny. Al visited me at the foster home a couple of times a year . He took to Penny right away. Twice my foster parents brought Penny and me to Huntington to visit Al. One year we went to a football game at Marshall. We even came to Ritter Park. Penny *loved* Huntington."

"Which is why she came here when she left Jeffrey," Diana said quietly.

"The main reason, but not the only one. She thought it was a city big enough to get lost in, but not overwhelmingly big. After all, she'd never been a single mother. She knew she could handle herself in a large place, but she wasn't as sure of herself with a child in her care. And she'd never told Jeffrey about her trips here because she was afraid she'd slip and mention Al or me."

While Tyler talked, Diana had forced down the rest of her warm milk and she now set the glass aside and put her hand on his tanned arm. "I called Al Meeks."

"I know. He told me."

"You know, I didn't trust you. I knew you were lying about not knowing Penny and Willow. I thought you might be lying about knowing Al. Anyway, he tried to give away as little information as possible, but he did say your grandfather's heart would have been broken if he'd known what happened to you when you were younger. He meant the last years with your parents and you ending up on the streets fending for yourself when you were only thirteen." Diana tightened her clasp on his arm. "Do you know what happened to your parents?"

"I know my mother died from an overdose when I was sixteen. I found out about that many years later. I don't know what happened to my father. He simply became one of the people lost on the streets—the kind I see so often in my job."

"I'm sorry, Tyler. Truly sorry."

Tyler took another sip of his drink. "Enough of my sad tale. Now tell me about Diana Sheridan."

"Diana Sheridan isn't nearly so interesting."

"I doubt that. Spill."

"My father was from a family with money. He and my mother married young, almost immediately had me, and were baffled by what to do with a child. So they left me in the care of my grandmother and they traveled a lot. And spent money. Too much money. By the time I was twelve, most of it was gone. They stopped traveling, stopped having parties, stopped enjoying life.

"When I was fourteen, my father had too much to drink at the first party he and my mother had attended in months, and on the way home, he missed a curve in the road and the car tumbled down into a ravine. They both died instantly. Grandmother was devastated—my mother was her only child and just thirty-four. I loved my parents and I missed them, but I wasn't as lost as most fourteen-year-olds would have been if their parents died. They'd been gone so much of my life, I'd learned to depend on Grandmother and myself. And Simon, of course. Also, I knew how unhappy they were with the life they had ahead."

"So you went to live with your grandmother," Tyler said. "And the two of you spent even more time with Simon, and when you were eighteen, he took you on an Egyptian expedition. Penny thought that was the most fabulous thing she'd ever heard."

Diana smiled. "It *was* fabulous. It was hard, but it was also wonderful." She sighed. "Penny and I used to talk about going on an expedition some day and taking Willow, of course. I always knew it would never happen, but we were like young girls planning what they were going to do when they grew up. It was fun."

Tyler grinned. "I know. She told me. You were her first real girlfriend, you know. She always sounded about sixteen when she talked of all the fun things the two of you talked about and did together."

"I had no idea, but I'm glad Penny enjoyed our friendship. It was the best one of my life, too."

A tear ran down Diana's face, and Tyler's eyes suddenly shone in the lamplight with his own unshed tears. He quickly glanced at his empty glass. "I think I'll take advantage of that fine bottle of Grey Goose vodka Simon left out in the kitchen and fix another drink. May I get you anything?"

"You may get me a glass of wine."

While Tyler was gone, Diana rid herself of the ridiculous ice pack and rested her head on the back of the couch. She didn't know how it was possible, but she was happy. In spite of everything, she was happy. "You must be crazy, Diana Sheridan," she said aloud, softly. "Only *you* would be happy two hours after someone tried to shoot you to death."

"Were you talking to me?" the object of her happiness asked as he strode back into the room. His face looked more relaxed, and his eyes no longer seemed to be probing every corner, searching for possible danger. He handed her a wineglass and walked to the front bay window, parting the draperies. "Good. Surveillance still in place, although I wish they were closer to the house. I looked out the kitchen window. They're still searching the woods, too."

Diana took a sip of her wine. "Ugh! Tyler, this is Willow's *apple* juice!"

"Yes indeed. Your uncle said no alcohol on top of a pain pill and a tranquilizer."

"An extremely mild tranquilizer."

"Be that as it may," he said, sitting down so close to her she could feel the heat of his body, "I've just won over Simon. I'm not going to lose his good will because of a glass of wine."

"You won over Simon the night you met him." Diana grinned. "You know that. He loaned you one of his cars. And I think Clarice fell in love with you."

"Well, I think Clarice is one hell of a gal, but she's not the one I'd like to have fall for me."

Diana had always felt disdain for women who acted coy, but she couldn't help herself. "What kind of girl *do* you have in mind?"

"One who's ambitious and wants to make her own good fortune, not have it handed to her. One who isn't consumed by her considerable beauty." He paused. "And most important, one who would risk anything to protect the people she loves. You risked your life to protect Willow."

"Yes, I did a wonderful job tonight, didn't I?"

"You woke up. You went after her. You shielded her with your own body. I'd certainly call those the actions of a protector."

"I woke up because of the cats. People who say cats aren't capable of heroic acts haven't read much about how many cats have saved their owners by alerting them of danger. And naturally I went after Willow and tried to cover her body with mine. Who wouldn't have?"

"A lot of people. I see it all the time."

"Well, the person who tried to kill Willow and me must have been the same one who tried to kill Penny. We can't have two potential murderers after this family."

Tyler smiled and took her hand. "I like it that you think of Penny and Willow as being part of 'this family.'"

"We felt as if she and Willow *were* family. We loved them." Diana looked into Tyler's eyes. "That's why I feel you should tell me the reason Penny ran away from Jeffrey instead of divorcing him. Why did she choose a life of hiding?"

Tyler glanced down, and Diana could almost feel him marshalling his forces to tell something he'd probably sworn *never* to tell. She didn't believe he broke promises easily. Then he began to speak in a low, hesitant voice.

"I hated what Penny was doing before her marriage. She was a stripper, plain and simple. Not a prostitute like some people said later, but a stripper. Then she met Jeffrey Cavanaugh. She'd been seeing him for over a month before she told me. She was in love, and I was horrified.

"I already knew all about Cavanaugh. His father, Morgan, was a rough customer with more criminal associations than the authorities probably knew about, but he was so devious, nothing could ever be pinned on him. He was also smart—enough to know if he wanted to start a legitimate business, he needed a partner with prestige. That's why he needed Charles Wentworth, Blake's father. People thought Wentworth had lost most of his money in bad investments or he would never have teemed up with someone like Cavanaugh. Anyway, together they formed Cavanaugh and Wentworth."

Tyler took another sip of his drink. "The business took off like a rocket. Morgan Cavanaugh actually began to earn some respect in the business world if not the personal one. He had a wife and two kids, but he was always involved with at least one other woman, and he had nothing but contempt for his son. I've heard some terrible stories about how he treated Jeffrey. That kind of treatment would leave scars on anyone."

"So you feel sorry for him."

"So I think his childhood might have warped him. That's too bad, but it doesn't mean I don't think the guy has some serious problems."

"I understand. You're not talking about causes. You're concerned about the result."

"Exactly, especially when that result affected Penny," Tyler said. "About ten years after they founded the business, Wentworth killed himself. Supposedly, he'd been caught embezzling and couldn't face the shame. A lot of people didn't believe the whole scenario. Wentworth had a spotless reputation, the business made so much money he didn't need to embezzle, and he was devoted to his wife and son. The police couldn't prove anything, though.

"Morgan now had control of the entire business. He provided well for Wentworth's wife and son, but the wife had a complete breakdown about six months after her husband's suicide and she never recovered. She's still in a sanitarium. Meanwhile, Morgan took Blake in, treated him like the son he thought he *should* have had instead of Jeffrey, paid for

Blake's Harvard education, just like Jeffrey's, and approved Blake's marriage to his daughter. Everyone thought Jeffrey must resent the hell out of Blake, but apparently he didn't." Tyler shrugged. "From what I've heard, they weren't close before Charles Wentworth's death, but afterward they became good friends in spite of the six-year age difference."

"That speaks well of Jeffrey," Diana said. "As long as it wasn't an act."

"With Jeffrey, you never know. The man is an enigma. Brilliant, reclusive, and strange."

"How strange?"

"That depends on who's talking about him. I've heard dozens of people talk about Jeffrey Cavanaugh and no one has given the same description of him. Some say he has a few minor eccentricities. Others say he's crazy. No one says he's just a friendly, normal guy."

"Well, that's comforting," Diana muttered.

"Isn't it? Just after Jeffrey turned thirty, his father was murdered—one shot at close range to the head. It looked like a Mafia hit, but people speculated that maybe Jeffrey had gotten rid of his father. Jeffrey hated Morgan, and with Morgan gone, the business fell to Jeffrey. He made a success of it and later brought in Blake as chief operating officer. In the meantime, he married a socialite named Yvette DuPrés. She was beautiful and definitely crazy—no one quibbles about *her* mental state.

"The marriage was a complete mess from the beginning. She started having affairs almost immediately. By the third year, she seemed to be doing everything in her power to humiliate Jeffrey. After one particularly bad evening in San Francisco, she left a hotel dinner party with Jeffrey and a bunch of bigwigs he hoped to reel in. She went up to her hotel room and half an hour later took a dive from her eighth-floor window."

"Lenore told me about Yvette's death," Diana said with a shudder. "She said the police didn't believe she committed suicide."

"That's because of the necklace." Tyler shook his

head. "You'd never believe the trouble that cursed necklace has caused Jeffrey. Even *he* doesn't know all of it."

"What's so special about a necklace?"

"It's a coincidence, but Yvette was fascinated by ancient
Egypt—the way people lived, their beliefs, you name it. I
can imagine how she would have loved to meet Simon. She
even had Simon's first book."

Diana nearly gasped. "You're kidding! Tyler, that's
just . . . just—"

"Creepy, in layman's terms."

"Exactly."

"Nevertheless, it's true. So, Yvette had a passion for
Egyptian culture and she especially loved some myth
about the Egyptian lotus. Lotus or lily? Does that sound
familiar?"

For a moment Diana was speechless. He could have
been spinning one of Willow's fabulous bedtime stories, but
he wasn't. "Are you serious?" she finally asked. Tyler nodded. "Go look at the center pane of the rear bay window."

"I already have," he said, smiling but going back to the
window anyway. He drew aside the draperies and tilted
his head, then said, "Just as Penny described it."

"You should see it when the sun shines through the
glass. It's beautiful. And Penny told you about it?"

"You bet she did. But I don't remember the myth. You
tell it."

As Tyler stood, looking at the glass as if mesmerized,
Diana said, "It's known as the myth of the blue lotus, although depictions in temples show that they were really
referring to a water lily. According to the myth, when the
world began, dark waters of turmoil covered everything.
Then the Primeval Water Lily surfaced from the waters. It
opened its blue petals, and inside sat a child-god on the
golden center of the flower. Light streamed from the child-
god's body and banished the darkness. He was considered
the source of all life."

Tyler turned and looked at her. "Did Simon write
about the myth in his first book?"

"He wrote about it in one of them. It could have been the first one."

"The one Yvette owned." He let out a low whistle and said, "Well, I'll be damned."

"Okay, you're damned, hopeless, a lost soul. Now get over here and tell me about Yvette's necklace."

"I'm glad you're so unconcerned about the state of my soul."

"I'm not at all worried about the state of your soul because you have one of the best souls I have ever encountered."

"Oh, I'll bet you say that to all the guys." Tyler grinned, but Diana thought he looked moved.

Diana patted the seat beside her and Tyler returned to the couch, once more sitting close to her, this time throwing his arm around her shoulders. "Cretin that I am, I only knew the necklace was a blue and canary diamond concoction Jeffrey designed for Yvette because of some myth that obsessed her. I think someone told me it was a Chinese myth. Anyway, what interested the cops the most was that it cost a fortune and that Yvette *always* wore it but it wasn't on her body after the fall. It also wasn't in the hotel room."

"What did the San Francisco police believe happened to it?"

"They thought someone had helped Yvette out that window and had kept the necklace."

"I take it Jeffrey wasn't with her when she went out the window."

"That's open to debate. Jeffrey, Yvette, Lenore, and Blake had gone to San Francisco to attend an anniversary party in the hotel ballroom for one of Cavanaugh and Wentworth's biggest clients. At the party, Yvette made one of many public scenes, but this was probably the worst. She screamed that Jeffrey had killed his father, that he was a thief, a sexual deviant, you name it. Then she threw champagne in his face and stalked out of room.

"Everyone at the party said Jeffrey just stood there. He

didn't answer her, he didn't try to shut her up, he didn't even wipe the champagne off his face. He didn't show any emotion whatsoever. I guess Lenore ran up to him and tried to dry his face, but he brushed her away. Lenore left the ballroom looking upset, then people started trying to act like nothing had happened—as if that was possible. Finally Jeffrey dried off his own face, downed another glass of champagne, talked to a couple of people, or rather talked as much as he ever does, and after about half an hour, he left the party. Everyone thought his behavior was almost as bizarre as Yvette's."

"Lenore says Jeffrey's odd behavior is the result of his father always tormenting him," Diana said.

"I wouldn't doubt it. I told you Morgan was a mean old cuss and he supposedly couldn't stand his son because Jeffrey wasn't at all like him." Tyler smiled pityingly. "The ironic thing is that Jeffrey's mother doesn't care much for him either because she thinks he's *exactly* like his father."

"That would have to badly affect him, Tyler. He couldn't win."

"Well, don't feel too sorry for him. We don't know which parent was right."

"Anyway, Jeffrey went to their hotel room after leaving the party. The police were certain that if he'd arrived before Yvette's plunge out the window, Jeffrey had jerked the necklace off her before he pushed her, or the necklace caught on his hand during the struggle. But someone in the next room claimed they'd heard Yvette shouting at somebody about ten minutes before Jeffrey could have arrived, and a man in the hotel lobby said he saw Jeffrey at almost the exact time Yvette fell, or jumped, or was pushed. That's where the matter ended. Again, no proof," Tyler ended in disgust.

"Two deaths—one appearing to be a Mafia hit, the other a suicide—and both benefitting Jeffrey," Diana said slowly. "That's stretching coincidence a bit far."

"I'll say it is!" Tyler's voice had risen. His distrust of

Jeffrey Cavanaugh and anger that no one could prove anything against him couldn't have been more obvious. "So you see why I didn't want Penny involved with him? He'd lived like a hermit after Yvette's death, then he and some client went to see 'Copper Penny'—that was her stage name—and suddenly he started dating her. You can probably imagine how the tabloids loved it."

"You read the tabloids?" Diana asked teasingly, trying to lighten Tyler's mood, which seemed to be teetering on the edge of fury.

He smiled for the first time in twenty minutes.

"Of course. I read them voraciously," he said, tongue in cheek. "I'm much more interested in who's just married for the sixth time than I am in Ahab chasing a white whale."

"It sounds to me as if Jeffrey has become your white whale," Diana said softly.

"I guess he has." Tyler grew serious. "I knew a lot about him after the Yvette business. Then to find out Penny was involved with him threw me for a loop, as my grandpa used to say. I begged Penny to stop seeing Jeffrey. Instead she married him. Diana, I would rather she had kept stripping than be married to him. I was afraid for her."

"No wonder. But you didn't interfere. Did Jeffrey know about you?"

"No, he didn't. Because of his suspected underworld associations inherited from his father, I couldn't have him knowing about me. Penny kept assuring me Jeffrey was entirely honorable, but frankly, Penny could be incredibly naive. She knew how important anonymity was to me, though, and she kept me a secret. We talked on prepaid cell phones so calls couldn't be traced. We met briefly in Central Park. Later, Penny would bring Willow to the park for me to see, and as she got older, we taught her to call me Badge so that if she ever mentioned me, Penny could say she meant the cops wearing badges that patrol the park."

"When Willow kept saying 'badge' in the emergency

room, the doctor and I thought she was referring to the badges worn by police at the scene."

"Even now she doesn't know my real name. Penny said Willow could start calling me Tyler as soon as they were safe."

"Safe from what? I still don't know why Penny ran away."

Someone rapped softly using the knocker on the large, wooden front door, and Diana jumped. "Oh God, who's that?" she asked, grabbing Tyler's arm.

"Well, most killers don't knock to announce their arrival. It's probably a cop."

Diana huddled on the couch while Tyler strode to the door. He was at least six-foot-one with wide, muscular shoulders, a toned body, and an almost catlike grace—the kind that in an instant could turn into the strong, agile moves of a dangerous adversary. Diana realized how much safer she felt with Tyler there tonight. If he hadn't stayed, she would have lain in her bed wide-awake and trembling all night, even if Simon had allowed her more than one tranquilizer.

Tyler opened the front door, and Diana crept to the entrance of the library. A patrolman said, "They're finished searching the woods for tonight. Just thought I'd tell you they'll be leaving now."

"Find anything?" Tyler asked.

"Some kind of white robe. Big thing." *Flowy,* Diana thought, remembering how Willow had described it. "It's bagged as evidence and forensics will see what they can recover from it. Other than that, they didn't find anything. They're going to take another look around tomorrow in the daylight, though."

"Good. And you're going to keep twenty-four-hour surveillance on the house."

"Well, we'll do the best we can, but I don't think we have the manpower for constant surveillance."

"Do you mean that after what happened, you're going to leave these people unprotected?"

"That's not what I said." The patrol officer sounded nettled. "I said we're going to do the best we can. I know you're from New York City and this isn't New York, but that doesn't mean we don't have crime here—it's not confined to the Van Etton house." The man apparently took a deep breath. "Look, maybe you should take this up with the sheriff tomorrow."

"Okay," Tyler said easily. "I didn't mean to jump down your throat. I just care a lot about these people."

"I understand." The patrol officer's voice sounded more affable. "I'll be leaving now, but we've got two guys in the car out front. Hope the rest of the night goes well."

"I don't see how it could get much worse," Tyler said dryly, and the patrol officer laughed as Tyler shut the door. He turned and looked at Diana hovering in the door. "He said they found a white robe in the woods."

"I heard. The one worn by Willow's guardian angel, of course."

Tyler's gaze traveled over her, swathed in heavy blue fleece. "My, you do go in for the sexy nightwear, don't you?"

"Clarice and I have traded robes. You should see the one I gave her on the first night she stayed here. It was a gift from my ex-mother-in-law meant to inspire unbridled passion in her son. I think Clarice took one look at it and was ready to run for what was left of her home."

Tyler walked toward her and put his arm around her waist. "Well, she didn't, and from what I've been able to see, she seems to fit right in with the Van Etton household."

"Especially its master. Do you know Simon not only took her to church yesterday but also stayed for the service? I can't remember the last time Simon entered a church."

"Not for your wedding?"

"I was married in a judge's office. No frills. I didn't feel like I'd even gotten married." She steered Tyler back to the couch and they both sat down, their bodies touching, their faces inches apart. "Now tell me about Penny's marriage."

Tyler reached for his glass and emptied the remaining vodka. "Well, Penny seemed really happy the first year of the marriage. She immediately went on a self-improvement kick. She took lessons to lose her New York accent, which was fairly strong. She spent hours reading etiquette books and books about gourmet foods and fine wines. She seemed more eager to become a 'lady' than to run around buying expensive clothes and jewelry. She wanted Jeffrey to be proud of her. Of course, she was never going to be accepted by high society—not a former stripper—but she didn't know it, thank goodness. That would have broken her heart because she thought Jeffrey was an integral part of that world." Tyler rolled his eyes. "He wasn't. Blake Wentworth was, but not Cavanaugh."

Diana frowned. "Did that bother Jeffrey?"

"I don't think so. He's not a social creature, if you haven't noticed. But Wentworth lowered his participation in that world nevertheless. I think he did it out of consideration for Jeffrey."

"Also Lenore?"

"Probably. I don't think she's considered one of the social elite, either," Tyler continued. "Anyway, Penny was thrilled when Willow—or Cornelia, as Jeffrey insisted she be named—was born. She doted on the baby and she was disappointed that Jeffrey didn't. She said he loved Willow but he just wasn't demonstrative. Still, things began to go downhill after that. Jeffrey spent more time away from the apartment. He'd work until ten at night and leave at seven in the morning. When he went on trips, he took Lenore and Blake but not Penny. I could tell she was unhappy. Then Jeffrey assigned Penny a bodyguard. She wasn't supposed to go anywhere without this guy."

"Are you certain Jeffrey wasn't just overprotecting her, especially because they had a baby?"

"She believed he thought she had a lover."

"Did she?"

"If she did, she didn't tell me about him."

"Are you sure she *would* have told you?"

"No. In fact, she probably wouldn't have. She wouldn't want another lecture from me about playing with fire, especially because she wasn't good at sneaking around. Well, the question of a lover aside, one day over a year and half ago, she called me, frantic. Penny had always been intrigued by a wall safe in Jeffrey's study that he never let her look into, saying it was full of boring business papers. While he was gone on one of his trips, she searched his study and under a heavy piece of sculpture, she found a piece of paper with numbers, which she thought were the combination to the safe.

"She was right, and inside the safe she found Yvette's necklace. Penny had heard so much about it over the years, she recognized it instantly. The clasp was broken and the chain twisted almost in two. She said the damage didn't look like what could have happened in a fall. To her it looked like the kind of damage the necklace would have sustained if there had been a struggle and someone had twisted it off Yvette's neck.

"The fact that Yvette's necklace was missing was the only reason the police didn't immediately rule her death a suicide. They believed if she'd jumped out the window, the necklace would have been on her body. But Jeffrey—and several of his lawyers—claimed the necklace could have been stolen after Yvette hit the street. Before the police could arrive, a lot of people had gathered around her body and somebody did CPR and checked her pulse and God knows what else. Also, Yvette was drunk that night, she'd threatened suicide many times—even the day before her death—and it was fifty degrees outside but her window was wide open. Everything except the missing necklace pointed to suicide."

Tyler's expression hardened along with his voice. "Over the years, Jeffrey kept talking about the necklace, supposedly wondering what happened to it, as baffled as everyone else. And all along it had been in his safe. When

Penny found it, she knew Jeffrey must have struggled with Yvette and pushed her out that window.

"That alone frightened and horrified Penny, but what really terrified her was that she finally believed all the things people said about him—that he'd killed his father and Yvette. She talked hysterically about the way Jeffrey had begun acting with her—the moodiness, keeping her a near-prisoner in the apartment, paying no attention to her or to the baby. She thought that because he believed there was another man in her life, she was going to be his next victim."

"Why didn't she take the necklace to the police?"

"I told her the necklace wouldn't convict Jeffrey of murder. He'd just left his guests at the party when a man in the room next to Yvette's heard her shouting at someone in her own room. Then the guy in the lobby claimed he saw Jeffrey heading to the elevators right before she would have gone out the window. If what the witness said was true, Jeffrey wouldn't even have had time to make it to the hotel room, much less struggle with Yvette and toss her out a window then hide the necklace. As for Jeffrey having the necklace years later, he could say it come into his possession after the murder. He might claim someone stole it and sold it back to him.

"Mainly, I didn't want Penny's knowledge to become public, because I was afraid Jeffrey might still have contact with some of his father's mafia connections. I thought if he didn't shut her up, they'd do it for him."

"So you told her to run away."

"No," Tyler said emphatically. "I told her to get a divorce. If Jeffrey didn't care much for Willow, he probably wouldn't fight for custody. Penny said he'd fight for the sheer hell of it, but she didn't think he'd let things get that far. She thought he'd kill her before he'd let her leave him, especially if he thought there was another man. I told her, 'Penny, you can run, but you'll never be safe.' She was determined, though. She begged me to help her. She said she'd do it alone if I refused."

Tyler gave Diana a despairing smile. "Penny was smart, but she didn't know the first thing about pulling off a disappearance. She would have bungled the whole process, Jeffrey would have found out, and God knows what he would have done to her. So I relented.

"I got her all the fake identification and bought the Social Security cards from a homeless woman—they are so desperate, they're more than willing to sell Social Security cards. I couldn't believe my luck when I found a woman with a child almost the same age as Willow." A smile flickered across his face. "Penny insisted I give the woman twice the money she asked for the cards. No one could say Penny wasn't a generous soul." The smile disappeared. "Penny told me she intended to come to Huntington, primarily to be near Al Meeks although she had other reasons, too. So Jeffrey returned from his trip to find absolutely no sign of his wife and daughter."

"That would seem cruel if you didn't know Jeffrey's history," Diana said gravely. "But I'm not certain I wouldn't have done the same thing if I had been in Penny's place."

"I didn't think it was the way to ensure her safety, but I think like a cop. Anyway, we kept in touch and I even came to Huntington to see her a couple of times—it was easy for me because I could stay with Al."

Tyler looked away from her, his face etched with pain. "Then I got a hysterical call from Penny about two weeks ago. She said someone was asking too many questions. I had a feeling there was more going on, but she wouldn't give me more details. She just insisted she'd been found out. She said she had to get away, which broke her heart because she'd have to leave you and Simon. Of course, I agreed to help her again. I couldn't come immediately— I needed time to gather false IDs again. When I finally got here, Willow was in the hospital with appendicitis. We were going to leave Sunday morning." Tyler drew a long, shaky breath. "But Sunday was too late."

Tears glittered in his brilliant blue eyes. Diana put her arms around him and lay her head on his chest. His arms immediately enfolded her and she felt a tear fall onto her forehead, just as her own tears spilled onto his T-shirt.

Finally, when she could speak, Diana asked, "Do you have any idea who found out about Penny?"

"No. She knew, though. She said she'd tell me when she got away from here. I think she was afraid if I knew who it was, I'd go after the person. I might even kill someone. I wouldn't have, but Penny could get carried away, exaggerate." He sighed. "But she sure wasn't exaggerating the fact that she was in danger."

"And not from Jeffrey if he didn't know where she was until after the explosion, when her fingerprints were sent to a national database."

"Even if he wasn't directly responsible for that bomb, Diana, he killed her just the same. If he didn't have the necklace, if he hadn't given her good reason to feel her life was threatened . . ."

"I know." Diana raised her head. "I know."

Tyler stroked her hair then pushed it behind her ears and kissed her neck, slowly, gently, trailing kisses from her collarbone up to her ear lobe. Diana closed her eyes, heat flowing through her, as she ran her fingers delicately over his chiseled features, lingering at his lips.

"A few years ago, Penny said there was one girl in the world for me," Tyler murmured. "She told me, 'She's out there somewhere, Tyler, and I know one way or another, you're going to find her.' " Diana opened her eyes and he looked into them so piercingly, she felt as if he could see her soul. "About three months after she started working for Simon, she told me on the phone, 'Your girl *does* exist, Tyler, and I've met her. Her name is Diana.' "

Diana's eyes filled with tears again although she smiled. "She thought I was the one for you?"

"Absolutely. When I met you the night of the explosion, I felt like I already knew you. I think I was halfway in love with you from the first minute."

"And now?"

Tyler smiled seductively, the tiny crinkles at the corners

of his eyes deepening. "And now I know Penny was right. I have met the girl for me. I just don't know if she thinks I'm the guy for her."

"Oh, she does," Diana said with a rush of feeling. "She most certainly does."

"We've only known each other three days."

"Penny told you there was one girl in the world for you. My grandmother told me love strikes as quickly as a lightning bolt. It doesn't matter if we've known each other three days or three years—my lightning bolt has struck."

Tyler lowered his face and kissed her deeply, making her feel as if she'd never really been kissed before tonight. His fingers tangled in her long, curling hair, and her palm closed around his strong, hot neck. They kissed until the grandfather clock struck three. Tyler pulled away from her, his breath coming fast, his face flushed. "I'm being incredibly selfish," he said in a breathy, reluctant voice. "You should go upstairs and try to get some sleep."

"I'm not leaving this couch," Diana whispered in his ear.

He smiled. "And I'm not leaving this house."

She sat up, reached for the beautiful crocheted afghan, and pulled it over them. "Then it's a good thing this couch is wide enough for two."

Shortly afterward, Diana laid her head on his chest, feeling his heart beating and the tingle of his kiss on her lips. In spite of everything, with his arms wrapped around her, she had never felt so safe and happy in her life.

CHAPTER FIFTEEN

1

Eventually Diana drifted into a dream in which she sat on her bed as Clarice told her a story about Glen and Penny, about Glen coming to see Penny several times. Clarice was worried Diana would be hurt, but Diana had merely been surprised that Penny had not told her.

In dreamtime, Diana suddenly sat in the park, a picnic hamper beside her. As she took pictures of Willow, a woman chattered beside her. Then a man stormed up to them, furious. He wanted to know the identity of someone. Diana didn't know. He didn't believe her. He was going to hit her then abruptly he kneeled on the ground while the woman ranted.

Another time shift and Diana suddenly faced Nan in the kitchen. Nan seemed different—deferential and emotionally beaten. "I need to tell you something," she said. She talked about Glen. Nan also needed to tell her about someone else. Penny.

Now Diana sat in the library. A handsome, dark-haired man talked to her and to Simon. He apologized for how another man had acted in the park. He said the man had suffered a shock—the doctor had said Penny was pregnant. Pregnant.

And then a glass had shattered in the kitchen.

Diana awakened with a start. She looked at Tyler pressed against the back of the couch, his socked feet hanging over the armrest, one arm thrown possessively across her, blondish hair covering one closed eye, his mouth slightly open. He wasn't snoring. *Thank goodness he doesn't snore,* Diana thought absently. She wanted to wake him. She wanted to tell him that her memory was returning. But did she remember anything important? Did she remember what had happened to her last night, why she'd fallen? *No, let him sleep,* she thought. He looked peaceful. Cramped but peaceful.

Diana, on the other hand, knew she couldn't lie on this couch one more minute. She was too restless, her mind too agitated. Besides, dawn hovered—she could feel it. Slowly and gently she lifted the afghan off herself and draped it over Tyler. With equal care, Diana moved his arm. He murmured but did not open his eyes. She then slid off the couch and stifled a cry of pain as she stood up . . . and felt as if a hot poker had been thrust into her hip and partly up her back. Diana's sprained wrist throbbed. Her head ached. Her mouth was drier than the desert. Running around dodging a killer's bullets hadn't been the best therapy, she thought ruefully. But a painkiller would take off the edge. Yes, she definitely needed a painkiller, a glass of ice water, and at least one cup of hot coffee. Immediately.

Diana made her way slowly to the kitchen. She took a painkiller and thirstily downed a whole glass of water. Then she reached for the airtight coffee canister and frowned. Propped against the canister was a legal-sized envelope with DIANA written on the front. *Nan's handwriting,* Diana thought. What could Nan possibly have wanted to say in a letter that she couldn't say in person?

2

Blake heard a clatter at his hotel room door and opened his eyes to see Lenore dragging in two small pieces of luggage. "Am I forgiven?" he asked.

"You're getting there." Lenore's hair hung messily around a tired face. She'd put on a slash of rosy lipstick that didn't improve the look of her ashy complexion or slightly sunken eyes. "I know I look like hell, but I didn't sleep much."

Blake sat up but didn't offer to help with her luggage. "You never do when you don't sleep with me. I don't think I did anything so awful you had to remove yourself from the marriage bed."

Lenore faced him, her hands placed on her hips. "You nearly choked my brother to death because he was understandably furious with Diana Sheridan."

Blake's dark eyes widened. "I did not nearly choke Jeff to death and he wasn't understandably furious with Diana! What did *she* do to make him furious?"

"She withheld information a husband has a right to know. If she'd told Jeff about Penny's lover, the news of her pregnancy wouldn't have sent him into a tailspin. Diana knew and she didn't have the decency to warn Jeff."

"You have decided Diana knew. You have no proof, Lenore."

She flung the smaller piece of luggage on a chair, and ran a hand through her tousled hair. "And now you're defending her. Why? What is she to you, Blake? Why are you taking her side rather than your own wife's?"

"Because my wife's side is . . ." Blake broke off.

Lenore looked at him challengingly. "Your wife's side is *what*?"

"I can't talk to you when you're like this. I'll say something I regret." Blake closed his eyes and shook his head as if trying to clear it. "I'm going to order us some breakfast. What do want?"

"Coffee."

"That's it? Just coffee?"

"Yes," Lenore snapped. "I suppose you're stunned because I don't want my usual lumberjack's breakfast."

Blake gazed at her for a moment then burst out laughing. "Lumberjack's breakfast! Lenore, what are you talking about?"

"You wish I hardly ate anything so I'd be all skin and bones like Diana Sheridan. Or Penny."

Blake put his head in his hands and moaned, "Oh God, here we go again. I should have expected it." He lowered his hands. "You think I wanted Penny? An ex-stripper who crawled out from who knows what gutter?"

"I'm not saying you wanted to marry her. I'm saying you wanted to have an affair with her."

Blake closed his eyes for a moment then said with strained patience, "Penny was—is your brother's wife. No one has ever accused me of being stupid, and having an affair with your brother's wife would have been *extremely* stupid. Not to mention that your brother is my best friend. Also not to mention that I could never look at Penny without seeing her sliding down a stripper pole, and I don't find that sexy. God only knows how many men she slept with before Jeff came along."

"You certainly gave Jeff an impassioned speech about how much she loved him."

"And what exactly does that have to do with me? He was satisfied with her. Good for him. I couldn't have spent one night with her, but he doesn't have to know how I felt."

Lenore stared at him for a few moments, hope, reassurance, doubt, and unhappiness all flashing through her gaze. Finally she said, "I still think you'd rather have someone else. If not Penny, then Diana. I don't think Diana Sheridan has slid down any stripper poles!"

Blake stared at her steadily. "Lenore, I do not want Diana Sheridan. Also, when you talk like that, you sound like you're five years old. Willow probably sounds more mature."

"Her name is Cornelia. That's what Jeffrey named her and that's what I'm going to call her."

"Well, that's very grown up of you, darling. You make me proud when you take an important stand like that—just gosh-darn proud!"

Lenore looked at him furiously. "I know you think all of this is very funny—"

"I don't think it's funny at all. I think it's pathetic. Lenore, you and I have been married for twelve years and during that whole time, you've thought I want a younger woman. You're four years older than I am. *Four* years. That's nothing! I know when we got married a few ignorant people made remarks about how I was marrying you for your money and to get my foot in the door of the company. Well, Len, I happened to be Jeff's best friend—my foot would have been in the door of the company if you and I had never said more than hello. And I've insisted we live on what *I* make—your money is tucked away in stocks, bonds, and trusts. I have never given you reason to distrust me—to think I'm using you, to think I'm having affairs—and I'm getting extremely tired of these scenes."

Some of the rigidity left Lenore's back, and her shoulders slumped, almost as if her confidence was draining away with her anger. "What about Jeffrey? Is he all right?"

"He was fine around midnight when we talked and he drank some bourbon before going to bed."

"So what you did to him in the park didn't hurt him?"

Blake took a deep breath, looking like someone desperately fighting for control. "I temporarily cut off his breath and he dropped to his knees. I didn't break his neck, Lenore. And I'll tell you what I did for him—I prevented him from hitting that woman, in which case he would have been arrested for assault. *He* knows that, Lenore. Why don't you?"

Someone tapped on the door. Lenore looked at Blake, who said, "I haven't called room service yet."

Almost immediately they heard Jeffrey say, "Hey, it's

me. I know you're awake. I can hear you next door. Arguing."

Lenore opened the door. Jeffrey strode into the room dressed in casual clothes, his thick hair still damp from the shower, his face ruddy from a recent shave. His eyelids looked heavy, though, and the eyes themselves slightly bloodshot.

"You didn't stay up and drink half the night, did you?" Blake asked.

"No. Just had trouble sleeping."

"So did Lenore. She's afraid I hurt you yesterday." Blake threw back the sheet. He wore only black pajama bottoms and a look of annoyance on his handsome face. "She's still angry with me, Jeff."

Lenore gazed up at her brother. "He threw you down—"

"He did not *throw* me down. I outweigh him by a good thirty pounds, Lenore." Jeffrey put his hands on his sister's shoulders. "I appreciate your concern for me, but as I told Blake last night, he did me a favor. I was out of control. I almost made a very big mistake."

"Wanting to punch Diana Sheridan? I'm not certain that would have been a mistake."

Jeffrey held Lenore out from him and looked into her eyes. "I thought you kind of liked the woman. You were having a picnic with her, for God's sake."

"I was trying to have a picnic with my niece."

"And to pump Diana for information about Penny," Blake added, searching for his robe in the tumble of clothes he'd left at the foot of the bed. "It's my guess Lenore's sudden dislike of Diana springs from the fact that Miss Sheridan wasn't as compliant as Lenore expected." Lenore looked at him in surprise, her color heightening. "Bingo." Blake laughed.

"Things started out all right." Lenore sounded defeated. "I was being witlessly charming, for which my husband says I have a knack. Suddenly the look in Diana's eyes changed. She knew exactly what I was doing. I don't know what happened. I've pulled off that trick with people a lot smarter than her."

"Maybe they *weren't* smarter than *she,*" Blake said.

Lenore gave him a deadly look and said to her brother. "He not only feels free to correct my grammar but to let us both know how *deeply* he admires Diana."

"I just said—"

"Lenore, you're tired and edgy," Jeffrey said kindly. "My God, who wouldn't be? You spent nearly two weeks with Mother, which would put me six feet under the ground. On your way home, I called with the news about Penny and insisted you and Blake come here with me. You've been doing your best to get through to Cornelia." He drew his sister to him and hugged her. "You're exhausted, kid. We all are."

"What are you suggesting?" Lenore asked. "That we go home?"

Jeffrey smiled at her. "For once I'm going to be unselfish and suggest that you and Blake go home."

Lenore blinked in surprise. "And just leave you here?"

"I'm not a teenager, Lenore. At forty-six I should be able to handle myself in a city the size of Huntington." His puffy eyelids lowered. "Besides, I'm not leaving here as long as Penny is still alive."

"And what about little Cornelia?" Lenore asked anxiously. "She's terrified of you. She won't go anywhere with you."

Jeffrey's expression hardened, "Maybe she won't go willingly, but she'll go. Van Etton and his niece act like she's theirs, but according to her birth certificate, she's *my* daughter. The law can't change that, and I have absolutely no intention of leaving her with those people much longer."

3

Diana looked with foreboding at the letter while the coffee dripped into the carafe. Somehow she knew she would need strong coffee to help her deal with whatever Nan had written. She didn't know why the letter filled her with dread, it just did. Finally she poured an insulated mug full of coffee, certain that a dainty china cupful wouldn't be enough. She sat down at the wide table in the big kitchen, tore open the envelope, and pulled out three pieces of yellow, lined legal-pad paper. Nan's letter began,

Dear Miss Sheridan,
    I thought you might not be home when I came by or you might not have time to talk to me so I decided to write everything down and leave a letter if I have to because I won't have another chance to tell you what I've *got* to tell you. I won't be back to work ever. I have to go away. Far, far away and I'm not even telling my mama where I'm going. Not for now at least.
    I'll just come out with it. I've been having an affair with Glen Austen since April. He said you're in love with him and he was afraid if he tried to break things off, you might try to kill yourself. That's why he said we had to keep our love affair a secret.

"Glen, you piece of slime!" Diana exclaimed in shock then hoped her voice hadn't been loud enough to wake Tyler. Having Glen even pretend Diana cared that much about him was infuriating. His having an affair with a student was unscrupulous, but taking advantage of one as unsophisticated as Nan was disgusting. She gritted her teeth and continued reading.

    I told Glen we couldn't protect your feelings forever. You'd have to know some time. That's when he told me about his other problem. His gambling. He said it started when he was in college and it just crept up on him. He tried to get ahold of himself but he just couldn't. He said now he's over a hundred thousand dollars in debt! He said he just barely scrapes by on his college salary and he gives every extra penny to a loan shark, but he's not making much progress on his bill and he's afraid they're going to come after him. He said he lived every day in terror and he loved me too much to drag me into that world. I felt so sorry for him. I worried all the time, trying to figure out how I could get money to help.

Well, I know you'll have trouble believing what came next. I sure did, but then I decided it must be a miracle. Mama had her heart attack in May and she made me come work for you. I know I'm not insulting you by saying I didn't like the job. I don't like being told what to do. Anyway, I did it to please Mama and because we needed the money. I met Penny. I could tell she didn't care for me much more than you did and I didn't like her. She was perky all the time. I hate perky people.

Anyway, after I'd spent a day at your house that seemed as long as three days, I was laying on my bed feeling like I just couldn't bear to go back to work. I was depressed so I dragged out all my magazines I've saved for years. Mama calls them trash, but I like reading about the movie stars and rich people and all the crazy things they do that I'll never get to do.

I'd read about six of my magazines when I finally came to one way over a year old. I saw an article about a millionaire's wife who was an ex-stripper and she'd just run away from him, took their little girl but no money. I wondered what kind of stupid woman would pull a trick like that. An ex-stripper married to a millionaire? She'd struck gold! Then I looked closer at the picture of the man and woman together. He was all right but nothing special—kind of old—but she was gorgeous. Long blond hair, real blue eyes, big diamond earrings, great makeup job. Then something about her struck me as familiar. It wasn't her hair. It sure wasn't her diamonds. I put my hand over her hair and something sort of chimed in my head. I took a pen and made her hair short and dark and I made her eyes dark, too, instead of blue. And guess who I was looking at? Penny Conley.

At first, I couldn't believe it. It was just way too weird to be true. I didn't think I was seeing straight, so I took the article to Glen. He looked at it in every direction and said yeah, it did sort of look like Penny, but not really. He said he just didn't see it. But he hadn't spent as much time looking at Penny as I had. And what about Willow? The article said the woman had taken their kid—a three-year-old girl. The article said the girl's name was Cornelia or something like that, but I figured she'd be about five by now, just like Willow. I didn't care what Glen said. I *knew* what I'd discovered without anybody's help!

Diana stopped reading and picked up her coffee mug with a trembling hand, her mind doing quick calculations. She and Glen had taken Penny to the country club in early May. She hadn't sensed tension between Glen and Penny—just fascination on Glen's part, which hadn't bothered her. Nan had come to work for Simon in late May, and soon after she must have seen the article about Penny and Jeffrey. She'd told Glen.

Something niggled at Diana's brain. A thought. A returning memory. Someone saying something . . . Clarice! Sometime, probably yesterday, Clarice had told her that Glen visited Penny in June. Had he gone to her home because he was romantically interested in her? Diana didn't think so. Penny would have told her, knowing Diana would not be hurt by Glen's wandering attention. No, Glen had gone to Penny's because he *did* believe Nan—he knew she'd managed to locate the missing wife of millionaire Jeffrey Cavanaugh. What did he say to Penny that night? Had he asked for money in return for his silence? No. Glen knew Penny didn't have any money. So what could

he have asked for? *Sex,* Diana thought. If Glen was unscrupulous enough to seduce poor, dim Nan Murphy, was
he capable of demanding sex from Penny in return for his
silence? Or had he played a same of vicious cat tormenting helpless mouse?

Diana didn't want to keep reading Nan's letter, but she
had no choice. She, not to mention the police, must know
everything Nan had to tell about Glen.

      I was mad because Glen didn't believe me—he
acted like I was just a kid imagining things. I knew I
was right, though, so I did more research on this millionaire Jeffrey Cavanaugh and found out about his
big business in New York, the address and everything. It took me until late July to get up my nerve,
but when I did, I typed a note to Mr. Cavanaugh
telling him I knew where his wife and kid were and
that I wasn't a crank or anything, I was real reliable. I
told him if he sent $150,000 to a post office box, I'd
see to it that he found his wife. I could've asked for
more money, but I didn't want to sound greedy like
an unreliable person would and also that was enough
money to get Glen out of trouble and have some left
over—I would've given Mama about $10,000. So I
rented a PO box just across the river in Ohio so he'd
think I was from Ohio, and I sent the note.

      I waited about three days before I told Glen.
He got so mad! He said I'd get caught and arrested. I
told him I did it for him and he got even madder and
said I'd drag him into it and he'd get arrested, too.
He hardly even spoke to me for a couple of weeks. I
kept checking the box regular, though, and there was
never anything—no money, not even a note from
Mr. Cavanaugh. And I was always real careful to
make sure no one was hanging around the post office
waiting to see who went to that box. I told Glen there
was no money and he didn't seem disappointed. He
said he was relieved that I'd just been dismissed as

some money grubber. That hurt my feelings, but I told him we'd get the money some how and that I would never, *never* let him go!

Then I started noticing him paying a lot of attention to Penny when he'd stop by your house. Whenever you were out of the room and she wasn't working, he'd be talking to her. Then he came by a couple of times when he *knew* you weren't home. I don't know if Simon noticed or not—he's pretty old. I got suspicious, though and I started following Glen whenever I could. And finally I saw him go to Penny's. I started to go bang on her door and tell her I knew what was what, but I knew Glen would get furious. Besides, that old bat you dragged home with you Friday night was peeking out her windows, taking in everything. Why can't she just watch television like a normal person? Anyway, that was Thursday night. And you know what happened Friday night. I had on my police scanner and I heard right off and I called Glen and told him about the explosion. He just hung up on me. He wouldn't talk to me the next day when he came to see you. He wouldn't talk to me Sunday, either.

Diana, I think he set that bomb. Either him or that Mr. Cavanaugh. Maybe I went to a post office too close to home. Maybe someone did follow me. I don't know, but I'm too smart to believe that bomb didn't have something to do with my scheme. I didn't like Penny, but I didn't want anything like *that* to happen to her. I'm real sorry about the bomb. I know this is going to come back to haunt me, though. I've got a feeling. Either Glen or that Mr. Cavanaugh will know I've figured out everything and one of them will want to kill me. So I have to leave. I'm not telling you where I'm going. I've learned my lesson about keeping my mouth shut.

Nanette Murphy (I'm going to change my name so don't try to track me down.)

Diana, shaking so hard she couldn't move, dropped the piece of paper on the table. With frightening clarity she suddenly remembered going to Nan's, hearing the music, entering the house, and finding the attic stairs pulled down. Her stomach turning, she recalled blood dripping onto her head, foolishly climbing the attic stairs, and looking at Nan's lifeless eyes. Then someone had kicked dirt into her face, put a foot on her chest and sent her crashing off the stairs onto the hard, uncarpeted floor.

"Oh my God," she murmured. Then she cried, "Tyler!"

CHAPTER SIXTEEN

1

Twenty minutes later Diana was sitting in the sunny kitchen with Tyler and Simon, both of whom had read Nan's letter. "Simon, Clarice told me about seeing Glen at Penny's and also about Nan watching them one night," Diana said when Simon had finished the letter. "The coincidence is that Nan dropped by yesterday afternoon and *she* wanted to tell me about her and Glen. She didn't get out much except that the affair had started in April. Then Blake came and I left her sitting in the kitchen. I knew she had more to tell me and I just left her sitting, waiting, while you and I spoke to Blake." She looked at Tyler. "He told us Penny was pregnant."

Tyler stared at Diana for a moment, obviously stunned. Finally he said desolately, "I had no idea Penny was pregnant."

"I'm sure it's Glen's child," Diana said flatly. The doctor thinks she's about two months along. Clarice said Glen first visited Penny's house two months ago. Thanks to Nan, Glen knew who Penny was. I think he was keeping his silence in return for sex."

"Dear God," Simon said in disgust.

"I believe that's why Penny never told me about seeing him," Diana went on. "I think his knowing about her past and the pregnancy were the reasons Penny was leaving. Anyway, Nan was here when Blake told us about the pregnancy. I heard Nan drop her glass. She was eavesdropping, as usual. I'm certain she didn't know Penny was pregnant. I don't know if she felt shock, or hurt, or both, but something sent her right out the back door.

"To make things worse, Glen called and I stupidly told him Nan had been here and that she wanted to tell me something important." Diana paused and took a breath. "I think Glen knew Nan had found out about him and Penny. He would have been humiliated if Nan told me about he was having an affair with Penny, but I believe he would have thought I'd keep it quiet for Penny's sake.

"But how would he have felt if Penny had told me about the sexual blackmail? You know Glen, Simon. Reputation is everything to him. He would know I'd tell you and you would be certain to inform the university administration, and worse still, if I thought he had anything to do with Penny's death, I'd go to the police. And finally he had Nan who wouldn't let him go and who knew too much." Diana looked into Simon's narrowed, dark green eyes. "If Glen placed that bomb in Penny's basement, just how far do you think he'd have to be pushed to get rid of Nan, too?"

2

"Who wants to get rid of Nan?"

Simon, Tyler, and Diana looked at Willow with various levels of shock and dismay. Simon was the first to recover. "Nan's mother is coming back to work next week and we'll all be happier. At least I will. How about you, Willow?"

"I'll be *lots* happier," the little girl said. She looked at Tyler and frowned. "How come you're still here?"

"Uh . . . because Diana asked me to stay."

Willow immediately looked wary. "Diana did? Why?"

Tyler took a deep breath, left his chair, and kneeled down beside the girl. "Your mommy didn't want you to talk to people about me. I was supposed to be a big secret. But the secret's out, kid." He grinned. "Everybody here knows all about me, and your mommy would be glad they do. She told you to call me Badge just like she did. My real name is Tyler, but Badge was her nickname for me because I'm a police officer. I live in New York City, where you used to live. Your mother and I are like brother and sister, and I consider you my niece, just like Simon does. We all love you and we're all here to protect you. But I'm the policeman, what they call an undercover cop, so I don't wear a uniform."

Willow reached out and touched his earlobe. "Is that why you have a little hole there? So you can wear an earring sometimes and look like a tough guy?"

"That's exactly the reason. How smart of you. But whether I wear a uniform or an earring, it's my job to keep bad people away from good people. I spent years training how to do it. I did it last night, didn't I?" Willow nodded. "And you weren't surprised. You said you knew I'd save you." He reached out and touched the end of her nose. "Somehow, you sensed that's my purpose in life—to protect pretty, smart little girls like you."

She giggled. "Mommy never told me, but I knew *she* thought you could do just about anything. That's how I knew you'd always protect me."

Afterward Willow seemed slightly buoyed by Tyler's presence, and managed to wolf down three doughnuts before Diana said, "I think we should save some for later, honey. You don't want to get a tummyache."

"Okay," Willow agreed affably. "Thank you for lettin' me eat doughnuts instead of scrambled eggs, Uncle Simon."

Simon beamed with pleasure. "You're most welcome, sweetheart, and I agree pastry tastes better than eggs, but we do need eggs sometimes."

"That's what Clarice says." Willow scooted off her

chair. "I'd better go upstairs and check on the cats. They might need me."

She'd barely exited the kitchen before the phone rang. Simon answered the kitchen extension. Diana could hear a woman's loud, excited voice. Simon remained calm, saying, "Yes . . . Of course . . . I understand perfectly— she must take care of her own health now. . . . I will be at the airport tomorrow to collect both of you. Just call me back and let me know what flight she'll be taking."

When he hung up, he looked at Diana. "That was Martha Murphy's sister. She says Martha is in quite a state today—who wouldn't be after just finding out their daughter has been brutally murdered? We let her know last night, Diana, before you remembered what had happened. Anyway, the doctor advises that she not fly back from Portland until tomorrow. Her sister is coming with her, thank goodness. The last thing the poor lady needs is to be alone. I will be picking them up at the airport. I won't have them out there trying to manage luggage and find a taxi." He looked down at the elegant satin robe Diana had bought him the previous Christmas. "And now I believe I should put on more mundane attire and leave you young people alone to talk."

After Simon left, Tyler looked at Diana and quirked an eyebrow. "Well, young person, what do you think?"

"I think I definitely need to give Nan's confession to the police when I go in to make my statement today." Tyler nodded. "And I'm now even more afraid of Jeffrey Cavanaugh than I was before. Tyler, thanks to Nan he might have known where Penny was for a couple of months before he showed up."

"Then why *didn't* he show up?"

"You sound like you're defending him."

"I would be the last person to defend Jeffrey Cavanaugh for anything. I hate him. But that's my emotional side. My logical side tells me something just doesn't fit." He sighed and ran a hand across his forehead then over his cheeks. He looked at her with slightly bloodshot eyes and smiled. "I had a perfectly lovely evening, Miss Sheridan. I've never enjoyed a night on a couch with a woman as much in my life."

Diana grinned. "I'm not certain how to take that statement."

"In the best possible way. But, my darlin' girl, I need a shower, and a shave, and a change of clothes. Then I'm going to escort you to police headquarters so you can give your statement."

"Oh, Tyler, I've imposed on you enough."

"Shush. You haven't even heard the rest of my plan. We aren't going alone. We are going to take Willow with us."

"To the police station? It will scare her."

"I'll bet it won't. She'll get a kick out of it. Then we're going to take her out to lunch and then maybe you can show me Marshall University. Simon taught there. You attended it, didn't you?"

"Of course. So did Penny."

"Then Willow will love going there. You can take pictures of her."

Diana frowned. "With everything going on, don't you think Willow might be safer staying here?"

"No, I don't. If Jeffrey or his relatives read the newspaper, they'll know Nan was murdered. I talked to a couple of the reporters and pleaded that your name be left out as the person who found her, but I don't have any influence around here. And if Jeffrey gets wind of what happened at this house last night, he'll be here banging down the door until he gets Willow. He might have some trouble actually taking her away after that scene in the park yesterday—in a way, he did us a kindness—but that child doesn't need to be frightened any more. She already looks pale and worn. She just had her appendix removed last week and now she's going through hell with no recovery time. She needs to get out of this house, Diana. She needs to have some fun. I know you tried with her yesterday, but it didn't work. So let's try today."

"But she'll be right out in the open, Tyler."

"That's the point. Jeffrey was in a rage yesterday or he wouldn't have almost hit you in public. He won't repeat the mistake. And who else is going to try *anything* in front of a hundred witnesses?" He lowered his voice. "Whereas if Willow stays here, she'll be under the protection of a man and woman in their seventies. Do you want them having to face down Jeffrey Cavanaugh?"

Diana took only a minute to make up her mind. "Come back in an hour, Tyler. Willow and I will be ready to go."

"That's my girl," he said, standing and drawing her up, pulling her against him and giving her a deep, lasting kiss. "That's the girl Penny said was the one for me."

3

Diana informed Simon of her and Tyler's plan, downplaying the suggestion that he and Clarice might not be adequate protection for Willow. If the man realized the implication, he didn't reveal himself. "I think that's just fine," he said heartily. "Clarice will fret over Willow all day, wanting to check on her every fifteen minutes, and the dear woman needs to rest. Yesterday was a bit much for her—the arthritis is causing her pain. And Willow could certainly use some fresh air and some fun. The three of you go and have a wonderful day."

Tyler left and Diana went upstairs to tell Willow the plans for the day. Her face brightened considerably at the thought of going on an adventure with Diana and Tyler, and she immediately selected a pair of bright-yellow shorts and a T-shirt with color blocks of yellow, white, and blue. After her bath, she requested that Diana pull up her long strawberry-blond hair into a ponytail with a yellow ribbon. They gazed at the finished product in the mirror.

"You look stunning, *mademoiselle*," Diana said. *"Trés elegante."*

To her surprise, Willow's smile faded. "What language was that?"

"French. I took it in college, but I don't speak very well. Why?"

"'Cause Mommy was tryin' to learn a different language. She called me mamadosel once, too, so it must have been French." She frowned. "And someone else said some words to me in that language, I think."

"Who was it?" Diana asked.

"I don't remember, but Mommy was tryin' to learn the language for him." Usually anything Penny liked intrigued Willow, but now the vague memory seemed to trouble her. "Mommy said some day I'd be able to talk in that language."

Diana turned the little girl around to face her. "It was a man who spoke the language to you?"

"Yeah."

"Do you know who?"

"I told you I don't remember."

"Was it when you lived in your house in Huntington?"

"Yeah, but it was a long time ago. Maybe when we just moved here."

"It wasn't Badge?"

"Tyler," Willow corrected. "We're s'posed to call him Tyler, remember? And it wasn't him." Willow's earlier brightness seemed to diminish. "Maybe I just dreamed it or I heard it on TV." She rubbed her forehead. "I think I'm gettin' a headache."

"Why don't you sit on your bed and watch television while I get ready?" Diana suggested briskly. "If you still have a headache when I'm finished, I'll give you a pill for it." *Get Willow's mind off this subject,* Diana thought. Something about this memory disturbs her. "Oh, honey, don't let me forget to take back the clothes the nice nurse at the hospital loaned you to wear home. I washed the dress and the underwear, and the nurse's little girl might want to wear those clothes this week. I can't forget the sandals she loaned you, too."

"Do we have to stay at the hospital?" Willow asked cautiously.

"No. You don't even have to go inside. I'll just drop off the clothes at the front desk."

Willow looked relieved to know she didn't have to venture inside the hospital walls. *No wonder,* Diana thought. She probably remembered only the sound of firecrackers going off in a metal waste can and the ensuing pandemonium.

Diana left Willow discussing her plans for the day with the cats, consoling them for not going along by telling them the streets of Huntington would be *really* hot and crowded and someone would be sure to step on Romeo. Smiling as she stepped into a hot shower, Diana imagined the two cats sightseeing like tourists.

Lost in thought, she put on too much shampoo and spent five minutes rinsing it out of her hair and another five trying to flush it from her stinging right eye. Finally she emerged from the shower to blow-dry her thick golden-brown locks, so like her mother's, then use a flat iron to smooth the unruly curls.

Diana certainly didn't feel like wearing dark, heavy jeans, so she chose a pair of white cotton-sateen slacks that showed off her flat abdomen, and a lavender, pale-green, and blue tank top to wear beneath a delicate, white georgette blouse. She then swept some light-green shadow on her eyelids, a gold-apricot blush on her cheeks, sheer apricot lip gloss, and a coating of black mascara, and finished by pulling back the sides of her hair and fastening them with two faux-pearl combs.

"What do you think?" she asked, stepping into Willow's room and twirling.

Willow quickly slid off the bed. "Gosh, Diana, you look be-*u*-ti-ful!" she exclaimed. "I can't wait till I get to wear high heels like you."

"After you've spent a day in high heels, you might change your mind," Diana said, looking down at her strappy sandals with the three-inch cork heels.

"And your toenails are painted pink!" Willow laughed in glee. "Mommy's are always painted pink or red. *Always!*"

"Then we'll paint yours pink tonight. Would you like that?"

"Oh yes." Willow sighed. "I just can't wait to be grown up."

"Don't wish away your time, honey" Diana said softly. "Being grown up isn't always easy or fun."

Willow looked at her solemnly. "Neither is bein' a kid, Diana."

4

"Are you sure they won't put us in jail, Badge—I mean Tyler?" Willow asked as they pulled up in front of the building housing the Detective Bureau of the Cabell County Sheriff's Department. "I can't think of anything I've done wrong, but maybe they have a file on me."

"A file?" Tyler asked.

"Yeah. On TV the cops always have files on people."

Tyler and Diana both tried not to grin. "I think most of those people are older than five, Willow. You and I are just going in to look around while Diana talks to a detective."

Willow looked at Diana and warned urgently, "Don't say anything incinerating."

Tyler had to turn his head so Willow wouldn't see him laughing, but Diana managed to keep a straight face. "I'm glad you reminded me, Willow. You certainly must watch a lot of police shows."

"I do. I might want to be a detective."

"I thought you wanted to be a photographer like me. Or sing in a rock group."

"I can do all those things," Willow said confidently. "Tyler can help me be a cop and you can help me be a picture-taker. I'll be a rock singer at night." She drew a deep breath. "Well, let's get this over with so we can go have lunch."

Inside the building, Tyler told Diana she would be talking to a Detective Silver. "Tell her everything you know. Oh, and be careful not to incriminate *or* incinerate yourself."

"I'll try, but I'm so nervous, I'm not making any promises about the latter. I might just spontaneously combust at any moment."

Detective Miriam Silver—slim, fortyish, with silver threads in her short black hair, and lively hazel eyes— immediately put Diana at her ease.

"So you're Diana Sheridan, the photographer," Detective Silver said, smiling as she leaned toward Diana who sat beside her cluttered desk in a large room with several other detectives' desks. "My husband and I saw a display of your work in the Huntington Museum of Art in February. We both fell in love with a photograph called, 'Willow in the Wind.' "

"It's one of my favorites," Diana said, thinking of the early-November day when she'd been taking shots of the red, gold, and bronze leaves of the woods near Simon's house. Suddenly Willow had wandered into the shot holding a yellow chrysanthemum. A gentle breeze had blown up, and Willow tilted back her head and closed her eyes, her profile perfect, her hair seeming to float against the background of vivid leaves. Diana had immediately shot the frontlit scene, firing off several frames.

When she'd shown the photo to Penny, she had been delighted at first. Then she'd asked Diana not to display it in any of the big cities like New York. Not understanding the problem at the time but still wanting to please Penny, Diana had said she'd put it only in her local showing at the museum in February. After the showing, Diana had given the framed photo to Penny, who had thrown her arms around Diana and cried. *I should have known then something was wrong,* Diana thought. *I should have known when she acted so nervous about the photo being shown anywhere except locally.*

"Are you all right?" Detective Silver asked.

"Yes. I was just remembering when I took the picture. The little girl's mother, Penny Conley, or Cavanaugh, didn't want me to show it in New York. Of course, that's where her husband and his sister and friends live. The child's real name is Cornelia, but Penny called her Willow. Willow loved the book *Wind in the Willows,* so I used it to come up with the title for the photo."

"Beautiful photo, beautiful title, beautiful little girl." Without making a fuss, Detective Silver handed Diana a tissue.

Diana dabbed at her eyes. "I've never been much of a crier, but I feel like all I've done for the last few days is cry or scream." She blew her nose. "I'm sorry."

"Don't be. Crying is a release. Besides, you didn't blow your nose on someone's embroidered handkerchiefs—the kind I don't even own." Diana laughed. "Willow was the little girl somebody tried to shoot at your house last night."

"Yes. She's been staying with us ever since the house explosion. Her mother is in the burn unit. Willow had nowhere else to go. Then the police discovered Penny is the runaway wife of Jeffrey Cavanaugh of New York City, and Willow is his daughter. Jeffrey and his sister, Lenore, and brother-in-law, Blake Wentworth, arrived Saturday." Diana was certain Detective Silver already knew this, but telling it helped her lead into what frightened her the most. "Jeffrey Cavanaugh wanted to take Willow then, but she had a fit. She was *terrified* of him, and he made things even worse yesterday when Willow, Lenore, and I were trying to have a picnic and he arrived, shouting at me that I'd kept information from him. He almost hit me."

"Yes, we got a call from Tyler Raines about that incident. He phoned from the park." Diana almost smiled. Somehow, she'd *known* he'd made that call. "Now what went on last night, Ms. Sheridan?"

"I'd gone out Sunday evening. Something happened. Later, I couldn't have told you what happened because when I woke up in the hospital, I had a concussion and no short-term memory. I remembered that I'd gone to the home of our temporary housekeeper, Nan Murphy. I found her in the attic, murdered. Her head looked as if it had been nearly severed. . . ." Abruptly Diana's voice began to shake. Detective Silver reached over and touched her hand. Diana took a breath. "Whoever had killed Nan was still in the attic. He kicked dirt into my eyes so I didn't get a look at him. Then he pushed me down the attic steps.

"I returned home remembering nothing about the whole thing," Diana went on. "Then about two in the morning, our cats woke me up. Well, actually I think a sound had begun to wake me before the cats did, but I'm still fuzzy on that point. I kept thinking I heard raindrops, but it wasn't raining. I rushed to Willow's room. She was gone. Her window was up. She never sleeps with a window open, so I knew something was wrong.

"I went outside. I thought I saw Willow running on the edge of the woods, and went after her. As soon as I'd gotten her, someone started shooting at us. I pushed her to the ground and tried to cover her with my body. I heard the shots coming closer and I could tell someone was standing almost directly over us. I thought we'd be dead in less than a minute. I heard another shot and shouting. Lights from the house came on, I heard yet another shot and someone running. . . . It just all went so fast. Then I heard Tyler Raines's voice telling Willow and me we were safe. He also told me he was a New York City detective and Penny's foster brother. He helped her disappear."

Silver nodded. "I know. Of course, there will be some consequences for his part in creating Penny Cavanaugh's false identity."

"What kind of consequences?" Diana asked alarmed.

"The New York authorities will have to decide that. He

wasn't helping a criminal escape. He has an otherwise spotless record. He's even been decorated for bravery."

"He didn't tell me about being decorated for bravery." Diana smiled. "Clarice will be delighted."

"That would be Clarice Hanson?"

"Yes. She's been living with my great-uncle and me since her house was damaged by the explosion. She helps us take care of Willow."

"That's nice. I'm sure she enjoys it." Detective Silver gave her an absent smile then asked, "Ms. Sheridan, why did you go to Nan Murphy's house?"

"Nan had come by earlier in the day. She said she had something important to tell me about Penny. I thought I already knew what that was. As I'm certain you know, Nan was nineteen and a student at Marshall last year. She was in Glen Austen's history class. I've been seeing Glen for about seven months. Nan told me she and Glen began an affair in April."

"Were you upset about this?"

"I was upset that a thirty-five-year-old college professor was taking advantage of a nineteen-year-old student. I know student-professor affairs are rampant, but I thought Glen was too—oh, I don't know—noble. I was not hurt, though."

"Really? You found out a man with whom you've had a relationship for a year has been sexually involved with a student and you weren't hurt?"

"No, I was not." Diana leaned a bit closer to Detective Silver, sensing other people close by might be listening. "I started seeing Glen in January, not a year ago. I was never serious about him. Our relationship was not even sexual, which may be why he turned to someone else. I could have understood that. If he'd been involved with a woman, not a teenager, I probably would have been relieved. I've been trying to think of ways to gracefully break off our relationship because I live with my great-uncle and he and Glen are friends. Or were friends."

"So you've told your uncle about Glen and Nan?"

"Actually Clarice did. She had seen a man come to Penny's house a few times—a man Penny didn't seem happy to see. Clarice had no idea the man was my 'admirer,' as she put it, until he came by Uncle Simon's house and she saw him there. Anyway, Nan and I talked in the kitchen. She told me about her and Glen.

"She had more to say but Blake Wentworth stopped by. He said he only had a few minutes and he needed to see me and I excused myself from Nan. He wanted to apologize for the way his brother-in-law had treated me in the park. Then he added that while Jeffrey Cavanaugh had been with Penny earlier in the day, the doctor had told him Penny was pregnant. I heard a glass shatter in the kitchen. When I ran in, I saw Nan was in her car, leaving. I went to her house that night to find out what she had wanted to tell me."

Detective Silver's dark eyebrows drew together. "Do you think Nan knew Penny was pregnant?"

"No, I don't. I believe she overheard Blake telling Simon and me. That's when she dropped her glass in surprise."

"I see. So what she wanted to tell you was not that Penny was pregnant."

"I don't think so."

"You know that her house showed signs she was leaving?"

"I noticed a suitcase out that night. I think she'd brought it down from the attic."

"Do you believe she was leaving because of Mr. Austen? Do you think she didn't want to be around him when she was certain he'd been having an affair with Penny?"

"I believe she wanted to get away from him. I don't think it was because of the pregnancy, though. She'd already made her plans before she found out Penny was pregnant." Diana reached in her bag and pulled out the letter Nan had left for her. "This morning I found this message for me. In it she says she's writing down what she wants to tell me because she thinks I might not be home when she comes by, or I might not have time to hear her whole story."

Diana took a deep breath. "Anyway, Detective Silver, Nan tells a story I could hardly believe at first. I still have trouble believing it or thinking of how many consequences her actions could have had. Of course I want to turn it over as evidence, but I'd like for you to read it right now." She handed the letter over.

Diana sat very still at first. Then she sorted through her tote bag, looking for nothing in particular. Nan's confession held Detective Silver's complete concentration, so Diana finally stood up and walked over to the window. "Would you like a cup of coffee?" Detective Silver asked. Diana said yes, and the woman nodded to an automatic coffeemaker with Styrofoam cups beside it along with packets of artificial sweetener and nondairy creamer. Diana fixed herself a cup, glad that the pot had just finished brewing, and immediately took a gulp, burning her tongue and swearing. It seemed as if everyone in the room looked up at her, and blushing like a young girl, she gushed an apology, feeling even more conspicuous. She walked back to her chair and sat down, determined not to make another sound.

Detective Silver looked up. "Well, from everything I've heard about Nan Murphy, this comes as quite a surprise. I didn't think she was a take-action kind of girl."

"She was a girl madly in love," Diana said. "Emphasis on *mad*. I think she'd taken leave of her senses."

"Or this wasn't her plan at all. It was Glen Austen's."

"Maybe it was. Maybe Nan saw a plan gone wrong and decided to blame it on someone else. Maybe the whole thing is a lie to make Glen look as bad as possible." Diana set down her cup of steaming coffee. "But if she isn't lying, Jeffrey Cavanaugh could have learned the whereabouts of his wife and daughter weeks ago."

"Then why didn't he do something about it?"

"Maybe he did. How do we know he didn't plant the

bomb in Penny's basement? He's been around construction all of his life. I'm sure he knows how to build a simple bomb."

Detective Silver stared at her for a moment then asked sternly, "Are you a parent?"

"You know I'm not."

"Because if you *were,* you'd understand how unlikely it would be for Cavanaugh to blow up a house with his daughter inside. His five-year-old child. I would die a thousand deaths before I'd hurt one of my children."

Diana knew that Silver was smashing her idea from pure reflex. She was not only putting Diana in her place, she was also telling her what it meant to be a parent. The woman's breath had quickened and her color rose.

Diana leaned back in her chair. "Detective, I know you're good at your job whereas I have no experience with murder cases, but I believe you're being a bit self-righteous. You seem to think that because I don't have a child of my own, I can't possibly know how much a parent can love a child. I believe I can. I believe I love Willow as if she were my own. And you're also comparing yourself to Jeffrey Cavanaugh just because you're both parents.

"Last night I heard the story of a thirteen-year-old boy whose crack-addicted parents simply moved one day when he was in school," Diana continued. "They left him alone to fend for himself on the streets. Would you do that? No. But they were parents and *they* did. So just because *you* would 'die a thousand deaths' before you'd hurt one of your children doesn't mean Cavanaugh feels the same way. Not all parents are alike, Detective Silver."

The woman had crossed her arms over her chest, her eyes narrowing, her face hardening as Diana talked. Dislike—even hostility—had flared in her hazel eyes. But in the minute of silence after Diana stopped talking, the hardness softened, the hostility lessened. Finally she looked down at some papers on her desk, then back up at Diana. "All right, Ms. Sheridan, you've made your point.

And much as I hate to admit I can be wrong"—a tiny smile here—"it's a good point."

"I'm sorry I offended you."

"I'm getting over it, but if you really want to get in my good graces again, you'll let me take a sip of that coffee you're not drinking." Diana smiled and nodded. Miriam Silver took a good-sized drink of the steaming coffee without the slightest indication of pain. "For now, I only want to go over two things with you. Both are pieces of evidence. One was found last night and is already stored. It's a white robe—something like a choir robe—made out of a heavy cotton-polyester blend. We found a few hairs on it, but of course, they must be tested for DNA, which doesn't happen overnight like it does on television. However, we did identify an iridescent white paint—the kind that glows when you shine a black light on it."

"The angel!" Diana exclaimed, and Detective Silver tilted her head. "Willow was lured outside the house by what she thought was her guardian angel. She said it wore a white robe and a light shined on its face and the face *glowed*. Those are her exact words."

"Someone put iridescent white paint on their face and held up a black light to it," Detective Silver said. "You can buy miniature black lights only five or six inches long. Was this person a man or a woman?"

"Willow got rather huffy about that question. She said angels aren't boys or girls—they're just angels."

"She said nothing about the way the angel moved? Its voice?"

"It ran. It called for her to follow. But she wasn't looking for male strides versus female. The same with voices. She's five."

"And when this *angel* got closer to you?"

"I saw nothing before the *angel* started shooting at us. When the first bullet rang out, I pushed Willow to the ground."

Detective Silver drained the coffee cup, and Diana briefly wondered if the inside of the woman's mouth was heat resistant. She tossed away the Styrofoam cup then picked up a plastic bag. "I know you have a bee in your bonnet about Jeffrey Cavanaugh, but our men were back searching the woods beyond your house early this morning. They found this."

She handed Diana a small, sealed plastic bag. Inside was a stainless steel, curb link bracelet with a foldover clasp. The bracelet bore a raised red emblem with a silver caduceus in the middle. A medical ID bracelet. Diana maneuvered the bracelet in the bag until she could see the engraved lettering: GLEN AUSTEN PENICILLIN

He'd told her that he'd worn the bracelet every day since a penicillin reaction nearly killed him when he was fifteen.

CHAPTER SEVENTEEN

1

"Gosh, I love Heritage Village!" Willow exclaimed as the three of them—Tyler and Diana each holding one of her hands—ambled into the plaza on Veterans Memorial Boulevard across from the Riverfront Park. "I haven't been here for years!"

Diana smiled. "You were here two months ago with your mother and me."

"Yeah, well it *seems* like years," Willow maintained. "Tyler, did you ever come here with Mommy?"

"No. I'm afraid when I came to visit we didn't do much sightseeing. Will you do the honors of being our tour guide, Diana?"

"Hmmm? Oh, sure." Diana had left the Detective Bureau shaken. Although she'd marched in with Nan's damning evidence against Glen in her hand, seeing his bracelet had made her picture him standing over her and Willow in the bizarre white robe, his face painted white, ready to shoot them to death. Obviously he had no reason to kill Willow. He had thrown pebbles against Willow's window to wake her up, then thrown more pebbles against Diana's window. After all, he couldn't have known the cats would awaken her. He'd assumed that once awake, she would check on Willow, and finding her missing, come in search of her. Diana had been Glen's real target either because he thought she'd seen him at Nan's, or because he didn't want her telling anybody that he'd been involved in the scheme to get money from Jeffrey Cavanaugh, or maybe both. Willow would have been merely collateral damage.

"Ma'am," Tyler said loudly, "I'm afraid we're not getting our money's worth. You're very pretty but you're a lousy tour guide."

"Oh! I'm sorry." Diana felt flustered, as if she'd really been leading a whole group of tourists. She had to put this morning's interview with Detective Silver out of her mind. "I'm afraid being with the two of you is so overwhelming, I just don't know where to start."

"She has stage fright," Willow said sagely to Tyler. "That's when you get scared and can't talk in front of people. Clarice told me all about it. She said it happened to her in a church play when she was a little girl. That must have been a *long* time ago."

Tyler grinned. "Yes, well, let's not remind her of exactly *how* long ago it was." He looked understandingly at Diana, as if he knew what preoccupied her thoughts. "Perhaps you might begin by telling us the history of this place, ma'am."

"As you wish," Diana said brightly. "You probably know that the founder of our city was Collis P. Huntington. He bought the Chesapeake and Ohio Railroad and laid the railroad from Richmond, Virginia, to the Ohio River. Huntington became a transfer point between the riverboats and the railway lines."

Willow pulled her hands free and clapped. "That was good, Diana! What's it mean?"

Both Tyler and Diana burst into laughter. "It means the train brought much more business to the city and many people came here and Huntington got *lots* bigger and more important. The importance of the railroad to this city is demonstrated by"—she waved her hand grandly—"the renovated railway station, an authentic locomotive, as well as a renovated Pullman Car."

The three of them toured the attractions, Willow asking politely why people would want to drag along in a train when they could fly in a jet and go way up in the clouds. Finally, they visited Huntington's first bank, built in 1873. Diana told Willow that Jesse James supposedly had robbed the bank in 1875. This brought on a barrage of questions for Tyler about Jesse James, the James Gang, and if Tyler had ever chased them.

At one o'clock, Tyler announced he might keel over from heat and starvation. They let Willow choose the restaurant—The Boston Beanery Restaurant and Tavern—and walked into the cool, antique ambience. They bypassed the long bar and went into the subdued second room. Diana had always favored the thick dark-green carpet, the brick walls, and especially the tin-plated, embossed panels on the ceiling. She ordered a large salad with grilled chicken while Tyler and Willow ordered cheeseburgers. "I warn you," Diana said. "Those aren't regular-sized cheeseburgers." Both assured her they could eat every bite.

"What was the name of the policeman who talked to you?" Willow finally asked.

"I gave my statement to a lady detective named Miriam Silver."

"A *lady* detective," Willow said in awe. "Was she nice?"

"Very. And smart. She told me she has children."

"Wow. They let you be a detective when you have kids?"

"I hope so," Tyler said, giving Diana a look full of meaning. "I'm a detective and I want to have kids some day."

"You have me." Willow's voice sounded half statement, half plea.

"Well, of course, but you're not considered my daughter, honey. Some people would say you're my niece."

Willow looked down, her smile flagging. "People will say I'm the Bad Man's kid and make me go with him. I *know* it."

Willow's lower lip trembled. Tyler looked at Diana helplessly. Diana could think of nothing both comforting and true to say, so she decided to pursue the subject. "Willow, who taught you to call Jeffrey Cavanaugh the Bad Man?"

"Mommy."

"Oh. Did she show you a picture of him?"

"Yeah. Just one picture but a lot of times. She said I should never go anywhere with him, but if someone *made* me go with him, I shouldn't talk to him because he's *so* bad. She said I should be afraid of him."

"Willow, did the man in the picture ever hurt you?" Diana asked. "Did he ever hit you or smack you or do things to you that you didn't like?"

Willow looked confused. "Things like what?"

"Oh, touch you or . . ." Diana was surprised by her embarrassment. "Did he just make you uncomfortable?"

"Diana," Tyler said in an almost-warning voice while Willow scrunched up her face in deep thought.

Finally Willow said, "I don't think he did anything. I don't remember."

"Did he hit your mommy?"

"Well . . . maybe he did, but I don't remember about that, either. How come you're askin' me all these questions?"

"I just wondered why your mommy thinks that man is bad."

"What about how he acted in the park?" Willow asked defensively. "He was gonna hit you. Besides, Mommy knows when people are bad. She wouldn't tell me he was bad if he wasn't."

Their glasses of iced tea arrived, breaking the tension of the moment. Tyler made a great production of asking Willow if her tea was sweet enough, cold enough, and if she had enough lemon, while he kept flashing mildly critical glances at Diana. She wished she hadn't asked Willow about her father, but she'd done so without thought, or so it seemed. Maybe she'd been thinking about the questions ever since she'd left Detective Silver.

2

"As your tour guide, may I present Marshall University," Diana announced. "Willow, this is where Uncle Simon taught, where I went to college, and where your mommy took classes last year. The university was first a college founded in 1837 and named for Chief Justice John Marshall. You are standing in front of its first building, known as Old Main. If you will kindly pose, I would like to take a picture of you."

Willow, always a willing subject, gave Diana a demure pose in front of the three-story building with its two gothic-inspired towers and the bust of John Marshall. She then insisted that Diana take another shot that "makes me look like I go to school here like you and Mommy did." This required Willow to carry a steno notebook that Diana found in the depths of her tote bag, and wear a look of frowning concentration as she climbed the steps to the building's entrance. Diana didn't have the heart to tell her that administrative offices now filled Old Main rather than classrooms.

"You're quite the actress," Tyler said after the photo shoot. "You looked just like a teenage girl going in to take a *very* hard test."

"Thank you," Willow answered modestly. "I just copied how Mommy looked whenever she was gonna have a test. She always worried."

"And she always did well." Diana smiled. "I wish she could have come here full-time instead of just taking one class a semester."

"But then she wouldn't have worked for Uncle Simon

and I woulda never got to meet him and you and Romeo and Christabel. That would have been a tragedy," Willow pronounced solemnly.

Diana smiled. "It would certainly have been a tragedy for the four of us if we hadn't met you and your Mommy." Diana felt the damnable tears rising in her eyes again and said, "Let's go explore some more of the campus."

An oddly luminous aqua sky stretched clear and low beyond them, and Diana couldn't resist taking more pictures than she'd intended. She did not ignore Willow and Tyler, though. She caught both of them in front of the graceful Drinko library. She told them that because of the prominence of glass used in its architecture, at night the building glowed with light from top to bottom.

Tyler suggested they go to the student center that Penny had described to him. Willow agreed, saying that her mother had promised to show it to her when Penny went back to school. Tyler and Diana exchanged looks, Diana swallowing hard knowing that Penny would not be starting school in two weeks. When they entered, Willow's eyes widened as they traveled around the large central lounge. Diana told her the center also contained a cafeteria and three dining rooms.

A few students were already visiting the bookstore in the student center, and Willow suddenly turned shy when a beautiful young student with long black hair and torn jeans said, "Oh, my, what a pretty little girl! You two must be proud of her!"

Tyler merely said, "We sure are," but both Willow and Diana blushed, Willow seeming to realize for the first time that she was only five, not eighteen, and Diana suddenly aware that they did look like a family.

Diana hurried them down to the basement to see the pool tables—where Tyler challenged Diana to a game she unfortunately didn't play—the table tennis tables, the lounge, and the large-screen television. The tables weren't in use, but Diana knew that would change in a couple of weeks.

When they emerged from the campus side of the student center, Willow pointed to the large copper-patina fountain. "How come they put a fountain there?" she asked.

"This is the Memorial Student Center Plaza," Diana answered. "They built the entire student center to commemorate the football team who died in a plane crash in November 1970."

"The whole football team?" Willow gasped.

"Yes. Along with coaches and supporters of the team and the crew. The crash killed all seventy-five people aboard the plane."

Tyler shook his head. "From the time I was old enough to get interested in football, I read about that crash. As I remember, the plane coming in for a landing hit some treetops about a mile away from the airport. They were so close to being safe."

"Did you know anybody on the plane?" Willow asked Diana.

"No. It happened before I was born. Uncle Simon knew a few people, though. My grandmother told me he was very sad when it happened."

"You see the points at the top of the fountain?" Diana asked Willow. Willow nodded. "Each of the points represents a life lost on the plane."

"Oh, my," Willow said mournfully.

"After they built the student center and installed the fountain, they constructed the amphitheater and laid bricks instead of concrete, for the floor of the plaza. I think it's a beautiful memorial," Diana said.

Willow turned to Diana. "Will you take a picture of Tyler and me in front of the fountain?"

Diana smiled. "I would be most pleased to oblige."

"Does oblige mean 'yes'?" Willow asked. Diana nodded. "Great. Then Tyler and me will have a picture of us at Marshall to give to Mommy when she gets well."

In their first shots by the fountain, both Willow and Tyler looked almost woebegone. Diana stopped snapping pictures and said, "It's all right to smile, you two. A picture of you both smiling in front of the fountain would be much nicer."

At first both their smiles and postures looked stiff. When Diana once again called for some joy to match the dancing, glittering water behind them, Tyler lifted Willow up to his shoulder and the pose seemed to do the trick. Diana managed to get several shots of the two looking cheerful, and one shot of them looking downright ecstatic.

"That last one was a winner," she told them. "In the first ones you both looked like your faces would crack if you smiled."

"We professional models have to get in the mood, Diana," Tyler told her haughtily. "We can't just turn the charisma on and off like a light switch. We're a temperamental bunch."

"That's why I usually do landscapes, smart alec."

The whole time they'd been touring the campus, Diana had been on the lookout for Glen. She knew that the police had not found his medical ID bracelet until this morning, and she didn't think that would warrant more than a questioning from them. She hadn't given Nan's confession to Detective Silver until nearly three hours ago. Would the police act on that immediately? After all, it was just Nan's word against Glen's. Still, Diana didn't want to run into him on campus. Autumn classes hadn't started yet but they would in two weeks, and by this time, professors who'd chosen not to teach summer classes often began readying their offices and class materials for the next semester.

Professors such as Glen, who was fanatically organized. Many people admired his stringent order, but Diana had always thought it resulted from his lack of self-confidence. If he didn't have everything planned to the last degree, he was lost. Glen could not speak or act extemporaneously. He lived by routines, schedules, habits, and almost fanatical preparation.

Thinking of Glen gave Diana a sudden, uncanny desire to return home. She didn't want to scare Willow, though. In a light voice, she said, "I don't know about you two, but I'm getting a little tired."

"Oh, my God!" Tyler burst out. "Your head! Your hip! You're supposed to be resting and I've dragged you all over the city. Doctor Evans would kill me."

Diana laughed. "I'd hardly say we've been all over the city and I don't believe Doctor. Evans would kill *anybody*. I've really enjoyed today. I needed to get out in the fresh air and have some fun, and so did Willow. But I think I have reached my limit. Do you mind if we go home now, Willow?"

"Oh, no. You need your rest, dear," she said, sounding remarkably like Clarice. "We can come back and see the rest of Marshall next week. Does your head hurt real bad?"

"Not yet, but my hip hurts some. And so do my feet." She held out a high-heeled foot. "I told you what this kind of shoe will do to you!"

They were all laughing when someone shouted, "Diana? Diana Sheridan?"

Diana looked up. A colleague of Glen's strode across the plaza toward them. She desperately tried to come up with his name but the best she could do was Frederick. He stopped in front of them, looking at Diana inquiringly.

"Uh, yes, I'm Diana Sheridan. Frederick, isn't it?"

"Can't believe you remembered. I wasn't sure at first it was you when I saw you with a little girl and this great strapping man by your side instead of Glen." Frederick was short, round, jowly. "You *are* still dating Glen, aren't you, Diana?"

"Well—"

"Sure you are. He told me you were going to some shindig at the country club over the weekend. I'm a bit shaken about . . . well, have you seen Glen today?"

"No, I haven't."

"Talked to him on the phone?"

"No. Is something wrong?"

Frederick's expression went from carefully bland to distressed. "Is it all right to talk in front of the little girl?"

Without waiting for an answer, Frederick ploughed on. "The history department had a faculty meeting scheduled for one o'clock. Glen didn't show up. In the five years he's been here, this is a first. He didn't even call in an excuse."

"Maybe he forgot the meeting," Tyler said.

Frederick looked at him as if he were an intruder. "And you are?"

"Tyler Raines. Good friend of Glen's."

Willow looked up at Tyler in surprise, but Frederick didn't notice. "Oh. He's never mentioned you." Frederick dismissed Tyler with a flick of his gaze. "Anyway, Diana, when Glen didn't show up at the meeting, the head of the department asked one of us to check his office. Glen can get caught up in all of his filing and note-making and— well, you know Glen. I went and knocked on the door. No answer and the door was unlocked. Naturally, I opened it and—"

All three of them leaned toward the round man. "And what?" Tyler finally demanded.

"The office has been trashed. Not just messed up. *Trashed*."

"Good heavens!" Diana exclaimed. "Did vandals damage other offices?"

"No. At least not in our department. We all checked. Just *Glen's* office!" Frederick shook his head. "The cushion on his desk chair had been slashed, someone had carved on the desk, and every book had been tossed from the bookcases. That photo you gave him of the cable-suspension bridge downtown with the sunset behind it was covered with ink. Ink was splattered everywhere. Ink! Who uses jars of ink these days?"

"How could someone have gotten in?" Diana asked, shocked. "He keeps the office locked."

"That's just one of the odd things about this. The lock wasn't broken. Someone had a key. And the damage must have been done in the night otherwise the secretary would have heard. We tried calling Glen to tell him about the office but we only got the answering machine."

"Have you called the police?" Tyler asked.

"Of *course.*" Frederick's tone indicated Tyler must be an imbecile. "I was just going back to the building to see if they've come, yet."

"Maybe it would be best to stay out of their way," Tyler said.

Frederick ignored him. "Oh, Diana, there was one more thing. Well, really two." He paused, making everyone wait in suspense once again. "Pictures of two girls were flung all over the place. One had light-brown hair, not so pretty—I think she's a student. The other had short dark hair and she was a real looker. Oh, sorry Diana," he said absently. "They were Polaroid shots, but there must have been at least twenty pictures of each girl—different poses."

"You handled the pictures," Tyler said with disdain. "Didn't you think you might be destroying evidence?"

"There's more than enough evidence in that office to satisfy the police," Frederick returned, offended. "And finally, Diana, if you can believe it, handwriting had been spray-painted in red on the wall. It said, 'They destroyed my life.' "

CHAPTER EIGHTEEN

1

Diana expected a barrage of questions from Willow after Frederick's badly timed description of the damage inflicted on Glen's office. Of course, they would not have wanted Willow to hear about it, but he hadn't given Diana a chance to say she'd rather talk to him alone. Frederick was so full of the news he'd simply told everything he knew, as unstoppable as a tidal wave. And what bothered Diana most was that he'd seemed more gleeful than upset.

After hearing about Glen's office and the inability of anyone to reach him, they'd headed back for the car. Diana wished she'd started complaining about pain ten minutes earlier and they'd completely missed Frederick, but she couldn't change what had happened. She could only deal with its aftermath.

She looked back at Willow, sitting quietly in the backseat with her seat belt fastened around her. Her earlier joy had vanished. Her face had turned tight and pale. She looked down at a blue-and-white crystal stretch bracelet that Diana had bought for her, turning it slowly on her small wrist.

"Did you have fun today?" Diana asked cheerfully.

Willow looked up. "Yeah. Lots. Thank you for taking me."

Her voice held no vibrancy, no hint of little-girl happiness. Diana tried again. "I can't wait to develop the pictures I took of you. I'm going to develop them even before I develop the ones for that awful man at the tourism center I went to last week. If he calls up saying he wants his pictures right *now,* I'll tell him he has to wait until I develop my pictures of the prettiest girl in the world."

"But I'm not," Willow said desolately. "Mommy and you are the prettiest girls in the world." She looked up with fearful eyes. "Do you think somebody hurt Glen like somebody hurt Mommy?"

"No. I think somebody tore up his office—maybe a student who was mad about the grade he gave them."

"Do bad grades ruin your life? That man said somebody wrote on the wall somethin' about his life gettin' ruined."

Diana tried not to look at Tyler. "A student who was really upset might think one bad grade had ruined his life, but that's silly."

"Glen was s'posed to go to a meeting but he didn't. How come?"

"I don't know. Honey, why are you so worried about Glen? I didn't think you liked him very well."

"I don't. Oh, he's okay, I guess, but I could always tell he really didn't like kids, so I tried not to bother him. I told Mommy and she said that was best. I said, 'How come Diana loves a guy like him? What if she marries him?' And Mommy said, 'She doesn't love Glen one bit. She's just going out with him till she meets the *right* guy, someone special I have picked out for her. When they finally meet, they're gonna love each other like crazy and they're gonna get married and have a little girl like you.' " Willow went silent again for a moment, then said, "Diana, was Mommy talkin' about Badge—I mean Tyler? Are you two in love?"

Diana, blushing, hesitated, but Tyler loudly announced, "I am so in love with Diana I could just burst! She's the most wonderful, beautiful girl I ever met and I'd marry her tomorrow if she'd let me. Would you come to the wedding,

Willow? Because neither one of us would want to have a wedding without you there. And the cats, of course. Do you think Romeo would be my best man?"

He'd done it, Diana thought as Willow began clapping, her face breaking into a wide smile. He made her happy again. But was that his only reason for saying he wanted to marry her? She looked at him, still embarrassed, and he reached over and took her hand. "Just how big a diamond do you want in your engagement ring, future Mrs. Raines?"

Diana still didn't know if Tyler was serious, so she tossed back, "As big and gaudy as possible. Something people will need to wear sunglasses just to look at it! And Willow will be my maid of honor and Christabel will be the flower girl."

"But what if Christabel and Romeo wanna get married then, too?" Willow asked.

Tyler pretended to think. "Then it will just have to be a double ceremony! Are we going to take our honeymoons together, too? Where do Christabel and Romeo want to go, Diana?"

For the sake of Willow, Diana and Tyler continued bantering until they pulled up to the Van Etton house. They went in to find Simon and Clarice in the library, drinking iced tea and talking quietly. While Willow sat down and immediately began telling Clarice all that she'd seen downtown, Simon walked back to the kitchen with Tyler and Diana.

"Something happened," Simon said. "You two can smile all you want, but I know when things aren't right. Just give me the bad news now."

Quickly Tyler told him about Glen missing the faculty meeting, being unreachable by phone, and finally about the office. Simon seemed most dismayed about the pictures. "They were all of Nan and Penny?"

"I suppose," Tyler answered. "This Frederick guy bursting with all his news said one girl had lighter hair, she wasn't pretty, and he thought she was a student. He said the other had short dark hair and was, in his words, 'a real looker.' He also said there must have been twenty pictures of both women. He wouldn't know there were twenty of each unless he handled all of them, which should delight the forensics people, and I don't know if they were twenty pictures of each in the same pose or different poses. He did say they were Polaroids, though."

"I'm sure Glen had no trouble getting Nan to pose for him, but what about Penny?" Diana asked. "Either he would have forced her or he would have taken shots of her when she didn't know he was around."

"The kind of thing a stalker does," Tyler said.

Diana shivered. "I cannot believe I dated this pervert for seven months and my only opinion of him was that he was boring. My God! What was I thinking?"

"Not about him, obviously," Simon said dryly. "And you must remember he was always on his best behavior with you. *You* were the woman he wanted to marry."

"Why?" Diana asked. "I gave so little—he didn't even *know* me."

"Status, dear girl. You're the beautiful, captivating, world renowned photographer from what he considered 'good stock.' "

Diana made a face. "I don't think the director of the tourism center considered me captivating and world renowned."

"Well, that man was an idiot. Nevertheless, when I first met Glen, I was rather charmed by his boyish wish to live in the world of some old movie. It was as if he thought somehow people really did live the way the characters did in *Dinner at Eight* or *The Philadelphia Story.* Later, I began to worry about him. He didn't seem to be maturing. He still didn't see life clearly. I wasn't overjoyed when you began dating him, Diana, but I didn't think any harm could come of it." He shook his head. "Hindsight is twenty-twenty."

"I'm just glad he didn't sweep Diana off her feet,"

Tyler said. "What would have happened if your relationship had gotten serious and you'd married him?"

"He would have been disappointed," Simon intoned.

Diana looked at him. "Thank you."

The older man laughed a little and put his arm around her shoulders. "My dear, he would have been disappointed with *anybody* because they couldn't make life into what he wanted it to be. I've no doubt that even if you'd been wildly in love with him, he would have been seeking out the Nan Murphys of the world, still looking for that intangible something he so desperately wanted."

"Well, so much for psychological analysis," Tyler said. "I'm going to call Detective Silver and see what's going on."

"Will she tell you?" Diana asked.

"Depends on her mood. She might feel like sharing information with another person on the job, or she might tell me I'm out of my jurisdiction and to leave her the hell alone. At least I can give her the details about Glen's office, just in case Frederick managed to leave out anything."

"I'm sure he didn't," Diana said wryly. "This is more excitement than he's probably had for years."

Diana quietly fixed three glasses of iced tea while Tyler called Detective Silver. Apparently she trusted him enough to give him her cell phone number because she had left the office for the day. Tyler's questions were abrupt and his answers muted. Diana knew he feared having Willow walk into the kitchen any minute.

At last he hung up and turned around. Diana gave him a glass of iced tea and he took a large swallow before he began to talk. "I don't know if this is all the police know, but it's all Silver was willing to tell me. First of all, *you* didn't tell me about the guys finding the medical ID bracelet this morning," he said to Diana.

Simon looked at her. "The one saying he's allergic to penicillin? He never takes it off.

"The police found it in the woods this morning," Diana

said. "I'm sorry I didn't tell you, Tyler, but we were with Willow constantly and—"

He held out his glass. "No need for apologies. I didn't mean to sound like I thought you were withholding evidence."

"Are you certain it was Glen's?" Simon asked.

"His name is printed on the underside of the red emblem with the caduceus on it."

Simon raised his eyebrows. "Well, I suppose that says it all."

"Yes, but . . ."

Tyler and Simon both looked at Diana. "But what?" Tyler asked. "Are you going to say there could have been two Glen Austens with an allergy to penicillin in your woods last night?"

"Certainly not. I guess I still find it difficult to picture Glen running around in a white robe pretending to be Willow's guardian angel. I didn't think he had that much imagination, but then I'm finding I didn't know Glen at all. Go ahead with what Detective Silver told you."

"They went to Austen's house—no one home. The bracelet gave them enough evidence to get a search warrant. They found nothing unusual in the house. They didn't find any luggage, his wardrobe looked on the skimpy side, and apparently the man used no toiletries."

"He ran," Diana said flatly.

"So it would appear. His car wasn't at the house and they even looked for it at the airport, even though no one by the name of Glen Austen had booked a flight yesterday or today. As for the office, they have a lot of forensics to look at. They will also have to take the fingerprints of the buoyant Frederick because he seems to have touched most of the stuff. Doesn't the guy ever watch television? Doesn't he know how important it is not to contaminate a crime scene?"

"He probably only watches shows on the History Channel," Diana said glumly. "And even if he knew better, he seemed too elated to have used good sense when he looked at that office."

Simon frowned. "I keep thinking about the writing in spray paint. 'They ruined my life.' That must refer to Nan and Penny with their pictures lying all around." Tyler nodded. "Why weren't there any pictures of Diana?"

"You sound disappointed," Diana said, smiling.

"Oh, never, child. *Never.* The point I'm making is that he seems to believe Nan and Penny ruined his life—Nan with her scheme, Penny for—I don't know what. Being the object of Nan's scheme to make money? Not turning herself over to his protection—rejecting him even when she was in deep trouble? But what about Diana?"

Tyler drained his tea, then said, "All I can say is that I'm glad Diana's picture *wasn't* there because it seems fairly obvious Glen trashed his own office, and when he wrote 'They ruined my life,' he was referring to the women whose pictures were lying all over his floor."

"And what about the attack on me last night?" Diana asked Tyler. "Me *and* Willow."

"I think he was still trying to get out of this mess unscathed but he couldn't with you around because you might remember seeing him in the attic with Nan. You were a witness he had to kill. When he failed, he threw in the towel and ran. At least that's how I see it."

"It does make sense," Diana said. "But I still feel that there's something we're not seeing, Tyler."

"We're probably not seeing a lot," Tyler answered. "We're guessing on the little bit of evidence we have, but what else can we do?" He set his glass on the counter, making the ice cubes rattle. "Detective Silver said she did have something she particularly wanted me to tell you, Diana."

"Me? Why me?"

"I don't know. I guess it's because of your talk with her earlier. Anyway, it's important. Silver talked to people at the hospital about the week Willow had her appendix taken out. She asked if anyone besides Penny had come by or called about Willow. A young nurse right out of school admitted that someone claiming to be Penny's brother, *Tyler*, called about Willow on Thursday. The man wanted to know when the child would be released. It was the nurse's first week, she was overwhelmed and she made a mistake." Tyler paused. "She told *Tyler* that Willow would not be released until Saturday morning instead of Friday morning, meaning that whoever blew up the house Friday night expected Willow to be safe and sound in the hospital."

2

Diana gasped. "Tyler, you and Penny thought *no* one knew about your connection, but someone did. He said he was Willow's *uncle*. Who could have known?"

"Jeffrey Cavanaugh could have known," Tyler said. "I was fairly certain a man like Jeffrey would have done the research on his soon-to-be wife. I just let Penny think I believed he knew nothing about me. As for me, I hoped he thought that once I'd left the foster home, Penny and I had never seen each other again. Obviously, even I underestimated Jeffrey."

"Detective Silver and I had a slight clash over Jeffrey Cavanaugh, Simon. That's why she wanted Tyler to give me this information. She had Glen tried and convicted of the attempted murder of Penny. I kept harping on Jeffrey Cavanaugh. She asked if I had children, then essentially told me a parent would *never* try to kill his own child. I, with all of my experience as a parent, pretty much said she didn't know what she was talking about—that maybe most parents wouldn't harm their children, but a few of them were capable of not only harming them but killing them."

"And now you think you were wrong about that?" Simon asked Diana in disbelief. "You think *no* parents are capable of killing their own child?"

"I believe that if Jeffrey Cavanaugh did set that bomb, he thought his daughter wouldn't be in the house."

"Oh. What a fine fellow," Simon pronounced sarcastically. "He wouldn't hurt his daughter but he would blow his wife to bits. None of us need to fear him any longer. He poses absolutely no threat. He—"

"Uncle Simon, Detective Silver was just making a point," Diana said. "We clashed over the issue of Cavanaugh. I've always been certain of his guilt and she's certain of Glen's." Diana paused. "Tyler, what *about* Glen? What if he was the person who tried to kill Penny. How would *he* have known about you?"

Tyler shrugged. "I don't know," he said tiredly. "Maybe if he was sexually blackmailing Penny, she got hysterical and pulled the 'My brother, Tyler Raines, is a New York City detective' card to intimidate him."

The phone rang and Simon answered it. Before Diana's eyes, her great-uncle seemed to shrivel inside his clothes as the fire left his gaze and the color drained from his face. He said, "All right. Thank you." Then he hung up.

Diana and Tyler looked at him anxiously. "Information about Penny is supposed to be for family only, but I cajoled someone into giving me a word if she took a turn for the worse." Simon's resonant voice had turned flat and lifeless. "Well, she is worse. The doctors say within a few hours, Penny will be dead."

Diana, Tyler, and Simon walked back into the library to find Clarice sitting alone in a chair looking out the window, her expression weary and distant. She tried to smile when they came in, but the smile lacked sincerity. "Willow was worn out," she said. "The child put out a mighty effort to act happy and carefree today, but she's tired and she's scared. She doesn't want us all to see how scared she is, and it breaks my heart that a little girl is trying to look out for the adults." Clarice's eyes filled with tears. "I took her upstairs in the elevator. She said she wanted a nap and she wanted to be alone with the cats, so I left her.

I didn't want her to feel that she had to keep talking, had to keep trying to entertain *me*. . . ."

Clarice's tears spilled over her cheeks. Diana made a movement toward her, but Simon reached her first. He kneeled beside her chair. "We can't blame ourselves for this situation," he said. "I say that because I know you are somehow blaming yourself. But you've done more for that child than a real grandmother could have done. You've loved her and comforted her and spent endless hours with her watching those scintillating movies. . . ."

Simon had managed to make Clarice smile. "Yes, my knowledge of movie trivia has vastly improved."

"You've been wonderful, Clarice."

She frowned. "You sound as if it's over."

"Not quite." Simon took her hands into his own. "We just got a call from the hospital. Penny is dying."

"Oh no!" Clarice cried.

Simon pulled her hands to his lips as tears ran down her face. "Yes. We all knew it was coming, but even when you know, you're never prepared. Penny was a bright light in all of our lives, but she could never be that again, and I know she wouldn't want to live the way she is, especially for Willow. She would know how terribly unhappy Willow would be every time she looked at her mother. Don't you think so?" Clarice slowly nodded. "I'm going to the hospital. I know I'm not family and they probably won't let me near her, but I feel I should be there."

"And so should I," Tyler said, his voice sounding thicker than usual as he held back his own tears. "Maybe I'm not legally her brother, but I'm her brother in every other way."

Simon nodded then looked at Diana and back at Clarice. "You two must stay here to look after Willow. Will you be all right while we're gone?"

"Of course," Diana said. "But promise to call and . . . and keep us apprised."

"I will," Simon told her briskly. "I'll call your cell phone so the house phone doesn't wake up Willow. Keep the cell phone with you and the doors locked."

Diana walked them to the garage. "Take the Porsche, Uncle Simon," she said. "Penny loved the Porsche."

He smiled and went to the Peg-Board for the keys. Meanwhile, Tyler hugged her tight. "I'm so sorry," she murmured in his ear.

"I know. And I'm sorry this is happening to you, too. But you must know you and your uncle gave Penny the best year of her life. Never forget that, Diana."

Tyler kissed her fiercely, then walked to the Porsche and climbed in the driver's side, since Simon insisted that he take the wheel.

CHAPTER NINETEEN

1

At six o'clock Willow was still sleeping and neither Diana nor Clarice had any appetite. They each drank a cup of coffee and sat in the library, talking quietly about everything except Penny. Clarice told Diana about her honeymoon with Henry, how they had started out for Niagara Falls and Henry's old car broke down a hundred miles out of Huntington, so they'd stayed in a tiny town with one diner and one theater while the car was being repaired at the town's one garage. Diana described how two days after her wedding, her husband came down with measles. They tried to laugh, but neither was really concentrating on the other's story.

At seven o'clock Simon called to say that Penny was still alive, but failing. They were basically on a deathwatch. He said Jeffrey simply sat like a man carved out of stone and had raised no objections to Simon's and Tyler's presence. Simon emphasized that Jeffrey hadn't even asked Tyler's identity, as if he already knew. Blake and Lenore also sat vigil, Lenore hovering over Jeffrey, Blake looking like he was steeling himself for a storm that lay ahead. "I have no idea when we'll be home, Diana," Simon told her. "How is Clarice?"

"All right. We've just been talking about old times."

"You're too young to remember old times," Simon informed her crisply. "And Willow?"

"Still sleeping. We decided not to wake her to force dinner on her."

"Good idea. Well, love to you all. I'll call again as soon as . . . well, soon."

As soon as Penny dies, Diana thought, feeling oddly numb. She supposed the body could withstand only so much stress, and then it simply went into a hibernation mode until it could gather enough strength to face another blow.

"Clarice, Penny is still alive but she won't be for long," Diana told the woman gently. Clarice's face puckered. "Jeffrey isn't putting up any fuss about Simon and Tyler being there, thank goodness. They both *should* be with her."

"Yes, they certainly should. I suppose you and I should, too, but I'm such a weakling. I'm so ashamed of myself. What kind of friend am I to Penny?"

"The same kind of friend I am," Diana said. "We love her. She knows we do, but I don't think she'd want either of us at the hospital. She'd want to know we're here with her little girl."

Clarice wept into a handful of tissues for a good five minutes. Diana made no move to comfort her, knowing nothing could comfort the woman. When her sobs finally began to lessen, Diana said, "I think you should go in your room and rest for a while, Clarice. I know your arthritis has been worse and you look exhausted. I'll make some tea. Chamomile. It's supposed to be relaxing. Want to see if the claims are true?"

"They are, dear. I've had the tea before and I suddenly feel as if I'd like a cup. Or a whole pot."

Even with Diana's help, Clarice had to use the walker to reach her bedroom. Diana turned down the bedspread, blanket, and sheet, helped the woman take off her shoes, and tucked her in as if she were a child. "Be back in a jiffy with the tea."

Later Diana sat in Clarice's room while each drank tea
and talked desultorily. Soon the elder woman began to
look drowsy. Diana told Clarice to nap if she could. Clarice
put up no argument—she just nodded and closed her eyes.
Diana left the bedroom door opened an inch and ambled
back into the library. As soon as she sat down, she heard the
elevator descending. She rose and when she reached it, she
saw Willow standing inside with Romeo and Christabel.

"You've never worked the elevator by yourself," Diana
said.

"I didn't wanna bother anybody." Her clothes were
rumpled and her cheek bore a pillowcase crease. "I
haven't heard Tyler and Simon talkin' for a while. Did
they go someplace?"

"Yes." Diana's thoughts scrambled as she anticipated
Willow's question of "Where?" Instead the little girl held
up one of Diana's CDs. "I got this in your room. I hope that
doesn't make you mad, but the picture of the big yellow sun
and the beach on the front is just like a CD Mommy has. It's
her favorite by some boys who live at the beach. Would you
play it for me, Diana?"

Diana took the CD—a compilation of songs by the
Beach Boys called *Sounds of Summer.* "Certainly I'll
play it for you, honey. Uncle Simon has a big stereo in the
library."

Diana put in the CD, then honored Willow's request
that they sit on the window seat beneath the pane of glass
with the blue-water-lily inlay. Willow leaned against Diana, who stroked her hair as they listened to the happy-
go-lucky sounds of "California Girls," "Surfin' Safari,"
and "Fun, Fun, Fun." When "In My Room" began to play,
Diana felt teardrops on her arms. She put her fingers under Willow's chin and raised it.

"My mommy loves this song." Willow wept. "She plays
it when she was sad, though. She kept playin' it the day our
house blew up. That's how I knew somethin' was wrong.
That's why I went out to get her some sparkle bugs. She

liked sparkle bugs almost as much as I do." Willow's chin drooped. "But she didn't get to see the sparkle bugs."

"But if you hadn't gone out to get them, you would have been caught in the explosion, too, and that would have made your mommy *so* unhappy."

"I guess." Willow stroked Christabel who had jumped up to sit on her lap. "Diana, when I was asleep this afternoon, I had a dream."

"About what?"

"About Mommy. I've been tryin' real, real hard to act happy 'cause everybody looks all upset when I don't, but today I felt weird. When I said I wanted you to take a picture of me and Tyler so I could give it to Mommy, I knew I'd never get to give it to her. Then when I went to sleep, I dreamed of Mommy dancing. Did you ever see Mommy dance?"

"Just at the country club with Glen."

"That wouldn't be a real dance. Sometimes she danced at home just for me. She'd put on a dress with a real full red skirt. It even had ruffles. And she'd put on red lipstick and dangly earrings and she'd dance so beautiful you wouldn't believe it. Some of it she said was ballet, and some was what she called Latin. I never saw her look so happy! And she'd dance over to me and end up bowing down at my feet. I always clapped and then she'd try to teach me how to dance like her, but I wasn't very good. She said I would be when I got bigger."

Willow paused. "In my dream this afternoon, she was dancin' but she didn't dance over to me. She was dancin' *away* from me. She went farther and farther away and I kept chasin' her and askin' her not to leave me, but she said, 'Don't be sad. We'll dance together another day.' And she said she loved me and then she was gone." Willow looked up, dry-eyed and bereft. "My mommy's dyin' tonight, isn't she?"

Diana had an overpowering desire to tell the child, *No. Of course your mommy isn't dying.* But she knew that would be the cruelest thing she could do. Simon and Tyler would be home soon, when Penny was gone, and Willow would be totally unprepared.

"Willow, darling, I'm afraid you're right," she said softly. "Someone from the hospital called earlier. Tyler and Simon went to be with her. Your mommy isn't gone yet—"

"But she will be soon. I knew it. Diana, I wish people and animals didn't have to die," Willow said brokenly.

"Me too, Willow. Me, too."

"Can we just sit here and listen to the music until Uncle Simon and Tyler come home?"

"Honey, we can sit here and listen to the music all night long, if you want."

2

Almost an hour later, the music was still playing while Diana sat on the window seat with Willow lying asleep with her head in Diana's lap. The child had never cried— she'd simply folded up nearly twenty minutes earlier and drifted off. Diana was relieved that Willow could find comfort in the oblivion of sleep. She, on the other hand, felt as if she'd never sleep again.

Even with daylight saving time, dusk was beginning to fall. Far earlier than this, Simon always turned on the lights in the library, the drawing room, the stairs, and the second-floor hallway. Without the lights and the enormity of Simon's personality that permeated the whole dwelling, the house had an empty, desolate aura. Diana had never experienced a moment of uneasiness in this house, but tonight she felt small and alone in a house large, dark, and somehow threatening. Fleetingly, she thought the house wanted her to leave then told herself she was being absurd. Too much sadness and turmoil had turned her foolish.

Her cell phone rang and she jerked then grabbed it before a second ring could awaken Willow. She expected to hear Simon's voice. Instead, silence followed her soft "Hello?" Nothing. "Simon?" she asked.

At last came a thin, distant, whispery voice. "Diana. Diana."

Her heart thudding, she looked at the caller ID. It read GLEN AUSTEN.

CHAPTER TWENTY

Diana sat frozen, holding the phone to her ear, for at least two minutes. Glen. He was coming. Or he was already here. What was he going to do? What *could* he do when the house was locked tight and a police surveillance car sat at the base of the long driveway leading to the house? Still, the police *must* know she'd just gotten a call from Glen.

Over the sound of the music, she heard with relief the roar of Simon's Porsche. He had said he would call from the hospital, but maybe he'd decided to come home and tell everyone in person that Penny was dead. Diana gently scooted Willow's head off her lap without disturbing her sleep, turned off the music, laid the cell phone on a table, and hurried to the front door.

She looked out one of the sidelight windows flanking the front door to see Blake Wentworth stepping out of the Porsche he'd parked in front of the house. For once he looked drained and slightly disheveled, not quite dashing but still tiredly handsome. Diana opened the door. "I didn't expect *you,*" she almost cried.

Blake stopped in his tracks and stared at her. "Diana, are you all right?"

"Glen just called."

"Glen?"

"Glen Austen. The man we're sure killed Penny and Nan and tried to kill Willow and me last night. You don't know about last night—we didn't want Jeffrey to know—but the police know all about it. They haven't been able to find him, but he's around here. At least I think he is. I don't know what he's going to do. I have to call the police—"

Blake held up his hand. "You have to get your breath before you faint. There's a police car at the foot of the driveway. I'll go back down and tell them. If you call nine-one-one, you'll have to go through a complete explanation of the problem." He started backing toward the Porsche. "Close the door and lock it while I go down and tell them. I'll be right back, Diana. Right back, I promise."

Diana closed the door and locked it just as Blake had ordered. He slid into the Porsche, made a sharp U-turn in the driveway, and headed back for the main road. When she went to the front bay window, Diana could see the Porsche stopped beside the patrol car. Blake stood beside the car, talking, gesturing, once leaning down, probably resting his elbows on the edge of the door while the police called in the report of Glen's call. After what seemed like an hour, Blake returned to the house. Diana unlocked the door and motioned for him to come in.

"Okay, mission accomplished. Those guys were told to stay here, but they reported the call. I think some backup will be here soon if we're lucky. And I'm glad I got here when I did. You must have been scared out of your mind."

"Yes. He didn't make any threats, but—"

"But anyone would have been frightened. Lenore would have probably screamed her way right down to that patrol car. She scares more easily than you."

"Oh, I don't know about that," Diana said without really thinking about Lenore. "My God, I didn't even ask. Penny?"

Blake nodded sadly. "Penny died about half an hour ago."

"But Simon said he would call."

"Simon is in the middle of a most unseemly fight at the hospital over who gets control of Penny's body." Diana's eyes widened. "I know. It's awful but it's happening nevertheless. May I come in and sit down before I fall down?"

"Oh, of course," Diana said, ushering him into the living room instead of the library.

"I've never been in this room," Blake commented.

"We seldom use it. My great-grandmother called it the drawing room and it's always struck me as unbearably cold and formal. Maybe Simon will let me redecorate it some day. Anyway, Willow is asleep in the library. I'd rather talk with you before I wake her."

"I understand. And before you offer me anything to drink, I will decline. My stomach is on fire from the awful coffee offered by the hospital vending machine." He drew a deep breath. "We've been at the hospital for hours. I don't think Jeff said one word until the doctor told him Penny was drawing her last breaths. He went into the burn unit and stood by her bedside. Lenore couldn't bear it, I just didn't want to see Penny that way again, and your uncle and that guy named Tyler Raines stayed with Lenore and me." He looked at her. "I told you Jeff didn't say anything all afternoon, but I was mistaken. When Raines walked in with your uncle, I asked Jeff who he was. He said, 'Tyler Raines. He's Penny's foster brother.' Did you know she had a foster brother?" Diana nodded. "Have you ever met him?"

"I met him the night of the explosion. He just showed up out of nowhere, carried Clarice out of her house that was beginning to burn, went back and helped the firefighters at Penny's house, and then later found Willow in the woods. I didn't know who he was then—only his name. It wasn't until last night I found out he was Penny's foster brother."

"And what's he doing here?"

"I guess he's been coming every now and then since Penny moved here. And he'd come this time to help her move away."

"Why was she moving away?"

"She thought someone had found out her true identity. That's all I know, Blake. Please tell me what happened at the hospital."

"Yes, well, when the doctor pronounced Penny dead, Jeffrey acted like he did the day she woke up, only worse. He roared past us like an enraged bull. He's big, you know, and it was frightening. Lenore just stood frozen for a minute, then went after him. As soon as she left, the doctor asked where the body was to be sent. Jeff was gone, so was Lenore, so Raines stepped forward and said he was Penny's foster brother. He'd make arrangements. The doctor said no way—Raines wasn't family. Your uncle pointed out that Penny's only family had vanished. The doctor said they'd just send Penny to the hospital morgue.

"Tyler got furious. He kept saying she *was* his sister, no matter what the courts said, and she was not going to lie in some awful morgue until Jeffrey Cavanaugh decided what to do with her body. Another doctor came to back up the first one. I thought Tyler was going to get physical. I will say he looked like he was at the end of his rope. Finally your uncle called his lawyer to come down and straighten out the mess."

"Oh, my God," Diana moaned. "How awful for this to happen right after Penny's death. I hope the strain isn't too much for Simon."

"I think he can hold his own. I said I'd tell you and Willow about Penny's death in person and Simon agreed. Raines was still yelling at the doctors and the hospital administrator. I went down to the parking lot. Jeff's car was gone, and so was the second car I'd rented. I suppose Lenore missed Jeff's exit and went after him in the other car. I went back up and told your uncle, who was back on his cell phone with his lawyer. He tossed me his keys and said, 'Take the Porsche.' And that's how I wound up here in your uncle's car. Also, I have one of the worst headaches I've ever had in my life. I know I turned down refreshment, but could I have a couple of aspirins, or better yet Excedrin and some water?"

"Right away." Diana jumped up and went to the kitchen, glad that she could concentrate on getting water and Excedrin rather than thinking about the ruckus going on at the hospital, not to mention the fact that Penny was actually dead. She'd known since Friday night that Penny couldn't live. Still, the news of her death came as a bludgeoning shock.

Blake swallowed the pills and took only a couple of sips of water. "God, what a day," he murmured then said, "That must have sounded unforgivably self-centered. I'm so sorry about Penny. That she was in the explosion, not that she's dead. You must think me cold, but she's out of her suffering, and if she'd lived—"

"I know. The suffering wouldn't have ended in a few weeks or months. The physical pain would have gone on for years. The psychological pain forever. I can't even bear to think about what her life would have been like." Blake gave her a sympathetic smile. "Would you do me a favor in spite of your headache?" Diana asked.

"Name it."

"I heard Willow beginning to stir in the library. I'd like to take her back up to bed, but I don't want to wake her completely. Would you carry her up for me? I have a sprained wrist. Besides, I'll have a cat to carry."

"A cat?" Blake asked.

"You'll understand when you see him," Diana said.

They walked quietly into the library. Romeo had curled into an unrecognizable mass of gray fur on the floor and Christabel sat beside him, alternating her gaze between him and Willow, her two charges. Willow lay curled up on the window seat beneath the water-lily glass inlay she'd always loved. She wasn't awake, but she was murmuring and twisting uncomfortably. In a minute, she would fall off the seat.

Blake stood and looked at her for a moment, a soft, unreadable smile on his handsome face. "She's a beautiful child," he murmured.

In a flash, Willow turned over and nearly fell off the window seat. Diana stooped and caught her before she hit the floor. When she stood up, Blake reached out to take Willow. Diana had caught her at a bad angle and now nearly dropped her. Blake stepped closer, his body almost touching Diana's as she began slipping Willow from her arms into his. Diana bent her head to kiss Willow at the same moment as Blake. Their faces met, lips pursed, arms touching.

And suddenly Lenore stood midway inside the library, her face twisted with rage, a gun pointed at the three of them.

CHAPTER TWENTY-ONE

1

"You really should lock your front door, Diana," Lenore said. "Or were you so excited when *my* husband appeared, you forgot?"

Diana and Blake stood still, both holding Willow who had finally opened her eyes although she wasn't fully awake. *I did forget to lock the door,* Diana thought. I was so frightened about Glen that when Blake came back from talking to the police, I was too distracted to think about the door.

"Well, nothing to say? Either of you? Aren't you going to offer me tea or some of that wonderful lemonade and a peanut butter and jelly sandwich, Diana?"

Finally, Blake asked evenly, "Lenore, how did you get here?"

"Jeffrey is at the hotel. I gave him a couple of tranquilizers and left in the Lincoln—the *nice* car he got for himself. I drove straight here."

"Why?"

"To end my pain." Her voice was loud, her blue gaze slightly wild and unfocused. "Penny's pain is over. Why shouldn't mine be over, too?"

Her words struck Diana dumb. Blake's voice remained calm and smooth. "What are you talking about, darling?"

"I'm talking about you, *darling.* You and your affairs. Ever since we married, I've put up with them because I loved you so much. I told myself I could bear them if you just stayed with me. But *this* is too much. I've known for years you were having an affair with Penny, no matter how many times you denied it. Yet she hasn't been dead an hour and here you are, wooing another woman, kissing her while the two of you hold Penny's child, for God's sake! Don't you have *any* shame? Either of you?"

Blake gently shifted Willow into Diana's arms. The child murmured sleepily, "Wha's goin' on?"

"Nothing, honey. Just be still right now," Diana almost whispered. "Don't say anything."

"No, don't say *anything,* Willow," Lenore snarled. "I won't call you Cornelia because that's my mother's name and you have *no* blood relationship with my mother! Now Blake's mother is a different matter. You've never met your Grandmother Wentworth because she's in an insane asylum!"

"Lenore!" Blake's voice cracked like a whip. "Are you saying Willow is *my* child?"

"I *know* she is. I've known since Penny gave birth to her. It was all I could do, but I always made a fuss over her because she *is* your child whereas I can't give you one. Barren. That's what I am. My mother always told me that was *my* cross to bear for being the child of Morgan Cavanaugh."

"For the love of God, Lenore, your mother belongs in a mental hospital more than mine does." Diana heard the tightly controlled fury in his voice. "Barren? I knew when I married you that you couldn't have children. It didn't make any difference to me."

"No, because you married me to secure your place in the business. You could always find other women to bear your children. Women like Penny. And Diana? She looks like good breeding stock to me."

"Stop it, Lenore." Blake's voice had turned to ice. "Willow is *not* my child. *Nothing* romantic is going on between Diana and me. We're barely friends. You, on the other hand, have been my wife for twelve years. I've done my damnedest to make you happy, but I can't make you happy because of all your crazy suspicions."

"They aren't suspicions!" Lenore shouted, coming closer, waving the gun. "They're *true!*"

Willow, wide-awake, had begun to cry. Diana jiggled her as if she were a baby and told her everything was all right, which was absurd. The child could hear.

"Diana is lying to you even now, Willow!" Lenore yelled. "Everything isn't fine for you. Penny is dead! Your mother is *dead!*" Lenore took two more steps toward them, the gun shaking. "You will *never* see her again, Willow. *Never!*"

Willow let out a piercing cry of sheer agony and suddenly the gun went off in Lenore's trembling hands. Diana felt nothing for a moment. Then pain erupted in her left shoulder and seared down her arm. The shock of pain loosened her hold on Willow and they both crashed to the floor. Lenore screamed, and with catlike grace, Blake lunged at her and grabbed the gun.

Diana watched as Blake pointed the gun at Lenore. She stood white-faced and shuddering, and Diana thought, *Thank God. Blake has saved us. Lenore could have shot Willow next. I'm only injured. Everything will be all right as soon as he calls the police.*

"The cell phone is on the table behind you, Blake," Diana said. "You can't leave us to get the surveillance guys at the end of the driveway."

Blake didn't even look at her. He made no movement to pick up the cell phone. He simply stared at Lenore, a small, pleased smile forming on his face. "You are so incredibly stupid, Lenore," he said calmly. "What did you hope to gain by this ridiculous show? Did you think you'd frighten me back into your arms? Because I know you weren't going to kill me. You'd never set me free so easily. Maybe you only meant to cripple me, turn me into a paraplegic or, better yet, a quadriplegic. Then you'd *really* have me,

wouldn't you? You'd have me with you all the time, de-
pendent on you, unable to escape you. That's what you've
always wanted, Lenore, but you won't get it. You've *never*
really had me and you *never* will."

The Lenore of ten minutes ago had wilted like a flower
hit by a blast of freezing air. "Blake, I'm sorry," she said
pitifully. "I don't know what came over me."

"A stunning defense, dear. No, you can't talk your way
out of this one by playing the innocent little girl. You will
go to prison just like your father should have. People think
Morgan and Jeffrey are two of a kind. They're wrong. It's
you and Morgan who are two of a kind. You always were
like him."

"I'm not!" Lenore protested. "I know my father did
awful things, but I haven't."

"Really? How about helping him make my father's
death look like suicide?"

Diana gasped. What was Blake saying? What in
heaven's name was he doing? He looked as if he were enjoying himself. With a stunning shock, she realized he had
no intention of calling the police.

"I helped my father make your father's death look like
suicide?" Lenore repeated. "I don't know what you mean.
I was just a teenager. . . ."

"A teenager who wanted to get into Daddy's good
graces. And you did, Lenore. *You* were the son Morgan
never had." Blake looked at her with cold, black hatred.
"Get over there and sit on the floor by Diana. Sit close to
the woman you thought was your rival. She never was your
rival, you know. Not that I don't find her extremely attractive. Not that I haven't fantasized about what she would be
like in bed. Magnificent, I'm sure. But I've had a plan for
years and I've never veered from it for simple sexual pleasure. Diana didn't fit into my plan. And be sure to sit to her
right side, Lenore. Diana's left shoulder is bleeding rather
profusely."

Lenore crept toward Diana, not meeting her eyes, and
lowered herself to the floor. Willow no longer sobbed. After

hearing that her mother was dead, she'd gone still and quiet, withdrawing into a world of her own. *Good,* Diana thought. *I don't want her to see or hear any of this.*

"What do you mean when you say Lenore helped Morgan make your father's death look like suicide, Blake?" Diana nearly jumped at the sound of her own voice. She hadn't planned to speak—she'd only thought she needed time until the surveillance police officers realized there was trouble at the house.

"My father? I thought everyone had forgotten about Charles Wentworth. They'd simply brushed him and his disgrace under the rug," Blake said.

"His disgrace?" Diana asked.

"Father made some bad business investments. He lost a lot of money. He was desperate, or he would never have accepted Morgan Cavanaugh's offer to go into business. He'd heard bad things about Cavanaugh—he didn't trust him. But Father's pride and his concern for his family got him into trouble. He joined Cavanaugh and, remarkably, the business was a huge success."

Blake shook his head slightly, his eyes seeming to glaze for a moment. "But once Cavanaugh and Wentworth had exceeded even Morgan Cavanaugh's expectations, he decided he didn't want a partner anymore. I wouldn't know all of this if my father hadn't gotten extremely drunk one evening and told me everything. He said Morgan had fixed the books to make it look as if Father had embezzled over a million dollars from the company. He told me Morgan made a great show of trying to cover up for his friend, but of course, the board members saw right through Morgan's sham cover-up because it was so deliberately clumsy.

"Father resigned. He talked about moving away because all of our friends—those fine society friends—had deserted us. Mother was beginning her nervous breakdown. He was worried about paying for my Harvard education." Blake stopped. "But even that night, my father was not beaten. He was injured, but not beaten. He was already making plans for turning our lives around. Then he told me he had an appointment with Morgan. He was going to make some kind of deal. I was worried. It was pouring snow and he was drunk." Blake's eyes clouded. "He never came home that night. Lenore, I'm sure you remember the next day—someone found him in his car on a little side road about two miles from our house, where apparently he had shot himself in the head."

"That's terrible," Diana said weakly.

"I'll tell you what's terrible," Blake snapped. "My father didn't commit suicide. Morgan Cavanaugh killed him because he was afraid my father was going to keep telling his story and eventually someone was going to believe him!"

"Wasn't there a police investigation?" Diana asked, feeling the silent Willow beginning to tremble beside her. "Didn't Morgan tell the police he and your father were supposed to have a meeting?"

"No, he did not. He said he didn't know anything about a meeting. His wife and Jeffrey were not home that night, but Lenore was. Our little Lenore, who swore on a Bible her father had not left home all evening. They'd watched television together, she said, as if Morgan would ever sit and watch television with one of his children."

Diana stole a look at Lenore, who huddled on the floor, head bowed, and she knew what Blake said was true. Lenore had provided her father with an alibi for that night. Diana wondered how much pressure a man like Morgan had exerted on her to do so. Blake obviously didn't care.

"My parents were deeply Christian," Blake went on. "My father actually *believed*. He would never have committed suicide because then he couldn't be buried in consecrated ground and he couldn't go to heaven. My mother was convinced he was burning in hell—that's what broke her mind. So Morgan managed to kill two birds with one bullet, shall we say. And what was his punishment? He got Cavanaugh and Wentworth all to himself."

"But Lenore said something about Morgan taking you in, giving you the same education he gave his own son," Diana said desperately.

"Of course he did. People thought he was a saint. His trusted partner steals from him then kills himself leaving no money and a crazy wife, and Morgan becomes poor Blake's salvation. What a prince of a man!"

Diana heard scuffling, gasping, and muttering in the hallway before Clarice stumbled in through the rear door of the library. Diana had forgotten the woman was in the house, but there she stood wearing the horrible billowing, flounced, ruffled pink robe that Diana had loaned her on her first night in the house. She glanced blankly at Blake then looked at Diana. "So much noise! What's happening?"

Blake pointed the gun at her. "And if you want to stay alive, you will keep your mouth shut."

"Oh! There's so much blood!" Clarice slurred. She wavered, a tiny woman lost in a mass of pink satin, holding her hands behind her. "I'll be quiet," Clarice whispered, her eyelids fluttering, her violet eyes rolling before she sank to the floor beside Diana.

2

"I think she's had a heart attack!" Diana exclaimed.

"She just fainted. If not . . ." He shrugged. "She just saved me a bullet."

Diana wanted to scream at him, but she knew that would probably mean instant death. She swallowed, glanced down for a moment, then raised her eyes and asked softly, "Blake, I know you're doing this because of Jeffrey. Why? Jeffrey is your friend."

"Jeffrey Cavanaugh? *My* friend?" Blake laughed without mirth. "*I* am a Wentworth. Who is he? No more than a man of common intellect, manners, and birth whose only redeeming feature is his money. He's just a gutter-born, ruthless thug like his father. And I had to be beholden to *him,* just like I did his father! I hated owing Jeff anything even more than I hated his father, so I decided I'd make

Morgan *and* Jeffrey pay for the destruction of my family and the humbling of our pride."

"I give myself a great deal of credit for waiting as long as I did, for planning as carefully as I did. It wasn't easy, but it worked. First, I romanced the less-than-lovely Lenore. She had boyfriends, but she knew they just wanted her money. What else was there to want? Besides, she'd been in love with me since I was twenty. She couldn't hide it. When I asked Morgan for her hand in marriage, he could hardly contain himself. His plain, ordinary Lenore married to a Wentworth!"

"Oh, Blake, please don't say things like that," Lenore begged. "You cared for me."

"I tolerated you. And don't ever think I didn't love you because you can't have children. I would never allow you to be the mother of *my* child. You're not worthy."

Lenore bowed her head and began to cry. In a gesture of disgust, Blake rolled his eyes and threw back his head with its thick black hair. At that moment, Clarice moved just a fraction of an inch closer to Diana. Diana almost glanced at her before she realized the woman's eyes were still closed as if she was unconscious, and from the folds of the hideous pink robe she was pushing something hard and cold against Diana's left hand. Diana moved her hand slightly against the object. It was a gun.

Blake looked back at Diana suddenly and she was afraid he'd seen her move her hand. She quickly asked, "Was Morgan's death really a mob hit?"

"No. I knew Morgan went to the same seedy little bar every Tuesday night. I made certain Jeff was occupied *alone*—no alibi—and I simply waited for Morgan to come reeling out of the kind of place that was his true home. I stepped out of an alley right beside the bar, and stuck the gun to his head, just like he did to my father, and I shot. Of course, Jeff had everything to gain by his father's death. He and his father hated each other and everyone knew it, and Jeff had no alibi. I made certain there was no incriminating evidence, though. And *I* started the rumor of the murder being a mob hit. Couldn't have old Jeffrey hauled off to prison and ruining my plans."

"So he took over the company at age thirty, when you were fresh out of the Harvard MBA program he gave you a nice job at Cavanaugh and Wentworth, and later he married," Diana finished for Blake.

"You certainly have your chronology down, Diana."

"This family fascinates me. Were you jealous when Jeffrey married Yvette?"

"Jealous? She was the most beautiful woman I've ever seen—she married Jeffrey only for his money, obviously— but I wouldn't have *married* her for a million dollars. She was a schizophrenic. I know some schizophrenics function in society quite well if they are careful to take their medication and follow doctor's orders, but Yvette did only as Yvette pleased. She wouldn't take her medicine because she said it made her drowsy. She drank more than I thought it possible for anyone to drink and stay on their feet. But she did have her good points. Aside from being stunningly beautiful, she was a fantastic lover. The best I ever had.

"But her illness was taking over. She couldn't control her behavior or her tongue. She was going to tell Jeffrey about us. I saw it coming so I got her wound up at that party in San Francisco. I told her Jeffrey was going to have her institutionalized as soon as we got home. She caused a scene. As soon as she left the ballroom, I intercepted her and told her to go to their room and order some champagne. I went back in and maneuvered Jeffrey into a conversation with an incredible windbag I knew who would keep him busy for at least twenty minutes. I went to Yvette's room. She was so drunk she was not aware of me opening the window. After a struggle in which I managed to tear off that fantastically valuable necklace, I tossed her out of that open window. Good-bye, Yvette. And once again, the police could almost make a case for Jeff's guilt, but not quite. I didn't want him to go to prison. I still had plans for him."

Carried away with his boasting, Blake didn't notice Diana subtly pushing the gun behind her. She cursed the wound in her left shoulder. It hurt terribly, and she felt as if she had little control left in the hand. Still, she had to keep subtly sliding the gun to the right.

"And then there was Penny," Lenore said out of the blue. "I always wondered why you didn't object more to that marriage. Now I understand. Penny was the next Yvette."

"Right, Lenore. At first, I could tell she really did love Jeff. No one ever said Penny was smart. I bided my time. Then she had Willow and things began to shift my way. She was unhappy with the way Jeff responded to the baby. She didn't see him crying like a baby himself when the kid was born—he wasn't one of those men who watch the delivery. But she didn't know how much he talked about the baby—on and on and on. I thought I'd lose my mind.

"Penny just didn't understand that although he adored Willow, Jeff was almost afraid of her—afraid he'd hurt her physically if he held her, afraid he'd be a father like his was and damage her psychologically. So he decided to inflict himself on her no more than necessary. It was crazy—it was perfect. Penny started talking to me about the problem. Then Jeffrey began spending more time away from home. He treated Penny like a prisoner. The more unhappy she became with him, the better my chances with her." He looked at the four faces in front of him. "I guess I don't have to tell you what happened."

"Penny ran away because she found Yvette's necklace in Jeffrey's office safe," Diana said coolly.

"Ah, Tyler has been telling secrets. Penny had decided she was in love with me—that she was going to leave Jeffrey for me. I couldn't have that! Jeffrey would have gotten me out of that company faster than I can imagine. I couldn't kill her—a murdered father and *two* murdered wives might have finished Jeffrey. If he'd been arrested and charged with murder, the business would have suffered badly.

"Instead, I decided to play on Penny's fear. I knew she didn't believe Jeffrey had ever harmed anyone, but I kept casually bringing up Jeffrey and Yvette. Then, when Jeffrey was gone on an extended trip with Lenore, I planted the necklace in his safe and kept bringing the necklace into the conversation. I knew Penny had always been curious about that safe. I even gave her a hint about where to find the combination. She found both the combination and the necklace. She was terrified.

"I convinced her not to go to the police. I told her it would be safer to run. She'd told me about Tyler, I knew he could get her false ID. I bought the house for her. I helped her move in."

"I saw you!" Clarice cried, leaning forward and waving her arms. "I thought you looked familiar. I saw you when she first moved in, but just for an instant and you were wearing a cap!" Clarice fell back, as if exhausted by her outburst, but she'd managed to move more of the robe onto Diana's lap. Diana was able to give the gun a shove to the right without Blake seeing her arm move at all.

"I knew I'd have to get rid of Penny eventually, but just having her disappear had the desired effect on Jeffrey. He was devastated, yet this time there was no police scrutiny. He'd been in France. People had seen Penny early on the day she and Willow disappeared—a time when he and Lenore were staying in the home of a client.

"Things went well for a while. Penny found a job she liked. She was happy with the town. I came to visit about once a month. Then Lenore began noticing my frequent absences. I couldn't visit as often. Penny started applying pressure about when I was going to tell Lenore, when was I going to tell Jeffrey we were in love and getting married. A month ago, she announced she was pregnant—pregnant with *my* child. I knew it was mine. I've always known Penny wouldn't let another man touch her, although she'd told me when Glen Austen started bothering her in late May.

"And then a note came for Jeffrey. He was having one of his usual cases of the vapors and working out of his apartment, so I opened his mail. The note said a *reliable* person would give the location of Penny and Cornelia Cavanaugh for $150,000. The sender had enclosed a picture taken with a disposable camera. It showed Penny and Willow in a yard, playing ball. The picture was taken inside because the photographer had caught that stained-glass water lily in the shot. Penny had even told me about the water lily. She said it was a constant reminder from Yvette of how evil Jeff was, of how he'd murdered her." Blake's laughter sounded raw and uncontrolled. "Penny could be *such* a ninny! Anyway, I was damned lucky to have intercepted that piece of mail, but I was also certain more would follow. I knew the time had come to get rid of Penny."

Diana's cell phone rang. Five sets of eyes fastened on it—four with hope and one with annoyance. It rang a second time. "That's Uncle Simon," Diana said.

Blake sighed. "I know. Tiresome Uncle Simon finally calling to tell you Penny died almost an hour ago."

The phone rang a third time. "He'll know something is wrong."

"He'll think you've misplaced the phone. You're careless, Diana. Just look at how you left the door unlocked when I came back the second time, making access so easy for Lenore."

"And if I hadn't, you wouldn't have a gun," Diana said.

Blake smirked. "Don't you think I brought my own? Well, really Penny's. I took it from her house." The phone rang for the third time. "Oh, give *up*, Simon!" Blake yelled as he aimed at the cell phone and shot, blowing it to pieces. "There. Now for some peace."

Diana could see that for all of Blake's bravado, he was unraveling, tiring of explanations, growing weaker from his long day of waiting for Penny to die. Still, he wanted everyone to know how very clever he had been.

"You came here and set the bomb," Diana said hastily. "While Penny was at the hospital with Willow, you went into her house and set the bomb." Blake nodded, pleased with himself. "You called the hospital and asked when Willow would be released. Why?"

"I wanted to kill Penny but not Willow. His child's death would have been the end of Jeffrey and the end of me at Cavanaugh and Wentworth. It seems some people aren't too pleased with the job I'm doing, but Jeff has my back. I hadn't planned on losing him yet."

Although Willow seemed to be in a world of her own, she held Diana's right hand. Diana tried to free it, but the child held fast. "And what about Nan?"

"Penny had already told me all about you and Simon and Nan. When I saw that stained-glass window in the picture, I knew someone in this house had taken it. Now who would call themselves a *reliable* person? That idiot of a girl. Penny had also told me she thought Glen was involved with Nan. She didn't want to tell you until Nan had left this house and her mother had resumed her old job—it would be too awkward for you. But I thought Glen was probably involved in this brilliant scheme to make $150,000."

"After the explosion, Jeff was notified and here we came, the Three Musketeers." He rolled his eyes again. "I couldn't count on Nan to keep her mouth shut about her letter to Jeffrey. She *knew* she'd set something bad in motion with her money-making scheme. I also knew she would have told Glen all about it. Both have numbers and addresses listed in the phone book. I went to Nan's. She was packing to leave, but she was too late. I got to her first.

"I was outside walking to my car parked a block away when I saw a man pull into Nan's driveway. He went inside. I knew it was Glen. I was going after him when *you* pulled up, Diana. You went inside. Apparently you trapped Glen in the attic with a dead body—not the most comfortable situation. When he came running out of the house, I was waiting for him in his car. I forced him to drive someplace. Then I didn't have to worry about Glen anymore."

"Glen has been dead since Sunday night?" Diana asked. Blake nodded. "Then who—"

"Came to your window? Me. You still knew too much

about everything. I had to kill you. I really didn't have any choice. So I put on the absurd costume and pretended to be Willow's guardian angel, then threw pebbles at your window to wake you. I knew I could use Willow to lure you outside. But then Tyler came to the rescue."

"And you didn't get us," Diana flashed back, immediately regretting her words. Blake's eyes narrowed. "But you planted Glen's ID bracelet in the woods."

"And predictably, the police found it."

"The bracelet bothered me," Diana said, beginning to feel dizzy from blood loss. "Glen always complained about how hard it was to unclasp. He said he almost had to use a screwdriver to pry it open. Yet we were supposed to believe it just fell off his wrist."

"I didn't care what *you* believed," Blake said. "The police believed he dropped it. And I used his cell phone to call you a while ago."

"So the police and I would think he was still around. That's why you ran down to the surveillance car to tell the police officers."

"There was only one and, unfortunately, he's dead, Diana. Right after he reported Glen's call, I was forced to kill him. I had no choice."

"The police believed Glen was guilty of everything, so why did *you* come here?"

"When I cornered Nan in her attic, she said you were suspicious of me. She said you knew I'd tried to kill Penny and you'd know I killed her."

"She was lying," Diana said flatly. "I didn't suspect you of anything except not being quite as patient with Jeffrey and Lenore as you seemed."

"I thought she was probably lying, but I knew I couldn't live comfortably if I had a shred of doubt. I always tie up loose ends, Diana. The police were supposed to think Glen came here in a rage and killed you for breaking his heart." He paused, his teeth clenching. "However, my darling wife fouled my plan. Now I will have to kill all of you and then go away. No one will ever find me. They shouldn't even try, but they'll waste hundreds of man-hours and thousands of dollars. I suppose I should be flattered." He paused then smiled. "Who shall I kill first? Willow."

He shifted the gun and pointed at the child, who screamed shrill and loud. While he took his time aiming, Diana whipped out the gun she gripped in her right hand and, through dimming vision, fired. The shot only grazed Blake's thigh, but the pain threw off his aim and the shot hit the wall. With a shout of rage, he aimed again at Willow. Diana fired once more, her shot whizzing past his ear.

By now she was shaking violently and sweating so much from the pain of her gunshot wound, the gun was slipping from her hand. The room seemed to spin around her and she kept blinking, trying to clear her vision, which she did enough to see Blake aiming at her. With the last of her strength, Diana pushed Willow sideways and closed her eyes just before she heard the sound of a gunshot. She felt nothing, and a second later she opened her eyes to see Blake weaving. Still, he aimed again at Diana. She looked beyond Blake. In the front entrance to the library stood Tyler Raines holding his gun.

"Stop Wentworth," Tyler said fiercely.

Blake's next shot was quickly followed by Tyler's. Blake jerked but managed to remain standing, ready to squeeze off another round.

"I said *stop!*" Tyler yelled.

Blake laughed raggedly. "Not on your life, Mr. Raines."

He pointed the gun at Willow. Diana closed her eyes, and her breath stopped as the sound of another shot crashed through the room. She opened her eyes to see Blake suddenly standing perfectly still and smiling. Then, slowly, his smile twisted, his beautiful ebony eyes went blank, he spun halfway around, and crashed facedown on the polished hardwood floor.

EPILOGUE

December Twentieth

"Well, I never thought my house catching on fire could lead to *this*!"

"Is this where I say God works in mysterious ways?" Diana said, as she tucked a wisp of Clarice's silver hair into her French twist then inserted a comb edged with iridescent amethyst-colored beads. "Perfect! Do you want to see?"

Diana gave Clarice a hand mirror, and the woman stood up and looked at the back of her hair in the vanity mirror. "You did a beautiful job, Diana! At the beauty shop they pull my hair so tight I feel like my mouth is stretched into a hideous grin!"

Diana laughed. "Maybe I missed my calling. I should have become a hairstylist."

"Don't let Simon hear you say that, particularly after your last gallery showing in New York. No more tourist center pamphlets for you!"

"Just as well. That spiffy head of the tourism board with the bow tie said my pictures weren't 'up to snuff.'"

"He's a fool, as Simon would say." Clarice laid down the hand mirror and turned in front of Diana. "How do I look? And be honest."

Clarice wore an amethyst-colored satin sheath dress

with long sleeves and a boat neck. A twenty-two-inch strand of pearls hung from her neck, and pearls dangled from her ears, all belonging to Simon's mother, and his gift to Clarice along with an antique-styled diamond engagement ring. Clarice had allowed Diana to emphasize her violet eyes with some pink and violet eye shadow, a bit of eyeliner, and mascara. She wore dyed purple pumps with two-inch heels and had no need for a walker today.

"Clarice, you look absolutely beautiful. No wonder a seventy-five-year-old confirmed bachelor proposed to you."

Clarice smiled and blushed. "I was *so* surprised."

"I wasn't. I think I've expected it since the first week you spent here."

Clarice's smile dimmed slightly. "What a week that was! Every day something awful happened, and yet just four months later, look how happy we are. Especially little Willow. I cannot believe how that child is blossoming."

Frankly, neither could Diana. After the horrendous scene with Blake in this very house, they had all learned not only how Jeffrey Cavanaugh had been treated as a child by his father, but how Blake had set out to ruin the rest of Jeff's life. *Blake* had murdered Morgan. *Blake* had murdered Yvette. *Blake* had pushed Penny into deserting a man she believed was a killer, only to die at the hands of the only man besides Tyler that she trusted.

At first Jeffrey had been so stunned to learn the truth about Blake, that he had no wish to take Willow away from Simon and Diana. She still feared him, and he said he feared himself, particularly his bad judgment, which had resulted in the murders of his two wives. Even his sister had not been what he'd believed. He'd gone back to New York and dived into psychotherapy. Meanwhile Simon and Diana had seen to it that Willow also got the psychological help she needed.

Then slowly, father and daughter had begun to come together. At first Jeffrey made a few weekend trips to Huntington. Then Diana had taken Willow to New York for short visits. Jeffrey spent Thanksgiving with Simon,

Clarice, and Diana, and after Christmas, Willow would be going to New York for a week's stay with her father, while Diana would happily spend time with Tyler, whom Jeffrey had promised could always be part of Willow's life—although the two men would probably never be more than polite to each other. They all hoped that by early summer, Willow would once again be living with her father full time.

Smiling, Diana left the downstairs bedroom where Clarice had spent her first week with them and went into the kitchen, checking to make certain the caterers had everything under control. Tyler stood by the counter, dressed in his tuxedo, his longish hair combed back. "You look devilishly handsome," she said.

"And you look gorgeous," he replied, gazing at her green velvet dress. "Sure you're not upset about not being a bridesmaid?"

"Heavens, no. Clarice has a daughter and two granddaughters for that job. Simon, however, didn't let you off so easily. Best man! How impressive!"

"My first time." He paused. "Oh, gosh, I hope I didn't lose the ring!" Tyler looked genuinely alarmed, and Diana began patting down his pockets before he pulled out the diamond-studded wedding band. "Well, here it is after all, but you're welcome to keep searching."

Diana made a face at him. "We're supposed to be greeting guests."

They walked into the flower-filled library. Diana could almost forget what had happened in there back in August when Blake had stood with a gun pointed at her and Willow. Later, after the paramedics had come to her aid once again, she'd learned that Simon had expected Blake to return to the hospital with the Porsche. When he hadn't, he and Tyler had asked Simon's lawyer to give them a ride back to the Van Etton house. Simon tried to call her. No answer, then the abrupt loss of service when Blake shot the phone told them something was very wrong.

Urging the lawyer to drive faster than he ever had up the winding roads of Ritter Park, they reached the Van Etton grounds to find the surveillance patrol officer dead in his car. Simon had told the story a hundred times of how his lawyer stood blithering at the patrol car, while Simon and Tyler had jumped in the man's car, Tyler flooring it until they pulled up behind the Porsche, where Tyler jumped out and dashed into the house, gun drawn, and heroically saved the day. "He'll be telling that story for the rest of his life," Diana had told Tyler. "It's exactly what he always pictured himself doing."

All of the furniture had been removed from the library, and a carpeted aisle ran between chairs up to a small altar where the minister of Clarice's church would perform the service. People had gathered—more on the groom's side than on the bride's, but Diana knew Clarice didn't mind. Her daughter looked lovely in a dove-gray dress and her own imitation pearls. Clarice's youngest granddaughter, Sue, kept mostly to herself, admiring her bouquet and smiling shyly. The thirteen-year-old, Katy, kept fussing with her hair, which, as Willow had claimed, looked like a bird nest.

Finally Jeffrey Cavanaugh arrived. He had lost at least twenty pounds since Penny's death, and the perpetually angry, frustrated expression had left his face. Even his eyes looked gentler, their color dulled to soft pewter from glittering silver. "Hello, Diana. Tyler," he said with a slightly hesitant smile. He still wasn't confident that all was understood and forgiven. That would come, Diana thought, because she and Simon had no intention of cutting Jeffrey from their lives, and not just for the sake of Willow.

"How's Lenore?" Diana whispered.

"Much better. She'll be out of the convalescent home by the first of the year. I'm having a nurse stay with her for a couple of months, but she'll come out of this depression. She's already come a long way. My sister is a strong girl." He looked down. "And so is my daughter."

Willow had appeared at the door looking angelic in

dark-blue velvet with a matching ribbon holding back her hair. She'd completely lost the tight, gray, haunted look of the weeks after her mother's death. Her blue eyes twinkled, and her cheeks bore a rosy glow no makeup could copy.

"Hi . . . Daddy." Jeffrey blinked. She had not called him Daddy until today. "You look very nice."

"Well, thank you," Jeffrey said uncertainly. "You look beautiful."

Willow smiled. "Are we still havin' the big New Year's Eve party like you promised?"

"It might not be as big as you think, but we're definitely having a party," Jeffrey said. "The invitations have all ready been mailed."

"I know 'cause Diana got one." She looked up at them. "You're comin' with Tyler, aren't you?"

"I certainly am," Diana said. "Clarice and Simon will still be on their honeymoon. I sure can't stay around here and be bored to tears. And I'll bring along Tyler because he assures me he's fun at parties."

"You want to be *anywhere* with Tyler," Willow said impishly, then looked at her father. "Diana's movin' to New York real soon," Willow told him.

"I know. You'll get to see her all the time even when you come live with me."

"Yeah, and she and Tyler are gonna get married." She looked at Diana. "You *are* getting married, aren't you?"

"If he behaves himself until May," Diana said solemnly.

"Oh, he will 'cause he wants to marry you a whole lot and I want to be in the wedding like you said I could, so he'd better not mess it up for me. Besides, once Mommy told me a real big secret. She said she wished Diana and Badge would get married." Willow beamed. "She'd be *so* happy her wish is comin' true."

No one knew quite the right thing to say after Willow's pronouncement. Diana could have jumped for joy when, unbeknownst to any of them, Christabel and Romeo— winding their way through the obstacle course of feet— arrived unharmed to greet Willow. Diana had just noticed them before Romeo let out a boisterous *"Quack!"* People turned in their chairs to look in surprise, but Willow burst into giggles, stooped down, and kissed each cat on the head.

"Don't they look beautiful, Daddy? They're all dressed up!"

Jeffrey looked down at the two cats wearing large, white satin bows around their necks and broke into laughter. "I don't think I've ever seen cats in formal wear," he said.

The organist started to play and, with a wink at Diana, Willow led her father to seats on Clarice's side. She leaned over and whispered something to Jeffrey, who bent his head and kissed her cheek.

Tyler pulled Diana against him. "Do you remember the day after the explosion when I told you miracles exist and you asked me what was Penny's miracle?" he whispered in her ear. She nodded, and he looked at Willow and Jeffrey holding hands. *"That* is Penny's miracle—her extraordinary daughter holding hands with a good and loving father."